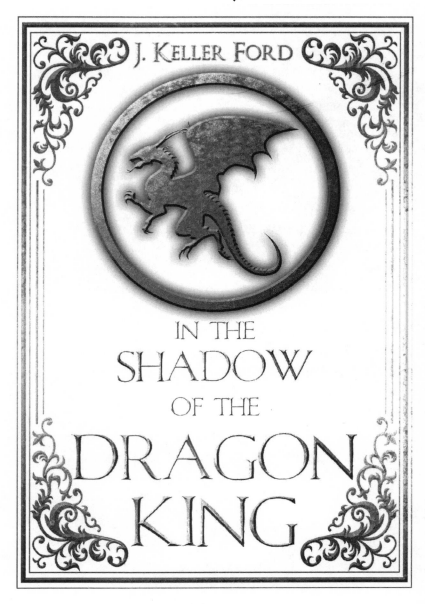

J. KELLER FORD

IN THE
SHADOW
OF THE
DRAGON
KING

Month9Books

To Diane –
my best and dearest friend.
You will remain forever in my heart and memory

"War is a necessary evil. There is not a day or time when each of us does not battle some sort of enemy within or around us. The true test of our character lies in the instant when we choose to either ignore or defeat that which seeks to destroy us. It is the same in our kingdom. Hirth has seen its share of battles, and this great province has ridden the wings of freedom for many an age; however, there will come a day when an evil so immense will seek to threaten our very existence. It is then the knights of Gyllen Castle will rise to the aid of Hirth and defend all that is dear— our families, our land, and our right to survive. When such a time comes, I will fight with honor and for glory and give my life, if my forfeiture of it will allow Hirth the chance to endure in peace. And while I know that the enemy may prevail, and my life be extinguished from this body, my death will not be in vain, for what is more honorable than giving one's life for love of family, country … and freedom."

Sir Trogsdill Domnall.

IN THE
SHADOW
OF THE
DRAGON
KING

"My shadow brings night, my footprints make lakes, my fire is brighter than a thousand suns. I am Einar. I am the Dragon King."

Chapter 1

Had Eric known what daylight would bring after the nightmares ended, he would have remained in bed, the covers pulled over his head.

Instead, he waded through the puddles of the castle's upper courtyard, each gong from the clock tower coiling his stomach into tighter knots. Sloshing beside him along the aisle of topiaries and statues was his best friend, a devilish lad with a cockeyed grin and unkempt hair the color of dirt.

"I don't know why you're in such a hurry," Sestian said, polishing an apple on his sleeve. "Weapons class began fifteen minutes ago. Master Mafi won't allow us in." The apple crunched in his teeth.

"You don't understand, Ses. I have to try." Eric swatted at the spindly arms of a willow tree. "This will be the third day in a row I've missed. If I don't go, word will get back to Trog, and he'll flog me. You know how he gets."

"You worry too much. He'd never physically hurt you. However, I do have to admit, he is quite an odd fellow. I saw him make another midnight trek to the fountain last night. He sat there all hunched over like he'd lost his best friend, and then he stood, dropped a rose in the water, and left."

Eric's muscles bunched under his light shirt, his brow pinched. "That is bizarre, even for him."

"Want to hear something even more bizarre?" Sestian paused, took another bite of the apple and buried the core in a potted plant. "I overheard Trog and my headache of a master talking this morning. I believe the exact words out of Farnsworth's mouth were, 'Fallhollow is under attack.'"

Eric came to a stop, his eyes wide. "Attack? From who?"

Sestian shrugged. "Don't know, but members of the Senate and the Mages' High Council arrived an hour ago, including the Supreme Master himself. They're meeting with the Order as we speak."

"What?" Eric's pulse quickened. "Jared's here? You saw him?"

The grand mage of all magical beings never involved himself in the affairs of men. Ever.

"No, but I plan to change that." An impish twinkle glistened in Sestian's eyes. "Are you game?"

"What? You want to—you mean—you're joking, right?"

The puckish grin on Sestian's face answered his question.

Eric shook his head. "Oh, no. There is no way you're going to get me to eavesdrop on a secret council meeting. I'd rather get hit by lightning than suffer punishment from anyone sitting in that room."

"Aww, come on, Eric. Must you always be so dull? Aren't you the least bit curious?"

"That sort of curiosity will land us in the pillory at best." Eric pushed past his friend through the carved citadel doors. Sestian darted in front of him and stopped.

"Your point?"

"My point is that I value my life."

"And what of Fallhollow? Don't you value our home?"

"Of course I do, but—"

"Then what are you waiting for?" Sestian punched Eric's arm. "Let's go."

"Ses, no!" Eric's protest fell on empty ears. His friend was gone.

Eric brushed past the lapis columns of the marble vestibule into the Great Hall, a wide-open space topped by a domed ceiling so high its ornate detail became lost in the darkness. Nobles and servants milled about, coming and going out of the many rooms, laughter echoing off the walls speckled with massive tapestries and oil paintings. A flock of girls dressed in aristocratic finery stood upon the majestic staircase, twittering like excited canaries. One of them, Lady Emelia, a startling girl with red hair and striking features, waved at him and winked. Eric rolled his eyes and scurried down the hall past the stairs. The last thing he wanted or needed was a flighty girl choking his freedom.

He passed several lavish rooms before spotting his friend at the far end of the music room, leaning on a harp.

"What took you so long?" Sestian grinned, then pushed aside a wall tapestry and vanished through a secret door.

"Drat you, Ses. How do you find these things?" Eric glanced over his shoulder and followed.

Inside, Sestian struck a wooden match against the stone wall and lit a torch he plucked from an iron sconce. They climbed a set of narrow steps. The guttering flame of Sestian's torch cast shadows on the walls. More than once the passageway twisted and turned as they ascended.

"Are you sure you know where you're going?" Eric asked.

Sestian laughed. "We're in the heart of the castle, and you're going to ask that question now?"

They continued upward. After what seemed an eternity, the steps emptied onto the landing of a dark corridor filled with cobwebs. Sestian stopped and thrust the torch at Eric.

"Hold this." He spun a wall sconce in a combination of left and right turns until a latch popped, and a hidden door opened inward, exposing a small room filled with wooden crates.

"What the—?" Eric stepped inside, his mouth open.

Sestian placed his finger to his lips and motioned to a jagged hole the size of a man's fist in the wall.

Curious, Eric squatted and peered through a banner of delicate silk hanging on the other side.

"Dragon's breath," he whispered. "That's the king's arbitration room!" He flicked a sideways glance at Sestian. "How did you find this?"

"I don't sleep much, remember?"

"Dragon's breath, you *are* crazy."

A chair scraped across the wood floor below. Four mages, recognizable by their golden skin, turquoise eyes, and sapphire–blue garments sat on one side of an immense oval table. Four senators clad in similar garments of purple and gold sat across from them. At one head of the table sat Trog and Farnsworth. At the other, a sojourner shrouded in black with silver rings on his fingers and tattoos etched upon his hands. And at one of the five arched windows stood the sorceress, Slavandria, her thick lavender hair plaited in a single braid to the floor.

"Jared," Eric said under his breath, offering Sestian a view.

"Yep," Sestian said. "That'd be my guess." He sat against the wall, his knees to his chest.

Below, Trog leaned forward, his massive hands clasped together, and addressed the cloaked figure opposite him. "We will heed your warnings, Master Jared, and dispatch a legion to Their Majesties. Latest word is they have left the kingdom of Banning and should arrive in Gyllen by tomorrow evening. I also think it wise to notify our neighbors to the north of the encroaching threat. If this enemy's intentions are to see Hirth fall, he will attack our allies first to render our kingdom helpless."

"Agreed." Jared's voice resonated deep within the chambers, and into Eric's core. "Master Camden, see to it the kingdoms of Trent and Banning are informed of the possible threat. Also, instruct the shime to dispatch regiments and secure the borders of Hirth."

"Do you feel that necessary?" replied a bald man clad in blue. "There is no proof the kingdom of Hirth or the realm of Fallhollow, for that matter, is under attack. There have only been a few isolated incidents of bloodshed, nothing that could be construed as acts of war."

"Master Camden," Jared said, "several families of barbegazis, a herd of nine unicorns, and over a hundred humans are dead, all in the course of four days. This morning, patrols rescued a herd of pixies from a crow's cage in the Elmwithian Marsh. They were swathed in dragon's blood. Might I remind you, a single act of brutality, especially one steeped in black magic as these incidences are, is one violation too many. Our job is to protect this world, and more so this kingdom, from any dark sorcery that may threaten it. If this directive is in any way unclear, I will be more than happy to personally instruct you on the importance of upholding your defensive role."

A chill crept up Eric's spine.

"Oh, come on. Instruct him," Sestian said quietly, a grin

stretched across his face.

A palpable silence fell over the room. Master Camden shifted in his seat and wiped the beads of sweat from his forehead. "Personal instruction is not necessary, Supreme Master."

"I find that to be a wise decision."

Eric exhaled. *Yes, so do I.*

Jared stood and pulled the hood of his cloak forward. "Since we are in agreement, I believe we can disperse. Sir Trogsdill, if I may, I'd like to speak with my daughter alone."

"Of course," Trog said, standing. "The rest of you, follow me to the dining hall where you can feast before your journey home."

"I don't believe this," Sestian whispered as Trog ushered the last of the visitors out and closed the door behind him.

"Shh," Eric said.

Down below, Slavandria said. "What is on your mind, Father?"

Jared strolled past her, his hands tucked into his voluminous sleeves. "I have given this a great deal of thought, and I have reached a decision. Considering all that has happened, I have no other choice than to order you to summon the paladin."

Her gasp could have ripped leaves from their stems.

"Father, no! I can't! The paladin is only to be summoned in the direst of circumstances. While these attacks are horrid, they are far from extreme."

"Daughter—"

"Father, please. The ramifications will be devastating to all those involved. Together with the shime, we'll find this enemy and bring him into the light. I beg you. Please do not do ask me to do this."

"If that were true, they would have done so by now. As such, your arguing is futile. My decision is made. By sunset within three days, you as queen of the Southern Forest and Protector of the realm must fulfill your duties. I will have the document drawn and sealed. Have Mangus deliver it. So it is said?"

Slavandria's jaw tightened. "You're being unreasonable."

"And you are bordering the line of punishment."

Eric shuddered at the menacing tone.

"Do I have your word?" Jared asked.

Slavandria straightened her back and steadied her voice. "Yes, Father. So it is said. So it shall be done, but do not think for one minute I won't improvise when the time presents itself."

"You have always been my challenge, child. I would expect nothing less from you. Now, if you will forgive me, I must go."

"Where this time?"

"Home to Felindil for a day. Afterward, I will be in seclusion, communing with the heavens before taking to the sea."

"What? And leave me here to set the world right once the paladin arrives?"

Jared's full-bodied laughter filled the room. "You sound as if the demon of the underworld will rise, spewing fire and ash."

"And how do you know he won't?" She paused, her fingers steepled to her lips before continuing. "Father, please. All I ask is, for once in your long, stubborn life, listen to me. The people of this kingdom and all of Fallhollow are innocent. They need our protection. I fear what the paladin's presence will do. You can't bring such devastation upon Fallhollow and then leave me to salvage whatever is left."

"I bring nothing upon this realm; therefore, I leave you with nothing to clean up. The course of the world is set. Events will unfold as they will. The paladin will not change that which is in motion."

"You're wrong, Father." Slavandria brushed past him.

"Disagree if you must. You always do. For now, go home. Wait for my summoning papers and prepare the traveler. I will come to you in Chalisdawn three days hence."

Jared snapped his fingers. White shards of light crackled and zapped around him, and he was gone.

Slavandria shook her head. "You have no idea what you've done, Father." She gathered her cloak from the back of a chair and incanted some strange words. A swift pale-blue mist rose from the floor, swirling, engulfing her in a vortex. The air sizzled and splintered, and she too disappeared.

"Whoa," Sestian said. "This is worse than bad."

"No kidding," Eric stood and brushed the dust from his breeches, "and I have a feeling it's going to get a lot worse."

Sestian withdrew the torch as they left the room and shut the door. "You do realize we're going to have to find out who this paladin is, right?"

Eric walked down the steps. "Why is that?"

"Come on. Are you that daft? How else are we going to prove to Trog and Farnsworth that we're deserving of becoming knights? Right now all we are to them is a pair of imbeciles worthy of nothing more than polishing armor and performing the duties of a valet."

"We're squires, Ses. That's what we do."

"And it's all we'll ever do if we don't prove ourselves. Don't you get it? When was the last time Gyllen Castle or Hirth saw battle, hmm?"

"You sound as if you want war."

"No, but I haven't trained all my life to become a knight only to end up as a fat, lazy, well-paid manservant."

Eric turned a corner and continued downward, his voice hollow in the muted dark. "I don't think you'll ever be fat or lazy."

"Eric, come on. Why must you be so difficult? Without a skirmish or two, acts of heroism for us are limited to rescuing girls from over-zealous drunkards and protecting the royal dinner from the palace dogs. I want more than that. When I die, I don't want to be remembered for how well I polished a sword, but for something grand and heroic. Don't you want the same?"

"Of course I do, but I don't sit around thinking about what legacy I want to leave behind when I die."

"Liar. All you ever talk about is how much you want to be a knight like Trog." Sestian shoved past Eric and blocked his descent. "Think about it. You know as well as I that we'll be relegated to saddling horses and packing rations and bedrolls if there is the slightest hint of a conflict. They won't let us anywhere near a battlefield, especially you. It's like you're some poster boy for squire school."

"I know, but—"

"No, there are no buts. Don't you see? Now is our chance to show our mettle. If we team up with this paladin, we have a chance to prove ourselves. Trog and Farnsworth will have to take notice."

"Yeah, after they flog, tar, and feather us. Besides, what makes you think this paladin will want us, huh? He's probably some powerful sorcerer like Jared."

"No one is as powerful as Jared, but I'll bet you a rooster against a duck this savior dabbles not only in white but black magic, too. That's why Jared needs him."

"Which is all the more reason for us to keep our distance."

"No! It's all the more reason for us to find him. He'll need guides to help him maneuver through our lands. We'll be heroes for saving Fallhollow from a murderous foe. King Gildore will praise us. They'll write songs about us."

Eric rolled his eyes.

Sestian snorted. "Don't think I can't hear your eyes flipping around in their sockets. You know I'm right. We know every crack in the earth Fallhollow possesses. The very best knights in the world have trained us. On top of that, I have a knack for getting us in and out of places unseen. You're extraordinary with a blade. Together, we're dangerous. We can be his eyes and ears. And when we defeat whatever is out there, Trog and Farnsworth will have no choice but to admit our accomplishments and recommend us for knighthood."

Sestian's stance and the set of his eyes conveyed an intensity Eric admired and feared. He sighed aloud. "All right. You win, but we say nothing. If Trog and Farnsworth found out, they'd roll us in dragon dung and set us on fire."

Sestian punched Eric playfully on the arm and smiled, wide. "Ha! I knew I could break you."

They hurried from the music room and fell in with other students leaving classrooms. In the sunlit courtyard, Eric stopped short. Sestian plowed into him from behind.

"What's wrong?"

Eric gritted his teeth. "Do you not see who is standing in front of us?"

Sestian turned his gaze to their masters leaning against the balustrade, their arms folded against their chests, waiting. "Great. Let me handle this."

Trog stood upright and adjusted the sword on his hip, flexing the intersecting scars on his arms—reminders of dozens of battles fought. He took a step forward, and a gust of wind blew his dark hair back from his weathered, sun-darkened face, exposing a high forehead, square jaw, and intense peridot eyes. Eric gulped as a childhood tale about a sly mouse captured by a blind owl scampered through his brain.

"You're late," Trog said, tossing Eric a suede satchel weighed down with sheathed knives. "Where have you been?" He spoke softly, but his voice reverberated through the crisp morning air.

"Listening to Magister Timan's lecture on ceremonial magic," Sestian replied. "Did you know there are magical portals that allow us to travel between realms?"

"Did you know I have a magical foot that can disappear up your backside if you don't get down to the stables right now?" Farnsworth asked. His brow furrowed beneath a curtain of wavy straw-colored hair. He walked toward Sestian, the seams of his green tunic strained over his wide shoulders, his eyes as brown and penetrating as a wolf's.

"So I've heard. Several times." Sestian grinned and tapped Eric on the arm. "We'll get together later and go over what we learned today, eh?"

Eric nodded and shuffled his feet under the weight of Trog's stare. He waited for Sestian and Farnsworth to get far enough away before lifting his head and meeting Trog's gaze. The knight lifted a brow.

"Are you going to tell me where you really were, or are you going to hold to your story that you were listening to a lecture that ended this time yesterday?"

"Which one will get me in the least amount of trouble?"

Trog placed his hand on Eric's back and edged him down the stone steps to the lower courtyard. "The truth, Eric. Always the truth."

"What if I promised not to tell?"

"Secrets are grave burdens to bear."

"I can't betray his confidence, sir. I promised."

Trog nodded. "Then you'll sleep in the stables tonight as punishment."

"What? How is that fair?"

"You know the rules as my squire, and you still choose to withhold the truth. Therefore, you shall be punished accordingly."

"But the rules of knighthood require I not reveal confidences or secrets under any circumstance to anyone at any time, even under pain of death."

"Nice try, lad, but the last time I looked, you have not been captured nor are you under pain of death." Trog placed a heavy hand on Eric's shoulder. "I'm going to give you one more chance. What will it be?"

Eric clenched and unclenched his fists at his sides. "With all due respect, sir, I cannot and will not betray my friend."

Trog removed his hand. "I commend you on your loyalty, son, but you have made your choice. Therefore, you will suffer the consequences of it. Now go on and get busy with your chores. I want each of those blades in your hand sharpened and polished by morning—"

"But, sir—"

"And for protesting when you should not, you will also sharpen and polish Sir Farnsworth's blades. I'll see to it they are dropped off." Eric opened his mouth to speak but changed his mind when Trog dipped his brow in warning. "Would you like me to add Sir Gowran's and Sir Crohn's weapons to your load?"

Eric bit back the irritation boiling below the surface. "No, sir."

"Very well. Bring the blades to the farrier's stall in the morning around eight. It will be a dual-fold meeting as you can visit your father at the same time."

Trog paused for a moment, his expression thoughtful, and then turned and strolled across the courtyard. He hoisted a young page from a game of marbles and lectured him on the pitfalls of wasting time. Eric snorted at the boy's bewildered expression and the speed at which he ran once set down upon his feet. *Been there, boy.* He cursed beneath his breath. *What am I talking about? I'm still there.*

Eric's boots clicked on the cobblestones as he plodded toward Crafter's Row. He passed beneath the archway connecting the cathedral to the knights' quarters and turned left down the tree-shaded lane toward the royal stables. After informing the stable master of his upcoming sleeping arrangements, Eric returned the way he came. At the crossroad, he turned and made his way toward the smithy. Horses clomped and wagons rattled over the pavers while thick clouds gathered overhead, suffocating the sun. A light drizzle set in as he entered a stone building marked by a metal plate engraved with a hammer and anvil. The blacksmith wiped the sweat from his brow and motioned Eric to a table set with vials of oils, and various whetstones.

Eric sighed. *Lovely.*

He settled into the monotonous task of sharpening and polishing, taking on Farnsworth's load a few hours later. He finished his arduous task just after dusk. Cursing his sore muscles, he packed up the satchels and shuffled to the stables where a plate of bread, cheese, and a pint of goat's milk waited for him.

Great. Is he trying to starve me too?

He ate his rations and settled into the hayloft, his stomach a knot of protests. He sighed. Who was this paladin, and from who or what was he destined to save the realm? There was only one way to find out. Tomorrow he and Sestian would devise a plan, and it would be worthy of a knight's tale. When all was said and done, Trog would have no other choice than to see him as a worthy knight instead of an incompetent fool. An image of Trog groveling for forgiveness appeared in his mind. Eric snuggled into a bed of hay and fell into a blissful dream, a wide grin on his face.

Chapter 2

Your time is nigh. Be brave.

David stood with eyes closed; his palms pressed flat to the shower walls. In time, the haunting words that hijacked his dreams dissolved and washed down the drain. He banged his fist against the knob, turned off the water, and stepped into the steamy bathroom. An offhand glance toward the mirror set his mind on edge.

A whispered expletive escaped his lips as he wiped a thin layer of moisture from the glass. He stared at his reflection, confusion and sleepiness riddling his comprehension. Running his fingers across his chest, he probed a dark tattoo of a bull standing on its hind legs, an eagle perched on its head, wings spread. A Celtic braid entwined with ivy circled the animals like a shield. His stomach clenched. The tattoo hadn't been there when he'd gone to sleep. "What the hell?" David soaped up a washcloth and scrubbed the blotch, but it refused to budge.

His pulse raced.

Inside his dressing room, he rummaged through the cedar drawers and color-coded hangers, clothes flying everywhere. "Crap! Where are they?" David spun around and honed in on the laundry basket sitting on the half-moon leather seat. He dumped it over like a wild dog scouring for scraps. Moments later, he scrambled into his room clad in a pair of jeans, sneakers, and a white sweatshirt with the words Air Force emblazoned in blue letters across the front.

Phone, phone. Where did I leave my phone?

He scanned the room in which he'd grown up. The Tinkertoys, Nerf basketballs, and glow-in-the-dark stars of his youth had been replaced over the years with posters of F-22 Raptors, archery and track trophies, and an entertainment zone that would make the most serious gamer, music lover, and movie freak, drool with envy.

Where did I put it? Think!

He swept back the dark strands falling into his eyes. His memory jogged. He'd sent a midnight text. He leaped on the carved antique bed and uncovered his lifeline to the world buried in the folds of his burgundy comforter. He fell back and pushed the number one.

A sleepy voice answered after four rings. "Hel-lo?"

"Charlotte?"

"David? Do you have any idea what time it is?"

"Yeah, it's seven thirty-three. I need you to come over. Something's happened. I'll open the door for you, but be quiet. Lily's still asleep."

"Wha—? No. Go back to sleep. I'll call you later."

"No, Char!" David bolted upright. "Please, don't hang up! It's important. I swear it. Please."

A long pause followed. "Oh, all right," she said. "I'll be there in a minute, but this better be good."

He ran his palm across his chest. "You have no idea. See you in a few. You remember the code to the gate, right?"

"Duuuh." Her sigh swelled in his ear. "You owe me, David Heiland."

"I kn—"

Click.

David stuffed the phone into his pocket and stretched his Aviator Rolex over his wrist.

Outside, several crows squawked in agitation, the noise incessant and loud.

"What is their problem?"

He rolled off the bed and crossed the room, the floorboards creaking beneath his feet. Cold January air blasted over him as he flung open the double doors to the balcony. Perched above him on a thick snow-covered branch were no less than a dozen crows, their wings flared, their beady eyes focused on something behind the house. David craned his neck to see what had their feathers ruffled, but saw nothing more than bare tree limbs and a snow-dusted roof.

"Stupid birds. Get out of here." He threw a couple of snowballs in their direction. The birds scattered, protesting as they flew beneath the canopy of naked oaks branching over the driveway. Beyond the iron gates, a row of five houses lined up along the east side of Chestnut Circle—minuscule sentries and rooks facing off against the encroaching Cherokee National Forest. Charlotte's house was the third one in, and she was nowhere in sight.

Come on, Char.

David slipped downstairs, and unlocked the front doors, then returned to the bottom step of the staircase, and waited. Ten tortuous minutes passed before the door opened and Charlotte stepped inside. She removed her white, puffy coat and crocheted cap, spilling coffee-brown hair over her light blue sweater to her hips. David's heart fluttered as she flicked him a smile.

"Hey, Firefox." His heart leaped at the special nickname she'd given him in third grade.

No one else was allowed to use it. "What's got your boxers in a bunch?"

Other than the smell of your hair and the way your smile turns me into jelly?

The stray thought stunned him into momentary silence. He rubbed the back of his neck. "I'll tell you in a minute. Come on."

Charlotte followed him up the staircase that curved to the second floor, her eyes fixed on the gigantic Christmas tree brushing the banister. "I thought you said you were going to get rid of this thing before school starts on Monday?"

"Yeah, I might have said that."

"Need help?"

"Only if you have the hotline number to dial-a-servant."

"I don't believe you just said that."

"Whatever." At the top of the stairs, David glanced over his right shoulder at his godmother's closed door. With a finger to his lips, they tiptoed across the landing to David's room and closed the door.

"You know, sometimes you can be such a snob." Charlotte tossed her coat and hat on the beanbag and sat on the edge of his bed.

David picked up Charlotte's belongings and placed them on a chair. "Yeah, so you keep telling me. Can we focus here? I have a serious problem."

"So said the frantic voice on the phone. What gives?"

David took a deep breath. There was no way to explain other than to show her. He pulled the sweatshirt over his head. "This," he said, pointing to the new addition on his chest.

He stood half-naked in front of her. Had it been any other time, any other circumstance like in one of his dreams, he would have appreciated, even welcomed the holy-crap-oh-my-God, Cheshire cat grin on her face. As it was, he wished she'd quit staring and say something, anything to make him feel less *exposed*.

She rose from the bed and chuckled. "Oh my gosh. I don't believe it. You got a tat." She traced the mark with her fingertips.

Her touch surged like warm currents through his body. David swallowed and pulled the sweatshirt back over his head in hopes she didn't notice the goosebumps spreading across his flesh.

"What happened to being afraid of needles and catching the plague?" Charlotte asked.

"Still there," David said.

She sat back down. "So why did you do it?"

"I didn't."

Charlotte smiled. "Your chest disagrees."

"I woke up like this."

Charlotte laughed. "Right, and I suppose the tattoo fairies came in your room in the middle of the night and inked it there." Her blue eyes twinkled. "Come on. Wipe away the scowl and tell me what happened. Did you do it on a dare?"

"No," David said. "Didn't you hear me? I. Didn't. Do. This."

"Oh, come on. It's me, David. Tattoos don't appear out of thin air."

"This one did, and it's not the only thing that showed up without explanation." He pulled an open sketchpad from beneath a stack of books on his desk and handed it to her. "Check this out. I drew it yesterday."

18

A black dragon with small horns and merciless cat-like eyes clung to a castle's battlement. A boy bearing a striking resemblance to David was clutched in one talon. Crouched in the shadows were a man and a woman, terror etched on their faces.

Charlotte stammered. "David, this-this is amazing. Creepy, but amazing. The detail is incredible. Who are these two people?"

"My parents. Look." David plucked two framed pictures from the nightstand. "You can see the resemblance."

"Holy cow. This is whacked." She glanced sideways at him, her eyebrows pinched. "When did you do this?"

"Yesterday, after Lily and I got back from visiting my parents' graves." David put the photographs back and sat beside her, his elbows on his knees, his hands clasped together. "The bad thing is, I don't even remember drawing it."

"What?"

"All I remember is sitting down to draw and then signing my name to the bottom. Everything in between is a blank, like last night. I don't remember leaving the house. I don't know if I walked or drove or if I let someone in." There was a strained silence. David took a deep breath and exhaled. "I'm scared, Char. What's wrong with me?"

"I don't know," she said, rubbing his back, "but we'll figure it out."

David stared at the floor, his nerves stretched tight like a rubber band waiting to snap. Charlotte's presence was the only thing keeping him from breaking. With her, he was complete, like he'd found a missing piece to a puzzle. If only he could tell her how he felt. If only—

Crack!

A branch splintered and crashed onto the balcony with a heavy thud. A diminutive but forceful, "Ouch!" followed.

19

Charlotte jumped. "Who said that?"

David stood, his gaze fixed on the balcony doors. *Your time is nigh. Be brave.* He shook the words from his head and took a deep breath.

"There's someone out there," Charlotte whispered. "I can see the shadow through the curtains."

"I know." David moved around the edge of the bed to the loveseat, opened a black case, and removed a longbow. He wrapped his fingers around the leather grip and pulled an arrow from the quiver.

"Really?" Charlotte quipped.

"Someone just dropped onto my balcony from a tree," he said. "You think I'm going out there unarmed?"

"Don't you have a bat?"

"I'm an archer, Charlotte, not a baseball player."

"And whatever that is is not a paper target."

David snorted. "Thanks for your overwhelming confidence in me."

"Hey, I'm just saying, but please. Go on, Sir Robin Hood. Go for it. Do your thing. Lady Marian awaits your victory."

David ignored the quip and crept forward. With a deep breath, he flung open the doors.

A patch of rust-brown corduroy sailed over the railing. Footsteps pounded the porch below.

"Whoa! Did you see that? He just jumped!" David ran back inside, scrambled over his bed and out his bedroom door.

"Who did?" Charlotte asked, following behind.

"I don't know. Some short little dude."

David barreled down the stairs and out the front door, Charlotte on his heels.

"There!" she said. "Darting between the trees!"

David took off down the long drive, the cold air stinging his cheeks and burning his throat. The stout figure, no more than three feet tall, ran faster, his shape blurring with the surroundings.

"He's getting away," Charlotte said a few feet behind David.

David willed his legs to go faster. Up ahead, the trespasser turned sideways and slipped through the narrow bars of the gate without slowing down.

"What the—" David skidded to a stop and typed in the security code on the control box. The motor engaged. The giant scrolling black rails churned open.

He blew into his freezing hands. "Come on, damn it. A sloth moves faster than this."

Ten. Eleven. Twelve seconds passed before David slipped through the opening and onto the cul-de-sac. His breath hung in plumes above his head. Two houses down, old lady Fenton, a spidery old woman with crooked fingers and waist-length strands of silver hair as fine as mist, shuffled back to her house with a newspaper tucked under her arm. There was no sign of the mysterious stranger.

Charlotte jogged up behind him breathing hard. "Where did he go?"

"I don't know." David bent over, his hands on his knees. "I've never seen anything move that fast in my life. And how did he—I mean—did you see him pass through the rails? It's like he morphed or something."

"Impossible," Charlotte said.

"What? Didn't you see it?"

"Yes, but there has to be—"

A limb in the giant oak tree above them groaned. David turned his face skyward as the branch splintered.

"Get out of the way!" He shoved Charlotte into his neighbor's yard, slipped on a patch of ice, and hit the sidewalk with a thud.

"Ouch!"

The wood missile plummeted toward the ground.

"David, look out!"

He rolled out of the way just as the limb hit the pavement.

David swallowed, hard. His heart beat like a jackhammer.

"Holy crap!" He stood and brushed the snow off his jeans.

Deep laughter boomed from his left. "Sidewalk slide out from beneath you there, son?"

Mr. Loudermilk from next door stood on the stoop of his house, his mouth twisted in a sadistic grin.

Very funny, you nutter. David dusted himself off, frowning at the lanky old man's brown plaid pants and purple striped shirt. His white hair was wilder than usual, standing on end like he'd rubbed his head with a hundred inflated latex balloons. His gaze fixed on David like a buzzard's to fresh road kill. David's insides gnarled. How the real-life Indiana Jones archeologist turned history teacher had turned into such a fruitcake he'd never know. It was if a switch turned off in his head toward the end of August and never turned back on.

Whatever. It didn't matter, so long as Mr. Loudermilk stayed on his side of the hedges, everything would be right with the world.

David stood and pulled Charlotte up. "You okay? No bones broken?"

She glanced up at the tree, then back down to the remnant blocking the sidewalk. "I don't know about you, but that was a little too close for me."

"No kidding."

Out of the corner of his eye, a red flash caught David's attention. The small figure darted across the lawn and around the backside of his house. "Holy crap, he's in my yard!"

David and Charlotte bolted over the limb and ran up the drive.

"Geez, how does he move so fast?" Charlotte said.

"I don't know, but he's getting away. Let's go!"

They took off together, rounding the mansion. The mini Flash Gordon disappeared into the forest.

"Oh, no, you don't!"

David broke into a full run, his track training kicking in. He dashed past the greenhouse and the overseer's cottage, leaping over fallen trees. Twigs and leaves crunched beneath his feet. Branches snapped. Birds took flight. Charlotte yelled for him to stop, but he kept running, the cold air burning his nose and throat.

To the north, he made out the Antylles River rushing toward Lake Sturtle. A flash of red zoomed off to his right. David turned, zigzagging past trees, leaping over boulders. Sweat beaded on his brow despite the cold stinging his skin. The trickle of a creek grew closer. He ran, faster, faster, until he reached the embankment of Wilder Creek. Out of breath, he pressed his palms to his knees and scanned the forest. On the opposite embankment stood a young doe, alert and unsure, her ears twitching. A rabbit darted off to his right. A squirrel scampered up a tree. Charlotte rushed up behind him and hunched over, out of breath and holding her side.

"Did—you—not—hear—me?" She staggered forward. "I—called to you—"

Behind David came a sound akin to hundreds of spiders crashing through the underbrush. David turned as a reddish-brown blur no more than three feet high barreled toward him at lightning speed.

"David! Move!"

Charlotte shoved David, knocking him several feet back. He tumbled to the ground with an oomph.

And then she was gone.

"Noooo!" Charlotte screamed in one long, sustained note as the creature carried her off. Her voice grew further away. "Daaa-viiid!"

David scrambled to his feet and half-ran, half-slid down the slippery slope and across the rope bridge toward her voice, his heart racing, and his throat burning. "I'm coming, Char!"

She screamed from the darkness of the old gristmill ruins. David vaulted over fallen trees and slipped as he swerved around a corner. Down he went, careening to the bottom of the creek. Covered in muck, he darted around the dilapidated water wheel, feeling along the vine-covered walls of the mill until his fingers found an opening. Charlotte sat inside in a heap against the wall.

"Char!" David skidded to a stop beside her, panting. "Char, are you okay?"

"Yeah, I'm fine." She grimaced as she pulled her left leg to her chest.

"Which way did he go?"

Charlotte pointed to her right. "The doorway. I'm sure he's gone by now." Her hand clasped around his wrist as he jerked to leave. "He's gone. Don't bother going after him."

David collapsed beside her, counting backward from ten in his head to calm his pulse. "Did you get a good look at him?"

Charlotte shook her head. "No. He moved so fast. Everything was all a blur. He had a very distinct voice, though. Scottish or Irish, I think."

David leaned forward, his arms perched on his drawn-up knees. "He spoke to you?"

"Not me, I don't think." Charlotte lifted her hip to one side and withdrew a broken brick from beneath her, then tossed it across the room blanketed in dead vegetation. "It was more like he was angry at himself for failing to get you. He said the strangest word that sounded like 'Figbiggin,' followed by a very angry, 'Missed!' Then he dumped me here and took off."

David laid his forehead on his arms folded across his knees. "Who is he? What does he want with me? I don't understand."

"Me, either."

The Star Wars Imperial March blasted from Charlotte's coat pocket. "Oh, geez! Not now." She answered, her tone a bit terse. "Hi, Daddy—at David's—but I'm not hungry—but— okay, fine. I'll be there in a minute."

She hung up and turned to David. "Sorry. I have to go. We have to do the ritualistic Saturday morning breakfast thing with my aunt and uncle. Are you going to be okay? You want me to see if you can come along?"

David shook his head. "Nah. I'm good. Let's get you home."

They hiked back the way they came, and down the street to Charlotte's small brick house nestled in a bevy of bare dogwood trees at the bottom of a gentle slope. A birdbath surrounded by mangled, winter-ravaged flowers stood in the front yard. A maroon SUV sat in the driveway. A tall man with square shoulders and a jawline to match opened the driver door and got out. He wore that I'm-retired-military-and-you-better-not-mess-with-my-daughter look.

Yeah, that one.

David gulped.

"What took you so long?" Mr. Stine said, "and why are you such a mess?"

David jumped in. "It's my fault, sir. I suggested we take a walk down to the old grist mill and we sort of fell."

"Um-hmm," Mr. Stine said, he steely eyes pinned to David. "And you just happened to fall on my daughter in the mud?"

"Yes, sir, I mean no, sir. I mean I did, but not on purpose, sir." Damn, why couldn't he shut up?

"Daddy, leave him alone, Charlotte said. "We didn't do anything wrong." She pecked David on the cheek. "I'll come over as soon as I get back." She cast her dad a look, then ran into the house. David turned to head home.

"That's my little girl, there, young man," Mr. Stine said. "You disrespect her in any way, and you'll have me to deal with."

David gulped. "Yes, sir. I understand, sir."

His stomach fluttered. How, after all the years he'd been friends with Charlotte, was her father still able to set him on edge? David trudged home, his nerves like a bundle of fireworks ready to explode. He headed up his driveway, his eyes darting about, taking in the gargantuan three-story Civil War mansion with black shutters and more massive white columns than a house deserved.

His stomach knotted, as it often did, at the sight of his house—so grand, so majestic, and yet so empty. His wish to have a typical family like Charlotte's was nothing more than a dream. He wished for it anyway, and then chuckled at the absurdity of it all. He wasn't a child anymore. The days of bargaining with God to bring back his parents were gone. After all, God didn't negotiate. Dead was dead.

David climbed the steps of the porch and went inside, the heavy doors closing behind him. An ivory-colored envelope skittered across the floor in a slight undercurrent and came to rest at the curled feet of an antique side table. He picked up the crinkled parchment and read the single name written in sprawling calligraphy across the front.

Lysbeth Perish.

Weird.

The unmistakable aroma of brewed coffee enticed him down the long corridor beneath the double staircase toward the rear of the house. The morning news droned from the flat screen above the stone fireplace in the family room. Muted daylight spilled in through the floor-to-ceiling windows overlooking the manicured backyard and greenhouse. He tossed the letter on the breakfast bar as Lily pushed through the pantry door carrying a bag of potatoes. She glanced at him and set her load in the sink.

"Good morning," she said.

David set his bow and arrow beside the fireplace and took a seat at the breakfast bar.

Lily twisted her thick cherry hair with both hands and tacked it to the back of her head with a clip. How the weight of those locks didn't tilt her off-balance, David never figured out. She poured a cup of coffee. "So, what's with the bow?"

David considered telling her about the speedy man for a moment but then changed his mind. There was no way she'd believe such a story.

"Nothing. I thought I'd go out and practice later."

Lily raised one eyebrow and remotely turned off the television. "With one arrow?"

David poured a cup of coffee. "Less to lose, I suppose."

"Uh-huh," Lily said. "Why was Charlotte here?"

David's stomach lurched. *Do those funky turquoise eyes see everything?* "No reason. We were just talking."

She raised one eyebrow. "Talking? It sounded like a half dozen bowling balls thudding down the stairs."

"Sorry. We didn't mean to wake you."

"I'm not asking for an apology, honey, just some consideration. I was up late last night."

"Someone have a baby?"

Lily rubbed her eyes and yawned. "Yes. The Padgetts. A little girl, around 3:30 this morning."

"I didn't know. I'm sorry."

Lily smiled and tousled his hair. "It's all right. I needed to get up anyway. I have to run into town a little later and pick up some supplies from the hardware store. We're due for a bad snowstorm in a couple of days, and I want to be prepared. Which reminds me, when you're done with breakfast and target practice or whatever it is you're really doing with that bow and one arrow, I'd like you bring up some firewood from the shed, and start taking down the Christmas decorations."

David rolled his eyes.

"I saw that, young man." Lily stood. "Tomorrow is the last day of winter break, and I need the bulk of the decorations down before you go back to school. You promised."

"Ah, come on, Lily," David said. "Why not hire some people to do it? It's not like we can't afford full-time staff to help with this sort of thing. Everyone knows there are tons of people out there who need a job. We'd be doing humanity a great service."

"As a part of humanity, you need to learn responsibility, David. You can't go through life thinking the world owes you any favors because of who you are or what you have. Trust me. It's not going to hurt you to do the few things I ask. Lily poured a glass of orange juice and slid it his way. "Tell you what, why don't you invite some friends over and make a party out of it. I'll pick up some sodas while I'm out. You can order pizza."

David buried his head in his arms folded on the counter. "Sure. Whatever."

"So, what is this?" Lily slid the envelope toward herself, the sound grating in David's ears. He lifted his head as she flipped the envelope over from one side to the other. Her brow furrowed. "This is rather cryptic. No return address. No stamp."

"Yeah, that's what I thought. Recognize the writing?"

"No, not at all. That's what makes it more intriguing, eh?"

Lily smiled at him, winked, and ripped open the envelope, withdrawing a single page from inside. Her fingers touched her lips. The color drained from her face.

David stiffened. "Lily? What's wrong?"

She shook her head and folded the letter in half. "Nothing." Her voice trembled. "Just some unexpected news, that's all." She shimmied around the bar and hurried down the hall toward the foyer. David followed her to the library, but the stained glass doors shut and locked in his face.

He jiggled the door handle. "Lily, what's going on? What's wrong?" He could hear her scurrying around inside. He banged on the door. "Lily!"

A few minutes later the door opened, and Lily headed back to the kitchen, her lips stretched into a fine line, her hands empty.

"Hey," David said, following on her heels. "Talk to me. What's going on?"

"I need to take your car." She collected her coat, purse, and gloves from the coat rack. "The heat in my car is out again."

"Sure. You want me to come with?"

She opened the back door and took his keys from the rack. "No."

"But—"

His protest fell on a closed door.

The rumble of his 1967 Shelby fastback filled his ears. David ran to the front door and watched the black Mustang pass through the gates and disappear. He turned to the library. *What is she hiding in there?*

He pushed open the double doors and stepped into the room rich in leather furnishings and mahogany bookshelves jammed with books. Some were so old he was afraid to touch them for fear they would disintegrate in his hands. With a push of a button on the wall, red velvet drapes, both upstairs and down, slid open, exposing a wall of windows stacked two stories high. Sunlight warmed the oiled portraits on the walls. David straightened the baseball cap on the suit of armor and wove around the plush wingback chairs to the antique desk carved with mermen, tritons, and sea creatures.

"All right. Think. If I were a mysterious letter, where would Lily hide me?"

David rummaged through the drawers and papers. Nothing. He panned the room, honing in on a small, curl-footed, single-drawer table tucked into an alcove under the spiral staircase. He hurried across the room and gave it a quick tug. Locked.

David bit the corner of his lip then snapped his fingers. He bolted upstairs to Lily's office, and from a hook inside a door hidden by a mirror in the closet, he grabbed an antique key ring heavy with brass keys and returned to the library. One after the other he tried them in the lock. The next to the last one popped the drawer open. David reached inside and withdrew a necklace with a heart-shaped lapis pendant, a small, dark-blue leather jewelry box, and the crinkled envelope. His stomach flip-flopped.

He turned the necklace over in his palm. "Why would she leave this? She never takes this off." He set it down on the table and picked up the box. The voice from the dream returned.

Your time is nigh. Be brave.

He cast aside the voice and flipped open the box. A black sickness filled his stomach. "What the hell?"

Perched inside upon a bed of dark blue velvet sat a man's

ring. A wide band of intricate scrolled silver held a dime-size lapis lazuli stone. Carved in its center was an eagle, its wings spread, perched on the head of a bull standing on its hind legs.

His gut lurched as if missing a step going downstairs. *That's my tattoo!* He touched his fingers to his chest.

An overwhelming ache, an intense desire, drew him toward the ring. He needed it, craved it like a junkie needs a fix. He bit his bottom lip and drummed his fingers on his thighs trying hard to ignore it, but the pull grew stronger, more intense as if drawn by a magnetic force. Unable to resist, David slipped the ring on the forefinger of his right hand.

A searing pain, like his skin being scorched from the inside out, shot like an arrow up his arm and hurled into the tattoo. David staggered forward, his hand clutched to his chest. He fell to the floor, upending a small table, and gasped for breath. Sweat poured from his brow. In the mirror over the fireplace, he caught a glimpse of himself and the blue glow beneath his clothes. He ripped off his sweatshirt. Both the ring and tattoo blazed an ice blue, two objects shimmering as one. The tattoo sank deeper into his skin, burning like a branding iron.

"Ahhhh! Make it stop!"

David bent in half, begging, crying for the pain to leave him. After what seemed an eternity, it subsided and let him go. He crawled to the table, snatched the letter and Lily's necklace, and then collapsed into the closest overstuffed chair.

Time passed with the speed of a turtle pushing a rock uphill. Question after question exploded across his tattered mind.

Breathless, David sat forward and withdrew the page from the crumpled envelope. Waves of nausea overtook him as the words reached into his subconscious, grabbing something he'd always felt was there but was never quite able to touch.

My dearest Lysbeth,

Please forgive my quick hand, but time is short, and the danger here grows stronger every day. It is difficult to recognize friend from foe, and I grow more convinced as time passes that Fallhollow sits on the brink of collapse. There are rumors that the Council is ready to turn elsewhere for our salvation. The thought torments me, for as much as his father and I wish to see our son, it pains me to think of David here, forced into the Council's servitude. The risk to his life is too great, yet I am no fool. It is inevitable. His time in Havendale is drawing to a close. Until the time he must leave, please keep him safe and sheltered in your love.

With deep affection.

There was no signature.

The words zoomed away from him, receding into a long black tunnel. His lips and hands trembled. The letter floated to the floor. His phone rang. He answered without speaking.

"David?" Charlotte said. "Are you there? Are you okay?"

He blinked and gasped for air, unaware until he did so he'd been holding his breath. He swallowed hard. An invisible fist clenched his throat and squeezed. Somehow he found the ability to speak. "I-it's my parents. They're not dead."

Chapter 3

Chickens squawked and scattered. Horses clomped, and grain wagons creaked over the cobblestones of Crafter's Row while children hurried toward the kitchens with baskets of freshly picked berries, apples, and vegetables. Men shouted orders, and servants scrambled to prepare the castle and its grounds. It would not bode well for King Gildore and Queen Mysterie to return home after a year away to find the castle in disarray.

Eric woke with a crick in his neck and his stomach rumbling like a wagon on cobbles. Excitement rippled through him at the thought of Their Majesties' return. They'd been gone far too long, and he ached to hear of their travels and adventures. It was one of the perks of being Trog's squire, and Eric enjoyed his talks with the king.

Much to his dismay, the welcoming festivities, along with the influx of thousands of jubilant and loyal Hirthinians, would provide little time to talk and socialize. He decided to wait until the following day to take them on a tour of the newly built university with its marble corridors and spindled turrets. They would be thrilled to see the progress, and he would have time to learn what he could about the danger lurking in Fallhollow.

Pleased with his plan, Eric grabbed his boots and climbed down from the loft. Sestian barged through the open barn doors, panting, with his hair a mess and his clothes askew.

"Eric, you've got to ask Trog for permission to attend the festival."

Eric grabbed a pitchfork and tossed some hay and alfalfa into the horse stalls. "Why is that?" The animals nickered with appreciation.

"The mages are gathering in Hammershire, waiting for the paladin's arrival."

Eric stabbed the pitchfork in a bale of hay. "I thought they had three days?"

"Don't know. I'm telling you what I heard Master Camden tell Farnsworth a few minutes ago. Come on! You have to ask Trog to let us go."

Eric considered the proposal but then shook his head. "I can't, Ses. Trog will never give me permission to go anywhere, especially today. In case you haven't noticed, he's a bit ticked at me."

"That's yesterday's news. Today is now. You have to ask."

Eric collected the satchels of polished knives and stepped outside into the bright sunlight. "Why don't you ask Farnsworth?" Eric walked across the road to the well and set the satchels on the ground.

"I can't. He put me in Trog's charge."

"Then ask Trog yourself." Eric splashed water on his face.

"Are you crazy? The way he looks at me with those little green eyes. They're like little sour grapes ready to burst, except instead

34

of spraying juice, they spew daggers. I don't know how you deal with it."

"I see. So you want his eyes to throw daggers at me?"

"He won't hurt you. You're his squire. You have clout."

Eric laughed and wiped the excess water from his face. "How do you figure? I slept in a barn last night with beggars' rations to eat."

"A minor setback."

"I doubt he sees it that way."

Eric gathered the knives and headed down Crafters' Row toward the farrier's stall. The brilliant blue sky sparkled. The birch trees along the road rustled in a warm breeze infused with the scents of hyacinth and wisteria.

"Eric, please," Sestian said, shuffling up from behind. "We may not get another opportunity like this."

They passed the fire pit where a whole hog and deer turned on a spit over an open flame. Eric tilted his head back and inhaled deeply, taking in the sweet smell of burning applewood mixed with roasting meat. Real food. His stomach grumbled.

A speckled dog ran out of the cordwainer's shop, overturning a workbench, before darting off with its tail between its legs. The shoemaker emerged from the stone building, cursing. Eric and Sestian set the bench upright and picked up the tools scattered about the ground. The wrinkled old man grumbled and snatched his utensils from their hands.

An imposing figure wearing all-too-familiar deerskin boots blocked out the sun. *Ah, great.* Eric gathered the knives he'd dropped, stood and met Trog's stern gaze.

"Well, well, I should have figured as much," Trog said. "May I ask why you were in such a hurry you knocked over this man's stand?"

Eric's eyes widened, and he shook his head. He glanced at his master and the cordwainer. "Oh. No. No, sir. It's not what you think. I—we—Sestian and I—we—we didn't do this. I-it was a dog; I swear it. We only stopped to help pick the bench up. Ask him." Eric pointed to the shoemaker.

Trog crossed his arms and fixed his green eyes on Eric. The seams of the dark-green broadcloth shirt tugged at his shoulders. After a moment, his gaze shifted to the shoemaker.

"Is what the lad says true?"

The man nodded. "Right bit of a helper them two is. Damn dog messed up me stand like he says."

"Hmph. Very well." Eric winced as Trog gripped the back of his neck. "Come with me. Sestian, stay put, understood?"

Sestian nodded, rocking from heel to toe. "Yes, sir. Here I am, and here I'll stay."

Trog guided Eric across the road to a wood bench beneath a large shade tree. "I take it you slept uncomfortably well last night?" Trog asked.

Eric rubbed his neck. "Miserably."

Trog nodded. "Are you ready to tell me the truth about where you were yesterday?"

"I can't," Eric said.

Trog's eyebrow lifted, and he said, "Were you sneaking a taste of mead?"

Eric shot him a wry look. "At nine in the morning? Please."

Trog leaned forward, his arms resting on his legs, his hands clasped between his knees. "Eric, I was young once, and I understand the need to protect your friend. However, you must keep in mind the secrets you keep now can come back to haunt you in the future. Now, I don't know what Sestian has pulled you into—"

"He hasn't pulled me into—"

Trog shot him a sidelong glance. Eric closed his mouth. Trog continued. "I don't know what he's pulled you into, but whatever it is, I need you to promise me you will remember what I've taught you, remain vigilant, and stay true to who you are … a future knight of Hirth. Don't ever lose sight of that or what it means."

"Is this a test?" Eric asked. "Of course I'll remember who and what I am. I've been training for it most of my life."

Trog nodded and looked down. "It is good to hear. Our world is changing, too fast for my liking. You and Sestian must remain steadfast and not be influenced by those with skewed visions of this kingdom. Keep your eyes and ears open. Be smart." He tapped his forefinger on his temple.

Eric furrowed his brow. "Have you been sneaking some mead, sir?"

Trog chuckled. "If only." He slapped his thighs and stood, his gaze settled on Sestian. "I need you and your impish friend to head over to the Floating Isles' welcoming docks. The Duke of Itas and his daughter are due to arrive any minute. I'd like the two of you to escort them to the castle and make sure they are settled in one of the third-floor apartments. Once everyone is tucked into their quarters, you and Sestian have my permission to attend the festivities in Hammershire." Trog glanced at him with amusement. "I assume that is acceptable to you?"

Eric grinned. "Yes, sir. Very much so. Thank you, sir."

"Then I suppose you should get going before I change my mind." The knight took the bundle of blades from Eric and tucked them under his arm.

Gladly!

Eric hurried across the road, grasped Sestian by the shirt collar, and shoved him toward the stables without a single look back. "Come on. We're going to the festival."

Sestian's eyes widened. "We are?"

Eric grinned. "Yeah. But first we have to do a little chore."

***

Eric and Sestian shouldered their way through the crowded cobblestone streets of Hammershire. All around them merchants hawked their wares from cramped wooden stalls decorated in bright fabrics. Magicians paraded their potions, amulets, and charms; entertainers dazzled their audiences with fire-breathing stunts, acrobatics, and magic acts. Tempting aromas of butter cakes, candied apples, and roasted chickens saturated the air. Outside the hatter's shop, Lady Emelia and a short, brown-haired girl with a round face and rabbit teeth began to follow them like hounds on a scent. Despite Eric's attempts to lose them in the crowd, they remained in tow, as if pulled along by an invisible rope.

"What is wrong with them?" Eric asked, stopping to examine an array of leather trinkets. "Do they not have anything better to do than follow us around like pups follow a bone?"

The girls stopped at the next stall over. Lady Emelia smiled and waved. Eric looked away.

"Aww, lighten up," Sestian said, flashing a big grin in the girls' direction. "What is there not to like? We're both devilishly handsome. We're privileged squires to the most elite group of knights Hirth has ever seen. Why, we're practically royalty."

"Key word, 'practically.' Besides, I would think you would want something more in your life, like perhaps a little conversation, some intelligence, not some shallow minx who finds status more appealing than principles." Eric picked up two pewter likenesses of King Gildore and Queen Mysterie and shook his head.

"Intelligence?" Sestian laughed. "What do I need with intelligence?" He patted Eric on the back and hurried off.

"What indeed." Eric paid the merchant for a leather pouch and caught up with his friend.

"Dragon's dung, have you seen so many people in one place?" Sestian asked. "It's complete and utter pandemonium!"

They dodged an intoxicated trio staggering from the Golden Finch Tavern, singing in imperfect harmony. A small boy in pursuit of a squealing pig shot between Sestian's legs, almost tipping him over. Eric laughed and watched the boy as he plowed past the row of inns before disappearing into the crowd. His smile faded. He tapped Sestian on the arm, gesturing toward three figures cloaked in sapphire-blue robes huddled at the intersection of Tavern and Medicinal Roads. Mages.

Someone poked Eric on the shoulder. He spun around to find Lady Emelia peering up at him; a cunning smile etched on her porcelain face. She took a step forward and linked her arm with his.

"Why, Eric Hamden, if I didn't know better, I'd say you were trying to avoid me."

He cringed inside. Silverware scraping across plates made a more pleasing sound than her nasal voice. He unwound her arm from his. A poisonous serpent would have been more welcome. "What do you want, Emelia?"

"Oh, don't be such a cad." She stroked his cheek and linked her arm once more with his. "It's a beautiful day. Their Majesties are returning home today. What do you say the two of you buy us an exotic blend of juices, then escort us to the pavilion to watch the acrobats?"

Eric stepped back, letting her arm fall away. It took everything he had not to spew ungentlemanly words at her. "I apologize, my lady. As tempting as your offer sounds, I am otherwise engaged. I'm sure you can find another more available suitor to buy you whatever your heart desires."

Lady Emelia's mouth fell into a pout. "But I don't want someone else." She drew the tip of her finger down his cheek. "Come with me. It will be fun."

Eric broke away from her once more. "I'm sorry, my lady. Another time, perhaps." He guided Sestian into the crowd and didn't look back.

"Perhaps we'll see each other again at the ball?" she called out to him.

"Not if I can help it," Eric mumbled. "Did you see where the mages went, Ses?"

"Never took my eyes off of them. Follow me."

Eric and Sestian darted alongside the A-framed buildings, keeping to the shadows as they pushed through the crowds. They turned left down Baker's Street and waited beneath the awning of a bread maker. Up ahead, the mages crossed the road and continued past the bustling clothier, tapestry and weave shops of Threadneedle Lane.

"Let's go," Eric said.

A grip upon his collar jerked him backward, the fabric choking his airway. A strong hand planted in the middle of his chest and pushed him against the building. Eric clenched his fist and raised his arm to strike, but changed his mind.

Fast.

"Sir Farnsworth." He glanced to his left at Sestian, pinned to the wall by the knight's other hand. Two other knights, Crohn, and Gowran, stood behind Farnsworth, their arms folded across their chests, smirks cocked on their faces.

"What are you two doing here? Don't you have work to do?" Farnsworth's eyebrows lifted up and down like hairy inchworms.

Eric gulped. "Sir Trogsdill gave us permission."

At the end of Threadneedle Lane, one of the mages glanced behind him before turning a corner and melting away into the tree line. Eric's stomach fell. *Drat rotten luck!*

"Then I suggest you get going before someone becomes suspicious and thinks you're up to no good." The pressure on Eric's chest lifted as the knight removed his hand. "We wouldn't want that, would we?" Farnsworth raised an eyebrow in Sestian's direction.

Sestian shook his head. "No, sir. Absolutely not."

Farnsworth stepped back. "Then get moving, both of you."

Eric and Sestian scrambled off without looking back, the knights' laughter resonating loud and clear behind them.

"I don't believe it!" Sestian said reaching the town square. "We were so close."

Eric smacked a wall and cursed beneath his breath. "We should have been more careful. Come on. Let's go."

"Yeah, yeah. In a minute."

A troupe of musicians arrived in the town square, followed by six dancers whipping around long, colorful ribbons attached to a stick. Sestian's gaze fixed on a particular raven-haired woman dancing to an energetic fiddle and flute.

Eric rolled his eyes and punched his friend on the arm. "Forget it, Ses. She's too old for you. Besides, you wouldn't know what to do with her if you had her."

"Speak for yourself. I *am* an apt pupil, you know." His smile grew wider if that was at all possible.

"You're an idiot, is what you are. Come on. Let's go before

41

we're accused of shirking duties we don't even know we have."

Sestian rolled his eyes. "Don't remind me."

They left the walled town and scampered up the hill, weaving in and out of the throngs of people trekking northward to Gyllen castle. The turrets of the sprawling limestone fortress pierced the sky while hundreds of arched eyes, stacked eight layers high, watched over all that lay below. Vibrant blue and gold silk banners hung over the palace walls; flags flapped in the persistent cool breeze.

Colorful tents and haystacks speckled the lush hillside. A breeze rustled from the east across the Northern Forest of Berg and the Domengart Mountains. The Cloverleaf River meandered southward, glistening in the afternoon sun.

Inside the castle grounds, Eric and Sestian stopped and stared. As if by magic, the royal wisteria tree, its branches so wide it embraced the entire courtyard, was in prolific lavender bloom. To their left, pages led commoners to the small but comfortable quarters beneath Festival Hall. A line of horse-drawn carriages wound along the outer rim of the courtyard, each filled with nobles ready for escorts to take them to their lavish apartments.

"Sestian!" The bark came from the jobmaster, a heavyset man covered in filth and sweat. "Where in flaming dragon's breath have you been? Get over here, now! Eric! You too!"

"What in creation does he want?" Sestian grumbled.

"Perhaps an audience with the privileged squires. We are practically royalty, you know."

They laughed and made their way across the courtyard. Sitting on the edge of the merman and hippocamp fountain was a short, stubby man, his feet barely touching the ground. His equally round wife, her hair piled high on her head in a beehive mess, sat beside him.

Sestian groaned. "Ah, the swine-bellied Baron von Stuegler and his haughty wife. Wonderful." His eyes drifted to the two large trunks and array of handbags stacked to their sides. "From the looks of it, you'd think they were moving in."

"Don't suggest it," Eric said. "They probably would."

"Sestian, hurry up!" the jobmaster ordered. "Take the von Stueglers to their quarters on the third floor. They're tired of waiting."

"What? I'm not a baggage hand—"

The jobmaster smacked Sestian on the head. "If I wanted your comments, I'd ask for them, now move! Eric!" He shoved a whistle into Eric's hand. "Take over for a bit."

"W-what do you want me to do?" Eric asked.

"You're an intelligent lad. Figure it out."

"But I should help Sestian. There are a lot of bags, far too many for him to carry alone."

Sestian glanced over his shoulder weighed down by two large paisley bags. "I've got this, Eric. I'll catch up later."

Eric's objections were interrupted by horns sounding from atop the gatehouse. The guard shouted, "The King's messenger arrives!"

The people scattered as the rider rounded the bend. His cloak flew out behind him as he brought his horse to a stop beside the waiting stable hands. The man dismounted and handed his steed into their care.

The jobmaster shoved Eric aside. "Captain Morant. Welcome back to Gyllen. What is the word?"

The rider stripped off his gloves. "King Gildore and Queen Mysterie are but two hours ride from here. They will arrive by sunset." The captain looked around, taking in all the decorations, and grinned. "They will be most surprised at what you have done to the place." He turned to Eric. "I need to speak with your master right away. I have a message to deliver to him from the king. Do you know where I might find him?"

"I'm not sure. You can try Crafter's Row."

"Thank you." Captain Morant's gaze traveled from the tip of Eric's head to his feet then back to his face. "You should get cleaned up, young man. You are a squire, not a stable hand. You cannot be first in line alongside Sir Trogsdill to greet Their Majesties looking like a bedraggled cat." He playfully punched Eric's chin. "Go on! Make yourself presentable!"

Eric grinned. He didn't need to be told twice. "Yes, sir, Captain." He flicked a sarcastic smile at the jobmaster and ran to his castle suite.

Chapter 4

David ran upstairs to his room, his phone pressed to his ear. "What do you mean your parents aren't dead?" Charlotte sounded as whacked-out as he felt.

He read the letter to her. His hands shook as the words faded from his lips.

"Shut up," Charlotte said. "This is so freaking weird."

"What do I do with this, Char? My brain can't process it."

"I don't know. Let me think. I'm still with my family. I'll call you when I get home."

David hung up and fell back on his bed. Unfolding the letter, he read it again. Three phrases stared back at him.

The risk to his life.

His father and I.

David.

No matter how he spun it, there was no room for misunderstanding. His parents were alive. His mother had written the letter, and he was in danger.

He dangled Lily's necklace above him. *Why did you leave this here?*

The woman's voice from his dream whispered deep in his mind two words he hadn't heard before. *Keep ... safe.*

The pendant swung from side to side in a gentle tick-tock motion. His thoughts traveled back in time to his first memories of Lily. Image after image flashed, and in every frame the necklace was draped around her long, regal neck. That is, until this morning. Until she drove away in his car. David bunched the necklace in his fist, his arm draped across his forehead. His forefinger pulsed. David sat up and removed the ring.

Hot molten fire shot through his veins, shooting down his legs, up his arms, through his neck. His blood turned to lava, burning, bubbling. An inhuman cry he didn't recognize as his own bellowed up from his throat. The room blurred. The ring rolled from his hand, and tinked to the floor.

"Nooooo!"

Fiery torture raged through his limbs. He dived from the bed, searching. Swimming. *Oh, God, make it stop!* Cool metal brushed his hand. His fingers curled around the band and slid it into place. An icy wave crashed through his veins, extinguishing the fire, soothing the burn, and calming his blood.

David stared at the ceiling, panting. "Jesus. What the hell?" His phone rang, but he didn't answer. Couldn't answer. His body failed to engage in movement. The grandfather clock did its musical gong thing twice, meaning thirty minutes passed before he could coerce his feet to allow him to stand. He hokey-pokeyed about and let out a long sigh. "Note to self. The creepy ring does not leave the finger." He checked his phone. Charlotte had called. No message. He grabbed his coat and fled downstairs. He needed to see her, and now, but she wasn't home.

He walked Chestnut circle from the cul-de-sac to the stop sign, counting his footsteps in his head. When he reached thirty-six hundre, he went home, his feet and legs cold and numb. In the warmth of his room, he crashed on his bed, a picture of Charlotte in one hand, his phone in the other.

***

A haze hung around David, lifting him to a green meadow, the morning sun bright and warm. In the distance, a farmer tilled a large field. Children laughed, a dog barked among clothes on a line. Beautiful. Serene. And then it came. Thunder. But it didn't come from the sky.

Hundreds of armored knights and soldiers clambered over the hilltop. On horses and on foot they charged one another, spears at the ready. Arrows flew through the air. The reverberations of the battle surged through his being. His heart was like a pendulum slamming against his ribcage. The ground shook.

Bark. Bark.

David turned to the children playing. Terror coiled around his spine. His feet left the ground in a sprint. His arms flailed in the air.

"Go! Get inside!"

They paid him no mind.

He ran harder, faster, his arms pumping at his side. An arrow pierced his thigh and agony ricocheted through his bones. He tumbled to the ground. Horses reared around him. Blood splattered his arm. A scream filled the air. He scanned the battleground looking for its source and froze as Charlotte came into view, tied to a lone tree in the middle of the field. The children disappeared, vanished as if never there. He pushed to his feet and ran to her, dragging his wounded leg behind. A man wielding a sword shouted his name, but David waved him away. He reached Charlotte and clawed at the knot binding her wrists, but it failed to budge.

A sudden burst of wind hit him from behind. Charlotte's face froze in terror; her expression ripped at his heart. Tears slid down her cheeks. He followed her gaze and stopped breathing as a huge shadow blocked the sun. A monstrous dragon, so plum-purple he was almost black, flew over the field, its enormous mouth open, fangs exposed. Flames bellowed inside its throat. And then it exhaled. Fire flooded the field. Men yelled, consumed by the blaze. The foul smell of death burned crisp and pungent in the air. David wrapped himself around Charlotte, her body buried beneath his, the intense heat on his back.

A downdraft of wind enveloped him. The earth reverberated as the dragon touched down. The beast snorted, its horrid breath brought the stench of rotten eggs. David turned and blinked several times to clear the stinging smoke from his eyes and gasped. A talon twice as long as he was tall poised above him. His reflection, wide-eyed and open-mouthed, stared back at him from the dragon's triumphant slit amber eyes. The talon fell. A scream echoed through the chaos on the field before the world went black.

**

David startled awake, sweat pouring from his brow, the nightmare still vivid in his mind. He shielded his eyes from the afternoon sun glaring through the windows. Clutching the mattress, he stood and gathered his wits. Downstairs, the grandfather clock struck two. Lily. He needed to talk to Lily. He needed answers. As if on cue, the Mustang rumbled up the drive. He thundered down the servants' steps to the kitchen as Lily walked through the back door, her face drawn as if she'd lost her best friend. She flicked him a furtive glance as she hung up her coat.

"W-where have you been?" David asked.

"I had to see someone." She padded down the hall to the library and stopped on the threshold. She turned to face him, her eyes wide. "David, what have you done?"

David stretched out his arm, her necklace dripping from his fingers. "We need to talk, Lily, and I want the truth."

Lily took the necklace, her gaze frozen for a moment on the ring. Her jaw tightened. "What possessed you to go through my things? When has that ever been okay to do in this house?" She stormed off toward the kitchen.

"When was it okay to lie to me?" David followed her.

She spun around, her palm held up in front of her. "Give me the ring."

"I can't, but you already know that, don't you?"

Lily swallowed.

He pulled the parchment from his pocket. "Now, tell me the truth about this letter, and while you're at it, the meaning of this symbol and why it's branded on my chest." He pulled the sweatshirt over his head and threw it on the stool behind him.

Lily's eyes widened, her mouth quivered at the corners. Wispy stray hairs flew wild about her face. She straightened. "When did it happen?" Her words sounded like she'd swallowed a pack of sandpaper.

"It showed up this morning out of nowhere, like your letter, and before the short little dude fell on my balcony then morphed, and vanished into nothing."

"A short man?" Her words reeked with worry. "Did you see what he looked like?"

"He was short with red hair."

"Oh, no." She turned around.

"Oh, no, what? Do you know who he is?"

She hugged her shoulders. "The traveler."

"The who?"

"The time is nigh," she whispered, tears in her eyes. Lily took a seat at the breakfast bar and motioned to the seat across from her. "Put your sweater on and sit down."

David did as she asked.

Lily put her elbows on the table and buried her face in her palms. "There is so much to tell you; I don't know where to begin."

"You can start by telling me if my parents are alive."

She paused and closed her eyes. The words fell from her mouth in a whisper. "Yes, they're alive."

The shockwave hit him full blast. The bottom fell out of his stomach. "W-what?"

Lily reached across the table and took David's hands in hers. "Honey, I'm sorry. I wanted to tell you for so long, but I was sworn to secrecy."

David ripped his hands away. "Y-you lied to me?"

"To protect you."

"From what?"

"From what's happening, from the ring, from the talisman on

50

your chest." She paused for a moment as if trying to find the right words. When she did speak again, her voice was soft, her cadence slow and calculating. "Honey, your life is ... complicated. There's more to who you are than I am allowed to tell you. Those were your mother's wishes, and I will not betray the promises I made to her. Your parents made a very difficult decision. Please believe me when I say neither of them wanted this to happen. They love you very much." Lily wiped a stray tear from her cheek. "It was because they loved you so much they put your life and well-being before their own. For almost seventeen years, you've been safe."

"And now I'm not?"

She shook her head and wiped her cheek. "No, you're not. Something is terribly wrong. The letter—it's not from your mother. That much I know for certain."

Something icy flooded the pit of his stomach. "Then who's it from?"

"I don't know. I wish I did."

"Are you telling me someone is pretending to be my mother?"

Lily nodded. "Yes."

"Seriously?" He leaned back in his seat and folded his arms across his chest. "Why would someone do that?"

"It has to do with who you are, what you are. I believe this is somehow a test. I'm still trying to confirm my suspicions. That's why I left today. I had to talk to someone, someone who can help me."

"Who?"

"Names don't matter, but I trust him with my life."

David leaned forward and picked at his nails. "Why did you leave your necklace?"

"It's a talisman, a safety charm. Through me, it provides a shield of protection to keep you from harm, to keep you safe. I

51

thought by leaving the necklace locked up with the letter and the ring, I might be able to afford you a little extra protection while I was gone."

David snorted and shook his head. "A talisman? Like in a magic stone that brings good luck?"

"In a sense, yes."

He laughed. "Yeah, okay. Whatever. And the tattoo and ring? What are they?"

"They are symbols of your destiny, of your true calling. Apart, they are useless. Together, they are invincible. More importantly, they are bound to you, to each other. They cannot be removed without suffering immeasurable pain."

David turned the ring on his finger, his attempt to remove the silver band still sharp in his mind. "Yeah, I kind of figured that out."

Silence fell between them as David sifted through the information. None of it made sense, and yet, at the same time he knew it all to be true. At the moment, all that mattered was that his parents were alive. His wish, his impossible dream, had come true. There was one thing left to do.

"Lily, where are my parents?"

She paused for a moment before she said, "Somewhere I will keep you from going with every breath in my body."

"Why? What are you afraid of?"

Lily's eyes pooled with tears. "You dying."

Chapter 5

At sunset, Eric and Sestian took their places in the receiving line beside Trog, Farnsworth, and the knights and soldiers of Hirth. Cheers erupted in the streets of Hammershire and rolled in a wave up the hill to the castle. Eric's skin tingled with excitement as he stood straight and tall between Trog and Gowran. He shot a furtive glance at Sestian who stood opposite him, flanked by Farnsworth and Crohn.

Festival trumpets sounded as a dozen guards rode through the arched entrance. Behind them, the royal carriage made of rare red Elven wood rumbled into the courtyard amidst the ringing of the cathedral bells. The coach circled the drive and came to a stop before Festival Hall. The coachman opened the door and offered his hand to the queen as she emerged amidst a shower of rose petals and cheers.

With an exuberant ruby smile on her lips, Mysterie greeted her people dressed in a low-necked, velvet gown of daisy-yellow, her abundant, ebony hair, braided with strands of pearls and ribbons of gold satin.

"Welcome home, Your Majesty." Trog folded into a deep bow.

Eric followed suit. The queen lifted Eric's chin and kissed him on the cheek. "I cannot believe how much you have grown. I hardly recognized you." She motioned for Trog to draw nearer. "Are you responsible for all of this, my dear Trogsdill?" She smiled and held his gaze, her fingertips lingering on his cheek.

Eric's breath hitched. *Whoa, what's that look all about?*

"No," Trog said, shifting his eyes for a second before glancing back at her. "I'm afraid this welcoming was the brainstorm of Lord Donegan and Lady Ashley."

"You must remind me to thank them. What an enormous undertaking. It seems as if the entire kingdom is here."

King Gildore stepped from the carriage amidst loud applause. He smiled and waved to his people.

Eric's insides fluttered. The once round man was almost unrecognizable. His beard was gone, exposing a chiseled chin and dimpled cheeks that deepened when he smiled. He was thinner and very regal in black trousers and a blue silk shirt. A light breeze played with his dark hair, the silver strands glistening in the evening sun. It was obvious the time away agreed with him.

"Your Majesty." Trog bowed once more.

Gildore embraced the knight in a hearty hug. "It's been too long, my friend. I see you've done your job well, and my castle still stands." Gildore winked at Eric, patting him on the shoulder.

"Yes, my liege," Trog said. "The only disaster to report occurred with your cook. It seems after all these years he's discovered a propensity for catching himself on fire."

Gildore glanced at Eric. "Flint caught himself on fire? Is this so?" A broad smile stretched across the king's face, and the mischievous twinkle Eric loved hovered in his blue eyes.

"Yes, sir," replied Eric. "Twice. The kitchen staff had to toss him in the horses' trough the second time to douse the flames."

King Gildore roared with laughter as did the other knights and squires. "I would have paid a hundred trallons to see that old badger thrown into the watering hole! Come, Eric. Alert those in charge to open these doors. I'm famished!" He leaned in toward Trog and said in a low voice, "I am assuming there is food behind these doors?"

"Yes, sire," Trog said with a smile. "Plenty."

The carriage rolled away. Eric and Sestian, along with the knights, led the royal party through the two-story-high mahogany doors of Festival Hall and down the center aisle inlaid with lapis tiles. Brilliant tapestries hung on every wall. Fires burned in the eight hearths, and the twenty-tiered, crystal chandeliers, each possessing more than a hundred lit candles, hung from the high, domed ceiling in sparkling brilliance.

The court musicians began to play as rows upon rows of tables, set with a buffet of food, filled up with guests. Eric waited for the king and queen to take their seats upon the raised dais before sitting beside Sestian.

"Did the von Stueglers give you a good tip, baggage boy?" A smile twitched at his lips.

"Two trallons." Sestian said, a cocky grin on his face. "Heh, you should have seen Farnsworth's face when he found out the courtyard troll turned me into a baggage hand. He got so mad I thought his brains would explode from his eye sockets."

Sestian waited for Eric to stop laughing. "Speaking of seeing people's faces, what's with Trog and the queen, eh?" Sestian nudged Eric on the shoulder. "The way he stared at her, you'd think he was the king."

Eric stared at his plate. "I'm not sure. I don't think it means anything. I mean, Gildore didn't seem upset by it, and they did it right in front of him."

"Still weird if you ask me." Sestian sipped his wine.

Eric acknowledged Sestian's curiosity with a nod and glanced around the room filled with close to a thousand souls. His gaze settled on the von Stueglers guffawing with some obscure landowner at a side table. Eric snorted. "I guess we should be thankful their son isn't here."

Sestian set down his chalice, its contents sloshing over the edge. "Bainesworth? Luck has nothing to do with it. I heard it from a reliable source that Gowran and Crohn took a trip to Faucher a couple of weeks ago and delivered a personal warning that he was not welcome. Need I say more?"

Eric snorted. "As if Trog needs their protection."

"Well, you know how the four of them are, all armed to the hilt and eager to ruffle some feathers."

"They must have anticipated trouble and put an end to it before it began." Eric put down his goblet and rotated it around on the tablecloth. He looked down at his plate of food and pushed it away, his mind elsewhere.

"What's the matter?" Sestian asked, taking a bite of bread. "Not hungry?"

Eric shook his head. "I can't eat."

Sestian's eyes narrowed with concern. "Why not?"

"I found out about an hour ago Trog and I are heading to Avaleen tomorrow."

Sestian's gaze fixed upon Eric. "What? Why?"

Eric folded his arms on the table and spoke just above a whisper. "I'm to spend the next twelve days in combat training with the mages."

Sestian sputtered, almost choking on his food. "What?" he

whispered back, his eyes wide with disbelief. He put down his napkin. "No one our age trains with the mages!"

"You sound almost jealous," Eric said. "I'll be more than happy to let you go in my place."

"No, no, that's not what I meant. This is incredible! Who will be your master?"

Eric kept his expression bland. "Mangus Grythorn."

Sestian caught his breath for a moment and let it go. "The general of the mage army? Jared's right arm?"

"One and the same." Eric swallowed his wine in one gulp.

"B-but. That man is a lethal weapon, more so than Trog!"

"Thanks, Sestian. You're doing a fine job making me feel better." Eric sat back, his arms folded tight to his chest.

"This is insane," said Sestian. "That man has the power to kill you with a look. Why would Jared hand over his top advisor and right-hand man to train you?"

"Do you have to say it like that?"

"You know what I meant. I wonder if it has something to do with the paladin."

"I doubt it. I think Trog feels he's taught me all he can."

"That's a load of dragon dung, and you know it," Sestian said. "You could spend a lifetime with Trog and never learn all he knows. No. There's something more to this. They must have hand-picked you for something."

"Like what? An early death?"

Sestian patted Eric's back. "You're going to be fine. I'm sure Trog won't let him scar up that pretty face of yours too bad." An infectious grin spread across his face.

Eric smiled despite himself. "I'll show off my battle wounds when I return."

"I'd expect nothing less. Now eat. You're going to need it."

***

The festivities continued in the adjoining ballroom where the royal couple initiated the first dance of the evening. Eric leaned against a marble column and watched, thankful to be a spectator. His contentment was short-lived when Trog arrived with Lady Emelia on his arm.

"Eric, I think you have met Lady Emelia, Lord Cameron's daughter." He gestured to the center of the room. "Why don't you take her for a dance?"

Lady Emelia smirked as she twirled a red ringlet around her finger. "Hello, Eric." She linked her gloved arm in his. "Shall we?"

Eric's insides boiled as he moved onto the dance floor. "I see you used your position to once again get what you want."

She laughed in his ear. "I always get what I want, haven't you noticed?"

"You won't get me."

"Ahh, but I have you now, don't I?" Her words brushed across his ear like a warm summer breeze laced with slivers of glass.

Unfortunately.

The music ended, and everyone clapped.

Eric bowed and escorted Lady Emelia to her father and exchanged a few moments of necessary pleasantries. Afterward, he returned to the dais where he bid goodnight to the royal couple. Trog caught up with him in the courtyard.

"I don't recall giving you permission to leave."

Eric continued walking, his temper ready to explode. "I

didn't think I needed your permission. I excused myself from the king and queen, as is proper etiquette."

"But it is not proper protocol. You know what I require of you."

Eric whipped around. "And am I required to be your pawn to move around at will, forced to do what you wish?"

"You were disrespectful to Lady Emelia at the festival."

"Me? Disrespectful to her? That spoiled cat?"

"Regardless of your personal feelings toward her, she is still a lady of this court."

"She's a snobbish tart," Eric snarled. "Her snout is stuck so far up in the air I'm surprised she doesn't suffer nosebleeds. You should have seen the way she ogled me like I was some prize at a fair. She walks and dances like an ass, and her face is in a constant state of puckered haughtiness. She is impertinent and would illuminate any room simply by leaving it!"

Trog stared at him hard. "Those words are most unbefitting of a future knight."

"I don't care. She's unbefitting of the title she holds."

"You had better care, Eric. She is, after all, of the queen's blood."

Eric gritted his teeth. "Just because she holds some distant and unlikely title to the throne means nothing to me. I will not be forced to engage in activities with a haughty, twittering, little bird whose only purpose in life is to wed and produce more twittering canaries!"

Trog jabbed his finger into Eric's chest. "You need to watch what you say and think. The very soul you loathe may be the one to save your hide someday."

"I shall ponder that thought as I prepare for our trip tomorrow. Now, if you don't mind, I'm going to bed."

Trog's nostrils flared like a horse's after a taxing run. "I expect you to be ready to leave at first light."

***

Eric retired to his chambers, his brain too busy and irritated to sleep. The day's events monopolized all of his time and the incidents with Lady Emelia served only to twist every nerve in his body into tightly wound knots. He clenched his fists and cursed her name each time he paced by his windows. Because of her, he and Sestian had lost track of the mages. Because of her, they never found out whether the paladin arrived. Because of her, there was now a rift between Trog and him that wasn't there before. The girl was trouble. She needed to go away. Far, far away.

Eric sat at the foot of his bed and stared at the floor. A knock at the door broke him from his thoughts. The door inched open, and King Gildore peered inside.

"You mind if I come in?"

Eric stood and bowed. "No, sire. Please." He scurried about the room, picking up his clothes. "I'm sorry about the mess. With everything going on today, I didn't get a chance—"

"I'm not here to lecture you on the cleanliness of your room, Eric." Gildore's eyes held a fatherly gentleness, his lips a warm smile. "Please, sit. I'd like to chat with you for a moment." He sat in a high-backed upholstered chair.

Eric dropped the clothes in a basket and returned to his bed. "Have I done something wrong, Your Majesty?"

Gildore chuckled. "No, no, lad, not at all. You seemed out of sorts, even a bit angry when you said your goodnights. I thought perhaps you could use a good listening ear. Was I mistaken?"

Eric breathed a giant sigh. "No, sire, you weren't mistaken. Does Sir Trogsdill know you're here?"

"Would it matter if he did?"

Eric paused for a moment then shook his head, his eyes turned downward. "No, I suppose not."

"If it makes you feel easier, I'm not in the habit of telling my knights, even those closest to me, where I go while in my own home." He smiled as Eric's gaze met his. "Talk to me, son."

Eric opened his mouth, and his frustration poured out of him as he explained Trog's infuriating hold on him, the constant pressure for Eric to be perfect in everything he did; his need to prove his worth to a man who deemed him to have none.

Gildore nodded, and when Eric finished, he said, "How well I can relate to what you say. Try not to hold it against him. He only wants what is best for you." The man stood, walked over to Eric, and sat next to him on the bed. "He also believes you might be in some trouble." The king lifted an eyebrow. "Are you?"

"There are many things Sir Trogsdill believes, sire. That doesn't make them true."

Gildore smiled. "Agreed."

"I'm trying to work something out on my own, that's all," Eric continued. "I'd like him to trust me enough to do so."

Gildore gave Eric's shoulder a reassuring squeeze. "I shall try to set his mind at ease."

"Thank you." Eric bowed.

"Let's get together when you return from Avaleen," Gildore said, "We'll swap stories from the past year."

"I look forward to it, my lord."

Gildore turned and walked out of the room, closing the door behind him.

Eric undressed down to his under tunic and breeches and fell into bed. Thoughts of the upcoming trip to Avaleen left him more than anxious. Perhaps Sestian was right. Maybe there was more to this trip than Trog let on. After all, mages were trolling Hammershire. A paladin was due to arrive any day. In a few hours, he would leave for the mage city to engage in what could only be military strategic warfare training with a man whose mere presence shattered his nerves.

Eric closed his eyes and pushed the thoughts aside, forcing his mind to focus on the music and laughter floating up from the courtyard.

A brisk breeze tinged with a hint of rain wafted through the open doors of the balcony as an echoing storm rumbled to the east. Chilled, he pulled the brocade covers over his shoulders, growing drowsy as a resonating purr boiled up, distinct and separate, from the growl of thunder. His weary mind whispered of an unseen threat and cast an image of living darkness crawling along the shadowed edge of the Northern Forest, waiting. Eric squinted the vision away and buried his head under his pillow. Tomorrow, he would come face-to-face with a killer more dangerous than Trog. The last thing he needed was an overactive imagination.

Chapter 6

David tossed the sketchpad to the foot of his bed. His head throbbed. His mind struggled to sort through the chaos flying around inside. For hours, he'd sat hunched over, his fingers tapping the keyboard, searching for the location of Fallhollow and possible meanings of the tattoo and ring. Only once did he venture downstairs to collect an armful of snacks and a six-pack of Coke. From the staircase, he spotted Lily in the library, an oversized, black, leather-bound book clutched to her chest. He'd never seen it before, and her protectiveness stirred more than curiosity. He made a mental note to go back and look for it.

It wasn't until the sky burned with a brilliant sunset that David stood and swept the dark strands from his eyes. He texted Charlotte, desperate to get out of the house, but she babbled back she was in the middle of doing chores and couldn't talk. Bored, he logged on to his favorite fantasy game, but the medieval world with its knights and dragons did little to calm his growing apprehension.

"I've gotta get out of here."

A gentle knock sent his nerves skittering.

"David, I'm going to grab a bite to eat. I'd like you to come with me."

Lily sounded sincere. It might be productive. "Will you tell me what I want to know about my parents?"

There was a pause, not a long one, but enough to give David an answer before she did.

"I can't, honey. Please, trust me."

Right. Trust someone who lied to him and continued to keep the truth away.

"I'm sorry, Lily. I can't."

Silence.

"Okay," she finally said. Disappointment flooded through the closed door.

David pulled his knees to his chest and buried his face in his arms. If only she would talk to him. If only she would acknowledge the betrayal.

If only his parents had never left.

His car rumbled down the drive. He jogged downstairs, desperate to feel the cold air on his face. To feel his skin freeze. That pain would be far easier to deal with than the ripping apart of his heart and soul.

He pulled down on the front door's handle.

The door didn't budge.

He entered the code into the security panel, but the red light stared back at him in mocking indignation.

A frustrated growl ripped from his throat. "Really, Lily? You changed the frigging code?"

He banged his fist on the door and sprinted upstairs. Back and forth he paced, clenching and unclenching his fist. It was bad enough she'd lied to him, but to keep him a prisoner in his own home?

He paused beside two black-and-white photographs on the wall, each paired with its newspaper article. The first: his father dressed in flight gear with a lopsided grin on his face, standing beside an F-18. The headline: 'Decorated Air Force Pilot, Edward Heiland, Lost in Tragic Accident'. David knew the article by heart: a training mission in the Gulf of Mexico. Two planes collided. His father's body never recovered.

His gaze flitted to the second frame, a photo of his mom in a floral dress, a contagious smile accentuating her sparkling eyes. The headline: 'Havendale Mourns the Loss of Widowed Philanthropist, Jillian Ashley Day Heiland—Infant Son to Inherit Millions'. According to the article, she'd died within hours of his birth.

But it was a lie. All of it. David swallowed the raw emotion choking his throat. He fought against the anguish, desperately wanting not to feel the torment. They'd left him, abandoned him, never wishing to be found. He clutched the bedpost.

Heartache pushed its way up, twisting and turning his insides. His bottom lip trembled. Why? Why had they left him? What could have been so bad they couldn't take him with them?

He took a breath and tried to rationalize, considering the puzzle piece by piece. Lily said they'd loved him. He knew Lily was afraid, afraid of him dying if he went where they were. If that was true, perhaps they were protecting him, but from what? He sat on the bed, the drawing of the dragon and his parents staring back at him. Enormous waves of energy and feelings crashed over him, suffocating him. Drowning him.

Beethoven's Fifth Symphony filtered through the pool of emotions. His stomach fluttered. He closed his eyes, swam to the surface and answered his phone.

"Hey, Char." He wiped a stray tear from his cheek.

"David! David! Oh my gosh!"

His heart leaped, almost stopped. "Charlotte, what's wrong? Are you all right?"

She sucked in a deep breath. "David."

Her sobs sucked years from his life. His nerves shattered. "Char, calm down. Take a deep breath and tell me what's happened."

Her voice lowered to a whisper, her words broken. "Mr. Loudermilk—Mrs. Fenton. They—they want to— "

"They want to what, Char? Slow down."

Charlotte inhaled, her breath so deep David thought for sure she'd inhale him through the phone. She paused for a moment. "Okay, okay." She exhaled. "I was outside about to roll the garbage cans to the curb when I heard Mr. Loudermilk and Mrs. Fenton talking in her backyard. Mrs. Fenton was arguing with him, telling him she didn't care if some guy named Bainesworth owed Mr. Loudermilk favors. She was tired and wanted to go home. Then she got all pissy. She threatened him. She told him if he betrayed her, she'd cut him from navel to nose. Then she wanted to know when they'd find out if you were the one, and how long would they have to wait to get rid of you. Mr. Loudermilk got all snarky and told her to shut up, and there would be hell to pay if she messed everything up. He said they'd know soon enough about you, at which time he would inform somebody called His Greatness, and they would go from there."

"His Greatness." David rubbed his forehead. "Who the heck is His Greatness?"

"Really, David? Is that all you got out of that?" Charlotte blew her nose in his ear. "Don't you understand? They want to get rid of you."

David stared at the floor and swallowed, hard. "Yeah. Right. That."

"D-do you think we should call the cops?"

"And tell them what?"

"I don't know. Maybe the truth?"

"And it would be their word against yours."

"So, we're going to do nothing?"

"I don't know what we're going to do, Char." He washed his palm over his face.

"We'll figure it out when I get there."

"No!" Visions of dark shadows assaulting her swarmed in his mind. "Stay where you are. Lily changed the security codes. The house is on lockdown."

A sigh of relief reached his ears. "Oh, good."

"Good for who? I'm a prisoner in my home."

"Maybe, but if you can't get out, they can't get in."

She had a point. He didn't like it, but she had a point. "Whatever," David said. "I'm gonna go. Keep your doors locked, too. We'll talk later."

"Okay. Make sure you tell Lily about our neighbors. Maybe she can find out what's going on."

Yeah, like the Grand Betrayer would do anything to help him figure out the insanity brewing around him.

"Bye, Charlotte. Love you." The words tumbled out without thinking, but it didn't matter. She'd already hung up.

David tossed the phone on his bed and stared at the floor, his hands clasped behind his neck. The empty house creaked around him. The pipes gurgled. The wind moaned, and the tree branches clawed at the sides of the house. Downstairs, the grandfather clock in the parlor struck seven. David shut his eyes to the four walls of his prison and collapsed from sheer exhaustion.

Chapter 7

E ric woke to the sound of heated voices.

He stole across the room and pressed his ear to the door connecting to Trog's room.

"Why? Why don't you tell him the truth?" the queen said. "He is a bright boy. He deserves to know."

"We have been over this a hundred times, my queen," Trog said. "He must remain protected."

"For how long?" Mysterie said. Her voice carried an edge like a well-sharpened blade, sharp and to the point. "You expect him to be a man, risk his life, fight in battle if need be, and yet you continue to treat him like a child. Where is your honor, Trog? When did you trade truth for lies?"

"Terie," the king said, "you're being unfair. You know the dangers if Eric learns the truth."

Eric's stomach pinched. *What truth?* He wiped the sweat from his palms and bit back the urge to barge into the room.

"Yes, I do," the queen said, "but I also know how that boy will react when he discovers the truth. He must hear it from Trog. We all know how secrets have an ugly way of divulging themselves at the most inopportune time. Goodnight."

Footsteps moved across the room, followed by the click of the door closing.

"Don't let her get to you," Gildore said. "You know how altruistic she can be."

"She's correct, though. If Eric finds out from anyone but me, he will never forgive me, no matter the reason."

Eric's shoulders stiffened. *I don't believe this! How dare he lecture me on the importance of honesty when he lies with such ease?* Eric swallowed hard, his heart thudding in his chest like a caged wild beast, and moved away from the door.

What secret are they keeping?

A hurricane of scenarios swirled in his mind until his brain ached and he could think no more. He had to get out of there, out of his room, away from the walls brimming with lies and deceit.

There was only one place he could go, only one person he could talk to who wouldn't lie to him.

Sestian.

Chapter 8

David woke and rubbed the sleep from his eyes. He glanced at the clock. Two a.m. As if a slave to his growling stomach, he made his way to the dark kitchen and gulped two glasses of orange juice and inhaled a donut. Heading back to his room, he passed the library and remembered the thick book with the black leather cover. After verifying he was alone, he slipped inside and closed the door. He withdrew a flashlight from the bottom desk drawer and shone it on the shelves. Finding nothing on the first floor, he crept up the winding staircase to the second. His fingers brushed the colorful bindings as he passed by them— Dahl, Dante, Defoe, Dickens —he'd read them all. If only he could find the one that mattered.

Overhead, footsteps moved across the floor. His heart skipped a beat.

Lily!

He shut off the light and listened. The front door opened. A male voice resonated in the darkness. "Hello, Lysbeth."

David's heart snapped into this throat.

"Thank you for coming, Mangus," Lily said, her voice low. "Please. This way."

David's heart plummeted. *Mangus? Who the hell is Mangus?*

The library doors opened. David pressed flat to the hardwood floor.

Lily stood in the middle of the room in a floor-length nightgown, a tall, clean-shaven man with plaited black hair beside her.

"I apologize for arriving so late," he said, stripping off his gloves. "I was detained."

David peered through the iron railing.

The man removed a full-length, black coat. His blood-red shirt shifted across his broad shoulders, accentuating a sheathed sword strapped to his hip.

David wrinkled his nose. *What the hell? Who is the Renaissance Faire reject?*

"I assumed as much," Lily replied, fingering the lapis pendant around her neck. "I had hoped you wanted to see me because you had good news, but I can see by the look in your eyes that is not the case."

He gestured toward an overstuffed chair. "Perhaps you wish to sit down?"

She shook her head.

Mangus perched on the edge of the desk. His leather boots squeaked as his ankles crossed. "I won't waste your time. The situation is grim. Murders and ill deeds are on the rise. The latest victims are from Falcon's Hollow and Brindle Greens. Seven little ones abducted in one night alone."

"No!" Lily's hand sprang to her lips. "Please tell me they were found!"

David knitted his brow. *Falcon's Hollow? Brindle Greens?*

The man shook his head.

"I don't understand," Lily said. "How can this person, this thing, wander about and no one witness a thing?"

"The shime have dispatched more guards. They are increasing their patrols as we speak, but that is not why I've come." Mangus hesitated for a moment, his arms splayed beside him on the desk. "I'm here to talk to you about the boy. He cannot remain here, Lysbeth."

David gulped.

"And just where is he supposed to go?" Their gazes met. Lily's mouth opened, and she shook her head. "No! I will not allow it!"

"It is out of your hands, my lady. The orders have been issued."

"I don't give a damn about your orders!" She cut the air with her hands. "He's not going anywhere!"

Go, Lily! David smiled against the rising panic.

Mangus slid from the desk and took her elbow in his hand. "Lysbeth, he must. If what you have told us is true, his location has been discovered. His life is in danger if he stays."

Lily jerked away. "His life will be in more danger if he goes back with you!" She shot him a vehement look as she walked past.

"I refuse to argue. I know you love him, but there is no time for hesitation."

"Do not patronize me, Mangus!"

"I would never do such a thing, milady," he replied in a measured voice.

"You have no idea what this will do!" she snapped. "There is far more at stake here than you know. The ramifications will be devastating."

"It will be devastating if we do nothing. This enemy must be stopped. The boy's time is nigh."

David's heart thumped against the floor.

Lily pulled her arms tight across her chest. "The boy has a name. It's David, and I won't allow you to put his life in further danger by using him as bait. My answer stands. He stays in Havendale."

Mangus pulled a rolled parchment from inside his coat. "Jared thought you would feel this way. He said to give you this. All the Council members signed it. I'm sorry."

Lily stared at it, wide-eyed. Her voice fell to a whisper. "Put it away."

She stood before the window, her slender body silhouetted by the moonlight. After several moments she said, "I don't believe this is happening." She turned to face him. "When must he leave?"

"In the next few hours—at sunrise."

David pressed his back to the baseboard, his head spinning. *What the—*

"Will I be allowed to say goodbye?" Lily asked.

What? I thought you said you'd fight for me, Lily! You said I wasn't going anywhere!

"Do you think it wise?"

"I don't know." She wiped a stray tear from her cheek. "All I know is I love him. How am I to let him go, knowing what faces him? I can't bear the thought. It breaks my heart."

David's temper flared in his gut. *This is how you love me, by betraying me? Lying to me?*

Mangus took her in his arms. "If it is any consolation, he will be well protected."

"That is little relief. How will he ever forgive me? He already knows I've lied to him about his parents' deaths, and now I am to walk away without fighting for him?"

"Time has a way of healing all pains, and you are fighting for him, in ways not even you cannot fathom. Now, I must ask—is the book secure?"

"Yes. It's in my room. I couldn't risk David finding it."

"Good. Keep it safe. I feel certain the enemy will come for it."

She nodded. "I understand."

Mangus glanced at his pocket watch. "I must go." He pulled on his gloves and coat and opened the door. Lily escorted him from the room. Moments later, the front door closed and the house fell silent.

David lay still, his breathing shallow. Fear merged with anger as he cast aside his first instinct to storm out of the room and confront Lily. Instead, he wiped his sweaty palms on his jeans and hurried out of the library's secondary door. With utmost silence, he dashed his way through the house to the servants' stairs in the kitchen. Back in his room, he shuffled around in the dark shoving clothes into his rucksack. *I can't believe she gave in! I can't believe I have to run away from everything!*

The hall light flicked on, its glow visible beneath the door. *Crap!*

He dove into bed and shut his eyes. The door opened, and Lily's nightgown rustled as she moved toward him. She set something on the nightstand and kissed his temple.

"I'm so sorry, honey. Please forgive me." A tear dripped onto his skin. "I love you."

Seconds later, she was gone.

David sat up and wiped her tear from his face as if it were poison. He glanced at the glass of ice water on the nightstand and guzzled it, his throat parched.

Instant dizziness crept into his brain. His mouth felt numb. Dry. His thoughts blurred.

You idiot! What were you thinking? What did she give me?

The glass clunked to the floor. He collapsed on his bed.

***

Charlotte's voice filtered through the daze. "David! Get up!"

David turned over and groaned. His head ached as if pressed in a vise. "Wh-what are you doing here?"

"Why didn't you answer your phone? I've been calling for the past half hour, ever since Lily hauled butt down the street in your car. I was worried out of my freaking mind."

David struggled to sit up. "Lily left in my car?"

"Yeah, she was driving like a lunatic, too. Why isn't she driving her car?"

"The heater isn't working." David combed his fingers through his hair. "What time is it?"

Charlotte propped some pillows behind him. "A little after seven."

David hugged his knees, his head resting on them. "Ugh."

"Seriously? What's wrong with you? You're usually up before the sun. Are you drunk?"

David shook his head. "I think Lily drugged me."

Charlotte laughed. "Don't be silly. Why would she do that?"

"So I wouldn't leave before he got here?"

"Before who got here?"

David relayed everything that happened.

Charlotte's jaw tightened. "This is twisted! How could she even think of sending you away? You're not going to go, are you?"

"No. I was packing when—wait a minute. How did you get in the house?"

"The door was open."

A loud crash came from downstairs.

Charlotte whirled around, her eyes wide. "What the heck was that?"

David sprang from the bed, his gut wrenched in a knot and crammed his feet into his shoes. "Stay here. I don't want anything to happen to you, got it?"

"Seriously? I'm not a fragile little girl, David. I can look out for myself."

David caressed her cheek, his fingers slipping through her hair. Out of all the insanity that had touched his life, she was his constant, and he loved her even more for it. "I know, but I would freak if anything happened to you. Promise me you'll stay here."

Charlotte rolled her eyes. "Whatever. Go!"

David kissed her forehead and headed downstairs. Lily's favorite antique white vase, hand-painted with baby rosebuds, lay shattered on the parlor floor beside the credenza.

David grabbed the poker from beside the fireplace. The parlor doors slammed shut.

Freaking A!

He glanced around, his chest rising and falling. "Where are you? Come out so I can see you."

A stout man, no more than three feet tall and dressed in a tweed suit sauntered from the doorway between the parlor and music room, a long-handled pipe in his hand. His ginger hair spilled over his collar while watchful, topaz-blue eyes took in all of David, appraising him as if he'd discovered a new species.

David swallowed. "W-what are you doing in my house? What do you want?"

The little man tapped his pipe into an empty candy dish and stowed it in his breast pocket. Despite his strange, gnomish appearance, he held himself with an air of importance.

"Now, now, dear boy," he said. "Is this the way you greet all your visitors? Appalling behavior, I must say."

"You're trespassing in my house. What do you expect?"

"A bit of propriety, young man. I was told you had impeccable manners, but it appears I was misled. Now please put down that iron. You look ridiculous."

"Not until you tell me what you want."

Toddler-man circled his finger in the air. The poker flew from David's hand and somersaulted back to the stand.

David gaped. His bones rattled. "H-how did you do that?"

"You wouldn't believe me if I told you, now close your mouth. It's rude to gawk."

"Who *are* you?"

The man stepped forward. "If you must know, my name is Twiller, and I am here to accompany you to safety."

"You? But I thought—" David wrinkled his brow.

"Now is not the time to think, Master David. It is time to say good-bye to your friend as you will not see her for quite some time."

The ceiling wavered and softened, melting away like warmed butter. Pink sneakers, followed by Charlotte's entire body, oozed through the pudding plaster. She dangled in the air, held in place by a spinning spiral of green threads sizzling with energy. Her face wore a terror he'd never seen before.

"David?" Her voice shook. Her fear plowed through him.

Rage swelled in David's soul. Twiller could do whatever he

wanted with him, but Charlotte was an entirely different matter. He pinned his gaze on the little man.

"Put. Her. Down."

"Say your fond farewell," Twiller countered. "*Arrivederci. Au revoir*. Whatever word you wish, but hurry on with it."

"I'm not going anywhere with you! Now put her down!"

Twiller shook his head. "I can't do that. You either come with me, or I will be forced to do unspeakable things to your friend. What will it be?"

David lunged at the man and fell flat on his face.

"David, please," Charlotte cried.

Twiller closed his eyes and chanted a string of peculiar words. Charlotte began to spin like a top.

"David, please! Get me down from here!" Her scream filled the room.

David rolled and swiped Twiller's feet out from beneath him. "Let her go!"

Twiller hit the ground with an oomph.

Charlotte crashed to the floor, shattering the coffee table.

David scrambled to her side. "Are you okay?"

She winced and stood. "Yeah."

A golden arc caught David on the forearm, launching him through the air. He crashed through the wall and landed in the entrance hall.

Twiller stood in the opening, a pearl of spittle crawling down his chin. Braided golden threads of light unraveled from his fingertips and spiraled toward David.

"No!" Charlotte yelled, throwing herself in front of David.

A loud boom filled the room. Charlotte vanished with a scream.

David's heart fell into his gut. "Noooo! What did you do with her?"

78

Twiller clutched his side. "Stupid girl!" Another braid unraveled from his fingertips and hit David in the back.

Pain spiraled up his spine. Time and space distorted like ripples across the water. The air around him exploded as he sped through a tunnel of darkness, a bullet through the barrel of a gun. His body twisted, turned, pulled, and elongated before crashing to the ground in a tumbling mass. Acid rose in his throat. His head throbbed, his vision skewed by hundreds of flashing lights. Stomach lurching, he rolled to his hands and knees and vomited.

Damn! What happened?

A lime-green creature no larger than a squirrel swooped down and landed beside his right hand. It stretched its long, sinuous neck and tilted its diamond-shaped, scaled head from side to side. Leathery bat-like wings folded at its sides while two talons gripped a broken branch on the ground. Its long, spiked tail swished back and forth.

David's breath hitched. He scuttled backward, kicking up leaves and dirt, adrenaline pouring through his trembling limbs. "That's—that's a—dragon!"

The small creature cocked its head from side to side. A twinge caught low in David's belly as he rubbed his palms over his face. "No. No. There's no such thing as dragons."

"Saying it won't make it so," Twiller said, straightening his jacket.

David stumbled to his feet. The small man walked toward him, his eyes on the darkening sky. The leafy canopy swayed in a brisk breeze tinged with rain.

David winced and clutched his hand to his chest. Fiery pain rippled from his tattoo, coursing down his right arm to the ring. The two objects pulsed in dull, but exasperating harmony. He counted to twenty and pushed the pain away. He'd dealt with worse in the last two days. He had to stay strong. The pain dissipated, and his thoughts trained on the only thing in the world that mattered. "What did you do to Charlotte?"

Twiller's heavy brows beetled together as if trying to assess David's condition. Apparently satisfied David wasn't about to die, he huffed and started walking. "Your friend is safe, have no worries about that. As to where you are," he glanced around the clearing, "Welcome to Fallhollow, Master David. Welcome home."

Chapter 9

Thunder boomed overhead, rattling the walls of the castle. Screams cut through the air, dragging Eric from a deep sleep. Heat and the putrid smell of rotten eggs wafted through the open windows. He rubbed his eyes, his lethargic mind barely registering the flames engulfing the sky over the courtyard. He dashed out of bed and ran to the balcony. A great, black shadow swooped in from the south and slammed into the northern battlement. Hunks of stone exploded and rained onto Crafter's Row. Sentries scurried along the southern battlement above Festival Hall shouting orders. The beast circled back around, this time plucking soldiers in its talons like apples from a tree, and snapping them in its gargantuan jaws.

Eric stood transfixed. He yelped as strong hands dragged him into the center of the room. A set of clothes and boots hit him square in the chest.

"Get dressed!" Trog shouted. "Now!"

Eric clambered into his trousers and boots. "What's happening? Why are we being attacked? I thought the kingdom was protected."

"So did I. Come!"

Eric belted his sword to his hip and followed Trog into the hall and up the stairs. Guests stampeded down the steps, the air impregnated with hysteria and smoke.

Kaboom!

Eric braced himself against the wall. The foundation of the castle rattled beneath his feet. "What was that?" he asked, catching up to Trog on the eighth floor.

"Sounds like the beast is having a temper tantrum."

They burst into the royal apartment, barging through five rooms until they reached the royal bedchambers at the rear of the castle.

Trog shoved the royal guards out of the way and shouted at them to leave.

"Majesties!"

"We're already awake, Trog. What is going on out there?"

"The Dragon King has attacked."

"What?" Gildore changed out of his undergarments and pulled a gray tunic over his head. "That's impossible. There is an accord in place!"

"You want to discuss that with him?" Trog said. "Hurry. We haven't much time to escape." Trog tossed Gildore his belt and sword.

Glass shattered several rooms away. The chains of the portcullis screeched.

Eric turned toward the sound, his overwhelming fear drowning in the pungent scent of spoiled eggs and burning flesh and wood.

"Escape?" Gildore said. "Are you mad? I have no intentions of scrambling like a coward. I won't abandon my people!"

Mysterie emerged dressed in trousers, shirt, and boots, with a dagger strapped to her side. "You'll do as Trog says, dear."

"Never!" Gildore retreated behind a tapestry and marched down a short, narrow hallway to the entrance of a tower. He flung open the door and hurried down the steps, barking orders as he went.

Eric's eyes widened. *Whoa. How many secret passages are in this place?*

"Trog, take Mysterie to the Southern Forest as arranged. Find Farnsworth, Crohn, and Gowran and have them—"

"That's not the plan." Trog snatched the king's arm and pressed him to the wall. "You both are to come with me. Those were the agreed upon terms."

Eric flicked his gaze between the two men. *What terms?*

Gildore grasped Trog's shirt in his fist. "Those terms were made under hypothetical scenarios. Reality dictates a different course of action. You will do as I command." He peered over Trog's right shoulder toward Mysterie. "If there is any love still left in your heart, take my wife to safety."

A flush of annoyance rushed through Eric, a sort of dogged euphoria. *What in dragon's breath are they talking about?* Someday, Trog would have to explain, whether he wanted to or not.

Gildore circled down the stairs in haste and barged through the door into the courtyard. Thick, acrid smoke slammed into them as they emerged. Overhead, the dragon circled, flames billowing all around.

Trog coughed. He covered his face with his arm and shouted, "Follow me!"

They hurried to their right in a tight cluster, hugging the

outer walls of Festival Hall. Swarms of terrified civilians ran past, shouting, screaming. Wounded cries for help carried through the asphyxiating haze.

"These poor people," Mysterie exclaimed.

Eric urged her forward, his eyes stinging.

The winged beast spiraled around. His talons grazed the ramparts above Festival Hall, catapulting stone into the courtyard, burying dozens of the castle's defenders within the rubble. White dust plumed around them.

Gildore coughed and shouted, "Trog, get the queen to safety." He pulled Mysterie to him and kissed her. "Go with Trog and Eric. I'll meet you in the forest. I swear it." With sword drawn, the king made for the pile of debris at the far end of the walkway.

Trog wrestled the king back. "Sheathe your sword now and come with me, or I will take you without your consent!"

Eric pointed skyward through the sulfurous smoke. An enormous shadow loomed inside the smoke. "Sir, we have to hurry. He's coming back around!"

Mysterie ran to her husband's side. "Darling, please. Trog is right. Your people need you to rebuild the kingdom, not die with its buildings. Let's go."

Gildore pursed his lips tight. His eyes shifted from the chaos to those around him. His nose flared. "Remind me to flog you when all of this is over, Trog!"

"With pleasure, sire." Trog pivoted on his heels and approached the wall. He pushed on two stones.

They failed to budge.

Eric squirmed. *Ahh, come on! Open.*

Trog pushed them again.

Nothing.

Everything was on fire.

Fear seared hot in Eric's blood, his bones, his skin. *Please don't let me die. I don't want to die.*

Another portion of the Hall tumbled around them. Mysterie glanced upward, her eyes widened as she flattened against the stone wall. "Holy spirit of the heavens."

Eric followed her gaze. All at once, his lungs forgot how to work. He'd seen sketches of the beast, witnessed its destructive powers, but nothing prepared him for its sheer size and magnificence as it landed amidst rubble and screams.

Dark purple and black scales covered its muscular body from snout to tail. Two horns protruded from its skull. Leathery wings twitched against its side. The beast measured half the length of the courtyard and stood half as tall. A stench of rotten eggs riddled the air. The dragon shifted. Shattered rocks tumbled in metallic clinks to the ground. The beast's amber eyes set wide in his head, blinked, snake-like. If Eric didn't know better, he'd swear the beast smirked at them.

Trog growled and turned back to the secret door. Once more, he shoved the stone with all his might.

The top one moved.

Einar stretched his thick neck, spread his wings, and bellowed an ear-splitting guttural shriek.

Eric and Mysterie pressed their palms to their ears. Trog and Gildore cringed beneath the sound and together pushed the second stone.

Nothing.

Dragon's breath!

Eric glanced at the dragon, his eyes burning as dark shapes floated out of the creature's wings. He tapped Trog on the shoulder and pointed. "What are those?"

Four ghostly shapes, black as obsidian, soared toward them.

With his heart thumping like a rat running from a snake, Eric pulled his sword, the metal hissing as it left the scabbard.

"Shadowmorths!" Trog drew his sword. "Go! Run! Eric, get the king and queen out of here!"

A shadowmorth swept toward Eric, a black fog on a swift breeze. Trog dashed forward, double-gripped his sword and sliced at its form. "Eric, Your Majesties, get out of here! Go! Meet in the Southern Forest. Falcon's Hollow!"

The creature turned, its onyx eyes fixed on the knight. Two wispy appendages extended forward; firelight glistened off their dual sawtooth edges.

Eric's body locked. His breaths came in strained inhalations. Beside him, the king and queen stood frozen. Paralyzed.

"Confound it, boy. Go!"

Two shadowmorths descended on Trog.

Eric's brain twisted. He yelled at Mysterie and Gildore. "Come with me!"

He fled across the courtyard, the king, and queen running behind.

He ran toward the stables, not looking back. A throng of women and children crusted in blood and grime, clawed at him, crying. Begging.

"Help us. Where do we go?"

A woman sobbed. A gray, lifeless child lay cradled in her arms.

Eric shook his head, his words stuck in his throat. A horse whinnied at the entrance to Crafters' Row.

"Please, sir. Please help us," another said, pawing at his shirt.

Eric unlatched her grip and backed away. Spires of the church came into view. He managed to find his voice. "Go—go to the cathedral. Hurry." He glanced behind him. "Your Majesties, come … "

But the king and queen were gone. Nowhere to be found. A glob settled in Eric's throat. "No. No, this can't be."

Heart racing, he pushed his way back through the crying, screaming masses, sweat pouring from his brow. He climbed a pile of stone and peered in every direction, but they were gone.

"No," he said, his hands pressed to the sides of his head. "How could I lose them? They were right behind me." Einar's sudden guttural screech forced Eric to his knees, his hands over his ears. The dragon stretched his wings and pushed off from his pile of rubble, the downdraft from his wings fanning the smoke, and fueling the fires. Eric jumped from his perch and ran to where he'd seen the horse, thankful it was still there. Scenarios of escapes ran through Eric's head. Maybe the king and queen turned around and managed to escape through the tunnels. Maybe they had found another way out and were on their way to Falcon's Hollow. He had to find out. Eric wiped the stinging tears from his eyes and approached the fretful horse. Moments later he was straddled atop the animal and was racing southward toward Hammershire and the Southern Forest.

An enormous winged shadow engulfed him.

Eric spurred the horse; his fingers wound tight in the steed's mane.

Faster. Faster.

Eric glanced over his shoulder as the beast swooped low, his talons outstretched like an eagle ready to pluck a fish from the water.

"Go! Go!"

The wind whipped his face. His hair flew back behind him as he sped down the hillside.

A black claw folded around his shoulder. A sharp, fiery pain plunged into his back. Eric howled as his body lifted from the horse.

He held tight to the reins.

Breathe! Breathe!

Eric grasped the hilt of his weapon. The horse ran harder, its muscular body gliding out from beneath Eric as the dragon tugged him upward. An inhuman sound wailed from his throat, his body hooked and dangling feet above the ground. He closed his eyes to the burning tears and lashed out with his sword, blind.

Must. Get. Free!

Swing.

Swoosh.

Contact!

The dragon screeched.

Forgetting his pain, Eric swung again and again, finding his mark each time. The scent of fresh blood filled his nose. His breath hitched as the dragon took to the sky, climbing straight up toward the clouds. Eric stabbed the sword into the ankle and held on. His skin tingled, his stomach lurched as the beast looped and dove to the ground, its wings stretched wide.

Dragon's breath! I'm going to die.

The hillside zoomed closer. Eric closed his eyes to the rush of wind. Tranquility found him beside a stream in a forest, rays of sunlight streaming through the canopy.

Please. Let it be quick.

Eric hit the ground and tumbled, the talon dislodged from his flesh.

Overhead, the dragon screeched and circled twice before retreating into the sunrise.

Eric lay still, unable to move, his eyes closed. Cold chills washed over him in waves.

Footsteps pounded toward him. Shouts bombarded his ears.

"Eric!" A large, calloused hand gripped his face.

Eric recognized the mild, granular voice as Sir Gowran's. With great effort, he pried his eyes open to find Trog's conclave of friends, Crohn, and Farnsworth, looming over him, their faces drawn with worry. But someone was missing. His heart jolted.

"Where's Sestian?"

"Don't worry about Sestian," Farnsworth said. "He's fine. You, on the other hand, need the care of a surgeon."

Gowran snapped his fingers and yelled at a boy behind him. "Bring me that horse!" He turned his attention back to Eric. The knight wiped beads of sweat from his forehead. Strands of russet hair clung to his face caked with blood and filth. His clothes hung in shreds. "What were you thinking, lad, running from a dragon, especially in an open field?"

A shiver ran out of Eric. "Trog told me to meet him in the forest. I have to go." He struggled to sit up, but Gowran pushed gently on his chest.

"You're not going anywhere, lad, except back to the castle and into the care of the surgeon."

A young boy limped toward him, a horse clomping behind him. "Your steed, my lord."

Eric shook his head. "No. I have to go to the forest. Trog is waiting for me."

"The matter is not open for discussion."

The man swept his hair from his eyes and glanced around. "Of all that is good in heaven, how could this happen?"

"Blast the heavens, Gowran," Crohn said. His black eyes bulged from behind the curtain of straggly black hair. "God's eyes were turned from Gyllen this night. Where were our sentries? Why didn't they sound the alarm? So help the wretched soul that fell asleep on watch for if I find him alive, he will wish Einar had killed him first!"

"Settle down, Crohn," Farnsworth said. The eldest knight's blood-and-sweat-soaked tunic adhered to his torso like a second skin. "Look around you." He worked the strands of his ashen hair into a frizzed plait. "This slaughter is not their fault. That beast caught us with our trousers off. He knew what he was doing." He adjusted the sword on his back and knelt beside Eric. "Son, I need you to tell me the last place you saw Their Majesties."

Eric swallowed. "They were with Trog at the entrance to the passageway leading to Hammershire."

"Did they go through?"

Eric shook his head. "I don't know. Everything got crazy. We were separated."

Farnsworth pressed his palm to Eric's forehead, the expression in his eyes tender. Fatherly. "It's all right." He glanced up at Gowran. "Help me get him on the horse."

Pain spiraled up Eric's spine as they lifted him on the animal. Gowran climbed behind him, his arms on either side to keep Eric upright.

"Take him to the surgeon and stay with him," Farnsworth said. "We'll meet at sunset in the upper courtyard."

Gowran guided the horse toward the castle. Sorrowful moans and sobs drew Eric's tired eyes to the bodies strewn about the hillside like broken dolls. The lifeless faces of the jobmaster, Flint, and the cordwainer held his gaze. A tear fell. "I know them," he said.

"There will be many you know who no longer breathe," Gowran said. "Might I suggest you put on blinders? Take everything you see, hear, and smell and store it somewhere in the recesses of your mind. There will be a time to revisit them later and mourn for what is no more. For now, you need to stay awake until I find the surgeon and get that wound stitched."

Eric shook his head. "No. You're going the wrong way. I have to find Trog. Must go to the forest." His head lolled to the side.

The horse picked up its pace. Eric groaned, his body angry at the increased bouncing. "Stop. I have to get down. I have to find Trog." His skin crawled with sweat. His bones burned.

The horse's hooves clomped over cobblestones. "Home," Eric muttered, half asleep.

"Yes. Home," Gowran said.

Eric's nose wrinkled. "What's that smell?"

Gowran paused, and then said, "War."

The horse slowed to a stop.

A girl yelled out beyond Eric's gaze. "Edgar, I need help over here. Now!"

Large hands reached for Eric as Gowran slid to the ground.

"Where is the surgeon?" Gowran asked.

"Inside," the girl said.

The men lifted Eric onto a litter and carried him into a room that smelled of tinctures and antiseptics. They rolled him belly down from the carrier onto a table covered with white cloth. Men spoke to him while hands tugged and pulled at his shirt.

"What happened?" the surgeon asked.

"Dragon caught him."

Eric groaned as the doctor's fingers probed the wound. "It's deep but fixable. Emelia, fetch me some ground redweed, comfrey tea, horseradish and fox's clote." Soft footsteps scurried away "Edgar. Gowran. As much as I love looking at your handsome faces, get out of my sight."

"If you don't mind, I'll take a seat along the wall," Gowran said.

"No, you won't," the doctor said. "I don't need your germs infecting the place."

"But—"

"He's not going anywhere. Now, get. You're wasting my time."

Metal instruments clanged together. Soft footsteps, along with clinking glass, approached.

"I have everything," Emelia said, setting the multiple glass containers at Eric's head.

"Good. Add four drops of redweed to the tea and give him two syringes full. That should do the trick."

Eric opened his eyes, his gaze wandering over Emelia's features, her hands.

One day, the very soul you loathe may be the one to save your hide someday.

He reached out and swept aside tangled strands of red hair from her eyes. She smiled at him and drew the liquid into the syringe.

"I need you to drink this, Eric. It will help with the pain and make you sleep."

She cupped his neck in her hand and drizzled the liquid into his mouth. After the second dose, she laid his head on the table and combed her fingers through his hair.

"You're going to be all right, Eric. I promise."

Eric nodded, the herbs taking effect. He reached for her hand. "Thank you."

She kissed his temple.

And the lights faded to gray.

***

Eric woke. His head pounded. His body throbbed. Various smells: sweat, smoke, medicine and food, all mingled together in a nauseating blend. To his left the surgeon worked on another patient. To his right, others lay on cots or in beds. Most looked to be recovering, but there was one, a male with gray, chalky pallor, who already seemed to have one foot in the grave.

Lady Emelia rinsed a rag and placed the wet cloth on the doomed patient's forehead. She turned, her red, swollen eyes meeting Eric's gaze. Tears rolled down her cheeks. She walked toward him, fidgeting with the handkerchief in her hands.

"You're awake," she said with a forced smile. "Here," she picked up a goblet from the table beside his bed. "Drink this. It will help with the pain."

Her hands shook. The liquid sloshed over the edge.

"My lady." Eric winced and pushed himself up. He took the cup from her and set it on the table. "What is wrong? Why are you crying?"

Emelia looked away, her chest rising and falling with her sobs. "I'm sorry, Eric. I'm so sorry."

She sat on the edge of the bed, her shoulders heaving.

"Sorry for what?"

Her eyes met his, the tears falling like summer rain. "It's Sestian. The surgeon tried everything—"

The words hammered a hole in Eric's chest.

"Move," he said, shoving her aside.

"Eric, you can't get up."

"Get out of my way!"

He slid out of bed and stumbled across the room.

His insides rattled. His limbs trembled. This couldn't be happening. There had to be a mistake.

The surgeon yelled for him to return to bed.

Eric ignored the shouts, as well as the pain slashing through his shoulder and back, intensifying with each step. It didn't

93

matter. None of it mattered.

"Ses." He reached the bed.

His friend groaned and turned his head. "Eric."

His whispered name shuddered through his entire existence. Eric's stomach roiled. Vomit rose in his throat. He looked up at the ceiling and blinked, blinked, blinked.

Emelia's hand rested on his shoulder. He flinched and turned his head, trying to find someplace to look other than at his friend. He breathed deep, pretending not to feel the pain caught in his chest.

"Eric," Sestian whispered again. "Did you see him?" His voice trailed off. "Did you see the dragon?"

Eric looked down at his friend's burnt, blistered face, the layers of bandages wrapped around the stub of his left arm. His limbs trembled and his knees buckled. He reached for a chair and sat down. Taking Sestian's right hand into his, he nodded. "Yes. I saw him."

Sestian smiled, and Eric was sure he heard a slight chuckle. "He. Was. So. Big."

Sestian's face contorted, and he groaned. "I stabbed him, you know."

Eric propped his elbows on the bed at Sestian's side, his friend's hand clutched in his own. He closed his eyes and focused on the beating of his heart slamming against his chest, the sharp breaths he fought to control. He couldn't lose his best friend. He just couldn't.

"What's wrong with him, Emelia?" Eric asked, tears dripping down his hands to his wrists. "How long before he is better?"

"It's his insides," she said. "The surgeon did everything he could, but he couldn't stop the bleeding." A tear slid down her cheek.

She placed another wet rag on Sestian's face.

Eric swallowed hard. Tears fell. He covered his face with his hands and tried to think of something to keep from fraying and falling apart, to keep from reliving every moment of insanity they'd shared together.

"Eric," Sestian whispered.

Eric wiped the snot from his nose with the back of his hand. "What, Ses?"

"Don't forget about our quest. Promise."

Eric wiped his face. "I promise, Ses, but you have to promise me you'll get better." He looked up to find Sestian's eyes shut, his features caught in an expression of pain.

"Can't do. You know how I am about making promises I can't keep."

"Ses, please." Eric fought the hole swallowing his heart. "Don't leave. Please, don't leave."

Sestian presented a weak smile. "It's okay, Eric. No regrets, right?"

Eric clasped Sestian's hand hard, his sobs ready to burst forth from his gut. He shook his head. "No regrets, Ses."

Sestian closed his eyes. "I'll be watching you."

Then, in a quiet whisper, he was gone.

Eric shook his head. "No, Sestian. No. Don't go. Please don't go." His lips quivered, his shoulders shook as the deluge of tears flooded from him. He dropped his head to the bed and wept.

Emelia cradled him in her arms.

"Why, why did he have to die? Why?" He clung to her, his heart ready to split at the seams.

Her fingers stroked his hair.

He sank to his knees, his face turned up to the ceiling, and wailed, "Damn you, God! Bring him back! He was my friend! You can have anyone. Why him? Why now? What am I to do?

I need him!" He gripped his belly and sobbed. "Please. I'll do anything. Please, just bring him back."

Eric crumpled in half, violent sobs decimating his body. His hand clutched at what was left of his shattered heart.

"Please, Emelia, make this pain go away. Give me something to make it stop."

He remained on his knees until he could sob no more.

"There is nothing for this kind of pain except time," Gowran said, his hands on Eric's shoulders. "Why don't you let me help you back to bed?"

"I don't want to go to bed. I want my friend back!"

Emelia kissed the top of his head and moved away.

"I know you do," Gowran said, "but—"

"Stop!" Eric half-stood and faced the knight. "Why did he have to die? It's not fair. It's not right."

"You're right. It's not."

"It wasn't supposed to be like this. We were supposed to be friends forever. Grow old and fat together. Get married to the girls of our dreams. Have families. But that's all gone. My friend is gone. I'll never hear his laugh. See that crooked smile. Why didn't anyone explain this to me? Why didn't anyone tell me about this hollow ache in my gut, this hole in my heart that is swallowing me?"

"No one can prepare for the loss of a loved one, Eric. You'd think after seeing many of my friends and loved ones pass on, I'd know what to expect. I could steel my heart, but each loss brings about a new kind of pain, touches a place inside that only they occupied."

"I feel so empty. So lost. Does he feel the same? Is he lost, too? Is he alone? What happens when we die?"

He couldn't stop the tears.

The knight shook his head. "I'm sure wherever he is, Sestian is not alone. No matter what, he will always be in here." Gowran tapped his chest above his heart. "Inside of you. Inside of all of us. As long as we remember."

Eric hung his head. His tears flowed in an endless stream. "I have to get some air."

He brushed past Gowran without looking up and left the infirmary, wincing as he bumped into tables and beds. He wandered into the cloisters and sat on a bench. Every inch of him hurt as if beaten with a club from the inside out. He pressed the heels of his hands to his forehead, folded in half and sobbed.

Chapter 10

David shielded his eyes from a ray of sunlight careening through the canopy. "Whoa, wait a minute. Did you say we're in Fallhollow?"

Twiller nodded. "I did. Is there something wrong with your hearing?" He waddled across the small glade and headed off down a narrow, wooded path.

"No." David followed. He scratched at his chest, annoyed by the tattoo's thrumming and prickling. "How did we get here? Where's my house? What happened to Charlotte?"

"Hmm, let me see. One," Twiller said, popping up a finger as he counted, "you ferried. Two, your home is where you left it, and three, Miss Charlotte is where you would have been if she hadn't jumped in front of the ferry stream meant for you."

David folded his arms. "That doesn't tell me anything. Where. Is. She?"

"Worry not. The lovely young lady is quite safe; you have my word."

"Your word? You just made my best friend vanish, and now you want me to trust you and your word? You are quite the jokester, aren't you?"

"Oh no, I never joke. I don't play games, either. Complete waste of time."

"Then what was all that magic crap back at the house?"

"Incentive."

David planted his feet in the soil. "What?"

"You refused to come with me. I had to change your mind."

"By vaporizing my best friend?"

"I vaporized no one. I simply ferried her."

"There's that word again? What does that mean?"

"Ferry. You know, travel, shuttle, traverse, go back and forth."

"I know what ferry means."

"Are you sure? You seem a bit confused."

"I'm confused about a lot of things," David countered. "Vocabulary isn't one of them."

"Ah yes, my humble apologies. I forgot you are quite the intellectual prodigy in your world. Tsk. It is a shame some qualities fail to carry forward."

The intense urge to play Whack-a-Mole with the pompous man threatened David's composure. "Are you always such a jerk? Why can't you just answer the question?"

"Oh, very well," Twiller said with a sigh of exasperation. He stopped and looked up at David, his round face pinched. "How can I explain so you will understand? Picture in your mind the universe as a colossal manor with endless rooms. Each room is a world, and each world occupies the exact same space in time as the one next to it or down the hall. While each room may be different, they still share the same geography."

"That doesn't make sense. This place looks nothing like my home."

"Pay attention, boy. As I said, décor varies, geography remains the same. Think of your home. In it, there are many rooms. The interiors are all different, but they share the same space and time."

"Fallhollow shares the same spot in time as Havendale?"

Twiller tapped his finger on his head. "Now you're beginning to understand."

"But how is that possible?"

Twiller returned to trekking the path. "I'm not a mage so don't ask me questions for which I have no answers. It simply *is*."

"So, whatever happens here, happens back home?"

"Only when the portals are opened. That is why they are hidden and traversable by only a few."

David chuckled. "And you want me to believe this." His words were more a statement than a question.

"Believe what you will. It changes nothing."

David's insides fluttered. His stomach sank. "Okay, so answer this. If you didn't obliterate my best friend, what did you do with her? Why aren't we together?"

"You know, that is a very interesting question. Something happened when I tried to return her to your room. The spell capped and forked. It's the first time that's ever happened to me."

"What in the heck does cap and fork mean?"

"When I cast the spell, the magic sensed something within her, a reason to bring her to Fallhollow. It acted on its own. I had no control. She ferried through the door I had opened for you. Since I do not possess the power to reopen a recently used portal, I had to open a new door."

Twiller came to a stop and peered into the forest and sniffed the air. A fine line formed between his thick, red brows. From his coat pocket, he withdrew a gold contraption about the size of an avocado seed and studded with red, gold, and blue jewels. It appeared to be a watch of some sort, with several layers of hands and peculiar lettering and numbers. He looked up at the sky again, now thick with billowing, lavender clouds, and dropped the contraption into his pocket. "We must hurry. We have tarried here far too long."

Twiller held his arms straight out to his sides and muttered a few words that sounded like German pig Latin. David's mouth dropped open as vines and roots slithered upon the ground and then raised upward, weaving and twining together until they formed an arched door strewn with leaves and moss. A baseball-sized knot in the wood served as a knob. Twiller pushed on the door and gestured toward the opening. "After you, Master David."

David glared through the passageway to the other side, which looked no different from where they were. He scratched his nose. "Umm, where does this go?"

Twiller smiled. "Where else? Your final destination."

***

David's breath hitched as he fell through a split second of cold, dark isolation. He emerged flat on his back, looking up at four stone warriors the size of two-story buildings, their swords raised and crossed, forming an archway over a path. Their human faces stared straight ahead, determined and unwavering. Enormous bat-like wings tipped in feathers arched from their shoulders to the ground.

David clambered to his feet and gulped. "W-what are those?"

"Ancient warriors, frozen in time," Twiller scurried ahead, leaves and twigs crunching beneath his feet.

"Frozen? You mean these things once roamed around like we do?" David marveled at one of the giant feet, part human, and part talon.

Twiller nodded. "They are Grids, warriors of the gods, brought forth by the great mage master during the last Dragon War. When the war was over, he hid them here, just in case."

"Just in case what?" David asked. "You mean, like if there's another war? And did you just say *Dragon War*?"

Twiller nodded. "That I did. I attest, you must get your hearing checked. Come, come. We're almost there."

David's brain flip-flopped. There was no way Twiller could be telling the truth. But then how could he explain the crazy weirdness around him? His head hurt just thinking about it.

Feelings of insignificance rushed through him as they walked the passageway between the Grids and into a dense part of the forest where trees seemed to swaddle them in a dark, spiritual cocoon. They soon came to a wide, arched, stone bridge and paused for a moment, taking in the roar of a cool waterfall cascading into a cerulean-blue pool. Spongy moss carpeted the ground. Boulders, like giant turtles, poked their smooth backs from the pool's depths.

Overhead, a flock of winged creatures, golden in color and double the size of an eagle, chortled as they glided from tree to tree.

"More dragons?" David said.

Twiller nodded. "Palindrakes. Messengers of the forest. You nearly crushed an infant earlier. Those are adults."

The path ahead narrowed into a tunnel of vines and flowers,

the trunks and branches braided so tight, their lavender blooms so thick, no light penetrated. David's stomach lurched at the scent. Wisteria. Lily had it everywhere back home, its sweet, intoxicating aroma almost nauseating.

David ducked as he followed Twiller inside. "I can't see a thing."

"The moon faeries prefer it that way."

"The who?"

His breath caught as hundreds of small, winged humans, no bigger than David's thumb, glimmered upon the woven branches. He peered closer. "Whoa! This is insane. May I hold one?"

"Not if you wish to retain your appendages."

David yanked back his finger and scurried forward, bumping into Twiller, who stood with his palms on a round, wooden door etched with strange writing. A latch gave way, and the door swung open into a cavernous room. Thousands of butterflies took flight in his gut.

Multiple levels of crystal walkways glimmered against slate-gray walls where thousands of books and parchments lay within niches. Hundreds of fiery orbs hovered in the air, casting the room in a warm, golden glow. Below, a wooden schooner, at least a football field long and half as tall—the name WindSong II etched on its bow—floated in a lake of sky-blue water, small waves slapping against its hull. Five masts, their sails furled, rose toward the vast ceiling flecked with twinkling stars.

David took deep breaths as he descended the crystalline ramp. Never had he seen anything so weird and wonderful. He clutched the smooth glass banister, terrified of missing a step. No sooner had he set foot on the deck of the ship than long, slender arms flew around his neck, almost knocking him over.

"David? Oh my God!"

The warmth of a thousand lifetimes engulfed him.

Charlotte kissed his neck, his cheeks, before squeezing him in a giant hug.

David wrapped his arms around her waist, his face and hands buried in her hair. Relief oozed out of him like jelly from a donut.

"Char," he whispered, pulling her closer. The urge to kiss her, devour her, tuck her away so no one would ever steal her away again, took over. No matter how close he held her, he couldn't get close enough.

"Where have you been?" She spoke into his chest. "I've been so worried about you. They kept telling me you'd be here soon, but it's been hours." She looked up at him, her fingers playing with the hairs on the nape of his neck.

His heart faltered at her warmth, her touch, a tingling reaction spreading throughout his body. *Get it together, David. Friends. Just friends. Don't eff it up.* He licked his lips, now as dry as a desert bed. "Twiller and I took the scenic route. I'll explain later." He pushed his need to kiss her aside and stroked her cheek. "Are you okay?"

Charlotte nodded. "I'm fine, although I'll never travel Air Warp Speed again. It made me sick to my stomach." She touched his arm. "Are you okay?"

"Yeah, I am now, but I am so weirded out. Did you know we're in Fallhollow?"

"Yeah, Slavandria told me."

"Who?" David ran his hand over the smooth, wood mast.

"That would be me."

David gulped at the tall woman who appeared out of nowhere. She walked toward him with an air of confidence and purpose, her shimmering white gown rustling along the planked floor. A smile touched her face as she brushed back waves of lavender hair that flowed over her golden skin to her bare feet. Her slanted turquoise eyes narrowed and shone impossibly perfect, yet frightening at the same time.

"Hello, David. My name is Slavandria. Welcome to my home. Welcome to Chalisdawn."

David forgot to breathe for a moment, and his heart hammered against his ribs. "H-hi."

The elegant woman motioned to four overstuffed chairs that hadn't been there moments before and took a seat. "Please, sit down. We have much to discuss."

David stood rooted to his spot, unable to peel his gaze away from the woman.

"Hey." Charlotte nudged. Her voice hovered near a whisper. "I appreciate beauty as much as the next person, but can you stop gawking? It's embarrassing."

He nodded and broke his gaze. "I'm sorry. It's just she looks so much like—"

"Like Lily, yes, I know. I thought the same thing when I first saw her, but trust me, she doesn't sound or act anything like Lily." She clasped his hand in hers and guided him to the chairs.

David stared down at Slavandria, the nerves twisting his gut into knots. "I-I'm sorry," he said, his gaze flitting around the room, looking at everything but his host. "I didn't mean to stare. It's just you remind me so much of my godmother."

Slavandria smiled. "As well I should. She is my younger sister."

David's lungs deflated. He put his hand out to the mast to steady himself.

Charlotte patted the cushion beside her and pleaded with him to sit. He gripped the edges of the chair to keep from falling to the ground and eased into the seat.

"I-I don't understand," he said. "Lily never mentioned a sister."

"There are many things she never mentioned, David, things neither of us ever wanted you to find out. Unfortunately, our father sees things differently and felt it was time for you to be educated."

"W-what do you mean, educated?"

"My father feels it is time for you to know who you are and why you're here, but before I enlighten you, I'd like to introduce you to someone. He will be overseeing you and Charlotte during your stay in Fallhollow." Slavandria called Twiller to her side. He'd been standing near the gangway, his hands clasped behind his back, waiting. She whispered something in his ear, and the little man disappeared below deck.

David turned the ring on his finger as his garbled mind worked to sort out the unbelievable mess going on inside. After a few moments, heavy booted footsteps sounded behind him. He turned as Twiller emerged from below deck followed by ... *the Renaissance dude from the library?*

The man was bigger than David remembered, huge, with a square, angular jaw, piercing, aquamarine eyes, and shoulders so wide they barely fit through the doorframe. He wore an outward expression that said don't mess with me. Beneath it, he wore another almost humorous one that said, come on, I dare you.

Slavandria gestured to the human tank. "David, this is Mangus Grythorn. Mangus this is David Heiland and his dear friend, Charlotte Stine."

David stood and locked stares with Mangus. The man circled him, rubbing his chin as if in deep thought. A chill crept down David's neck, and he swallowed with difficulty, certain the man could eliminate him with a whisper if he wanted to. He steadied his nerves. "What are you doing?"

106

Mangus ceased pacing, his gaze pinned to David's face. "So you're the one. He's a little scrawny, don't you think, Van?"

"Nothing you can't remedy, Mangus," Slavandria said with a teasing smile.

The man narrowed his eyes and laid a hand on David's shoulder, the weight of it like a boulder. "Tell me, young man, do you always eavesdrop on conversations that don't pertain to you?"

David sputtered. "I don't know what you're talking about."

The man furrowed his brow. "The library? You were there, weren't you? Upstairs?"

A flush crept up David's neck and into his cheeks. He'd been so careful. So quiet. "H-how did you know?"

Mangus chuckled and released his grip. "I didn't, until now."

David gazed at him, openmouthed. "What? You mean you tricked me?"

"I gathered information, and you tilted when you should have withdrawn."

David swallowed the cotton lump in his throat, unsure at what angered him the most: being suckered into revealing a secret or not seeing the trap coming.

"Don't look so dejected," Mangus said. "You learned a valuable lesson just now. In the future, when prodded, keep your mouth shut. Never admit or deny anything. Understood? Good. Now, how are you with a sword?"

"Swords?"

Mangus turned to Slavandria. "Is there an issue with his hearing?"

Twiller chuckled.

David spoke. "No, there's nothing wrong with my hearing. The question caught me off guard."

"Well?" Mangus peered at him, his blue eyes penetrating

David's core. "Can you use a sword or not?"

"I-I don't know. I-I've never tried. Not much call for them where we come from."

"You can say that again," Charlotte snorted, her arms crossed over her chest. "We use bombs instead. Why kill one when you can kill a hundred at once? Boom! Nothing left other than a bunch of mangled body parts to send home in a box."

David winced. Charlotte never talked of her brother's death or that his plane was shot down halfway across the world. He shifted his stance. "Charlotte, I don't think now is the time—"

"It's never the time, is it, David?" Charlotte snapped. "Ever since Daniel died, you've been tiptoeing around me, not wanting to talk about what killed him." Charlotte stood, and pulled her hair into a ponytail, and tied it into a knot. "Don't you see what's happening? This man is talking to you about fighting with swords, and you're not even questioning why? How dense can you get?" Charlotte turned on Mangus, one hand on her hip. "And you. I see what you're doing, and you can forget it. I already lost my brother to one stupid war that wasn't his to fight. I'm not going to lose my best friend to another one."

Mangus inhaled sharply and narrowed his eyes. "Young lady—" His voice had a dangerous barbed edge.

David stepped in front of Charlotte. "Leave her alone."

Mangus pushed David out of the way. "Stay out of this, boy. This is between this saucy lass and me."

Slavandria touched the man's arm. "Mangus. Stop. Be nice. They don't understa—"

The word froze in her throat. She clutched her chest, folded in two, and collapsed in Mangus' arms.

He guided her to a chair. "Van, what is it? What's happened? What do you see?" He caressed her cheek and brushed the hair from her face. Worry lines creased his brow.

She glanced up at him, her eyes brimming with tears. "Oh, Mangus. It's happened. A tear, followed by another, trickled down her cheek. "Gyllen castle has been attacked. So many are dead." She gripped his arms. "I have to go, Mangus. They need me." She turned to Twiller, who stood beside her, his face contorted with concern. "Escort our guests to their quarters at once. Go. Waste not a minute. Mangus, stay here and keep them safe. Protect them with your life." She wiped her cheek and stood. With a flick of her wrist, a green velvet cloak appeared out of nowhere.

Mangus held her shoulders. "With all due respect, my lady, you aren't going anywhere."

"I have to, Mangus. Don't you understand? Everything I feared has come to pass. The vision was there for just a moment, but it's gone again, hidden by a shime weave. I'm certain of it. They've woven it so tight it is impenetrable by my magic. I have no choice but to go."

"You have no choice but to stay. You are the only one who can protect these children. They are your priority, now. They need your protection as only the protector of the realm can give them. My skills would be better service to the people of Hirth."

"But—"

"This is not open for discussion."

"Mangus, please. At least let me speak with the Council, beg their intervention."

"Do you think they will rush to your aid? Unless the order to intervene comes from Jared, they are bound by our laws, as are you, to remain neutral."

"I can't stand here and do nothing!"

David jumped up. "What are you talking about? Who's been attacked?"

Mangus shoved him down, his gaze never leaving Slavandria. "Yes, you can. You have to. If Master Camden suspects even a smidgeon of rebellious blood in you, no matter how noble, he will throw you into the mage prison at Eisig faster than I can spit. You have to stay put. I'll contact you as soon as I have secured the royal party."

"But—"

Mangus touched a finger to her lips. "I'll see to it the king and queen are safe. Stay here and do what you do best."

Slavandria searched Mangus' face as more tears fell. Her shoulders slumped forward in defeat. "Very well. Go."

Mangus brushed the stains from her cheek, kissed her forehead, and bolted from the room using the way David entered.

Slavandria inhaled a sharp breath and righted herself. She disembarked from the ship and motioned to David and Charlotte. Come with me, please."

David linked his hand in Charlotte's and crossed the trestle connecting the boat to land. "What was that all about? Who attacked? What's going on?"

"All will be revealed soon," Slavandria said without turning around. "Right now, I must get you to safety."

"Safety from what?" Charlotte rubbed her arms as if chilled.

Slavandria cupped Charlotte's chin and said, "War."

***

A moonlight glow lit the twisting passageway into the heart of the mountain. David ran his hand along the cold stone walls, counting doors as they went. Were there others like him and

Charlotte hidden behind them, kids removed from their homes, waiting for someone to rescue them? Behind him, Charlotte ooh'd and aah'd at the living murals of sea life on the walls. Whales, dolphins, and weird creatures with odd shapes and breathtaking colors swam by only to disappear in the distant blue. After several minutes of walking, they reached an arched wooden door carved with mermaids, selkies, and hippocamp. Slavandria ushered David and Charlotte inside, into a round chamber where artificial stars twinkled in a fabricated indigo sky. Brown and green roots and vines wove together, covering the walls in intricate, braided patterns. A carpet of bright green moss covered the floor.

"There are two bedrooms," Slavandria said, pointing to the left and the right, "and, of course, all the food your heart desires." Trays of meats, bread, fruits, and tea appeared on a low table surrounded by plush cushions. "I'm sorry I can't stay and talk. I promise to explain everything, but for now I have to go. You'll be safe here."

"Safe from what?" David asked.

Slavandria walked from the room without an answer and locked the door behind her.

Charlotte folded her arms to her chest. "Well, that was rude. No explanations, no nothing, just here's your room, we'll talk in the morning."

"Uh-huh," David mumbled as his eyes honed in on a round table beside the sofa, more specifically a carved wooden statue of a bull raised on its back legs, an eagle with wings spread perched on its head. He knelt beside it. "Charlotte, do you see this?"

"Yeah, I see it." Her voice came from the other side of the room. "There's one over here, too. Are they making anything weird happen, to the, you know—"

"No, but this stinking tattoo has been throbbing like crazy

ever since I fell through the rabbit hole."

"It does feel a bit like that, doesn't it? Alice in Wonderland? Everything I see is more curiouser than the one before." She plucked a handful of grapes and sat on a green overstuffed sofa. "What do you think about that Mangus dude? He gives me the creeps."

"Yeah, me, too." David sat beside her and popped a few grapes in his mouth. His stomach grumbled with appreciation.

Charlotte ate a few more. "You know he's sizing you up for something dreadful, right?"

David nodded. "Yeah. I got that." He paused for a moment, then turned to her, his arm on the back of the couch. "Char, I'm sorry about what I said about Daniel. If you ever want to, you know, talk about it—"

Charlotte waved him off. "Don't worry about it. No biggie. I'm sorry I snapped. It's just, this is all so weird, and I'm irritated, and I want to go home. All I can think about is Mom and Dad and how scared they must be right now."

David grinned. "Your dad's probably already called the cops."

Charlotte snorted. "Cops? Try the military police and FBI." Charlotte nestled up to David and rested her head on his chest.

Tingles rippled through him.

"There is one good thing about all of this," she said.

"What's that?"

"Our crazy neighbors can't kill you."

David smiled. "True."

Her fingers drew circles on his chest, opening that secret place inside him he didn't want to go. Did she know what she was doing to him? She couldn't. They were just friends. They'd always been just friends. But her touch was so gentle. His heart fluttered. He snuck a glance at her lips. So full. So beautiful.

112

Her fingers moved to his neck. David froze. That was not a playful touch. She raised her gaze to his face, her blue eyes holding him hostage, her touch tantalizing every inch of him.

"Char?" he whispered, not sure what he wanted to ask her.

She smiled, and her lips replaced her fingers at his neck, gently dragging across his collarbone.

His eyes fluttered. A low moan escaped as her fingers crept into his hair.

An unbelievable pressure built up inside him. He pulled her closer, wanting her, needing her. His skin ignited, melting beneath her touch. He trembled as his heart thudded. Boom, boom, boom, boom. All of him ached. Everywhere.

"David."

Her breath fell over him like a warm, sweet embrace. Her lips pressed closer to his. He inhaled her intoxicating scent.

Her hand slid beneath his sweater, her skin like fiery satin against his. "David," she whispered in his ear.

His fingers traced messages only he understood on her body. His hands glided down her sides and slipped to the small of her back, her hips, her thighs.

Their lips touched, and he knew any moment he would explode.

Her hands wove through his hair, her body pressed tight to his he could feel every contour, every muscle, every heartbeat pounding in time with his.

He gasped, her lips hot on his neck. He pulled his sweater over his head. He could hardly breathe. His eyes closed. "Charlotte."

Her lips moved to his chin; her hands searched the slopes of his body.

He pulled her to him, his kiss urgent. Searching. His hands slipped beneath the thin fabric of her shirt, her skin hot and soft.

She moaned.

He frayed and fell apart. She wanted him as much as he wanted her.

Sweet pleasure spread through him. He could hardly breathe. His heart had taken flight without him. He was soaring. Floating.

He rolled her over, his hands firm on her hips. She wrapped her legs around him. "David." She tilted her head back and moaned as his lips found her neck.

Something like a leather strap snapped his brain. *No! This isn't right. What are you doing?* He leaped off her as if burnt, and scrambled away.

"I'm sorry. I'm so sorry," he said, looking around, stammering. "Oh, God. What was I thinking?" He pressed his palms to the sides of his head. "I wasn't thinking." He stood with his back toward her, gasping for breath. His body shook in agony. "That will never happen again, I promise."

"What are you talking about?" Charlotte said. "I've wanted you to kiss me like that for years."

He closed his eyes, the ache for her unbearable, but he couldn't risk losing her. He'd lost so much already, if he lost her to a stupid moment of lust, he could never live with himself. Yes, it might be perfect now, but what if this messed it up? No. He wasn't going to risk losing the best thing in his life.

His voice was thick when he finally spoke. "It went too far, Charlotte. We're scared. Life is weird and if I—we did, you know, *it*, I think we'd regret it. I also think there's something in those grapes."

Charlotte looked at the table and laughed. "Are you kidding?" She got up and strolled over to him. "Don't be silly. I've never heard of a grape that makes you horny." She touched her fingertips to his back.

He shivered under her touch and jerked away. "No, Char. I care too much about you to screw things up. I can't do this."

Charlotte stared at him as if he'd lost his mind. She scratched the back of her head and sighed. "I don't believe this. You're serious, right?"

"I'm sorry."

"You're sorry? We both ran to second base, almost third, and you're sorry? What's up with that? You didn't like what you felt?"

"No. Yes. It's not about that."

"Then what is it about?"

"It's—I—I shouldn't have touched you. I can't allow—I can't—"

"You can't what?"

David snatched his sweater from the couch. "I can't lose you like I did my parents. I would die. Is that explanation enough?"

He stormed off, barged into the bedroom to his right and slammed the door. He fell onto the canopied bed, the billowy mattress so soft it seemed to swallow him whole.

I'm such an idiot. What is wrong with me? What am I so afraid of?

Charlotte knocked gently on his door.

"David. I'm sorry. I didn't mean to upset you. It's just," her voice choked with emotion, "I love you so much. There. I said it. I love you. And if you're worried about me leaving you, don't. I'll never leave. I promise."

David's insides twisted and jumped. *Tell her you love her, idiot! Give her something for spilling her guts!* He wiped the tear from his cheek and said, "I'll never leave you either, Char."

He squeezed his eyes tight. Waiting. Listening.

Finally, her voice slipped through the door. "Good night, David. Sweet dreams."

The overwhelming sadness in her words ripped at his soul. He'd hurt her when all he wanted to do was protect her. He knew in his heart she'd forgive him, but how could he forgive himself?

He lay on his back and stared at nothing, the events of the last forty-eight hours playing over and over like a needle stuck in the same groove of an old vinyl record. He spun the ring on his finger and slipped into an uneasy sleep.

***

David woke to Charlotte's frantic whispers.

"David, get up! You've got to see this."

David moaned, his brain still in a dream fog. He yawned and rolled over.

Charlotte shook him again. "No! You've got to get up. We have visitors. Twelve of them. Come on."

David's pulse quickened. "What?" He fumbled out of bed and followed Charlotte into the common room engulfed in a shimmering green light. Along the walls stood a dozen slender beings with slanted eyes and pointed ears, their backs to the wall, their eyes straight ahead, focused. Each of them, cloaked in their green aura, was dressed in one-piece garments of green leather, strips of brown leather fingering through it like branches of a tree. Longbows and quivers were strapped to their backs.

"What the heck?" David asked. "Who are they? What are they doing here?"

"I don't know," Charlotte replied. "I got up to pee, saw the green light, and came out here to see what it was."

David walked up to the closest one on his left and peered

116

into his crystalline, lime-green eyes. The stranger didn't blink.

"Do you think they're elves?" Charlotte asked.

A palpable tension saturated the air. The hairs on David's skin stood on end as if rubbed by a balloon.

Charlotte slapped at her arms and yelped. "Ouch! Something shocked me."

David glanced down at the small green sparks dancing at her feet, swirling stronger and faster like a tornado. "What the hell?"

"Da-vid! I can't move!"

David's eyes fixed on her terrified face. He tried to lunge, but his feet remained planted to the ground. His pulse raced as panic rippled through him. "Charlotte!"

"David, help me!" The few sparks turned to hundreds, then thousands, wrapping Charlotte in a glowing cocoon. As if pulled by an invisible string, Charlotte lifted from the ground and tilted until her body was parallel to the floor. Like a guided missile, she shot across the room into her chambers, the door latching behind her.

Panic back flipped in David's chest. He willed his legs to move, but they failed. Anger reared its ugly head and raked its fingernails down his neck.

Strands of electricity arced through the air. The elf creatures clicked their feet together. Gold armor sprang from their leathers and snapped over their shoulders, all the way down their bodies. Their auras grew brighter, blinding.

David shielded his eyes. A strange sensation, like hundreds of needles poking his skin, swarmed around him. A cocoon of energy enveloped him and flung him into bed. The door slammed shut.

David struggled to sit up, but a great weight sat on his chest.

"Let go of me, and don't you dare hurt Charlotte!"

"Quiet!" A male voice replied in his head. "Be still and silence your mind. It is imperative you listen. Many lives are in peril, including your own. An enemy seeks you, and he will stop at nothing until he finds and kills you. He is on his way. His dark magic approaches. Sleep while you can. Gather your wits and strength. Everything you are and have been is about to change. There is no turning back. Your time is nigh. Be brave."

Sleep swept over David like a great swooping wing. A shadow man appeared in his dreams, his face hidden in darkness. He entered a thatch-roofed home, dragged its owner from the dinner table, and beheaded him in the street with a blade of light from his fingertip. He moved on, going home to home, ransacking each one and killing those who lived inside.

Women, children, it didn't matter. Afterward, the killer walked out of town and made for the neighboring forest, thrashing through the woods, his breath raspy.

"Where are you hiding, David? I know you're here. I can sense you. Smell you."

David yelled in his dream, "Who are you? What do you want from me?"

The man turned, changed his direction. Shadows played on his face. His eyes shone like two blue moons. "Keep talking, boy."

A soldier from the common room appeared in David's dream, blocking his view of the cloaked man.

No. Move! I have to see who's after me!

David's dream-self shoved away and ran toward the shadow of trees. The moon hung above him. Wide, dark wings crossed the clouds overhead.

The cloaked man yelled in the dark. *Remove the veil, boy! Show yourself! I swear to you your death will be painless.*

The green light of the elf grew stronger, brighter. A tingly, woozy sensation flooded David's mind, snuffing out the dream.

No! Stop!

The aura grew brighter. Leather, snake-like armor conformed to David's dream-self like a second skin, collapsing in layers from head to toe. The moon and stars of his dream gave way to the green canopy of a forest. The first shades of dawn arrived in his mind, rolling in on a mist. The cloaked man, audibly panicked and delirious, faded from view, his voice silenced.

David rolled over in bed and moaned. His eyes fluttered open long enough to see six elves encircling his bed, their backs to him, their bows drawn.

Chapter 11

Eric gazed down at the lower courtyard lit by bonfires, Gowran at his side. The frenzied search for survivors buried beneath the fortress walls continued as the subtle reds and purples of sunset gave way to night. Farnsworth and Crohn topped the steps, their expressions as worn and bedraggled as he felt.

The knights shared information they'd uncovered, which amounted to nothing much, and discussed their search efforts for Trog, King Gildore, and Queen Mysterie. Eric stared straight ahead, not looking at anything in particular, waiting for someone, anyone, to ask him how his day went. Apparently, the facts that a dragon talon had speared him, and his best friend had died were unimportant. He waited for a pause in the conversation, then said, "Sestian's dead." The words tumbled from his mouth with vacant emotion.

Farnsworth flinched as if struck with a poker across the gut. He hung his head and swallowed. His hands tightened into fists.

His gaze strayed to the lower courtyard. His voice rattled when he spoke. "I'm sorry, Eric. I know how close you were."

An ache spread from Eric's chest, and an unpleasant feeling over the knight's flippancy gathered in his gut. His nostrils flared with the sudden influx of anger. He straightened against the stabbing pain in his back, his eyes narrowed. "You're sorry? Is that all you can say?"

"Don't, Eric. Sestian was like a son to me. What happened isn't fair, it isn't right, but it is what happens in war."

"War? A war against what? What did Sestian die for? What noble cause? He was never at war with anyone."

Farnsworth straightened, his gaze meeting Eric's. "He died defending this castle, this land, his home."

"That's a lie! He died for nothing. All these people died for nothing!"

"How untrue."

Eric whipped around as the owner of the intrusive voice strolled out from behind a statue of a bull raised on its hind legs. He swallowed as if ingesting sandpaper doused with sheep gut oil. "Lord Seyekrad."

The horse-faced man dressed in blue leathers sauntered forward, his white hair tied back in a ponytail at the nape of his neck. His turquoise eyes glimmered like blue jewels in the moonlight. Farnsworth, Crohn, and Gowran shouldered together, blocking Eric's view.

Eric pushed through the formidable wall of muscle, irritated by their protectiveness.

Seyekrad chuckled as if amused by the display. "In war, people always die for *something*, even if that something was nothing. The innocent always die for a cause, wouldn't you agree?"

"Why are you here, Seyekrad?" Farnsworth's expression

remained impassive.

Seyekrad gestured toward the castle. "Let's discuss this in private, shall we?" His gaze settled upon Eric, his eyebrows raised just a hair. "Young man, you are dismissed. Tend to whatever activities benefit your soul at the moment while I speak with the Order."

Eric's lip twitched, his fingers curled into fists. How dare this cocky, arrogant creature order him about as if he were nothing more than a servant boy?

Farnsworth planted his palm square on Eric's chest, his eyes never leaving Seyekrad's. "I think you forget where you are, my lord. Your role of protector of the Northern Forest may benefit your position on the High Council, but you hold no sway here. While you're within the walls of Gyllen, we have authority, not you, and we say the boy stays with us. If you find this in any way unacceptable, feel free to leave."

Seyekrad's lip curled up in a snarl. "Very well. Lead the way. A private room away from prying ears is preferable."

The entourage entered the castle and turned right, following the gallery flecked with oiled portraits and porcelain statues. After several zigzag turns, they entered the Cedar Room, a resplendent chamber rich in velvet tapestries, dark wood furnishings, and a heavy atmosphere. Seyekrad spoke a single incantation, and the wall sconces and hearth leaped into fiery brilliance. The sudden warmth, however, did little to mask the formal chill in the air.

"Get on with it, sorcerer," Crohn said, closing the door behind them. "We're in the middle of a crisis."

"I can see that," Seyekrad said. "In fact, it is why I'm here."

Gowran huffed out a breath and took a seat beside Eric. "This should be interesting. Are you going to break your edict and protect Hirth from further attacks?"

Seyekrad let out a boisterous laugh. "Oh, my, what do you take me for, a fool? No, I'm afraid I'm here for something far less trivial."

"Trivial!" Eric sneered, his lip curled up in disgust. "We've been attacked by a monster. Hundreds are dead. More are trapped beneath the pile of mess out there. How is that trivial?"

Seyekrad smirked. "Well, well, what do you know? The fledgling has a backbone." He strode over to Eric, his arms crossed. "Let me put it in simpler terms so you can understand. This crisis, as you see it, is trivial when considering the urgent matter before the High Council and the Senate."

"Which is what?" Farnsworth asked.

A smug expression skewed Seyekrad's face. "We have it on good authority that your beloved Sir Trogsdill may have conspired with the enemy and planned this attack."

"That's a lie!" Eric shouted.

Crohn pointed a finger at Eric. "Quiet!" He directed his scowl at Seyekrad. "How dare you grace these walls and spout such vitriol. What proof do you have?"

Seyekrad flicked a glance around the room. "All you need to know is Sir Trogsdill faces charges of kidnapping, treason, and sedition. Once found, he will be arrested. If we discover you are harboring him, each of you will be charged and arrested for aiding and abetting a suspected conspirator to the crown."

Crohn lunged forward, his face like a puffed-up bullfrog. "Why, you—"

Gowran and Farnsworth grasped him by his collar and yanked him back.

Seyekrad fixed his eyes on Eric. "Of course, should you wish to come forward with any information, we will be more than happy to forgive your involvement in the matter."

Eric's temper smoldered beneath the surface. "There is no information to give. Even if there were, I wouldn't give it to you."

"Pity," Seyekrad said. "It is a shame your age and lack of wisdom will be no defense for your stupidity in this matter."

Farnsworth stepped forward. "I think it's time for you to leave, Seyekrad. I trust you know your way back to Avaleen."

Seyekrad smirked. "Indeed, but I have no intentions of returning to the mage city at the moment. This hovel fascinates me. I think I'll tarry, see how inferior beings survive under such harsh circumstances."

"I have a better idea," Eric quipped. "Why don't you do something useful and return Einar to the bowels of the earth? After all, the reason we're in this mess is because the mages failed to keep their magical creatures under control. Seems, you owe us a favor."

Seyekrad smiled. "Banishing dragons is not my specialty, pup. Neither is saving this kingdom. You have a paladin for that if he ever decides to show his face."

Eric held his breath for a moment. *Play dumb.* "What are you talking about? What paladin?"

"Oh, haven't you heard?" Seyekrad surveyed the other faces in the room. "Your guardian and savior arrived in the realm early this morning."

Eric's mind raced with excitement. In his despair, he'd forgotten the paladin.

"This is news to us," Farnsworth said. "Until he arrives, what do you or the High Council intend to do to protect us?"

"Why, nothing, of course. It goes against mage law to intervene in the affairs of men. But please," Seyekrad conjured several stacks of folded handkerchiefs on the table, "give the grief-stricken one of these for their tears, and don't forget to pass on my regards."

Eric lunged at Seyekrad, but the sorcerer backed up, and Eric fell face-first on the floor. The sorcerer laughed and vanished with a snap of his fingers. Eric cussed as Gowran helped him to his feet.

"I loathe that creature!" Gowran said.

"You're not alone," Farnsworth said, "however, if what he said is true, we have a serious problem on our hands. We must find Trog and warn him not to return to Gyllen." He walked to the window, his body a giant shadow in the firelight. "Gowran, send patrols into the Southern Forest. Elicit the help of the shime to ensure open communication between us and the centaurs, General Balendar in particular. We must know if Trog crossed into the forest."

"I think it would also be wise to find any one of our emissaries," Farnsworth continued. "I want Seyekrad followed while he's here. That shiftless goat is up to something. There is no reason he had to deliver the message himself when runners could have done it unless he's seeking something."

"Maybe all he wants is to gloat at our misfortune," Eric said.

"More like Seyekrad is hoping we'll lead him to Trog," Gowran said.

"Precisely." Farnsworth rubbed his chin in thought. "Eric, tell us what happened this morning. All of it."

They sat at the table, deep in thought, while Eric relayed the tale. When Eric got to the part about the shadowmorths, Farnsworth slammed his fist on the table.

"Shadowmorths, in Gyllen!" Gowran stood, kicking his chair with such vigor it hit the wall behind him. "You know this changes everything. Trog and Their Majesties could be in Einar's clutches as we speak."

"Perhaps the king and queen are," Crohn said, "but not Trog."

Farnsworth raised an eyebrow. "Why is that? He's not immune to the powers of the dragon."

'No," Crohn said, "but you have to admit he has more lives than a common housecat. He has overcome every obstacle ever thrown at him."

"And he has paid a severe price for each and every one of them." Gowran righted his chair and sat down.

Eric's thoughts strayed back to the conversation between the king and queen in Trog's room. What were they hiding? What price had Trog paid? How many pieces of the puzzle were missing?

Farnsworth placed a hand on Eric's shoulder, snapping him back to the here and now. He handed him a note.

"Find Captain Morant and give this to him. Afterward, get something to eat and go to bed. You're going to need your strength." He turned his attention to the dark-haired knight. "Crohn, come with me. We must seek an audience with the High Council and beg the mages for intervention as well as instate Lord Donegan as Steward. Hirth must have some semblance of leadership so that we may focus our attention on finding Trog and Their Majesties."

"Lord Donegan is dead," Eric said. "I saw him."

A vision of the man's twisted body lying on the ground flashed through his mind. He and his wife had done such a fine job of making Gyllen look so nice for the king and queen's return, only to suffer an untimely and vicious death. It didn't make sense. None of it. Eric pushed the repulsive image into the deep recesses of his mind.

Farnsworth scrubbed the back of his neck and cursed beneath his breath.

Eric stood straight and sucked in a deep breath. "I-I was wondering, sir, if I might have your permission to ride with the conscript."

"No!" All three knights chimed at once, their voices resonating off the tapestried walls.

Eric's stomach jolted, his pulse took off running. "Why not? I'm just as capable as the rest of them."

"No," Farnsworth said. "End of discussion."

"But that's not fair!"

Crohn flashed Eric a condescending smile and patted his cheek. "Who said anything in life is fair?"

Eric smacked the man's hand away. "Don't touch me!"

"Eric," Farnsworth clamped his large hand on the back of Eric's neck and squeezed. "It seems you have forgotten your manners. Crohn is a knight of Gyllen, and you will give him the respect he has earned and deserves. Is that understood?"

Eric glared at Crohn, his teeth clenched. "Yes. *Sir.*"

"Good." The man released his hold. "Now do as you were told. Meet us in the lower courtyard by the fountain at sunrise. We have a lot to do."

Eric scowled and scanned the faces in the room before he stormed from the castle. Outside the garrison doors, he paused for a moment, taking in the stars. "Tell me what to do, Ses. Guide me."

He stepped inside the rowdy quarters and approached Captain Morant. On the far side of the courtyard, someone blew the ceremonial horn five times, a message five more survivors had been found.

Eric looked around at all the faces plastered in smiles. The congratulatory hugs. The shouts of joy. It was only when that he saw what was in their eyes that he began to feel what was in his heart.

Hope.

It was all around him—in the cry of a new baby. In the first blade of grass after a winter's thaw.

And at the moment, it was the only thing keeping him from throwing himself off the Haldorian Bridge into the Cloverleaf River and floating away.

***

Eric woke at sunrise to find himself on the gazebo bench in the queen's private garden. His head pounded, and his stomach churned, a result of too much stress and not enough food.

The air was crisp and tinged with wood smoke and the sickly-sweet stench of burning flesh. His tongue folded against the roof of his mouth to keep the rancid odor from settling in his nose and mouth, but it didn't work. He leaned over the rail and vomited.

Off in the distance, the sound of hoof beats, joined by the rattle of harnesses and the creak of iron wheels, clomped and clattered their way across the courtyard. He shuffled toward the cherub fountain and splashed his face before collapsing on the dew-drenched grass. The sun did little to ease his sorrow, not just for Sestian and Hirth, but also for himself. His home, his family, his way of life, was gone, destroyed. He desired nothing more than to ride to Avaleen and bring the war to the mages, make them pay for what they had allowed to happen, but he stood no chance against them. He was mortal, and he was alone, and alone was a terrible thing to be.

Buck up and stop with the self-pity, Sestian bolstered from the recesses of Eric's mind. *You are the squire to the most revered knight in all of Fallhollow. Why, you're practically royalty.*

Eric wiped his face. *Shut up, Ses. You have no idea what I'm going through. If only I could clobber something to make it feel as terrible as I do.*

A maid entered the side garden, took one look at him, and then set about hanging the wash while humming a wistful tune. Somewhere nearby a baby cried. Children laughed and dogs barked. Moment by moment, the world returned to normal. Life continued, as it should. *So why do I feel so miserable?*

"Ah, there you are." Eric's heart leaped as Farnsworth padded across the lawn. "I've been looking all over for you. What in the devil are you doing back here?"

Eric stood and steadied himself against a weeping willow. "Hiding. What do you want?"

Farnsworth fixed him with a steady, shadowed gaze. "We need your help in finding Trog and Their Majesties, or have you forgotten?"

"I've forgotten nothing." Eric strode passed the knight refusing to make eye contact. "Where do you wish me to start?"

"We'll discuss that in a moment. For now, I'd like you to stop and listen to me."

Eric stopped and exhaled.

"I'm sorry about Sestian," Farnsworth said. "I know the raw, hollow pain in your gut. I know the ache, the emptiness. I grieve for him, too, Eric. Please don't mistake my silence for not caring. I don't have the luxury of mourning right now. I have to concentrate on the living, to find our king and queen as well as my dearest friend."

Eric turned around and met the same expression in Farnsworth's eyes he felt in his gut, the total sadness for what was, what should be, and what would never be again. There was also an expression of courage, hope, and compassion, sentiments out of Eric's reach.

Farnsworth approached and placed his hands reassuringly on Eric's shoulders. "I wish I could turn back time and undo what has been done, but I can't. Somehow you will find a way to cope with what has happened. You will never forget Sestian, but I can assure you this emptiness and sorrow will pass in time. Until then, I hope you know Gowran—"

Eric pushed away. "Yes, I know. All of you will be there for me. May I go now?"

Farnsworth paused, his eyes filled with an unreadable emotion, then nodded. "Of course. I want you to get something to eat, and clean your mouth. Your breath is horrid. Once done, search the passageway to Hammershire. See if you can find remnants of anything … clothes, buttons, the slightest hint they were there."

"As you wish." Eric bowed and followed the pebbled walkway around the rear of the castle to the cloisters surrounding the cathedral gardens. Up ahead, hidden in a recess, several men conversed in hushed tones. Eric ducked into an alcove and listened.

"My Lord, how can you be certain the paladin has arrived, especially since the Council has detected no signs of him?"

Eric's breath caught in his chest. *Bainesworth von Stuegler! What's that weasel doing in Gyllen?*

"Trust me, he's here," replied the all too familiar voice of Lord Seyekrad. "I sense his presence."

"Sensing him is not the same as knowing where he is," said the third man. Eric recognized the voice as Master Camden's, overseer of the High Council. "If we are to succeed in sequestering the kingdom, we must find him before Einar does."

Eric gulped.

"Don't presume to tell me what I already know, Camden."

"Then tell us how you intend to capture him," said Bainesworth. "It's obvious he's cloaked by powerful magic that far exceeds either of your *superior* mage abilities."

"Hold your tongue," Seyekrad countered, "unless you desire to witness firsthand just how superior my abilities are. And might I remind you of why you're here. It would be rather difficult for you to play your part of a worried son if you've been reduced to nothing more than worm fodder."

"Enough," Camden said. "Focus on what is important. We must ensure the prophecy does not come to pass. If the paladin joins forces with the heir, our plans will be ruined. We must find and eliminate them both immediately."

Eric fixed his gaze on the teary-eyed cherub plaque tacked to the limestone wall in front of him. *What heir? Gildore and Mysterie don't have children.* Heart slamming against his ribs, Eric tried to slow his breathing enough to hear. A sudden coldness hit his core. The air became quiet and still as if all living things had been silenced by the heavens. Footsteps hurried along the walkway, stopping briefly at regular intervals before continuing toward him. Eric cursed beneath his breath. He tried the door to his left. Locked. The footsteps drew closer. He grasped the hilt of his sword as a hand reached around the corner, grasped his shirt, and flung him into the courtyard. Eric stumbled, somehow maintained his balance, and faced the blond man dressed in black-and-gold leathers.

"Trogsdill's runt!" Bainesworth said. "I should have known!"

He clasped Eric's chin, his fingers digging into Eric's cheeks. "Are you spying for him? Where is he?"

Eric glared at the huge, powerfully built Fauscherian knight and Trog's lifelong enemy. Cold brown eyes stared back him.

Bainesworth tightened his grip. "I asked you a question, boy!"

Eric grunted and said, "Go crawl in a hole and die."

A backhanded blow sent Eric sprawling across the grounds. White lights burst in front of his eyes. He struggled to get on his hands and knees, but Bainesworth's fingers entwined in his hair. Eric's eyes watered with pain as he was drawn to his feet; the tip of a cold, silver blade jabbed into his throat.

"Talk," Bainesworth said, "or I'll cut you down here and now."

Eric spat and said, "Go ahead. I dare you."

Lord Seyekrad appeared at Bainesworth's side, his face grim. "Others are arriving. You must leave ... now."

Bainesworth sheathed his dagger and glared at Eric. "I'm not done with you."

Seyekrad uttered an incantation and in an instant, Bainesworth was gone, vanished. To Eric's left, Master Camden uttered a few words and disappeared as well.

Cowards.

Seyekrad's lip curled into a sneer. He stepped forward and clasped one hand on Eric's chest, the other on his back.

Agonizing pain ripped through his throat, taking his breath and preventing his screams. Intense waves of fire spread over Eric's skin. His blood burned. His knees buckled. Seyekrad knelt over him, his face twisted in demonic pleasure, his eyes glowing amber, and his mouth twisted in a malevolent smile.

A sword hissed as it left its scabbard. "Get away from him, Seyekrad!" Gowran warned.

Seyekrad's lips touched Eric's ear. "I know you heard things you shouldn't have. For that, your father will die. You will live only long enough to see his mangled body. Then I will come for you."

"You so much as look at my father and I'll kill you," Eric seethed.

Seyekrad sneered. "With what? Your toy knife?"

Two more swords hissed as they left their scabbards. The blades glistened in the morning light before coming to rest a hairsbreadth away from the sorcerer's spine. "Move away, Seyekrad," Gowran said. "Slow and easy."

Seyekrad raised his hands and stood, his gaze glued to Eric, his thin lips stretched into a satisfied grin.

Farnsworth and Crohn inserted themselves between Seyekrad and Eric, their weapons trained on the mage.

"You want to tell me what's going on here, Eric?" Gowran asked, his eyes fixed on the swollen, throbbing side of Eric's face.

"It was nothing," Eric said, licking his lips.

"I don't consider threatening me, *nothing*," Seyekrad said. "He came after me with this." He held up a small dagger.

Eric rose to his feet. "That's a lie."

Seyekrad handed the weapon to Farnsworth. "You really must keep this spoiled brat in check. It's time he learned his rightful place. Why, the way he carries himself and walks about, one would think he believes himself to be Sir Trogsdill himself and not the lowly son of a farrier."

"I know my place, Lord Seyekrad," Eric countered in a raised voice. "Perhaps you should learn yours and return to Avaleen, or better yet, your hovel in the Northern Forest. I'm sure there are one or two insects there that miss you."

Seyekrad glowered at Eric. "I'll be back for you, pup." He emitted a guttural growl, and with a two-word incantation, he was gone.

The knights rallied around Eric, bombarding him with questions.

"What did he want?"

"Did he do that to your face?"

"Was he alone?"

"Let me look at that cut."

Rage swelled in Eric's soul. "Stop it! All of you! I don't need your coddling. Please. Find something else to do and leave me alone."

He snatched his weapon from Farnsworth's hand and stormed off, praying they didn't follow.

Sestian's voice erupted in his head. *Wait. What are you doing? Go back. Tell them what you heard.*

Be quiet, Ses. I have another plan.

Farnsworth shouted, "Eric, get back here, now! We're not done speaking to you."

Eric ignored the demand and continued to the stables. After a great deal of effort, he climbed upon his saddled horse and rode to Hammershire.

A chill colder than death crept over him as he made his way through the charred town. Burnt and crumbled A-frame roofs reared against a crisp blue sky. Shops, vibrant and alive the day before with laughter and music, stood scorched and empty. Dogs rummaged among the ruins, snarling over scraps of flesh. The unmistakable stench of death mingled with the smell of rotten eggs.

Dragon's breath.

Eric dismounted and secured the horse outside the clothier's shop. He slipped into the room still smoldering from the attack and exited the backdoor onto a narrow dusty road bordering several detached farmhouse dwellings.

He hurried as fast as he could across the way and burst through a door, scattering a mess of chickens. "Father!"

A burly man emerged from the kitchen. "Eric!"

Eric hugged the man tight, ignoring the pain from Einar's

talon in his back. "Father. I was so scared. I was afraid the worst had happened to you."

The man held Eric at arm's length and looked into his son's eyes. "Ya sure are a sight for these ol' eyes, my boy. Thank the heavens you're alive."

Eric sat at a rustic wood table. "Are you okay? Do you need anything? Food? A doctor?" He clasped his hand around his father's. "Better yet. Why don't you come back to the castle with me? The grounds are a mess, but the palace stands intact. You can share my suites. You can sleep in a comfortable bed."

Eric's father smiled and stood. "I don't want no fancy suites, lad. I have my home. It's all I need. I survived this long, why tempt my fate, eh?"

Eric smiled. "I should know by now I can never drag you from this place." He glanced around, taking in the scorched walls. "Have you ventured out since the attack? Is there anyone else left?"

His father spooned some porridge in a bowl and gave it to Eric. "There are a few scattered here and there. Many of us sought refuge in the root cellar when it happened. Otherwise, ya might be speakin' to me on the other side of the flowerbed right now." He ripped a piece of bread from his bowl and shoved it in his mouth. "How bad is it out there?"

"Bad. Too many are dead that shouldn't be, including Sestian." Eric stared at his food and swallowed the pain rushing to the surface. He closed his eyes, squashing the tears before they could fall. He cleared his throat and said, "Many more are trapped beneath Festival Hall. They've got teams of men trying to free them."

The man patted his son on the shoulder. "I'm sorry to hear 'bout Sestian. He was a good friend to ya."

Eric dropped the spoon in his bowl and sat back. "What I don't understand is how any of this happened. That beast was supposed to be under a spell. How did that break? And why," Eric pounded his fist on the table, "when those stupid mages sensed the spell was broken, didn't they do anything to stop him?"

Eric's father laughed. "Ya don't think they have the means to stop that beast, do ya? They tried once before to kill him, and the best they could do was banish him beneath a stinkin' lake. Nah, my boy. Them magic folk might like to think they're mighty, but their magic ain't anything against that beast. It'd take something more powerful, maybe even other-worldly, to take on that dragon and kill him."

Eric stared at his bowl, his father's words sinking in. "Of course," he whispered. *The paladin.* He pushed his chair away from the table and jumped up, a sense of urgency flooding his body. "I have to go, Father."

"What? Ya just got here."

"I have to find someone." Eric kissed the top of his father's head and ran out the door. "I'll see you in a day or two."

Two hours later, after posting a guard near his father's home, he rode to Avaleen, the horse's hooves kicking up the dirt and ash behind him. All he had to do was get inside the heavily guarded city without drawing attention, and find Mangus Grythorn. Thank the stars he had a three-hour ride to figure out how to manage such a foolish deed.

Chapter 12

David tossed and turned. Slavandria spoke to a man on the far side of David's dream. They sounded faint, distant. He strained to listen past the ethereal veil separating him from consciousness.

"I told you this was not a good idea," Slavandria said, "but you wouldn't listen. Now look what's happened. We have to send them back before any more harm comes to Fallhollow."

"No," the man responded.

"How can you be so callous and cruel? He doesn't belong here. He'll die if he remains here. He knows nothing of our ways or what waits for him."

"You underestimate him, Daughter. There is a great power within him. He has been protected for far too long. It is time for him to discover who and what he is. The heavens chose him for this task two centuries ago. It is written. He stays."

David flinched. *Two centuries ago?*

"What about Charlotte?" Slavandria's tone was as sharp as an ice pick. "The words mention nothing of her being a part of this journey. Why can't you return her to Havendale?"

"The ancient magic took her on its own. Her purpose will unfold in due time. I suggest you stop worrying, my dear. All is as it should be."

"So you keep telling me." The air grew quiet. Footsteps padded around the room. "How is Mangus?" The words slipped from Slavandria's lips in a tremble.

"Mangus' brush with Einar was minimal. His burns are healing well. Thanks to his mage blood, there should be little scarring, if any. He is quite obstinate, like someone else I know."

"He has to be to survive you."

A new voice, a man's, spoke. "Supreme Master Jared—"

David's subconscious jerked. *Jared? I've heard that name before. Think.*

"The boy stirs within the weave. He can hear your every word."

Shut up, blabbermouth, David's subconscious said. *Go away.*

"Thank you," Jared said. "It is just as well. I need to return to Felindil and ready the WindSong. It sets sail in two days. I trust you have everything under control, and you will behave while I'm gone? Master Camden, the High Council, and the Senate have enough to deal with without you running amok."

"I cannot promise you anything."

Jared chuckled. "That will have to suffice coming from you. Goodbye, Daughter."

The voices faded into a sizzle. Slavandria whispered in his ear, her breath like a summer breeze. "I'm so sorry. I'll protect you as long as I can. For now, sleep."

Darkness swooped in, enveloping him beneath a protective

wing. He curled on his side and slipped into another dream. This time, he found himself aboard a schooner at night. Pelting rain blew sideways. Sails flapped in the battering wind. He clung to a mast as huge ocean waves tossed the ship about. Water sprayed over the sides with each tilt and dip. From the stern, a human figure cloaked in shadow glided toward him, hovering above the deck, eyes gleaming silver in the dark. David clutched the mast tighter. He squinted, looking for recognizable features. *Who are you? What do you want with me?* A black gossamer veil fell around him, shielding him from the elements and his assassin. A roaring scream filled his ears.

"They cannot protect you forever, David. I'm coming for you, and when I find you, death will be the least of your worries."

***

David woke to Twiller shaking him into consciousness.

"Go away. What do you want?"

"You have been asleep long enough. It's time to join the living. Her Grace awaits you and Lady Charlotte upon the WindSong. I've taken the liberty of running you a warm bath. Your clothes are on the chest at the foot of the bed. Please be ready when I return in fifteen minutes." The little man strutted from the room, closing the door behind him.

David slung his legs over the edge of the bed and eyed the gauze-like undergarments, nut-brown corduroy trousers, matching vest, and long-sleeved shirt the color of butterscotch. On the floor was a pair of calf-high leather boots. "You've got to be kidding me."

He hurried through his bath, mulling over the conversation between Slavandria and her father he'd heard in his dream. Two hundred years ago he'd been chosen, but for what? How was that even possible? He scratched at the marking on his chest, now set deep within his skin as if he were a marked brand of cattle. *What have my parents and Lily gotten me into? What did I get Charlotte into?*

David layered on the clothes, surprised at their comfort. He pulled on the last boot as Twiller knocked and announced it was time to go.

Charlotte faced him as he entered the sitting room. His breath hitched at the sight of her dressed in form-fitting wheat-colored trousers and a forest-green shirt with puffy sleeves. A plaid corset cinched her waist, popping her breasts over the top of the lace trim.

His mouth opened then shut as he struggled to find the right response.

"Don't say it," Charlotte warned, "and keep your eyes above the neckline. I already feel self-conscious enough without you staring at my boobs."

His cheeks flushed. "I wasn't—honest."

"Yeah, whatever. Come on. Let's see what the great and powerful Ozette wants."

"Don't get your hopes up. Somehow I don't think there's a hot air balloon or red slippers waiting to take us back home."

They followed Twiller down the twisting, turning, tunnel of stone until it emptied into the main room where the sails of the WindSong flapped in a magical breeze heavy with the scent of salt and sea. Slavandria emerged from below and joined them on the deck.

"Please sit down." She gestured to a settee. "I trust you slept well."

"Not if nightmares fall into that category." David leaned against the mast, his arms folded across his chest. Slavandria touched her fingertips to the table. A porcelain teapot and cups, along with a plate of sliced apples, cheese, and toast appeared.

"I'm sorry about yesterday and especially last night." She sat down across from Charlotte. "The world is turning on end, and I had to protect you."

"Really?" David said, sitting beside Charlotte. "You want to tell me what exactly *did* happen last night? Who were you talking to while in my head?"

Slavandria set the teacup on the upended leather trunk beside her. "David, your life is very complicated. I know you're aware of certain changes, many of which I'm sure have you baffled and confused."

"What gave it away?" David sat back. He inhaled a deep breath and rubbed his palms over his face. "Look. I'm not trying to be difficult, but we've been here for a day, and I have no idea what is going on now anymore than I did when we got here, so I'd appreciate a bit of honesty, okay. I'd like to start with the elven dudes in our room. Who were they?"

"Duwans, a conclave of fae from the mountainous regions of Felindil. I brought them here to protect you."

"Protect me from who? The man in my dreams?"

Slavandria nodded. "Yes, and any other beings who wish to see you dead."

"Why would anyone want to see me dead? What did I do?"

Slavandria placed her teacup on a table. "It is not a matter of what you've done but what you are capable of doing. You see—"

BANG!

The round door leading from the path of the moon fairies bashed open against the cave wall. David froze as a centaur with eyes the color of blue sea glass galloped down the steps and onto the ship. He carried an unconscious man, water-drenched and blood-soaked, upon his back. Flanking each side were two of the most bizarre creatures David had ever seen: luminous, almost translucent, human-like gargoyles, with round, amethyst eyes, square noses, and shimmering, green scales. Webbed, lime-green wings protruded from between their shoulder blades and crested above their heads before cascading to the floor, culminating in a rim of vibrant feathers. Crossbows hung at their sides. They dropped to one knee and bowed as Slavandria approached.

Charlotte was right. This place kept getting curiouser and curiouser.

"Balendar," Slavandria said.

"Your Grace." The centaur bowed. "I apologize for the intrusion, but your assistance is required in an urgent matter." The winged creatures lifted the unconscious man and laid him on the floor. "I hope I am not too late."

Slavandria gasped and dropped to her knees. "Sir Trogsdill!"

She closed her eyes and swept her hands over the still body. "He's been wounded by a shadowmorth's blade." Slavandria's gaze met with Balendar's. "Where did you find him?"

"These two shime came upon him while they were on patrol."

Slavandria stood and approached the creature nearest to David. "What is your name? Where did you find this man?"

"Taccar, Your Grace. Second Lieutenant, Fox Glen Brigade. My comrade and I found the victim along the banks of the Cloverleaf River along with this." He withdrew a long sword from a sheath at Balendar's side and placed the weapon at Slavandria's feet.

Slavandria's brow furrowed with worry. "Did you see others like him in the forest? Sense their presence?"

Taccar shook his head. "No, Your Grace, however, news has

reached the forest that Their Majesties are missing."

Slavandria closed her eyes for a moment and then turned to Twiller, who stood quietly in the corner. "I need you to escort David and Charlotte to Tulipakar immediately. Make room for them in the Elthorian Manor. I will meet you there tomorrow." She turned to the centaur. "You and the shime are to scour the forest. Elicit whatever help you can from Hirth. King Gildore and Queen Mysterie must be found. Also keep your eyes open for a young man, not much older than this one, (she inclined her head toward David), with dark hair and emerald-green eyes. He goes by the name of Eric. He is this knight's squire. It is imperative no harm comes to him. These two shime will remain with me."

Balendar bowed. "As you wish, Your Grace. I will send a message by palindrake as soon as the king and queen are secure."

The centaur retreated from the room.

Slavandria turned to David and Charlotte. "You are to go with Twiller. Do as he says. Do not stray from the path. There are too many dangerous things that wait for you out there."

"Like what?" Charlotte said.

"I don't have time to tell you. I'll explain everything tomorrow. Twiller, get them out of here. Hurry. Do not stop for anything. Use whatever methods you must to reach the safety of Tulipakar before nightfall. Go, and send in the moon faeries on your way out."

Slavandria knelt beside the injured man and ripped open his shirt, exposing a raw, festering wound that stretched from beneath his left armpit to his navel.

David glared over his shoulder as Twiller urged them to leave.

"You can't keep us locked up forever, you know. We'll find our way out of here, with or without your help."

"Hold fast to that determination, David," she said, pressing her hands to the bloody lesion. "You're going to need it."

143

Chapter 13

Dark clouds snuffed out the midday sun as Eric came in sight of Avaleen. He ventured off the dirt road and brought his horse into a thicket of trees to survey the city. Unlike the charred farmlands and towns he'd passed through on his journey, the sprawling white marble citadel with its bright-colored bulbous turrets rose strongly from the rolling hillside and surrounding lush forest. Eric held tight to the reins and clicked his tongue, urging his horse into the open. A cool breeze whisked in from the east. Thunder rumbled in its wake. His horse snorted, and a sinking feeling settled within Eric. No birds flew overhead. No chanting or singing emanated from within the city walls. Only immeasurable silence greeted him.

A cold chill rippled down his spine.

He rode through the city's arched gateway of ivy-covered marble, his horse's hooves clomping on the cobblestones. A bead of sweat crawled from his temple to his jaw. He swept it away with his arm. His senses heightened. His heartbeat drummed. Time crawled by as he maneuvered his way through the barren city streets toward the Hall of Reflection.

It was there he and Trog were to have met his lethal instructor, Mangus Grythorn. Of course, that was before Einar happened. Now all Eric had was a soul full of hope that the mercenary remained within the protective confines of the city. If not, finding the paladin might prove to be more difficult than anticipated.

Eric arrived at the Hall of Reflection and winced as he dismounted, the wound from Einar still barking out in pain.

A few large raindrops plopped on his face and skin. Foreboding poured through his limbs.

Leave. Get on your horse and go.

He bit his lip and pushed against the desire to flee. Only cowards flee. Trog wouldn't run.

He entered the Citadel.

The oblong reception room was as he expected—grand, its marble walls dotted with oiled paintings of famous wizards, mages, and kings, both past and present. On the frescoed ceiling, gods and mages battled the forces of evil alongside unicorns, dragons, griffins, and faeries. Three corridors fingered off the main room, each leading to places seldom seen by humans. It was the narrow corridor straight ahead, the one lined with dark woods and mirrors, that caught his attention, for beyond it came a voice he recognized as clear as his own. Eric crept closer and ducked into a cloakroom, leaving the door cracked.

"You know it will be difficult to convince the Hirthinian people there is corruption in the ranks surrounding the king." Eric didn't recognize that voice. "It will be even more impossible for the King to believe his most valued knight and General of the Army would do anything against the crown or his country."

145

"Don't worry about that." The voice Eric recognized as Master Camden's, chuckled. "It has already been addressed and taken care of."

"How so?"

"Let's just say it's fascinating what these humans will do when threatened with the lives of those they love. Even the strongest crumble beneath the hint of such, how should I put it—emotional terrorism."

The unknown man let out a mirthful chuckle. "Yes, I do agree. Who, might I ask, is the malefactor?"

"Why, the Dragon King, of course." Another round of laughter. "There are benefits to situating a quisling high within the ranks of Einar's entourage. Someone the beast trusts."

"And the evidence planted?"

"Could be refuted, but then again, it's them against us, and what would we have to gain by lying, especially since we've captured one of their spies!"

The closet door flew open. Eric's heart leaped as hands grasped him by the breast of his tunic and threw him into the center of the room. An army of feet and legs surrounded him, kicking him. Pain spiraled up his spine, out his ribs. Air rushed from his lungs. He struggled to his hands and knees. A sharp blow slammed into his back. Stars popped before his eyes. His body crumpled. His face smacked the cold floor. The metallic taste of blood coated his tongue and trickled from the corner of his mouth.

He couldn't breathe, and for a moment, he saw more stars.

Master Camden's full-bodied voice, deep and resonant, spoke from above him. "Pull the runt from the floor and bring him to the chambers right away. You," the mage snapped his fingers, "gather the rest of the Council. Inform them we have a spy in our midst." Master Camden knelt and clasped his hand around Eric's throat. "You will be sorry you ever stepped foot into Avaleen, young squire. But I'll save your worst punishment for when Sir Trogsdill arrives to save you, and believe me, he will come for you."

"You're wrong." Eric winced at the pain rippling through his body. "He'll never fall for your ruse, and I'll make sure he knows everything."

"Not if you're dead."

Fiery threads of magic flew from the mage's fingers and plummeted deep within Eric, burning and winding their way through his torso and limbs. His body lifted from the ground, and air sucked from his lungs as he was hurled across the room.

Pain splintered along his back, exploding in his head as he slammed into the wall. His vision blurred. Voices grew distant, muffled. Gruff hands took hold of his arms and dragged him across the floor into an immense room swathed in rose-veined marble. Statues of ancient gods stood poised in the golden light of the globes fastened to the walls. His captors dropped him to the floor like a sack of grain. His chin hit the floor.

He cursed at the man who dropped him and worked his way to his feet. His ribs pulsed in agony. Ahead of him, doors to the Council chambers opened and a blind, elderly man dressed in a flowing maroon robe approached. In his left hand, he carried a birch staff. "The High Council will see you now."

The guards jabbed Eric in the sides.

He wailed and collapsed to all fours.

"Get up! Let's see how fast you can move after you've been properly beaten."

Eric struggled to his feet and walked inside the circular chamber. They descended three flights of steps, passing rows of empty chairs. Torches, bolted by iron fittings to the walls, provided the only source of light in the cavernous room. The domed ceiling was lost in the dark and smoky haze. It was in this room that the High Council and Senate debated issues and handed down verdicts regarding their magical kind, both manufactured and ordained. Sestian's enthusiastic grin flashed in Eric's mind. He'd lived for moments like this, for the defiance, for the thrill. *Now would be a good time to help me out, Ses. Give me the strength to steel my nerves.*

They stopped before a raised dais where Master Camden sat among four men and three women, all dressed in flowing robes as blue as a midnight sky. Master Camden stood and glared down at Eric, his amber eyes gleaming with amusement. "Where is your master, Sir Trogsdill?"

Eric met the mage's stare. "Why don't you tell me? You're the magician."

The backhanded blow struck with the force of a sledgehammer. Eric stumbled, his face throbbing. Lights flashed before his eyes. He righted himself and swallowed the blood trickling down his throat.

Master Camden sneered. "That was my gentle touch, so if you know what's best for you, you'll answer my question. Where is Sir Trogsdill?"

Eric straightened up and positioned himself squarely before his abuser. Never in a million years would he give the cretin information, even if he had it. Even if it meant death.

Camden growled and raised both hands over his head, the tips of his fingers dancing with red sparks.

Eric steadied himself, knowing full well whatever came his way was going to hurt.

But the mage's hands froze in mid-air. The sparks fizzled.

Camden's face twisted with anger and confusion, his eyes wild. He whipped around, his gaze boring into the council member walking his way.

"Elizon, please," the intervening mage said. "Do not lose your head over this imp." He made a small circle with his hand, and Camden's arms fell limp at his side, pendulums without a swing.

"What are you doing, Aldrich?" Camden said in a menacing growl. "Release my arms!"

The council member stepped closer. "Why? So you can carry on with your temper tantrum? The rest of us have a better idea to bring our knight out of the shadows."

"Such as?"

"Send word throughout the Southern Forest that Sir Trogsdill's pup has been apprehended while spying, and is awaiting prosecution. He will come to us if he believes his prized squire is to be executed."

Master Camden's lips twitched, his shoulders relaxed. A mirthful chuckle escaped the corners of his mouth.

"Of course," he said. "That is a brilliant idea." He called out to a guard standing near a side door to send a messenger.

A moment passed before a girl with chestnut skin, pearl-white eyes, and a barbed collar inked into her neck entered the chamber. She curtsied before the mage as if he were king.

"What is your name, girl?"

"Ceylione, my master."

A smile emerged on Camden's face as he curled his right arm and flexed his fingers.

A hollow feeling settled in Eric's stomach. The mage had his powers back, and it wouldn't be long before they were trained on him again.

Camden ordered the girl to her feet and cupped her chin in

his palm. A small whimper escaped her lips as the collar darkened and protruded from her skin. No longer an image, the real metal spikes hovered above her delicate skin, poised to plunge in if the girl disobeyed. Her fingers twitched, and her eyes flicked in their sockets.

Eric willed his mouth shut and steeled his nerves. The desire to strangle the bald pig of a mage surged through his entire being, but now wasn't the time. Tactical training told him he was outnumbered, and the weapons they wielded were far superior to anything he had, which at the moment was nothing. There would be a better time, a better place, to avenge her and others like her, and he would make sure he was there to carry out the justice.

"Go into the Southern Forest," Camden said, "and locate an elder palindrake. You are to relay that Sir Trogsdill's squire is in the custody of the High Council on charges of espionage and is awaiting trial. If no one speaks for him within two hours, he shall be executed."

Camden released her chin and the collar melted into her flesh, fading to a dull gray. She curtsied and fled from the room. Master Camden turned to Eric and grabbed his face in one hand, squeezing his cheeks together. "You know, you could have made this so much easier and much less painful if you had told us what we wanted to know. Now look at all the trouble you've caused. I don't like trouble."

Eric's feet lifted from the floor. He dangled there for a moment before flying backward through the air. His body broke over a row of chairs, his arms doing little to break his fall. He yelled out as a rib, maybe two snapped.

Pain. So much pain.

He staggered to his feet, swaying where he stood, his hands

150

gripping his sides. He swallowed, hard, his lungs desperate for air. If only he could breathe deeply. If only …

A weave of magic twined around his neck, squeezing, choking. His eyes widened. He clawed at his throat.

"I—can't—breathe!"

Blackness crept along the edge of his vision. He crumpled, and fell, pain ricocheting through his knees, his side. His head. Teetering on the edge of consciousness, he whimpered, *Someone help me, please.*

A loud bang broke through the languid dark. Eric coughed and gagged for air as the hold on his throat released. Tears fell, the pain unbearable. Overhead, dozens of sizzling, crystalline-blue tentacles crackled and whipped through the air.

"Slavandria!" Camden shouted. Her name caught in his throat like a barbed hook.

Eric yelped as he struggled to his hands and knees. Using the seats to each side, he hoisted himself to his feet. He blinked to bring everything into focus.

The sorceress stood on the steps only a few feet away, her fingertips aimed at Camden's chest. Two Duwan guards stood at her side, their bows drawn and nocked with two arrows each, the remaining council members marked as their targets.

"Please tell me this is not what it appears," Slavandria said, her voice as smooth as laced pudding.

Master Camden sputtered, his finger pointed at Eric. "H-he was caught trespassing, trying to break into sacred vaults."

"That's a lie," Eric said, his voice weak and abraded. "He wants Trog, and he's using me as bait."

Slavandria's eyes narrowed. "What business does the council have with Sir Trogsdill?"

The mage swallowed. "He is wanted for questioning in

the disappearance of Their Majesties. We believe he may have information beneficial to discovering their whereabouts."

Eric sucked in a shallow breath, then another. "That's not true. They have someone in Einar's ranks, someone who will falsely testify against Trog." Eric shook his head, desperate to rid himself of the dizziness taking over. He pinched the bridge of his nose. "They want everyone to believe he had something to do with the king and queen's disappearance."

"You lie!" Master Camden bellowed.

The sparks at Slavandria's fingertips flared and crackled like embers in a flame. "Swear to me on my father's name these accusations are untrue. Swear it!"

Aldrich pressed a hand to Camden's shoulder, his gaze boring into Slavandria. "Do not answer, friend. She is intruding upon a private council meeting, which violates the sanctity of our laws and this chamber. She must be detained for interfering in Council matters that do not concern her or involve her area of expertise."

"Do not speak to me of violating the sanctity of this chamber," Slavandria said. "This is an unauthorized hearing where you are illegally torturing a human. As queen of the Southern Forest and daughter of the Supreme Master, I am well within my area of jurisdiction to not only intervene in this Council matter but to order all of you into solitary confinement until a tribunal can be held to ascertain your guilt or innocence." She gestured toward the Duwan. "Escort these recreants to the holding cells."

Master Camden dodged their grip, spun and thrust out an arm, his palm outward. "*Ignisvipera!*"

A barrage of flaming snakes volleyed forth, unfurling in the air. Arrows sailed into the darkness behind the dais, missing their targets. Slavandria's magic thickened and swelled. The air bent with her power, but three serpents made it through her defenses.

They latched onto her and sank their fangs into her flesh. Her limbs twitched as she collapsed to the floor, her skin chalky, her eyes open and void of life. The magic flickered at the tips of her fingers and then blinked out.

Eric stared, wide-eyed. He looked to the Duwan for help, but they were as rigid as stone, blood oozing from fang marks in their necks. He swallowed, terror clogging his throat. It couldn't be. Slavandria couldn't be dead. She was Jared's daughter. She was powerful. Nothing, no one could defeat her.

Another snake launched through the air and coiled around Eric's body. An inhuman cry, unrecognizable as his own, wailed from his throat as the serpent constricted. His heart thudded against his ribcage. Life seeped out of him.

From somewhere deep in his mind a memory of a training class flared. What had his teacher said? *Short, shallow breaths! Don't panic! Kick groin! Gouge eyes!*

Eric gasped. He couldn't. His assailant was too far away.

He thought about death, life, and the senselessness of it all. What was it for, living, if death was the reward?

A loud, echoing crack split the air. A sword hissed from its scabbard.

Swoosh!

The constrictor around Eric's neck disintegrated into powder.

What the—?

Chairs scraped the floor. A chorus of voices shouted, "*Incendium!*"

The room ignited.

A man dressed in black leathers, his face blistered and scarred, leaped through the flames and shoved Eric to the floor.

Eric screamed the pain in his ribs more than he could take. Tears fell as he lay on his back, drizzling down his face into his ears. Above him, the man dodged fireballs. He swung his sword to the right, then to the left, the veins in his neck bulging in tight cords. Sweat flung from his brow as he danced, deflecting the attacks in fluid, powerful twists, turns, kicks and slices. His blade glowed pewter-blue, and scrollwork etched in the steel flickered in the firelight.

Eric's breath caught in his chest. *No, it can't be!* He pushed up to a sitting position and wiped his face with the heels of his palms. He recognized the writing. Felindilian script. Every knight, every squire knew there were only two swords like it in the world. One belonged to the Supreme Master Jared, the other to the general of his army, the one and only … Mangus Grythorn.

One after the other, Eric's rescuer smacked the fireballs and laughed as they rebounded back to their makers. The mages yelled. Their fleeing footsteps vibrated the floor.

"Where do you think you're going?" the man said. "*Ventus!*"

Three mages dropped to the ground, their bodies flopping like fish out of water.

Master Camden backed down the steps, stumbled over his own feet and fell, his eyes wide. The man in black cleared five steps in one leap, and landed, one foot on the mage's chest, the tip of his sword at Camden's throat.

"Please, Grythorn. I beg you. Spare me," Camden cried, his arms extended.

"Undo your spells and I might let you live. Do it! Now!"

"I-I c-cannot, not unless I stand."

"I'm not a fool." Mangus Grythorn flicked the tip of his blade across the mage's cheek, cutting open a small wound.

"I-I swear it!" Camden sobbed. A tear trickled down his cheek. "I need to stand."

Mangus chuckled. "You need to release them, or I shall release your head from its shoulders. How is that for negotiating?"

Master Camden rolled to his left side and pushed up on his elbow. Tears dribbled down the coward's face. He snapped his fingers and waved his hand.

The air moved, like a wave through the water. The snakes fell in plops.

Slavandria gasped. The Duwan stirred to life. In seconds, their arrows were pointed downward at Camden.

"Bind them and take them to Eisig," Mangus said. "Shoot them if they try to escape."

Green threads wove through the air.

"You're going to regret this!" Camden yelled as the Duwan carried him from the room. "Jared will hear of your interference."

"Good. Tell him, and don't leave out the part where you attempted to murder his daughter, for I can assure you that will head my report to him." Mangus sheathed his sword.

Master Camden struggled as the Duwan led him away. "You cannot do this to me! I will have your head!"

Mangus knelt at Slavandria's side and swept the hair from her face. "Are you alright, Van?" He brushed a thumb over the apple of her cheek and the curve of her jaw.

She nodded. "Yes. How is Eric?"

"He's alive, but in desperate need of your help." He touched his fingertips to the fang marks on her neck. "I will kill Camden for this."

"You're sweet." Slavandria met his gaze, her eyes soft. She ran her fingers up and down his arm. "But I'm sure my father will beat you to it." She glanced Eric's way. "Help me to my feet. I have a rogue squire who needs a bit of attention."

Eric shrank as Mangus walked toward him. So much restrained power sparkled in the man's eyes. He offered his hand to Eric. "Go on, lad. Take it. I won't rip you apart unless you give me a reason to."

Eric clasped the man's hand and yelped as he stood, his limbs wobbling.

He flinched as Slavandria pressed her palms to his torso. She sighed and shook her head. "You have two broken ribs. I can take care of them if you like, but I'm afraid you won't like me for awhile."

Eric exhaled. "Is there no magic you possess that doesn't hurt?"

"There's quite a bit, actually," Slavandria said as she gingerly pried open his shirt, "but when you have bones sticking through your skin, I'm afraid you're going to feel pain."

Eric glanced down at the wound and swayed. There was so much blood.

Mangus moved behind him and wrapped his arms around Eric's shoulders. "It'll be alright, boy. Think of something else."

Eric bit his trembling lip. He was so scared. Scared of the pain that was coming. Scared of crying in front of Mangus Grythorn. He froze in place, his eyes closed, waiting.

Slavandria placed her hand on the protruding bones. She spoke soft and low. The magic slipped from her palms and seeped into his skin in waves of fire and ice. Eric listened and tried to attach his mind to her soothing voice, but the ripping agony came, and he screamed.

"Noooo! Please stop!"

Mangus Grythorn tightened his grip. "Hold on, lad. It'll be over soon."

Eric sobbed. Sounds warped, and images faded. His pulse pounded in his eardrums.

The bones moved deep into his chest and snapped into place.

He gasped as the magic sank deep into his body like warm, thick honey. He could feel it, sealing and buffering. Second by second, the pain eased until it was little more than a tolerable ache. He sniffled and stepped away from Mangus. What an ass he must have seemed. Such a fine, noble squire he was, crying like a baby.

Mangus patted him on the back. "You all right there, lad? You mind telling us how all this happened?"

Eric nodded. "I'm fine." He stared at the floor, his hand cupped on the back of his neck. No matter how he tried, he couldn't look his savior in the eye. He swallowed and looked at Slavandria. "Thank you, both of you, for arriving when you did."

"Think nothing of it," Mangus said, with a heavy slap to Eric's back. "I'm such a sap when it comes to a good mage fight. I had no idea how bored I was." His eyes twinkled with mischief.

Eric smiled. A lethal warrior with a sense of humor. What a dangerous combination.

"Are you okay to walk?" Mangus asked.

Eric nodded. "I think so."

They climbed the stairs and exited the citadel onto the sunny courtyard glistening with puddles. In the daylight, the blistered skin and fresh scars on Mangus' face were less menacing than they'd appeared in the shadows of the Council chambers. An unmistakable power emanated from his very being, confirming he was still quite dangerous despite his recent injuries. Slavandria faced him; concern ever-present as she stroked his cheek, touched his hands.

"Mangus, I'm so sorry. I should never have let you leave Chalisdawn. I knew you were no match against Einar alone."

Mangus laughed. "Is that how you think I got my injuries, by crossing billywogs with a dragon?" He smoothed her hair from her eyes and cupped her chin. "My dear Van, Einar didn't do this to me. It's my own stupidity, really. I decided to act all human and save a few wee ones from an inn engulfed in flames. I got them out, but not before the inn collapsed on me."

Slavandria's eyes widened.

Mangus shook his head. "Fear not. Jared heard my agony and ferried me from the wreckage. He took me home to Felindil where I was in the middle of intense healing until I sensed your distress." He ran his fingers along her cheek. "It's a good thing I arrived when I did."

Slavandria rubbed the fading marks on her neck. "Yes, I'm quite thankful for your help. Then again, you always did have a propensity for making grand entrances and rousing exits." Her turquoise eyes stared at Eric and narrowed. She sauntered toward him. "Now, the matter comes down to you. What are you doing in Avaleen? Why are you not at Gyllen where you belong?"

"I-I … I was looking for him." Eric pointed at Mangus. "Sir Trogsdill and I were to meet him here yesterday, but then everything fell apart. I thought —"

"Ah, yes." Mangus chuckled. "Sir Trogsdill's squire. I've heard good things about you, lad. Where is your master?"

Eric shook his head. "I don't know. He's missing. Maybe dead."

"And you thought he may have died here?" Slavandria raised an eyebrow.

"No, Your Grace."

"So why are you here? Surely you didn't think your training would continue after all that has happened."

"N-no, Your Grace." Eric's core liquefied beneath their stares. Internal alarms went off. He wasn't ready to answer more questions about his purpose in Avaleen. Was he even supposed to know about the paladin? He shifted beneath the weight of their gaze. "I came to Avaleen to find him." He pointed to Mangus. "I thought I could bring him to Gyllen. Maybe his presence would bolster morale. I mean, the High Council has no intentions to protect us. I-I thought he could help."

"Interesting," Mangus said. He turned to Slavandria. "What do you think, Van? Can your father spare me for a day?"

Slavandria shook her head. "Doubtful. Maybe I can find you an hour or two, but not a day. As it is, I must return to Chalisdawn immediately to see to an important matter, and then travel to Tulipakar in the morning. Father said he would see me there before he sets sail. Where are the two of you going?"

"It is best you don't know. Plausible deniability and all that." Mangus requested the stable hands to bring two horses.

"Does that mean you are coming with me to Gyllen?" Eric asked. Excitement rippled through his veins. His plan worked. They never worked.

Mangus smiled. "Either that or I have an obsession with horses. Do you think you can arrange a meeting with me and the Order while I am there?"

Eric nodded. "Yes. Of course, sir."

Mangus rubbed his palms together. "Good. It's settled then." He took Slavandria's hands in his and kissed her cheek. "Stay out of trouble while I'm gone."

She smiled. "I won't promise you anything."

"I would expect nothing less."

Slavandria stepped closer to Eric and touched his face. Pulsating warmth rippled through his veins, and all the soreness in his ribs faded. The puffiness around his eyes seeped away, his skin no longer taut and stretched. She stepped back and admired her work. "There. The swelling is gone. By tomorrow, the bruises should be gone as well."

Eric bowed his head. "Thank you, for everything."

Slavandria nodded, her eyes dark and narrow. "Eric, what you said in the chambers, was that true? Is the Council conspiring against Trog?"

Eric nodded.

Slavandria caressed his cheek. "We'll get to the bottom of this, I promise." She turned to Mangus and kissed him on the cheek. "Be careful. I will buy you as much time as I can. Give Farnsworth and the others my blessings and tell them I will see them soon. They may not have the Council fighting for them, but they will always have my support. Make sure they understand that."

"I will, my lady." Mangus mounted his horse, as did Eric. "Let's go, lad. I don't wish to be on the roads at night. There is no telling what boggarts Einar let in when he attacked, and I'd rather not find out."

"Agreed, sir." Eric turned his horse and spurred the animal into a run. Behind him, a crack splintered, its sound carrying on the breeze. Slavandria was gone, and the second most powerful mage in the world was at his side.

What a mess he'd created.

And how glad he was to have friends in high places.

Chapter 14

David and Charlotte trudged behind Twiller, their clothing soaked from the torrential rainfall that plagued them since they'd left Chalisdawn. For the last several hours, Twiller had become quiet, agitated, his temper short. He skirted the small towns and hamlets despite David and Charlotte's pleas to rest and eat.

"I don't know why you didn't just ferry us," David said. "It would have been much quicker."

"We are not in the Southern Forest anymore," Twiller said. "Ferrying outside the woods would be a death sentence."

"Why?"

"Ferrying leaves signatures, remnants of your presence. If anyone of a higher power chose to look for you, he could trace your essence, which would lead him to Tulipakar. As Tulipakar is my home, I do not wish it to be turned into a battlefield. Now please stop asking questions and hurry. The moon is rising."

***

They followed the road north. Beggars Field gave way to an expansive meadow and rolling hills. The forest on their right thinned out, and before long they stood upon a ridge overlooking a deep valley dotted with haystacks. Two silos stood like shadow giants in the night. Apple trees speckled the landscape, the scent of their ripened fruit sweet and pungent on the cool air. They plodded downhill along the muddy road dotted with puddles. At the bottom, the terrain evened out and a row of dense hedges, at least nine feet high, formed on their right. Twiller picked up his pace and stopped a dozen or so yards ahead, facing the endless row of verge.

"Here we are," he said, as David and Charlotte approached. Charlotte slid from David's back and leaned into him, his arm around her waist for support.

Twiller cleared his throat, held up his hands, palms facing the hedges, and chanted:

"Weeping willow, mist, and vine
Heavenly moonlit stars align
Verge of green in sea of grass
Permit Slavandria's guests to pass."

A golden glow fanned the branches aside, offering an entrance large enough for passage.

"Whoa." David helped Charlotte through the divide. The hedge rustled and snapped into place. "Sweet."

A landscape of rolling green hills stretched out before them. Winding narrow paths of glowing lapis lazuli wandered off in several directions leading to pastures, gardens, and round huts made of stones and thatched roofs. To the southeast, looming against a thick forest, stood a resplendent white palace, complete with domed turrets and minarets.

"Good God," said David, his mouth gaped open.

"What is that place?"

"That is the Elthorian Manor," said Twiller, "and it is where you will spend the night."

"You're joking, right?" Charlotte's eyes sparkled like a little kid's on Christmas morning.

"I never joke," said Twiller. "Come."

They trekked down the hill and through the monolithic gatehouse of stone and iron.

Towering hedges skirting the path turned into brick walls thick with ivy. They passed through another gate and came face-to-face with dozens of half-moon steps leading to the palace where a domed, copper roof rose like a puffed up penny from the center.

"This is beautiful," Charlotte said. "I bet you could fit your house in there a hundred times."

David nodded. "No kidding."

Twiller climbed the steps and waddled across the wide mezzanine. He touched his finger to the lock, and the two-story wooden doors opened inward. Wall sconces and candled chandeliers flared to life.

David stepped inside, his heart thumping madly. "This is sick!"

A gold-flecked marble statue of an armored soldier straddling an armored horse stood with honor in the center of the entrance hall. Off to each side, two sets of marble stairs swathed in dark-blue carpet swept up to the floor above. Hallways dressed in bold, blue carpet and oiled paintings led off to either side as well as straight ahead, all disappearing into a vast, velvety darkness.

"Whoa!" David turned in a circle, his head thrown back. "Check out the paintings on the ceiling!"

"It's even more amazing from up here!" Charlotte shouted as she clung to the second-story banister. "You've got to check out the tapestries and paintings!" Charlotte peered down the dim hallway behind her. "I wonder what's back there."

"I don't know," David said, jogging up the stairs. "Maybe Twiller will take us on a tour."

"I'm afraid that is out of the question," Twiller said as he reached the landing.

"Whose place is this?" David peered down the darkened hallway behind him.

"It once belonged to the Baron and Baroness of Trent, Fredrik Elthorian and his wife, Allena." Twiller waddled across the landing to the right and opened a door. "Lady Charlotte, this will be your quarters for the duration of your stay."

It was a grandiose room with painted murals of rose gardens. A fire roared in the hearth. A plush bed adorned with brocade covers nested upon a platform inside a white gazebo. David opened the balcony's double doors framed in dark blue velvet drapes with gold tassels and stepped outside, his breath momentarily taken by the view.

"Oh, my." Charlotte stood beside him, her mouth open. "Have you ever seen anything more beautiful in your life? Look!" She pointed to the right. "There's a huge pond and a gazebo, and look at all the little houses lit up. Can you hear the music and laughter? It's magical, don't you think?"

David nodded. "Yes. Magical." *So magical, I want to go home.*

Twiller, still standing in the doorway, cleared his throat.

"Master David, if you will, please walk with me to the other side of the landing, I will show you to your quarters."

Charlotte was the first inside the spacious suite with murals painted on the walls. She sat at the foot of a massive, canopied bed carved with foxes and dogs, horses and hunters. From the corners of the canopy fell drapes of purple and red silks and velvets. A gilded mirror hung above the fireplace that was roaring with a freshly started fire. Plush sofas and armchairs formed a half-circle in front of the hearth. In the center was an oval table dressed with a fresh pot of tea, and a tray of rolls, jam, and tarts.

David sat in a chair and leaned back. "Twiller, this is amazing. Thank you."

"Do not thank me. It is Slavandria who has provided such hospitality."

Charlotte sat on the couch and plucked a tart from the tray. "You said this house once belonged to a baron and baroness. What happened to them?"

"They perished at sea while on holiday, leaving behind three sons. The two oldest moved to Hirth a few years after their parents' death. The youngest, Devron, remained behind, befriended the king of Berg, and when the king passed away, Devron inherited the entire estate and title to the throne. Devron ruled for several years, returning now and then to the manor to escape the demands of the kingdom. Several years into his kingship, he married, and his queen had their only son here in this very room. It was a glorious day."

"You remember it?" David asked.

Twiller smiled. "Oh yes. It was a grand affair, but the joy did not last. No more than six months after Master Cole turned three, the greatest known enemy to the five realms of Estaria attacked Berg. Within hours, the enemy's army decimated the kingdom; every inhabitant, including Devron and his family, lay dead. The enemy, known only as Einar, took possession of the castle where he remains today, his eyes set firm and strong on the kingdom of Hirth."

"Why? What's so special about Hirth?" David poured three cups of tea and popped a tart in his mouth.

"Hirth is the seat of power in the realm of Fallhollow. It is the fabric that binds this realm, our world, together. If it should fall, all of Fallhollow as we know it will cease to exist. Einar will rule all. With Hirth and Fallhollow under his control, there will be no kingdom strong enough to protect the other four from crumbling. Einar will rule all things. There will be no place for any of us in his world." Twiller stood and straightened his vest. "Now if you don't mind, I must—"

"Wait," David shifted in his seat. "If Hirth is so powerful, then who or what is protecting it from falling into the hands of this Einar dude?"

"I'm afraid no one, Master David, except for a well-loved king, an exceptional army, and a faithful order of knights."

"That's it? No magic? No wizards? What about Slavandria?"

"As you will find out, the mages are forbidden to interfere with the lives of men, and they adhere to that rule above all others."

A suspended moment of silence followed before Twiller stood. "Master David, Lady Charlotte, it was a pleasure having this chat, but I am taking my leave. I have not seen my home and wife in several days, and my feet are aching for a nice hot bath. You will find lavatories in your rooms. Restrictions are in place on the house, limiting your access to your chambers, the upstairs landing, and the entry hall. I suggest you get some sleep, as Slavandria will arrive first thing in the morning." Twiller left and returned within seconds. "I almost forgot." He withdrew a small black rock with silver streaks from his vest pocket and set it on the chest at the foot of the bed. "Should an emergency arise—you fall, break your neck, that sort of thing—throw this at the wall. I'll be here before you can utter my name. Goodnight."

Moments later, the manor's front doors closed. David collapsed on his bed, his hands clasped on his stomach. Charlotte sat cross-legged beside him. "You okay?"

"Yeah."

She tore off a piece of bread and poked it in her mouth. "I don't believe you."

David stared up at the carved canopy. "I'm trying to piece together everything, Char, and the more I try, the more effed-up it becomes. I mean, where do centaurs and fae exist? Nowhere and yet … " He rolled out of bed and walked to the balcony doors and opened them. "I feel as if I'm losing my mind. Nothing makes sense, and I'm losing track of time. On top of that, this damn tattoo keeps pulsing and sending out these warm tingly feelings."

Charlotte slipped her arms around David and pressed her cheek to his back. His heart skipped. His skin electrified. "Does it hurt?"

"No, not really." His breathing became harder. Why couldn't she understand what her touch did to him? The urge to kiss her intensified. He had to make her stop or else …

David turned around and cupped her hands in his.

Her eyes. So blue. So deep. They darted back and forth, searching his face as if waiting for him to say something. Do something—something he couldn't afford to do. *No, David. Friends.*

The heat of her body tumbled into his. "I'm sorry." She

gripped her fingers tight around his hands and pulled into him. "I wish there was some way I could help you."

David dropped her hands and walked inside, the memory of his hands all over her body fresh in his mind. *Breathe, damn it. Breathe.*

She walked past him and sat on the bed. A moment of discomfort lingered between them and then vanished. "David, have you thought what we're going to tell people when we get home?"

"A little. I suppose we'll have to make up a story that's simple and easy to stick to."

"Yeah, I suppose." Charlotte got up and walked to the sitting area. "It's not like we can tell people we met a sorcerer and saw a centaur. Speaking of which, who do you think that guy the centaur delivered was?"

"From the sounds of it, someone important. Did you see the cut across his stomach? I'm surprised his guts weren't hanging out."

"I tried not to look. There was so much blood. I almost puked."

David tugged on her hair as he walked around her. "You almost puke over a hangnail."

"Like it's my fault I have a queasy stomach." Charlotte flashed him a coy smile.

His heartstrings tugged at his soul, and his skin tingled as heat spread through him from head to toe. Once again, she'd managed to turn him into a gooey mess with just a smile. He had to find a way to turn the attraction off.

He poured a cup of tea and raised it to her. "It's my last one. Do you want another?"

"No, I don't think so. I think I'm going to get cleaned up and try to get some sleep. Are you going to be okay?"

David nodded and wiped the dribble of tea away on the back of his hand. "Yeah, I'm good. I think I'll turn in, too."

Charlotte glanced at the floor, a strand of hair twisted around her finger.

Was she waiting for an invitation? No, she couldn't be. She understood his need to stay just friends, didn't she?

"Okay," she said. "You know where I'll be." She shuffled to the doorway and paused. "David. Do you think we'll ever get home?"

David met her gaze and hoped his tone didn't betray his doubts. "Yes. We have to. You?"

Charlotte smiled and nodded. "Yeah. Sure. Night."

David waited for Charlotte's door to close before settling back on his pillow. Moonlight carved patterns on the walls. Dirt and sweat clung to his body like a repulsive second skin, and his mouth tasted like something had crawled inside and died. What he would give for a toothbrush.

He turned on his side and stared at the sky, and for the first time since he and Charlotte arrived in Fallhollow, he allowed the hovering shroud of fear to settle over him. Not fear for Charlotte, not for himself, but from the threat that had yet to reveal its true face. It was coming, it was all around him, but this time there was no one to protect him. He was going to have to face the danger like a man, perhaps even die like one, but not before he got Charlotte home. That was his priority. After that, nothing else mattered.

Chapter 15

"What do you mean, you went to Avaleen?" Farnsworth's fist tightened around the finials on the high-backed chair, his knuckles white, his face as red as beet soup. "No one gave you permission to leave!"

"I don't need your permission!" Eric tried to shove the anger down into his gut, but it fought back and tumbled out of his mouth uncontrolled. "I don't need permission from any of you. I'm seventeen years old. I'm not a child, and if you'd stop for one moment and let me explain, you might realize I'm not as incompetent as you think I am!"

"Eric, it has nothing to do with incompetence. It's about you defying the rules. You know you are never to leave Gyllen without an escort. Ever."

"And why is that? Why am I always to be coddled and protected?"

"There are reasons, and that is all you need to know."

"Then I suppose you would like to accompany me to the lavatories to ensure I don't flush myself away."

"Eric, I'm this close to knocking that sass out of you," Farnsworth said, his thumb and forefinger pinched together. "Now tell me what you were doing in Avaleen and how you got that bruise on your face."

"Farnsworth, go easy on him," Mangus said, walking into the room, his lip curled up in a sly smile. "He managed to take quite a beating and still leave a very bitter taste in Master Camden's mouth as well." Mangus put his arm around Eric's shoulder and squeezed. "He's quite the young intrepid. He reminds me of someone else I knew years ago."

"That's what I'm afraid of." Farnsworth's features softened. He embraced Mangus. "It's good to see you again, my friend. We weren't expecting you. What brings you to Gyllen?" The knight's gaze wandered over Mangus' healing face.

Mangus sat in a chair and scratched his nose. "Don't look so concerned, Farnsworth. It's not as bad as it looks. A week from now it'll all be gone with nary a reminder."

"What happened?" Farnsworth sat across from Mangus, one leg crossed over the other.

Mangus relayed the story of his injuries once more, adding a few more details of Einar's destructiveness.

"I don't understand it," Farnsworth said. "That monster has been contained for the last seventeen years. Why? Why now?"

"I think the mages woke him," Eric said before he could stop himself. "I think they did it because they want a war."

Farnsworth rubbed his palm over his face. "Eric, I appreciate you wanting to help, but your overactive imagination is not what is needed right now."

Mangus sat back and tapped his fingers on the arm of the

chair. "I don't believe his imagination is overactive, Farnsworth. I think you should listen to what he has to say. You might find yourself a bit enlightened."

Farnsworth waved his hand as a gesture for Eric to continue. "Very well. I'm listening."

Eric paced back and forth as he relayed the conversation he'd overheard in the cloisters and the chain of events as they occurred in Avaleen. Farnsworth sighed and rolled his eyes as if the story was too impossible to believe. Several times he turned to Mangus, who nodded in confirmation. When Eric finished, the room fell quiet. Farnsworth stood and moved to the fireplace, one hand on the wall, the other on his hip. He stared into the flame, chewing on his bottom lip. Finally, he turned to Eric.

"Why didn't you say something to us when Seyekrad attacked you?"

"Would you have believed me? Besides, all of you were babying me, acting as if I had no mind of my own. Like I couldn't take care of myself."

Farnsworth's jaw tightened, the blood vessels in his temples bulged and pulsed.

"Regardless, you know your position as a squire and future knight of this kingdom requires you to inform us of any conspiracy you are witness to. You deliberately disobeyed that directive, and instead, decided to pursue your investigation that nearly got you killed."

Farnsworth folded his arms across his chest. "I am beyond angry with you, Eric. How dare you think of your personal gain at a time like this."

Eric sputtered. "My own ... are you kidding me? Did you not hear what I said? There is a council of mages out there who are determined to peg Trog with a crime he didn't commit, all because they want to take over Hirth. They're willing to risk open war to get what they want. They tortured me to get him to come to them, and all you can focus on is that I didn't tell you about the incident in the cloisters when it happened? Would you have believed me without proof or would you have told me like you just did five minutes ago that I have an overactive imagination?" His arms and hands trembled with stifled anger.

Mangus flicked a glance at Eric and gave a slight shake of his head before standing. "The boy has a point, old friend. As it is, the lad found out some very valuable information, and Master Camden, along with four other members of the Council, are now confined until Master Jared can address the issue."

"You're missing the point, Mangus. There are protocols all squires must follow, and he failed to adhere to them. He cannot go around thinking he is impervious to the rules."

Mangus waved his hand in a dismissive fashion. "Forget the rules for a moment and consider what the boy did. Look at him. He took a hell of a beating in the name of this kingdom, for Trog and Gyllen, and never once did he falter. The more determined they were to break him, the more steadfast he grew. Trust me. He looked a lot worse before Slavandria got hold of him. I'm telling you. I've seen less honor and resolve in grown men. Please consider my words before you pass down punishment."

Farnsworth threw up his hands in exasperation. "I don't believe what I'm hearing. I have a rogue squire who picks and chooses what rules and laws he wishes to abide by and you're telling me to ignore the blatant disrespect."

"Do not twist my words, Farnsworth, but consider this. He came looking for me, and here I am. What do you choose to do with this good fortune?"

"That's not exactly true." Eric swallowed, his chest rising and falling with his rapid breathing. He glanced between the two men. "I went to Avaleen to find the paladin. I'd heard he had arrived in the kingdom and thought, if I were a magical dignitary, Avaleen would be the place I would go."

Farnsworth flashed Mangus an I-told-you-so look. "See? He does as he pleases without a single thought to consequences."

"I was supposed to go there yesterday to train with him." Eric pointed to Mangus. "I didn't think there would be a huge problem."

"That's your problem, Eric. You act before you think."

"What was I supposed to do? I had to do something, especially since the mages have no intentions of helping us. I thought if I could bring the paladin here, he could help us."

"How do you know about the paladin?" Mangus asked, an eyebrow raised.

Eric's stomach sank. "Sestian and—"

Farnsworth threw his hands up in the air. "Sestian." The name rolled from his lips like venom. "You're going to tell me you acted on something Sestian told you?"

"No! I—"

"Did you make a promise to him to carry out one of his insane plots?"

"No, and he didn't have insane plots!"

"Eric, sit!" Farnsworth pointed to a chair. "I've heard enough. We'll discuss this later."

"But—"

Farnsworth shot Eric a glower that could set a hearth ablaze. An exhausted sigh heaved up from Eric's chest. It was no use. Sestian was right. No matter what Eric did, no matter what he said, Farnsworth and the other knights would never see him as anything more than a stupid boy incapable of doing anything more than sharpening knives and shining armor. He crossed his arms and slouched in his chair.

"Good heaven, how Trog manages I'll never know." Farnsworth sat in a chair and rubbed his brow. "Mangus, I don't suppose you know what the boy speaks of and where this paladin is, do you? We were hoping he would make contact with us by now."

Mangus shook his head. "I am not privy to that information, and to be honest, I'm not too keen on knowing. I'm more interested in who the traitor is inside Einar's circle."

"Do you have any ideas?"

"Only that it will be someone of little consequence. Someone expendable, either on the mages' or Einar's terms."

"I agree though I'm unsure as to what to make of Bainesworth's involvement."

Mangus snorted. "I wouldn't worry too much about him. My guess is he's in it to see Trog grovel and beg for mercy. He has no connections to Hirth. Therefore, he has nothing Einar wants or needs. My guess is that the Council is using him to stir up some ill feelings, to get all of you to focus on Bainesworth instead of the real threat wandering the halls of Berg."

"That still doesn't explain what Seyekrad was doing here," Eric said. "He's supposed to be one of the protectors of the realm, but it didn't look like he was doing much protecting."

"Seyekrad's taking care of something for Jared right now. That's all I can say."

Eric huffed. "Then Jared needs to re-evaluate his help. That's all I have to say."

Mangus laughed and stood. "I'll be sure to pass that along to him when I see him tomorrow."

Farnsworth raised an eyebrow. "Oh? Are you returning to Felindil?"

Mangus nodded. "For a short time. We are to set sail on a diplomatic mission to all the realms. Depending on how well we are received, the trip may last several months."

"I see." Farnsworth rubbed his chin, worry clouding his eyes.

"Is there something you need from me before I go?" Mangus folded his arms and stared down at Farnsworth.

The knight leaned forward, his hands clasped between his knees. An immeasurable pause followed before Farnsworth said, "Yes, there is, and I know I should not ask, but I have to."

Mangus sat in the chair across from Farnsworth, his position a mirror image of the knight's. "What do you need? You know I'll do whatever I can to help you."

"We need protection, Mangus." Farnsworth's voice cracked, the way a voice does when tears hover on the edge. "We are few. Many have died, many more are injured. We have a squadron of soldiers on their way to Doursmouth. We've dispatched as many troops as we can to the borders, but there are not enough to protect the kingdom. If Einar attacks again, we will lose."

Mangus clasped Farnsworth's hands in his. "I will see what I can do. I'm sure I can whip up a buffer charm and a repellant spell that Jared won't be able to trace back to me.

Unfortunately, I cannot do much more, as my supreme lord and master would view my help as interfering, which would not bode well for anyone concerned. I will tell you, though, he has placed a rather strong and complex verdaí around Berg which should hold the beast away from Hirth, but it never hurts to have an extra layer of protection."

The two men stood and embraced.

"Thank you," Farnsworth said. "Anything you do will be much appreciated."

The two men walked toward the door. Mangus laid his hand

on Farnsworth's shoulder and gave a reassuring squeeze. "I'll also speak with the shime's chieftain and secure their help. They've already been informed of the situation and are on high alert." He turned to Eric and pointed his finger at him. "And you, young man, do me a favor. You impressed me today, but let's not do that again, okay? I know you want to prove yourself, but let Slavandria deal with the paladin. Today could have ended up a lot worse than it did, and the next time, you may not be so lucky. Understand?"

Eric nodded, admiration puffing up like a pastry in his soul. Mangus Grythorn was nothing like what he'd imagined. Unlike Trog and the other knights, this man understood him. Sympathized with him. Defended him. Of course, he'd do whatever the mage asked of him. He'd be a fool not to.

Mangus patted Farnsworth on the back and said, "Remember, go easy on him. If you have any problems out of him, send him my way when I return."

Eric gulped as the man left the room.

Farnsworth turned with a grin on his face and motioned to Eric to get up. "Come on. Let's get out of here and get something to eat. I'll figure out what to do with you tomorrow."

Chapter 16

David woke with a start and sputter, his dreams washing away with the splash of cold water dripping from his hair and face. Twiller set a pitcher on the nightstand, his mouth curled in a triumphant smile.

"What are you doing?" David dabbed his face with the sheet. "Ever hear of waking someone with a simple 'Good Morning?'"

"I've been trying to get you up for the last fifteen minutes. I had no other choice. Slavandria is here and awaits you and Lady Charlotte on the terrace. You have twenty minutes to bathe and dress. When done, meet me in the hallway. Your clothes are on the foot of the bed." The door clicked shut as he left the room.

David leaned forward, picked up the dark brown leather pants and shirt, and groaned. *Whatever happened to a pair of jeans, a shirt, and sneakers?* He scratched the two-day old stubble on his chin and headed to the bathroom, hoping the toiletry gods were kind and had left him a razor. He wasn't so lucky.

David emerged from the room a few minutes later at Twiller's annoying insistence. His breath hitched as Charlotte stepped onto the landing dressed from top to bottom in a molded two-piece leather outfit in midnight blue. Her milk-chocolate hair was swept up in a ponytail and her blue eyes were deadly serious. His brain stumbled for the perfect word to describe the way she moved, graceful like a gazelle. Elegant. Poised. Determined. Her gaze met his and her lips parted as if daring him to make even the slightest off-handed comment. He'd seen that look before. He breathed deep, taking in as much air as her presence allowed. *Don't give your feelings away. Smile. Pretend you don't see.*

He blinked and walked toward her, his insides a trembling mess. "That's a new look for you. I take it there was a wardrobe glitch on your side of the cosmos, too."

His embodiment of perfection stood before him, a scowl on her face. "Shut up. At least you look presentable. Me, I look like a sausage wrapped in a latex balloon, not to mention my legs are sprouting, and I'm pretty sure there's a family of fuzzy caterpillars living in my pits." She scraped her thumb over David's stubbled cheek and snorted. "I take it there wasn't a razor in your bathroom either."

"Oh, blight me." Twiller rolled his eyes. "Now is not the time to discuss your hygiene. Slavandria is waiting." He waddled down the wide corridor toward the rear of the manor, his footsteps silent upon the thick red carpet.

"What's stuck up his pants?" David said, tugging his leather jerkin.

Charlotte smiled. "Shh. Be nice."

"He's annoying."

"And you're not?" She nudged him as they walked down the hall.

"I'm sixteen. I'm supposed to be annoying."

Morning, hidden in a veil of gray mist, beckoned to them through the wall of floor-to-ceiling windows at the end of the wide corridor. Eyes in oiled portraits seemed to follow their progress as they hurried to catch up to Twiller.

At the end, they turned left down another expansive corridor then walked through a glass door and down flagstone steps to a terrace below. Straggling vines and roses wove in and out of rotted trellises that barely clung to stone walls. A white gate leading to lower terraces hung lopsided on its weathered casing. In the center of the terrace, Slavandria stood beside a fountain of a trident-wielding merman surrounded by a sea of rambling weeds and honeysuckle. And in the corner, sitting upon the low stone wall, was the guy the centaur had dumped off in Chalisdawn. David gulped as the stare from the man's lime-green eyes darted toward him, pinning him where he stood.

Upon closer inspection, the guy had to be in his forties, thick, with nut-brown hair, a square jaw, and serious eyes.

The sleeves of his cream-colored tunic were rolled up past his elbows, the loose fabric doing little to conceal his massive chest and arms. A wide, brown, leather belt was cinched around his waist, and brown, leather boots covered his calves to his knees. The hilt of a sword glinted from a sheath on one hip.

"Well, he looks better than he did yesterday," Charlotte whispered, clutching David's arm a little tighter.

"Yeah, but yesterday he didn't look like he wanted to kill me."

Charlotte linked her arm around his. "Don't let him frighten you. He's only as scary as you let him be."

"Easy for you to say. You're not the chunk of meat being eyed by the hungry wolf."

Slavandria greeted them as they arrived. "David, Charlotte,

I'm glad you're here." She gestured toward the man in the corner. "I'd like to introduce you to the Grand Master Knight and General of the Hirthinian Army, Sir Trogsdill Domnall. Sir Trogsdill, this is Master David Heiland and Lady Charlotte Stine of Havendale."

David gulped, his insides fluttering as the man stood. He was way tall, like redwood-tree-tall, and just as thick. He nodded his head once in their direction. "Please, call me Trog."

His deep voice rumbled like an earthquake.

Charlotte clutched David's arm, the slight tremble in her body transferring to his. He squeezed her hand. *So much for not being afraid, Char.*

"Come, come," Slavandria said. "There is much to discuss, and we are on limited time."

"We're always on limited time," David whispered as they ventured across the terrace to a marble table laden with roasted quail, breads, figs, apples, and cheese.

From the surrounding verge a towering stranger appeared. His black robe shifted as he approached, his face hidden within the deep hood. Voluminous sleeves met at his waist, concealing both hands.

Charlotte oozed into her seat. David stood behind her, his sixth sense firing off all kinds of bad vibes.

"Good morning, Daughter," the man said.

The voice rippled through David. He recognized it, but from where?

"Good morning, Father," Slavandria replied.

David's heart jolted. *Of course! The man from his room who was talking to Slavandria while David slept.* He struggled to remember the name. *James. Jason.*

Jared!

A crippling sense of dread buried into his soul as the man approached and shed his robe as if it was a nuisance. Wavy hair as purple as winter plums framed his rugged face and fell to below his shoulders. Eyes like turquoise glass shone brightly against his sun-bronzed skin. Over his well-defined muscles, he wore a black leather vest, and heavy black trousers tucked into knee-high boots. Silver rings, weighted with jewels, adorned every finger. A sword rested on his hip, and mystic symbols stained his chest and arms.

David shuddered as the man walked around him. *What does he want? Why is he looking at me?*

Jared continued to circle, his eyes swirling like a hurricane at sea. He moved his arms through the air in a series of long pushes and slow pulls. A whispered chant in a strange language slipped from his lips. His fingers furled and unfurled and with a powerful thrust, he clasped the back of David's neck.

Cold terror crawled along David's spine. Every muscle tensed, his upper body heaved in an effort to breathe as his blood bubbled and oozed like lava through his veins. He reached behind his head, clawing at the man's hand, his body filling with fire.

From somewhere beyond his agony, Charlotte screeched, "Let him go! Stop it! You're hurting him!"

Ice-cold slush flecked with shards of glass plunged into his veins. Cutting.

A primeval cry like that of a wounded animal wailed from his throat. His mind retreated to a place of survival, where no anguish existed. An abyss where no one could reach him. A place where death would roll over him in calm, easy waves.

His eyesight faded as a new sensation like threads of electrical currents zinged through him. Power surged in his chest, building, spinning into a tight ball. Air siphoned from his lungs. Stars exploded in an enveloping darkness. His world spiraled. He wanted to run, to go, but his feet failed to move. He was trapped in a swirling hurricane of lightning. Up and up the current swarmed, electrified bees buzzing, stinging his limbs from within.

David dropped to his knees, his arms flailing at his sides. Burning tears spilled down his cheeks. The surge spun into a tighter, brighter ball, growing.

Spinning.

Whirling.

He gasped for breath. His eyes popped open as a shockwave swelled then burst through his chest, upending flowerpots, the table. Charlotte flew back, hanging in the air before slamming into the terrace wall. She lay crumpled on the ground, gasping for breath.

The hand of agonizing torture released his neck. Jared backed away. His words echoed in David's frazzled brain. "It is done. He is sealed."

Charlotte groaned and turned onto her side. For a moment, she hung poised on her hands and knees. "What—do you mean—he's sealed? What's done? What did you do to him?"

Looking shaken, she got to her feet and inched toward David.

Jared flexed his hand. "I sealed his destiny. He is now bound to this world as he is to his own. Everything he does from this point forward will affect both this world and his own. Every decision, every risk, every alliance he seeks, every friendship he tests will have a ripple effect." He planted his eyes on David. "Choose wisely. Most chances only come once in Fallhollow."

David shook his head, his body still in spasms from the pain. "What does that mean?" He pressed his eyes shut for a moment, trying to find his center, his thoughts, his mind. Heavy footsteps thudded around him. He looked up to see Trog staring at him as if thoroughly amused. The knight offered his hand. David took it and rose to his feet. He wobbled and grasped the table to keep from falling over. His gaze met Jared's once more, and he repeated his question.

The magic man uttered a scornful sound and turned to his daughter. "Explain things to him, won't you? My purpose here is done. I must return to the WindSong and ready its sails."

David sat down, his limbs trembling. "But—"

Slavandria flicked him a quick glance and linked her arm around her father's. "I understand. Please give Mangus my love and prayers for a speedy recovery."

Jared's eyes darkened, eying her with the look of a wild, angry beast about to attack. "Do not play innocent with me, Daughter. He told me of your escapades in Avaleen."

"Father, I—"

"You blatantly defied me!" His booming voice shook the universe. "I am tired of your flagrant disregard of the rules and abuse of your title. Disobey me again and you'll find yourself sitting alongside Master Camden in Eisig."

Slavandria laughed. "You don't mean that, Father."

Jared held up his index finger, his eyes dark. "Do not test me. I am no longer amused by your games."

Slavandria straightened and lifted her chin. "I suppose that leaves us at an impasse, Father. You do what you must, and so shall I."

Jared studied his daughter then growled. He flicked a glance at Trog. "I trust you will take care of your own troubles and leave my daughter out of your affairs."

Trog inclined his head. "I will do what I can."

The two men shared a long gaze, then, with a single nod and a crack like a whip, Jared vanished.

David's heart raced, his blood pumping too fast and too hard. "What did he do to me?"

Slavandria gathered her lavender hair over one shoulder. "He completed the dorna—a very special blessing only he can give. I'll explain while we eat. I hope you're hungry."

Trog piled his plate with food. David watched the man eat, his gaze caught on a cluster of seven visible white scars along the knight's jaw line, each of them about two inches long.

Trog licked his fingers and dropped a clean bone on his plate. "It's impolite to gawk. If you have a question, ask. I won't bite you."

David rested his arms on the table's edge. "I-I'm sorry. I don't mean to be rude, but those scars," he ran his thumb along his jaw, "what caused them?"

"I infuriated a dragon." Another bone clinked onto the plate.

Charlotte frowned and knotted her hands in her lap. "Did you say dragon?"

"I did." Trog wiped his mouth. "A Timberlake Smoothback to be exact. A fire-breather. Black as onyx dipped in liquid amethyst. He was a spawn of the underworld and wielder of the most malicious sort of black magic. He was a big one, too, a hundred or so feet long, half as tall with the eyes and tongue of a snake."

A slight cool breeze wafted through the terrace and toyed with the dilapidated gate, tapping it several times against the post. David's insides jumped. His heart thudded against his ribcage. An image of his parents cowering beneath a dragon appeared in his head. *No. It couldn't be. Could it?*

Trog glanced at Slavandria. "Do you wish to tell them the story or should I?"

Slavandria sipped her tea and set her cup on the table. Her

glance darted from David to Charlotte and her lips turned up in a smile. "If their bewildered expressions are any indication, I'd say you have a captive audience. By all means, continue."

Trog pinched off another quail leg and took a bite. "This dragon, his name is Einar, and he's about as evil as they come. Legend tells us, two centuries ago, a young prince of Berg found a dragon egg in the Elastine Forest while hunting with his father. He took it to the castle, hatched it and watched it grow. When the young man could no longer provide for the dragon's needs, Einar slaughtered him and the entire royal family." Trog sucked the juices from his fingers and threw the bone on his plate.

"After securing the castle and the lands around it, the beast proclaimed himself the Dragon King. For years, he ruled the kingdom of Berg. All those who defied him suffered his wrath. The mages did what they could to dethrone him, but Einar's magic was far too dark. A war broke out between the two, an ultimate battle of good against evil."

David gulped his tea. "The Dragon War," he said. Charlotte's arched brow begged for an explanation. "Twiller mentioned it on the way to Chalisdawn."

Trog nodded and reached for a pear. "After several years and much bloodshed, the mages defeated Einar and banished him beneath Lake Sturtle. The vile creature remained there until fifty years later when he escaped."

A shiver rippled out of Charlotte. She folded her arms tight to her chest as if cold. "How did he escape?"

Trog shrugged. "No one knows. What is certain, he returned to Berg Castle, killed the young king who once lived in this manor, and reclaimed the kingdom as his own. For fifty years, he reigned. All the lands from Tulipakar to the far reaches of the Northern Forest fell under his control. Greedy, he moved on to the kingdom of Braemar and reduced it to the smoldering ruins that remain today. It was then he made a very stupid mistake." Trog took a bite of pear and chewed.

"What mistake?" David asked.

"He went after Hirth."

"Why?" Charlotte asked.

"The kingdom is rich beyond your wildest imagination. Crops, minerals, precious metals, it's got them. But it's not that kind of wealth that has Einar biting at his tail. It's the abundance of human spirit that's got him in a tizzy. He can't stand humans being happy and content especially on a piece of land more valuable than any jewel he owns." Trog leaned forward, his gestures growing more animated as he spoke. "Einar thought if he claimed or destroyed the surrounding kingdoms, he could glide right into Hirth and take it. But he misjudged its people." He tossed the pear core on his plate and pushed it away. "They refused to live as slaves, to succumb to the beast's tyranny. They met him on the field of battle, prepared to die as free men, and you know what?" Trog pointed his finger at David. "They won the day. Einar retreated to Berg with a wound right here," Trog jabbed his chest with his fist, "no doubt to lick his wounds and plan his revenge. That's when the mages wove their spell around Berg to keep him isolated, which is where he stayed until a few days ago when he escaped his confines and attacked Hirth and Gyllen Castle."

"What set him free this time?" David wiped the sweat from his palms on his pants.

Slavandria glanced at him over her teacup. "You did."

The words hurled into David's chest like a cannonball. It was impossible. "How? Why?"

Slavandria hesitated for a moment. "You're the paladin,

David, the chosen guardian and champion of Fallhollow. Einar's bane. And he wants you dead."

A breeze sliced through the terrace carrying with it an ominous chill; its edge cut through to David's bones.

"There must be some mistake." He thought of the role-playing games he played online with Charlotte. He glanced at Trog. "Paladins are big and bulky. Strong, like him. I'm nothing like him, and I'm not hero material."

"You are more remarkable than you realize," Slavandria said. "Lily has told me of your accomplishments on the archery range, as well as your speed and agility training. I also understand you to have a keen understanding of military prowess and weaponry. Where do you think these abilities come from?"

David shrugged. "I don't know. My dad, I guess."

He lowered his gaze to his father's ring. *My dad*. The word stung his core. He thought back to Lily, the letter, the tattoo, which continued to prickle, as if asleep. The discovery of the truth seemed so long ago, like a dream from another lifetime, but he had it only been a day? Two? Three? He couldn't remember. All he knew was Lily had provided few answers. He needed them all. David looked into Slavandria's penetrating eyes, words forming on his tongue. She spoke before he could utter one of them.

"Yes, your father is well-versed in tactical matters. His prowess and tenacity are legendary. You mother is agile, sharp-minded, and to answer your next question, yes, they are both alive, though where they are, I do not know. I haven't heard from or spoken to them in some time."

David gulped. The words seemed surreal. He stilled the tremble in his voice. "Why did they leave me?"

"To protect you. Your mother hoped if you were tucked away, hidden, no one would ever find you and you could live a life of luxury and peace. You would grow up without a care, fall in love and have a wonderful family. Do something altruistic. My sister, Auruvalla — Lily as you call her — agreed to care for you. Protect you. She and I worked together your entire life to make sure you never wanted for anything. We both did what we could to keep this from happening, but we can't keep you from your destiny." Slavandria reached for David's hands, worry deep in her eyes. "The Dragon King must never find you, David. If he does, he will kill you."

"Why? What did I do to him?"

"It's not what you've done, David. It's what you can do. You're the paladin."

"So you've said, but I have no idea what that means."

"You're a guardian, David. You are also an executioner."

David choked on his spit. "Executioner? You're joking, right? Do you not know anything about me? I can't kill anything. Period."

Slavandria stood. "I'm afraid you're going to have to, David. It's in your blood."

"No it isn't. You can't force me to kill something I don't want to kill, especially a dragon the size of a freaking house. Now work your magic fingers, open a portal and send Charlotte and me home."

"I can't do that."

"Why not?" David hardened his jaw, ground his teeth.

"Because you're in danger if you go home."

"I'm in danger if I stay here."

"True, but you have more protection here. Lily is only a force of one, David. She cannot provide the protection you have here, especially since she and I believe someone working with Einar discovered your presence in Havendale. We believe the same individual is responsible for the attacks in Fallhollow, but we have no proof.

"I'll take my chances."

"Even if your parents are at risk?"

The question grabbed his gut and twisted his heart. "What are you talking about?"

"Your parents left you in Havendale to protect you. Now that you are here, what are you going to do to protect them? What are you going to do to protect Charlotte?"

David chuckled and shook his head. "Oh, no. I see what you're doing. You're trying to put some kind of guilt trip on me. Well, it's not going to work."

"David, listen to me. Even if I had the power to send you back, I wouldn't be able to until you do what is expected of you."

"Which involves killing a dragon."

"No. Your role is to guard and protect the realm, and there are only two beings with the power to kill the dragon."

"And who would they be?"

"The youngest heir to the throne of Hirth, or a direct descendent of Einar's, of which there is only one."

"Wait. You want me to find and make friends with a killer dragon's offspring?" David shook his head. "Are you insane?"

"David, it is imperative you find Einar's descendant and make him your ally. With him on your side, you can rid the path of enemy forces, including the man in your dreams, and provide your ally the perfect opportunity to kill Einar."

"And what's going to stop this dragon offspring from killing me?"

"He won't."

"How do you know?"

"Let's just say it's a hunch I have."

David laughed. "A hunch? You want me to risk my life and Charlotte's on a hunch?" He flicked a quick glance at the girl he loved. "Pfft. You *are* crazy."

"David, you need to do this."

David scowled. "I don't need to do anything."

"Yes, you do, if you have any hope of returning home."

"Are you kidding me?" David's temper gathered. "And can I ask how you expect me to do this? With my good looks? Oh, wait. I forgot. I have a box of lightning bolts in my pocket and flamethrowers embedded in my palms."

"This is no time for sarcasm, David," Slavandria said.

"The hell it's not! You're telling me I have to fight a war that isn't mine, kill enemies like they're nothing more than characters in a video game, and take Charlotte with me so she can watch! How am I supposed to react?"

A very large shadow fell over David. "Young man." Trog glared down at him, his brow drawn low. "Stop your barking and apologize for your temper."

David angled his body away. "What? No! She—"

"You will stop your yelling and apologize for your temper."

"No, I —"

The knight gripped David's shoulder and squeezed. Pain spiraled through his flesh down to the muscle. The terrace surroundings blurred. He hunched over. "Ow! Ow! Ow!"

"Apologize."

"Agghh!" Sharper, tighter pain flooded his senses. White lights danced in his vision, obscuring most of it. "Okay, okay! I'm sorry! Let go. Please."

"Do not apologize to me." Trog exerted additional pressure on David's shoulder, twisting him around until he faced Slavandria. "Apologize to her."

191

"I'm sorry," he said through waterlogged eyes. I didn't mean to yell."

Trog backed away.

David rubbed his shoulder and sat down. Charlotte reached for him, but he waved her away. "Don't."

She recoiled.

He gritted his teeth. How dare they manipulate him! He glanced at Slavandria as she sat opposite him. Twice in one day he'd been attacked, bruised, beaten, and he was certain it would happen again if he didn't do as she asked. He let out a defeated sigh and rubbed his shoulder. "What do you want me to do?"

"David, no!" Charlotte said. "You can't give in!"

"Do you have a better idea?" David cocked his head in Charlotte's direction. "I don't see you getting the crap beat out of you or being told you have to sacrifice your life for a battle that's not even yours!"

Charlotte rose to her feet, her hands clenched at her sides. "Don't you dare yell at me, David! I'm the only one who has been by your side since this whole mess started, so don't start throwing your poor pitiful David attitude at me. I'll whack you so hard it'll make what Sir Gorilla did to you feel like a smack on the hand with a wet noodle."

Trog chuckled.

David glowered at the knight, a snide comment burning in his throat. The dull throb in his shoulder made him extinguish it. He didn't need another lesson on when not to voice an opinion. He propped his elbows on the table and buried his face in his palms. His anger slipped away, but guilt wiggled into its place. He'd just yelled at his best friend, the girl he loved. The girl he'd go to the end of the universe to shelter and defend. What had this world done to him?

He turned and reached for Charlotte, his eyes pleading with hers. "I'm sorry. I shouldn't have snapped at you."

She took his hand and sat down beside him. "It's all right. I shouldn't have gotten mad at you, either." Her gaze darted between Slavandria and Trog before settling back on him. "I suppose this is the only chance we have to get home, huh?" She squeezed his hand.

David nodded. "Yeah, I think it is." He turned to Slavandria. "What do I have to do?"

The drawn lines in Slavandria's face softened. "Outside of finding Einar's offspring, you must locate a talisman lost during the first Dragon War. Once found, you must deliver it to Sir Farnsworth at Gyllen Castle where it will remain in the royal vaults until I can retrieve it."

David sighed. "And what does this talisman look like?"

"It's a circular piece, as large as your palm. Gold filigree threads swirl along the outer edges, forming a wreath. In the center is a vibrant red stone, a dragon eye. A sliver of gold forms the slit pupil. We call it the Eye of Kedge, and its last known location was the Domengart Mountains." Slavandria steepled her fingers and pressed them to her lips. "It is very important this item is found, David. Without it, Fallhollow stands little chance against the Dragon King. Without it, you can never go home."

"Why me? Why can't one of your magic friends find it?"

"It needs your essence to work. It is difficult to explain. It's something you have to experience to understand."

"Well, now, isn't that just peachy," David said, exasperation swelling. "And how exactly am I supposed to find a relic in a mountain range? That's like trying to find a grain of sugar in snow."

Slavandria paced and nodded. "There is one who may be able

to help you. He is the caretaker and overseer of the Doomideen Pass. He is the last known guardian of the Eye, but you must tread carefully for he doesn't take kindly to visitors."

"Am I supposed to kill him, too?" David folded his arms on the table and plopped his head down on top of them.

"No. Him you must not kill."

Charlotte rubbed David's back. "This is insanity. How can you do this to him? He has no weapons. He's not a fighter. You're going to send him into a battle with nothing to protect himself."

"Who said he will be unprotected?"

David lifted his head. "You're giving me weapons?"

A triumphant smile creased Slavandria's face. "No. I have something better. Come here. I have something for you."

Slavandria balled her fingers into a fist, blew on it, and then opened her hand. Piled inside was a ribbon of dark blue fabric. She unfurled it, shaking it out to its full-length. Gold threads shimmered along the outer edges of the wide band of silk. Golden tassels hung at each end.

David laughed. "You're giving me a scarf?"

"It's a sash," Slavandria said, tying it to David's waist. "It is made of asthirium, a plant found in my homeland of Felindil. Soft as silk, yet stronger than dragon hide. I have woven many counter-spells within the fibers to keep you from dying should Einar attack. This is not to say he cannot injure you, but as long as you wear this sash, you will not die, allowing you time to seek the help you need."

The thought of dying crippled his entire being. He'd never thought about it until now. Not really. He always thought he was too young to die. Death was something that happened to other people. Old people. Diseased people. Dragonslayers. Paladins. He adjusted the fabric on his hips. No matter what, he was never taking the thing off. Ever.

"Thank you," he said.

And for a moment, he felt invincible.

Slavandria smiled. "You're welcome. Now if you don't mind, I need you both to join me, please."

David and Charlotte exchanged a baffled look as they followed her across the open terrace.

"Charlotte, let me start with you. May I have your hands, please?"

Charlotte glanced at David, a questioning glint in her eyes. Despite his apprehension, he nodded, since there was nothing either one of them could do to stop the older woman.

Charlotte wiped the sweat from her palms and placed her hands in Slavandria's. Threads of blue light danced over their joined fingers. Charlotte giggled as the lustrous glow clouded their bodies. Electricity arced within the veil. Slavandria tilted her head back, her eyes closed, and chanted some foreign words that sounded like pig Latin. Seconds passed, and then the cloud dissipated.

Charlotte laughed. "Oh my gosh, what was that?" She shook her hands as if air-drying them. "That tickled."

Slavandria smiled, her eyes gentle and kind. Tender. "I bestowed a very powerful and important magical gift upon you — the gift of healing. From this point forward, you will know the properties of every root, every weed, every plant, and every animal in Fallhollow, and which ones will benefit you in the treatment of ailments and illnesses. In essence, you will be the healer, and responsible for the health and well-being of your companions while on your journey."

"Seriously?" Charlotte's eyes widened. "I can't look at a drop of blood without passing out."

Slavandria smiled. "That was then. Now you have the skills to patch the most despicable of wounds with nary a second thought." She tucked a stray hair behind Charlotte's ear and pressed her palm to Charlotte's cheek. She seemed to search Charlotte's face as if committing the lines of her face to memory. "Let's hope the wounds you see are small and few." Slavandria squeezed Charlotte's hand and turned her attention to David.

His heart jumped in his throat as her gaze fell on him. Mesmerizing amber and lavender flecks swirled in her pupils. No matter how hard he tried, he couldn't look away. A shiver raced through him as she took his hands in hers.

At her touch, the mark above his heart grew warm. Like an ember fed by a wind-blown fire, it grew hotter by the second, but it didn't burn like before. The air around him shimmered and distorted. Tingles spread through his arms and legs.

"What's happening to me?"

"The mark upon your chest is receiving the magic I'm spinning around you, preparing you for the magic I am about to awaken within you."

David's mouth fell open. "Huh?"

A cold sensation gathered at his feet and swirled upward until it exited his skull, leaving him with a dull brain freeze. The distortion faded. He marveled at his sense of clarity. Every smell, every object he saw was sharper than before, magnified many times over. He rubbed his chest, the sensations overwhelming.

"Your discomfort will go away with time," Slavandria said. "Are you ready to learn your first spell?"

"Spell?"

"If you are to have any chance of succeeding in your quest, you must learn to ferry, and not the sort you experienced with Twiller. This will require concentration and practice as the portals you use are ones you create with your mind."

David looked at Slavandria. Really looked at her. Like she'd lost her stinking mind.

"Repeating the words *Accelero Silentium* to yourself will ferry you from one place to another by merely thinking of where you want to be."

Okay. Now we're talking. David glanced over his shoulder at Charlotte and grinned.

Slavandria turned his face back to look at hers. "This is not a game, David. As with all magic, there are limitations to its use, and if done incorrectly, it can kill you."

There was that word again. Kill. He was beginning to develop a severe dislike for the four letter word.

"You may only ferry within Fallhollow," Slavandria continued, "and you may only travel to a place you can physically see, or to a place you've been before."

David rolled his eyes. "Figures."

"Shall we try it?" Slavandria asked.

David gulped. "What? Now?"

Slavandria gestured to the furthest point on the terrace. "Charlotte, would you please stand by the terrace wall?"

Charlotte glanced nervously at David as she passed and took up her position.

Slavandria paced before David, her fingers steepled against her lips. "David, I want you to focus on Charlotte. Imagine she's in trouble. You need to go to her right away, but you cannot use your feet, only your mind to get there. Repeat the following words to yourself, *Accelero Silentium*. Picture yourself rushing to her side. Go to her."

David laughed. "You're joking, right? I can't do magic."

"Yes, you can. All you need to do is believe."

"But there's nothing wrong with her. She's fine."

"I'm asking you to imagine she's in danger."

Charlotte hopped up on the wall and leaned back slightly, her hands in the air. A wide smile brightened her face. "Look, David, I'm going to fall."

David's stomach churned. "Come on, Char. That's not funny. Get down." He turned to Slavandria. "Look. I know you have this crazy amount of faith in me, but I'm not what you think I am. I can't just—"

Trog slapped his hand on the table. "We don't have time for this." He stormed across the terrace toward Charlotte. Her eyes widened as he grabbed her by the back of her leather shirt and lifted her in the air.

David stared, wide-eyed, her cry for help stabbing his heart. "What are you doing? Let her go!" His feet kicked out with the urge to run, but Slavandria held him with the touch of one finger.

"Concentrate and use the words."

Charlotte kicked and flailed. "Put me down!"

Trog held tight, his eyes on David, his brows arched in a taunt.

David swept Slavandria's hand from his shoulder and darted forward. "I said let her go!"

His contact with an invisible wall propelled him back several feet. He landed on his back with a thud.

Slavandria knelt beside him.

"Get away from me!" He scampered back.

"David, this could all be over if you would just use your words."

"I can't!"

"You must. *Accelero Silentium*. Say it."

David's heart rat-a-tatted away in his chest like never-ending machine gun fire. Sweat beaded his brow. How could he use words to conjure magic he didn't believe in? He wiped his palms on his leather pants.

"This is getting old," Trog said, studying his fingernails. He swung his arm to his left. Charlotte dangled over the edge of the terrace like a wrecking ball from a crane.

Terror struck, David dashed into and propelled off the invisible wall again. He pounded his fist on the ghostly barrier. "Please. I beg you. Let her go. I'll do whatever you want, just put her down."

"Ten," Trog said.

The blood in David's veins froze. *No. He wouldn't drop her, would he?* "Stop that. It's not funny."

"Nine."

Charlotte whimpered.

David jammed his fingers in his hair and spun around. This couldn't be happening. *Why? Why me?*

"Eight."

Charlotte screeched. "David, do something!"

"Seven," Trog said.

"Stop it! Just stop it!" David spun around, his eyes wild. He pressed his palms to the sides of his head, and shouted, "*Accelero Silentium!*"

Nothing happened. He fell to his knees.

"David, calm yourself," Slavandria cooed. "You must settle your mind."

"But those are the right words!"

"Six."

"Stop it!"

"You must settle your mind!" Slavandria said again.

"You settle your mind!" David locked eyes on Trog.

The knight opened his grip on Charlotte. She screamed as he let her fall a few inches before catching her again. Tears streamed down her face, her pleas painful to hear.

"Damn you!" David yelled, standing. "You're supposed to be a knight. Where is your sense of mercy, your honor?"

"Five." Trog swung Charlotte around, grabbed her with his other hand, and hung her over the steepest edge of the terrace. "I am growing tired of this. How long do you think it will take for her to hit the rocks below?"

Loathing settled in David's gut. His lips twitched before settling back against his teeth.

"Four."

Charlotte cried out. "David, please. Say the stinking words."

Trog cocked an eyebrow. "Three."

"I will never forgive either of you for this!" David closed his eyes and breathed through the emotions welling within him. *Accelero Silentium.*

"Two."

Warmth oozed over him as he repeated the words in his mind, each time, stronger and more focused. Energy swarmed like bees around him, the buzzing loud in his ears. It grew louder, tighter. Suffocating.

"One."

Save her. Get Charlotte.

The buzzing soared deep into his ears, shooting into his veins. His limbs stung and grew numb.

Slavandria's voice crept into his brain. *Drop her, Trog. Maybe I was wrong. Maybe he's not the one.*

David cried out in his mind, *Accelero Silentium* one last time. He shot across the terrace and hurled into an unforgiving object before crumpling to the ground. Nausea churned in his gut and burned upward into his throat. He got to his hands and knees and threw up. Twice.

Charlotte shrieked behind him. "I hate you! I hate you both!"

Trog chuckled as she stormed off.

David glowered at the knight. "Don't you ever touch her again!"

Trog sucked air through his teeth. "Or you'll do what, pup?"

David managed to find his feet and shuffled toward Charlotte leaning against the merman statue.

"Don't talk to me." Her hands were visibly shaking. Her voice trembled.

"I'm sorry, Char."

"Sorry doesn't cut it, David! All you had to do was say two stinking words, and you couldn't do that even while I dangled like bait over a shark tank."

"But I did do it." Realization bloomed in his mind. He held Charlotte's hands, his breath coming faster. "I did it. I rocketed to you like a freaking bullet! I was there, and then I was here."

"Yee haw." Charlotte folded her arms across her chest. "Excuse me if I don't celebrate in your newfound talent."

"Oh, come on, Char. Don't you see what this means? I did magic."

"And you're about to do some more," Slavandria said, joining them.

David shook his head. "No. No more. I'm not doing that again. I'm sore, and I still feel sick."

Trog's shadow engulfed David. "Your enemies won't care if you are sick or hurt. In fact, they'll count on it."

Slavandria nodded. "Trog's right. That's why you have to learn all you can to avoid any entanglements with them. The next spell will leave you feeling a bit dizzy at first, but like the spell before it, the more you practice, the less it will affect you."

"I doubt it," David said.

"The following spell works well in conjunction with *Accelero Silentium*. It blends you into your surroundings, rendering you more or less invisible. I don't think I need to explain to you the importance of being able to mask yourself to your enemies and having the speed to move away from them undetected."

"You know, if you just sent us home, we could avoid having to do this all together."

Slavandria ignored his comment. "I want you to stand here and this time, picture yourself as part of this fountain and repeat the following words in your head, *Ibidem Evanescere.*"

David closed his eyes and envisioned himself as stone. *Ibidem Evanescere.*

Nothing. Four more times, the words tumbled around in his brain, and still nothing happened. He shook his head and said, "I'm not feeling it."

"You must believe you can do it. Erase all doubt. It will destroy you. Try it again."

"Come on," Charlotte said, putting a great deal of space between her and Trog. "You can do it."

Charlotte's confidence in him drove back his doubt. He closed his eyes and pictured himself as the merman. Powerful, indestructible, with a triton in his hand.

He waited for the magical buzzing to attack him. Instead, it started in his veins and retreated, flying out of his body.

Charlotte gasped. "David! Where did you go?"

David opened his eyes and looked down. He looked no different. "What are you talking about? I'm right here."

"Where?" Charlotte asked, walking toward him, her eyes narrowed, searching. He shuffled quietly out of the way as she did her mime impersonation. "Okay, you're freaking me out. You were just here. I heard you."

David's spirit jolted, and he smiled. "Wait. You really can't see me?"

Charlotte spun around, searching for him with her hands. "No, I can't see you. Where are you?"

Daring to risk feeling sick once more, he closed his eyes and thought *Accelero Silentium.*

The buzzing returned, swarmed, but it felt different this time. The spell collided with the magic within, both springing off of each other like polar equals of a magnet. He shot across the terrace and beyond with unimaginable speed, and clung to a limb high in a nearby tree. Triumph muffled nausea. He hooted with delight.

Charlotte jumped and spun around. "David Heiland, this is not funny. Show yourself!"

David ferried back to the terrace, only feet away from Charlotte. "I can't. I don't know how."

Slavandria stepped toward him, a large smile on her face. "I believe the word you are looking for is *Andor.*"

David repeated the word. A cool chill, as if doused in a peppermint patty, spread over him. A thin film disintegrated from him and vanished in a poof at his feet. "Whoa. Awesome!"

Slavandria called for Twiller who trudged toward her dragging three rucksacks. He laid one at David's, Trog's, and Charlotte's feet.

"What are these?" David asked, picking his up.

"Items you will need for your journey, including some additional sundries you're accustomed to. You can go through it later. Right now, I have one last gift for you."

Slavandria conjured a longbow, the sleekest, most beautiful

weapon David had ever seen. It was almost as long as he was tall, red in color, and feather-light in his hand. She handed him a leather quiver with six arrows and strapped on him an armguard with leather lacing.

David shook his head. "Wow. I don't know what to say."

"Thank you would be sufficient. Oh, and as a special treat, each arrow you release will replenish by one. I gave you a few extra just in case."

"Limitless supply, huh? I like it."

"You will also need these." Slavandria rolled her wrist. Three full-length cloaks appeared, draped over her arm. She gave one each to Trog, David, and Charlotte.

"I take it we're going somewhere?" David said.

"Yes. It is time for the three of you to go. I have done all I can do for now. The rest is up to you."

Trog tightened his belt and adjusted the sword and dagger at his sides. "I take it you have alerted General Balendar and the shime we are entering the Southern Forest. Our journey will be much smoother if they know you have sent us their way."

"I'm afraid you will not be going through the Southern Forest, Trog. You are to travel by way of the I'ildril Road and make your way to Gable. From there, you shall travel the Domengart Mountains northward to the fields of Valnor and onward to Hirth."

Trog's brow furrowed. "I don't understand, Your Grace. That path takes us out of our way. I must return to Gyllen immediately. Their Majesties are counting on me to find them."

"Trog, I understand your desire to fulfill your duties as a faithful knight and general, but war has been declared. Your military expertise is now required of you in a different, but equally important, manner. You will accompany David and

Charlotte to Gyllen via the I'ildril Road. From there you will travel the Doomideen Pass, then to the field of Valnor, and then on to Gyllen."

"You're mad!" Trog said. "The Northern Forest will be teeming with shadowmorths and trolls. I don't care what sort of spells you've given these two; this tadpole will die before he gets within pissing distance of Gyllen."

"I'm not a tadpole," David said, "and what are shadowmorths?"

Slavandria raised an eyebrow. "Are you admitting you do not have the wherewithal to oversee two children, Trog?"

David turned to Charlotte. "They're ignoring me."

Trog's glare shot darts through him. David gulped and lowered his gaze.

Trog turned back to Slavandria. "I'm saying you should let me do my job, and perhaps *you* should escort these two to Gyllen. You can do it much more efficiently than I, and in far less time."

"I am not concerned with efficiency or speed of reaching Gyllen. I am concerned with learning firsthand what is happening on the ground. Who is teaming with Einar, and who is willing to fight for Gyllen. Only you can do this. There is no reason you cannot search for King Gildore and Queen Mysterie while assisting David in his quest, can you not?"

He growled, waved his arm in disgust, and turned away.

David glanced at the ground and shuffled his feet. How humiliating it must be for the highest-ranking knight and commander of an army to be ordered around by a sorceress.

Slavandria moved to stand before Trog, her eyes soft and gentle. "I know this is not what you expected, but I need you. It has to be this way. How else will David find what he must seek?" She touched his face, her eyes soft and pleading. "May I count on you to do what is required?"

"I cannot protect them as well as you think I can," he said.

"You won't need to. Charlotte can heal. David can ferry you out of any precarious situation you might find yourself in. They will, however, need your eyes, your expertise, your wisdom, and your guidance."

David affixed the quiver against his back.

Charlotte whispered in his ear. "She's got a lot of confidence in you and those magic spells."

David's stomach fluttered. "Yeah. I wish I did."

Trog brought Slavandria's hands to his lips and kissed them. "I will do as you request, Your Grace."

She smiled and withdrew an amber pendant dangling from a gold chain around her neck. She slipped it over his head. "In case you need to summon me. You know how it works."

Slavandria squeezed his hands and stepped back. "David and Charlotte, stay with Trog at all times. Listen to him. He knows what's out there. David, practice your spells until you can do them with ease and little discomfort." She turned toward the verge near the stone table and called out, "Agimesh. Tacarr."

Two humanoid gargoyles stepped forward. They were the same shime that had accompanied the centaur. Charlotte squeezed David's hand.

"These two will accompany you as far as the Doomideen Pass. From there, you are at the mercy of the Sankara Mountains and the Northern Forest. Go, and may the heavens be with you and guide you."

Trog guided David and Charlotte down the terrace steps and turned north to circle the manor, the two winged creatures marching behind.

"Is where we're going as dangerous as you said?" Charlotte asked as they left the green hills and meadow and stepped foot on the main road.

"More than you know," Trog answered.

"Are we going to make it?" Her voice trembled.

Trog pushed his way through them and picked up the pace. "Yes, provided we reach Gable before dark."

Chapter 17

Eric spent all day in the courtyard overseeing the clearing of debris, his mind reeling with a hundred different ways to find and team up with the paladin. Of course, each scenario devolved into one of the knights finding out and confining him to his room, or worse yet, the dungeons, so as to learn a good lesson. Sometimes he wished he could clap his hands and make them all disappear. It certainly would make his life a lot easier.

As he sat cross-legged on his bed, he pondered the box of Sestian's personal belongings before him. A young page had dropped it off just after sunrise, along with his tearful condolences. Eric had accepted both and set the box on the chest at the foot of his bed with no real intentions of digging into memories he'd rather not visit at the moment. Sestian's death was still too raw. Painful. But there was something about the box, something that called to him, like a warm vanilla cake swimming in drizzled rum.

He eyed the worn sole of a boot poking through the effects

and touched a slice in the scuffed leather, remembering with clarity the knife once lodged there.

It had started innocently enough— a jaunt through the castle in the dark on one of Sestian's many sleepless nights—when they came upon a fellow squire determined to have his way with an unwilling servant girl. A fight ensued, the girl's virginity rescued, and Sestian ended up with a knife in his foot from an ill-judged kick. It was one of the few times Farnsworth didn't punish Sestian for his roaming, believing Sestian had learned his lesson. But a knife wound to the foot was nothing to Sestian. He continued to break the rules, keeping life interesting at Gyllen.

Eric lifted a pair of suede shoes and the leather boots from the box and set them on the floor. Next, he withdrew a handful of lace handkerchiefs, no doubt mementos from pleasant moments of seduction steeped in heartbreaking promises. There were several knives, money, rocks, fencing gantlets, a few belts, coin bags, a leather flask, and a pendant the size of his palm made of spun gold with a ruby dragon eye in the center.

"Well, this is interesting, Ses." He placed it around his neck and tucked it beneath his tunic.

The last item, a suede-covered book, piqued Eric's curiosity. He flipped through the pages, uncertain why Sestian had it in his possession. His friend had detested books, saying they were distractions from the freakishness reality of life.

Tucked between the pages near the center of the book, Eric found a small sheet of parchment folded in half. His breath hitched at the handwritten note on the outside.

Eric—third one found. Must confront Trog!

"What in dragon's breath is this?"

The paper crinkled as he unfolded the page. He scanned the scribbled text.

Sir Trogsdill,

Einar is in possession of your most recent letter. He would like to remind you of your agreement and the consequences should you not follow through. The fact that all of Hirth will attend the festivities to welcome home the king and queen makes no difference to him. He has no need for their admiration, only subservience, and you will see to it he gets it. Present Their Majesties to the Dragon King in the manner upon which agreed. Otherwise, consider your accord vacated.

Senior Advisor to Einar, King of Berg

"King of Berg my ... " Eric turned the book upside down and shook it.

Two more similarly-sized parchments floated to the bed. On the outside were more notes written by Sestian, and they were marked as numbers one and two.

More? He clenched his hands to keep them from trembling.

Eric read the words. His jaw was tight. His temper continued escalating by the second.

He stared at a loose thread on his bedspread. What if more lies like this existed? Trog would be screwed. But of course, that was what Master Camden and Seyekrad wanted. They had done this. Damn them. They'd planted the letters so there would be inquiries. What a convenient, devious plan. They knew Trog would be arrested, charged with sedition. Treason. They would find him guilty, and he would be hung as a conspirator against the crown. Eric could feel his blood boiling. Yes. They'd had it all planned. The kingdom would be shocked, unwilling to believe, but unable to ignore, the written evidence. And the king? Why, with Trog out of the way, King Gildore would be devastated. His friend and confidant would be dead. Wrongly accused. The mages would deem the king unfit to rule in his grief and remove him from power, then take over until they appointed a new ruler.

Einar.

Anger exploded from his throat. The papers scattered in the air and floated to the floor. He stood and paced, huffing.

Damn those conniving, predatory bastards! How dare they!

Raging heat distributed throughout his body, his mind was in a whir. He had to stop it. He had to fix it, but how? Should he show the letters to Farnsworth and the others? Should he destroy them? The wrong choice could send Trog to the gallows.

He snatched up the pages and read them again and again. After some time, Eric ambled to the fireplace. Filled with an eerie calm, he cast the parchments, along with their handwritten lies, into the flames. They curled, sputtered and turned to ash, evidence gone.

Next he shuffled down the narrow passageway connecting his suite to Trog's. It was highly unlikely anyone would be able to plant evidence in Trog's room, but Eric couldn't take the chance.

Over the next hour, Eric scoured the rooms, careful to return items exactly as he'd found them. Every page of every book was turned, every mattress, every cushion searched. Twinges of guilt flared in his belly. He could almost feel Trog's eyes on him as he snuck around like a common thief, searching through drawers and clothes, looking for signs of a conspiracy.

Finding nothing, Eric sat for a moment on the edge of the bed and let out a heavy sigh. His thoughts rambled to his encounters in the cloisters and Avaleen, then to Sestian.

"Drat you, Ses. Where did you find those letters, and why didn't you tell me about them?"

Eric stood and picked up Trog's chemise that had slipped from the bed to the floor. A glint of gold beneath a chest under a window caught his eye. He got on all fours and pulled a small, wooden box from its hiding place.

He'd never seen such a beautifully carved box, the lid intricately crafted with a forest scene of a maiden, her hand on the neck of a large deer. Eric pulled out a chair and set the box in his lap. With great care, he opened it and withdrew a plain silver necklace, delicate in size. A tear-shaped filigreed pendant with a single sapphire dangled from the end. Next came a pressed pink rose and a sprig of dried wisteria. On the bottom lay a folded note, slightly yellowed and creased many times over.

Carefully, Eric withdrew the page, his hands trembling ever so slightly. He rubbed his hand over his mouth, his mind debating with his conscience about whether he should read it. He muttered a plea of forgiveness as he opened it and read:

My love,

How I miss your smile, your touch, your voice. Why must you be so far away? I lie awake at night and ponder how you are, wishing somehow I could release this burden from your shoulders. How lovely it would be to run away, to never look back, to be wild and free. Damn the restrictions of our stations in life. Why must we always do what is expected of us? When will we ever be free of the demands placed upon us? Please say you will dream of such freedom, with me at your side. My dearest, I shall never forget our moment in the garden. It is etched on my soul for all eternity. I shall never love another as I love you. Please write. If I cannot hold you, at least I can caress your words and sleep with them, pressed to my heart every night. Until such time we are together again, I shall always and forever be,

Your Gwyndolyn

Eric read the letter several times, each time choking back the emotion clumping in his throat. Trog had been in love, and someone had loved him, and yet he never uttered a word about it. How typical of the man to not speak of such a personal loss, as if he was immune to such things. It was one more secret in a puzzle of many. Eric folded the note and placed it in the box with all the other treasures and returned it to its hiding place. He thought upon Trog's solitary ventures to the fountain at night, the way he always set a rose in the water. Suddenly he understood. Trog, for all his harshness, was, as Farnsworth said, just a man, and he'd suffered a broken heart.

Satisfied the rooms were as he found them, Eric returned to his suite, packed Sestian's things away, and went for a walk. Later that night, when the moon was high, he sat on the edge of the fountain and set three red rose buds he'd gathered from the queen's garden adrift, one for each night Trog had been away.

In memory.

In hope.

Chapter 18

David and the others reached the I'ildril Road as the sun began its descent into the west. Through the thinning trees ahead, David glimpsed sunlight shimmering off the surface of the Gop River. A wooden arrow sign bore the names of three towns. To the east, over an arched stone bridge, lay Bybrook and Stonewater. To the west, down a narrow forest road, lay their destination, Gable. Trog shifted the bag on his shoulder and glanced behind him as if making sure all his ducklings were in tow, and bore left.

"Trog, can we rest for a bit?" Charlotte tossed her rucksack to the ground and sat on a boulder. "We've been traveling for hours. My feet hurt. I'm hungry."

A subtle vibration in the ground turned Trog around. Two riders, clad in studded leather armor as black as the horses they rode, thundered toward them.

The riders slowed and set their horses prancing in a circle

around Trog. Eyes peered out from beneath wolf-faced helmets. One of the horsemen pulled his sword and dropped from his saddle. He removed the metal helmet from his head. "Good day," he said, his smile devoid of any hint of warmth. "Where might you be headed this late in the eve?"

Trog's voice remained calm. "We're on our way home to Gable."

"Is that right?" He grinned. "I take it you've traveled this road before?"

"Many times." Trog's eyes narrowed. "Is there something I can do for you, sir?"

The man chuckled. "Now that is a question, isn't it?" He scooped Charlotte's bag from the ground.

Charlotte went to protest. David grabbed her arm.

"There is nothing of any value in there, good man," Trog said. "We're traveling empty but for a few coins, if it's money you seek."

The man plucked a cotton petticoat from the rucksack and held it up by the tip of his sword. "Well, what have we got here?"

"Put my things down!" Charlotte shouted.

David squeezed her arm. "Shh! Are you trying to get us killed?"

The man's mouth twisted in a malevolent smile as he stepped toward her. "Ah, what a pretty lass."

The shime snapped together, their crossbows drawn, their arrows nocked before David blinked. He nudged Charlotte further back toward the bank of the river and assessed their surroundings. He found a spot on the opposite bank of the river he could ferry if need be, but he didn't want to use his magic if he didn't have to. Even though he'd spent the last few hours honing his skills, much to Charlotte's and Trog's annoyance, they were far from perfect. He also had no idea how Charlotte would react to being shot a thousand feet in a split second. Still, the leer on the man's face ignited anger within him he never felt before, anger so intense it could light a bonfire without a match. He balled his right hand into a fist and imagined it planted in the man's face.

"I suggest you drop the bag and move along," Trog said. There was a smooth, sharp edge to his voice. He stood tall and straight, his shoulders squared.

Both men laughed. The one on horseback armed a crossbow and aimed the bolt at Trog. "You do not scare us, gypsy. Hand over your gold or we take your lives and the girl as a prize."

Charlotte's mouth fell open, her eyes filled with horror. David closed his hand on her wrist. "I won't let them hurt you. Do you understand?"

She nodded and gulped.

Trog looked around. "I am not inclined to fight with either of you." He withdrew a small leather pouch from inside his coat and tossed it to the ground. The coins clinked inside. "It's all we have, so how about you get back on your horse and ride away?"

"From where I sit, you are in no position to haggle for your freedom." The horseman pranced his horse around Trog once more. "I shall give you to the count of three to discard your weapons and the remainder of your money."

"Good man, I beg no trouble from you," Trog said. "I have nothing more to give you. Let us go, take the money, and I promise not to speak a word of this to anyone."

The man on the ground stooped and gathered the leather coin pouch. He tossed it a few times in the air. "Why, there's hardly anything in here. Where were you planning on staying in the river town with nary enough to you buy a pint?"

"We live there," Trog said. "We are returning from a trip to Bybrook."

"I don't believe you," the mounted horseman said, "and you know what I do with those I don't believe?"

Trog's sword hissed as it left its scabbard. The sound snaked up David's spine.

The man on the ground flicked Charlotte's garment into the air and charged forward.

Two crossbows fired. Two arrows whizzed through the air, both lodging in the man's chest. The impact pitched the man backward before he crumpled to the ground on his back.

Charlotte wailed.

David clutched her to his chest, his thoughts, his body, numb. Frozen.

Death.

Destruction.

Blood.

The horseman raised his crossbow and fired.

Trog barked as the bolt lodged in his leg. He came around, slicing his blade through the rider's leg.

Agimesh nocked another arrow.

Whoosh!

The horseman flailed back, an arrow to his heart. He teetered for a moment before he fell to the ground, his body still.

Trog bent over, his palms on his knees. Sweat dripped from his forehead. He grabbed the bolt in his leg, pinched his eyes shut, and wrenched it from muscle and flesh. There was a brief moan followed by a few curse words. He hung there for a moment before limping forward and collecting both horses.

"Agimesh. Tacarr, do something with this trash while I unload their belongings. David, gather both bags, and you and

Charlotte come here." He gimped back to his sword and wiped as much blood as he could from the blade with his shirt before sheathing it.

Agimesh holstered his bow and withdrew Charlotte from David's arms. He led her to the fringe of the road, shielding her eyes from the carnage. Tacarr secured both the coin pouch and Charlotte's bag and held them out for David to take. He tried not to look at the man sprawled on the ground as he collected his things, but the man's empty eyes made him ill.

Tacarr carried the dead man to the edge of the river and tossed him in. A life, only vibrant moments before, was gone. He glanced at Trog and the two creatures, hoping to find some remorse, sadness in their eyes, but there was nothing. How can one kill and feel nothing? How were Trog, Agimesh, and Tacarr any different from the nameless men who had tried to rob them? The thought perplexed him and rooted him to his spot.

A splash sounded behind him. Another dead body discarded, left to rot in the murky waters.

David's insides jumped as Agimesh placed his hand on David's back. Warmth, serenity engulfed him, soothing the tattered edges of his mind. "Come," Agimesh said. "It is time to leave."

David met up with Charlotte as Trog hobbled from across the road in a new set of clothes, a tourniquet wrapped around his leg.

"That looks pretty bad," David said. "Maybe you should help him."

Charlotte snatched her things from David's hands and shot him a look that could curl a lead pipe. "I don't think so."

"But you're a healer now, Char. You need to practice."

"No, I don't."

"But he saved our butts. It's the least—"

"Shut up, David." Her eyes were a conflagration of anger,

and sadness, so much so, it was difficult to tell which burned brighter. "It's not happening," she finished.

Trog shoved his soiled clothes in his rucksack and tied it to the saddle of one of the horses.

"David, you will ride with me. Charlotte will ride with Tacarr. Agimesh, if you don't mind, scout ahead. Make sure there are no surprises waiting for us."

David nodded, his voice taken from his throat. Death had a funny way of doing that, transfiguring spirited creatures into muted, tongueless souls.

They ventured onto the road bathed in twilight. A light evening breeze skipped through the leaves. Nightbirds echoed from some distance away. The horses snorted as they made their way toward Gable.

The road passed under the clip-clop of the horses' hooves. In time, it opened to fields and farms. Yellow light filled the windows of small cottages. The Gop River edged its widening mouth closer to the road. Cogs, bathed in torchlight and filled with raucous music and laughter, floated up and down the water.

"How much further, Trog?" David asked, his eyes on Charlotte, who had said little since the attack.

"Not far now." Fatigue adhered to Trog's voice.

Was the man made of stone? David yawned and scratched the mark on his chest, now itching from the inside out.

A horse-drawn wagon, weighted with a full load of what looked like wine or ale barrels, bumped and swayed toward them. The driver, cloaked from top to bottom, pulled the cowl so far forward no part of him showed. Though he could not see them, David was certain the driver's eyes locked on him as they passed. A shiver wiggled out of him. What had Trog gotten them into now?

The putrid smell of beer, rotten fish and sewage wrinkled David's nose before they topped the small hill, and A-frame buildings came into view behind a massive and sprawling stone wall. Light spilled in a rich orange cream from wide windows. The smell of meat roasting on open fires triggered a grumble in his stomach. Music and bawdy laughter saturated every molecule of air. Through the trees, warehouses and docks crowded along the water's edge and ships moored between spongy jetties. Two guards clad in leather and chain mail stood guard at the gates, pikes in their hands. Trog pulled up alongside David.

"I cannot stress enough the importance of staying close to me. Do not wander. Do not speak to anyone, not even a chicken. Understood?"

David sighed. *Like I would anyway.*

He and Charlotte nodded.

"Good. Let's go."

Agimesh led the way beneath the arched gates of Gable. They moved through a series of crowded cobblestone streets, bounded high on one side by warehouses, the other side by a series of bordellos and taverns. At the first cross street they turned left, past doorways marking the shopping district.

They continued uphill, meeting with a busy street bathed in orange lamplight. Laughter and music rang from the inns. In the center square, people gathered around a huge fire pit where a boar roasted over an open flame.

Trog's horse cantered ahead, and he dismounted outside a three-story stone structure with jutting balconies. David slipped from the saddle and glanced up at the oblong wooden sign. The Inn of the Nesting Owls.

Trog, Agimesh and Tacarr spoke in a huddle for a few moments, after which the two shime departed, taking the horses with them.

"Where are they going?" David asked.

"They will keep watch tonight."

"Why? Don't they need to sleep?"

"Not like you and I do," Trog said. "They can go days without sleep. Come."

David and Charlotte tagged along behind Trog, entered the crummy joint, and approached the bar.

Charlotte waved her hand in front of her face. "It stinks of sweat and vomit in here."

David nodded in agreement.

Raucous laughter rang out from a group of men sitting at a table in the middle of the grungy room. Along the walls stood groups of men in drunken stupors, weaving and laughing and falling. Crumbs of food fell from a man's wiry red beard as he bragged of his hunting adventures. Others shoveled food into their mouths while engaging in boisterous conversations.

A bald, burly man with a beak-like nose and tufts of hair protruding from his ears, stepped behind the counter. A single bushy brow shielded two small eyes, the right of which appeared milky and devoid of sight. He leaned on one arm and said, "What do you need, fella?"

"A room, large enough for myself and two other companions, as well as food and drink for one night."

The innkeeper's eyes narrowed as he licked his lips. "One night, you say?"

"Aye."

The innkeeper rubbed his chin. "That will be twelve dracots."

Trog leaned forward. "The sign above you says five dracots. I will be more than happy to give you seven for the extra arrangements, but no more." He pulled his knife and laid it on the counter.

The innkeeper glanced between the blade and Trog, his fingers tapping on the counter. His gaze flicked around the room as if searching for reinforcements. Not finding them, he rubbed his chin, then his nose. "Nine dracots."

Trog pulled a small leather pouch from the satchel and deposited seven gold dracots on the counter. He wore a look that said the haggling was over. "In which room shall we rest for the night?"

The innkeeper scooped the money and barked, "Garret?"

A tall, lanky boy about David's age emerged from a room behind the bar, his blond hair straight about his face.

"Take this man and his guests to the third floor and put them in room twelve." He handed the boy a key.

"Thank you," Trog said, sheathing his blade. He gathered David and Charlotte to him and followed the boy.

Room twelve was rather small, but it did have three beds, a table, and five wooden chairs. David collapsed on a mattress while Garret lit the lanterns. The boy turned to Trog. "Would you care for something to eat, sir? We have stew, pottage and pork pies."

"Stew for all. What have you got to drink?"

"We received a batch of coconuts from the Spice Isles three days ago. Outside of that, just the normal ale, tea, and cider."

"Bring us hot cider, please." He tossed the boy three dracots. "For your troubles."

The boy's eyes lit up. "Yes, sir! Thank you, sir!" The boy ran from the room, pulling the door closed behind him.

With great effort, Trog removed his boots. A painful sigh escaped his lips.

Charlotte sat on the bed in the corner of the room opposite the door, her arms folded across her stomach. She stared at the floor, rocking back and forth.

Guilt stabbed David in the chest. What had he done? He should have protected her from seeing. From hearing. He should have ferried her across the river, to the manor, anywhere so she didn't have to witness not one, but two vicious deaths. He sat on the bed across from Trog and yanked off his boots and wool socks. His feet were covered in raw blisters, but it didn't matter. He'd failed Charlotte. He'd failed to protect her.

I'm such an ass!

A knock sounded at the door.

"Who is it?" Trog asked.

Garret answered. David limped to the door and admitted a girl about their age with straw-colored hair carrying a tray of drinks. Garret followed with the stew, his stare stuck on Trog. They placed the food on the table and faced the knight.

Trog stood before the girl. "What is your name, miss?"

"Gertie, sir."

Trog handed her a handful of coins. "Give four of these to the cook. Divide the rest between you and Garret. Now, go, before you are missed."

Gertie curtsied and deposited the coins in her apron. "Thank you, sir."

Garret bowed, and followed the girl. David closed and locked the door behind them.

"What was that all about? Why did you give them all that money?"

"To gain their trust."

"I don't think you need to worry about that. Didn't you see the way they salivated over you? It was like they witnessed you parting the heavens or something."

Trog snorted. "You have an active imagination, David. Come, let's eat. Charlotte?"

"I'm not hungry." She folded in on herself a bit more.

"I doubt that," Trog said. "Come. You need to keep your strength up."

"For what? To watch you kill more people?" Charlotte glared at Trog as if he'd grown two horns upon his head.

Trog tore off a chunk of bread and dipped it in his stew. "I did what I had to do."

"Really?" Charlotte rose to her feet. "You had to kill them? You couldn't have knocked them unconscious or something?"

Trog swallowed his food. "Do you believe that is what they would have done to you, my lady? Knocked us all unconscious, rummaged through our things, and tootled off with a few coins?"

"It's not about what they would have done to us. It's about us being better than them. You didn't have to kill them. They may not have been good people, but they were someone's husbands or brothers or sons. Now they're dead because of you and those two shime murderers."

"And you and your friend here are still breathing because of me and those two shime murderers. I took a bolt in the leg protecting the two of you, my lady, so do not lecture me on what I should or shouldn't do to keep you both alive." He dunked another piece of bread in his stew and popped it in his mouth.

Tears crept down Charlotte's cheeks. "How can you be so cold? How can you kill people and then sit there and eat your dinner like nothing's wrong? You're a monster!" She folded in half. Her sobs ebbed out of her in waves.

"Call me what you wish, my lady, but I will not apologize for saving your life."

David gestured for Trog to stop and took Charlotte into his arms. "Shh, it's okay." He glanced over her shoulder at the knight and mouthed, *It's a long story.*

David had no words to soothe her soul, so he said nothing. He simply held her until she could cry no more. Once her tears dried, he tucked stray wisps of hair behind her ear and brought her food to her. "Here."

Charlotte blew her nose in a cloth napkin and sat across from Trog. "I'm sorry about what I said earlier. I know I must have come off sounding like an ungrateful brat. It's just—my brother was killed in a war, a stupid, senseless war that wasn't his to fight." She turned her eyes downward. "Seeing those men die ... it was too much. I saw Daniel's face on every one of them ... lying there bleeding ... just empty shells. Was that what it was like for him? Was he alive one minute, and dead the next? Did he suffer? Did he know he was going to die?" Tears began anew. "I just don't understand how someone can be alive one minute and dead the next. It just doesn't seem possible." She wiped her eyes and met Trog's gaze. "Thank you for saving our lives."

David stared at his food. "Yeah. Thank you." He shoved a forkful in his mouth.

Charlotte stood. "Would you like me to take a look at your leg?" She let out a nervous laugh. "I'm not quite sure what to do with it, but if I'm supposed to be a healer, I might as well get started."

Trog took Charlotte's hands in his. A lifetime of sorrow, anguish, and understanding peered out from behind his eyes. "Death is never easy, my lady, no matter how many times it visits us in a lifetime. As many times as I've seen it, you would think Death and I would be great friends, but in all actuality, I try to avoid it as often as I can. You have not seen the last of death, my lady, but I can promise you this. As long as I live and breathe, I will not allow it to take those in my care, not without a fight. Should death seek you or David again, I will not hesitate to provide it a substitute, even if the substitute is my life. Understand?"

Charlotte nodded.

Trog's words swelled inside of David. This man who barely knew them had just sworn his life to them. The thought blew him away.

"Good." Trog released her hand. "Now, eat." A wide smile creased his face. "My leg won't fall off while I'm waiting for you to fill your belly."

Chapter 19

Eric met Slavandria on the outskirts of Hammershire at twilight. Keeping to the shadows, they slipped into the clothier's shop. Glass, soot, and ash lay settled upon the floor. An emaciated cat in a windowsill offered up a scratchy guttural protest and darted off. Eric opened a door at the rear of the shop.

Slavandria stepped through into a tunnel lit by sputtering torches. "Thank you, Eric. I'm glad to see your wounds are healing well."

Eric closed and locked the door behind them. "Yes, Your Grace. I don't know what I would have done if you and Mangus hadn't shown up." He plucked a torch from the wall. "I hope you don't mind traveling underground to Gyllen. Sir Farnsworth said to make you as inconspicuous as possible."

"This is perfect. No magic, no traces."

They walked quickly, and in time, reached a set of stone steps rising into the darkness. At the top, Eric manipulated a series of stones until the door opened inward. If only it had opened so easily when they were trying to get the king and queen out of the castle. As they stepped into the courtyard, Slavandria paused, her eyes trained on a dozen men rooting through the wreckage of what remained of Festival Hall. She closed her eyes. A light breeze pushed against them. "They're still alive," she said. "All of them." She swept her palm above the ground. Her lips moved, but Eric couldn't hear the words. The earth grumbled ever so slightly beneath their feet. Slavandria cast a slight smile in Eric's direction. "Living is much easier when freedom is unobstructed, don't you think?"

"Y-yes, it is. W-what did you do?"

"I gave them hope, Eric. Everyone needs hope."

"And your father?" Eric guided Slavandria toward the castle. "Would he agree?"

"My father is a perplexing contradiction. Sometimes I wonder if even he knows what he wants or believes."

The warmth in her eyes made Eric smile. "That must be difficult to live with."

Slavandria laughed. "It has its moments."

They climbed the steps and made their way to the fourth-floor drawing room. Farnsworth greeted her as they entered. Eric closed the door.

"Thank you for coming," he said. He gestured to his friends in the room. "You remember Sirs Crohn and Gowran."

Slavandria nodded. "Yes, indeed."

Everyone exchanged pleasantries and sat in upholstered chairs placed around a table.

Farnsworth motioned to Eric. "Have a seat, lad."

Slavandria glanced at the knight, her eyes wide with surprise. "Eric's staying?"

Farnsworth nodded. "Yes. Is this a problem?"

"It has the potential to be problematic."

"I'll take the risk."

Eric sat beside Farnsworth. Sestian's voice crept into his head.

Well, well. What a tantalizing puzzle piece. How can your presence be problematic? Interesting. You know, for a group of folks who pride themselves on honesty, they sure do keep a lot of secrets. And have you noticed they all seem to center around you?

Eric closed his eyes and took a deep breath. *Go away, Ses.*

"Are you all right, Eric?" Slavandria asked. "You seemed irritated, upset by something."

"No. It's nothing." *Nothing but my best friend taunting me from the grave.*

Eric squirmed beneath the weight of her stare. *Does she know? Can she hear him?*

She steepled her fingers and turned to Farnsworth. "I suppose we should start this meeting with why you asked me to come, other than the obvious reasons."

Farnsworth propped his elbows on the arms of the chair, his hands clasped before him. "We need your help, Your Grace. Our borders are open to whatever Einar wishes to throw at us. We have it on good authority there is a coup in place with members of the High Council leading the way, including Lord Seyekrad. We need someone on our side, someone to intercede as well as reinstate the defenses that were in place before Einar's attack."

Slavandria's expression darkened. "I am confused. What information do you have of Lord Seyekrad?"

Farnsworth relayed the information given to him by Eric.

She took a deep breath and laughed. Relief washed over her face. "Dear Eric, what a fright he must have given you. Please accept my apology for his behavior. Sometimes he gets carried away in the parts he plays."

"What are you talking about?" Eric said with a scowl. "He held a knife to my throat and threatened to kill my father and me."

"Seyekrad is working for my father. Do you not think Jared hears rumors? Do you not think he senses treachery? Lord Seyekrad has deliberately put himself in this situation to gain the favor of those willing to see Gildore removed from the throne. It's all show."

"There was no one present when he threatened to kill me," Eric said. "There was nothing but hatred in his eyes and his magic reeked of death."

"Eric, I've known Lord Seyekrad for many years. He's eccentric, pompous, even ruthless, but he's not a murderer."

Eric nearly choked on his spit. "Don't tell me what he is! I was there. I saw murder in his eyes. I felt it in my veins."

"I have to agree with the boy," Gowran said. "I saw nothing but malice in his eyes, and when confronted, he lied. Said Eric attacked him."

"You should have heard that malefactor's vitriol, his disgust for the innocents," Crohn chimed in. "If he's pretending, I'd hate to see him when he's forthright."

"All right," Slavandria said, Eric surprised by the intensity in her voice. "I am to meet him after I leave here to discuss strategy. I will see what I can find out. If I detect anything that seems questionable, I will take action. As for protecting Hirth, you know I would love to help, but what you ask is impossible of me. Father has forbidden my interference. He would have no problem throwing me in Eisig alongside Master Camden if I defy him. I must be very careful."

"But the mages interfered once before," Crohn said. "Almost

seventeen years ago. Why should they not do so again?"

"The Council is not responsible for the verdaí," Slavandria said.

"Who, then?" Farnsworth raised an eyebrow.

"No one knows. The magic was dark, untraceable."

"Then how did it break?" Eric asked.

Slavandria let out a breath. "I'm afraid I'm responsible for that."

"What?" Gowran said.

All eyes turned to her.

Slavandria stood and flicked a quick glance at Farnsworth as she passed. "It happened when I summoned the paladin."

Farnsworth dropped his chin to his chest and sighed.

Slavandria faced the hearth. "As soon as the paladin arrived, I felt a shift in the realm. I could sense the verdaí crumbling, but the shime erected a shield, and I could not see or feel anything beyond Chalisdawn. It wasn't until the paladin arrived at my home that I saw the devastation. Felt the terror."

"Where is the paladin now?" Farnsworth asked.

Slavandria met his gaze. "On his journey to do what he came to do."

"Does his undertaking involve protecting Hirth in any way," Crohn asked, "or is he forbidden by your father to use his magic as well?"

"His skills will afford protection, provided certain criteria are met." Her gaze darted around. Her fingers flicked at her side.

She's nervous, Eric thought. *Why?*

"It is imperative he meets," she paused as if trying to choose the precise word, "the right people."

Crohn shifted in his seat. Gowran rubbed his temples. Farnsworth exhaled and rubbed both palms over his face. "Eric, would you excuse us please?"

The floor dropped out beneath Eric. His stomach went with it. "Why? What did I do?"

"Nothing. There are simply some things we need to discuss that do not involve you."

"In other words, I've become problematic, right?" Thick, searing, white-hot rage rushed through his body. His hands clenched at his sides. "What could you need to discuss that I can't hear? Oh, wait. More secrets and lies?" He was surprised by the cool, fluid tone in his voice.

Farnsworth stepped closer and shoved him into an overstuffed chair. He leaned over, his face inches away from Eric's. "I do not have to explain myself to you. I asked you to leave, and I expect you, as a squire, to do so without protest."

Anger flicked at Eric's composure, the steadiness in his voice running away with his fleeting self-control.

"I wouldn't protest if you treated me like I was something more than a piddly grunt boy, worthy only of sharpening blades and shoveling manure. If you would give me a chance to help instead of always treating me like I'm a festering sore on your backside, you might see I'm not the buffoon you think I am."

Farnsworth tightened his grip on the arms of the chair, the veins in his arms bulging. His mouth twitched at the corner. "This has nothing to do with your feelings of inadequacy and everything to do with your lack of respect and obedience."

Eric's anger seethed. "I am not a dog, sir. If you want obedience, find yourself a mutt." He shoved Farnsworth's arm away and stood.

Farnsworth grabbed Eric by the ear, his lips tight. "You are pushing me beyond my patience with your backtalk, young man."

Slavandria touched Farnsworth's arm. "It's all right. Let me handle this."

Farnsworth cursed beneath his breath and turned away, his hands clasped behind his head.

Slavandria touched Eric's arm. Threads of calm surged into him, cooling the flames of anger. He met the softness and compassion of her gaze. She cupped a hand on his cheek, the way a mother comforts her son. "Eric, I understand how angry you must be right now, to be told you can stay, then told to leave, but I must speak to the Order alone. It has nothing to do with you being untrustworthy or incompetent. In fact, I have a favor to ask of you. I need you to keep an eye out for something, an object of great importance. It is what I've sent the paladin in search of."

Eric's pulse quickened. A mage quest? He bottled his excited breaths.

Slavandria conjured a floating vision from her palms. "It is a necklace, a filigreed wreath, about the size of your palm. In the center is a ruby-red dragon's eye. It is called the Eye of Kedge, and it is imperative to the future of Hirth and all of Fallhollow that it is found."

Eric's heart skipped. Excitement tickled his belly so much he wanted to laugh. It took every bit of control to keep from smiling. *Oh, Sestian, you imp. You and your box of treats.* He reeled in his zeal; his attention focused completely on Slavandria and the item snugged safely around his neck.

"I have no idea where this relic is," she said, "but should you find it, please give it Farnsworth. He'll know what to do with it."

"What does it do?" Eric asked, doing his best to keep his voice steady.

"Think of it as a key," Slavandria said. "A very important key."

Eric feigned indifference. "A key to what?"

"Intense magic unlike anything you've ever seen."

He held her gaze, and for a moment his belly tingled as if she knew his secret. He tossed the feeling aside and inclined his head toward her. "Thank you for entrusting me with such an important task. I won't let you down, I promise."

His glance darted between the knights, and with a nod to them, he departed and hurried to his suite. Locking his door, he withdrew the necklace from beneath his tunic. He held it up, seeing its filigreed swirls as mere shadows in the moonlight.

"What were you doing with the mage stone, Ses?" Eric flipped the pendant over several times and brushed his thumb across the ruby eye. "Better still, what should *I* do with it?"

His thoughts turned inward and focused on the promise of something grand. If he turned the key over to Farnsworth now, there would be all kinds of questions. The knights would never acknowledge him for returning such an important artifact, only ridicule him for not turning it over sooner. If he could find the paladin, however, and present the stone in such a way the paladin believed he found it, then Eric would achieve something great. It would be such an altruistic thing to do, to allow someone else to take the credit for something he did. The paladin would achieve praise, and in turn, so would Eric, for being there at the right time, at the right place. Maybe then the Order would see he was capable of doing something paramount without ruining everything else, and Sestian's secret would remain buried forever in a box of worn shoes and memories.

Eric returned the pendant to the safety of his neck and fell back on his bed. Tomorrow, his adventure would begin. Tomorrow, he would find the paladin.

Chapter 20

David wandered onto the balcony and sat in the corner, his knees drawn to his chest. Below, the town lay quiet, save for the night birds and the gentle slosh of the river against the docks. He closed his eyes and inhaled. The crisp air, rich with the smell of pine, moist earth, and river tang, nose-dived deep into his lungs. The scent whisked away the remnants of yet another hellacious nightmare brimming with pale, lifeless eyes. He spun the ring on his finger, envisioned his bedroom back home and whispered, *Accelero Silentium.*

A swearword escaped his lips when all four depressing, dilapidated and oppressive walls of his prison remained. He clenched his fingers against his thighs.

"Were you expecting it to work?"

David's heart plummeted into his gut before it shot into his throat. He jerked his head to the right to find Trog sitting opposite him, arms folded across his chest, legs straight out in front. In the

235

dark, the human tree trunk appeared even more daunting than he did in daylight: congenial and generous as moonlight while burning fierce and merciless like the sun. He was a contradiction, one that demanded both fear and respect. David had no problem providing both.

"Yes." David swallowed. He rubbed his palms over his face. "No."

"Let me guess, you were attempting to return home."

David nodded. "Can you blame me for trying?"

"No, I suppose not." Trog paused for a brief moment. "What is it like, this Havendale? Is it much different from Fallhollow?"

David snorted. "Oh, yeah. Crazy different. Like night and day." He stared at the ground. "I miss it a lot, especially Jamocha Joe's." He hugged his knees. "I'd do anything for a cup of joe right now."

"Joe?" Trog's eyebrow lifted in confusion.

David smiled. "Coffee. It's this hot drink that smells like nuts and chocolate and caramel all mixed together, and it tastes like … like liquid heaven. I'll have to buy you a cup someday."

He mentally face-palmed himself, like Trog would *ever* step foot in Havendale. Well, maybe he would … when hamsters flew.

Trog nodded, his features softened. "I'd like that." He shifted his position, bringing one knee to his chest. "Tell me about this Havendale. What is so *crazy different*?"

David grinned at Trog's attempt to speak like him. He leaned back against the wall, the cold, sharpness of the stone digging into his spine. He gave Trog the five-dollar tour of his hometown, minus the cars, airplanes, and electronic gadgets. After all, it would be futile to launch into an exhaustive explanation of advanced technology to someone who didn't even know what coffee was. Before he knew it, his life story poured out of him, his words flowing like a rushing river, distinct and animated. When finished, the man knew the gist of David's life story, right down to the tattoo, the ring, and the fake foreboding letter.

David took a tight breath as Trog stood and walked to him. The man held out his hand, palm up. "May I have a look at the ring?"

David shook his head. "I told you, I can't take it off."

"I'm not asking you to. You can, however, stand and let me look."

David got to his feet and held out his hand, his fingers curled into a fist just in case Trog tried to go all Gollum over his *Precious*.

Trog held the specimen up to the moonlight, his brow beetled together as he scrutinized it. "Interesting. You said this was the same marking that appeared on your chest?"

David nodded. "Exactly the same. Have you seen it before?"

"The ring or the marking?"

David shrugged. "Either. Both."

Trog released David's hand. "The ring I have not seen, but I recognize the work as that of the king's goldsmith. His initials are etched in the vines. As for the markings, they are the same as those that appear in Gyllen's Coat of Arms. My sword is also engraved with the same mark."

David bit back a shiver. *A royal* ring. He paused, his brain clicking away. "So, does this mean my dad's a noble or something?"

Trog shook his head. "Doubtful. I've seen the royal family present such gifts to commoners who have displayed outstanding acts of valor. It is a treasure, to be sure. The fact the mages enchanted it makes it even more valuable. It also means you are quite special, beyond what Slavandria told you. For you to have both ring and mark means the mages bound you to our world through your father. I will be interested to see what becomes of you, young David."

"Yeah, me, too." David ran his thumb over the etching. "So, what do the markings mean? Anything?"

"The rearing bull represents strength and bravery; the eagle displayed—protection by the nobility, specifically the king."

"And the braided circle?"

"A symbol of eternal life, a reminder we are all one spirit within the universe, under the heavens."

Pride swelled inside David. His father was a hero, both in this world and his own, but what had he done to deserve such an honor? He had to meet this man. He had to find his father now more than ever.

Trog took two steps and poked his head in the room, then pulled the louvered doors closed.

"Is she still sleeping?" David asked.

Trog nodded. He walked to the railing and leaned against it, his hands clasped together. "Care to share the story between the two of you?"

"There's nothing to tell," David said, standing beside the knight. "We're friends."

"I see." A smile almost touched his lips.

"What's that supposed to mean?" David said, surprised by an unexpected flash of fury.

"Your eyes betray your words, young man."

"I don't know what you're talking about." David stared out over the shadow of a town, his eyes focusing on nothing.

"There is no reason to become defensive. I simply made an observation. Why do you not tell her?"

David picked at his fingernails. "It's complicated."

"Most matters of the heart usually are." Trog turned to David, his eyes so intense David had to look away. "May I give you a few words of advice? Tell her how you feel. She will appreciate your honesty."

"You don't understand," David said, his mouth suddenly as dry as a desert, "especially now that everything has changed."

"What's changed?"

"I'm bound to this place, Trog. She isn't. What if I have to stay here forever?"

"Then she stays, or she goes. At least she knows what you both face."

"But what if I don't want her to stay? I could never, ever make her go through another day like she did today. I'm surprised she's not flipping out and having nightmares right now. You have no idea how hard it's been for her, losing her brother. She hates war and death. Today, you made her look at it up close and personal. I'm not stupid. I know there'll be more. I can't let that happen. I have to get her home."

"Don't you think that should be her decision?"

"No. I have to make sure she's safe and has everything in life she deserves, someone who will care for her and protect her."

Trog scratched his chin. "What if that person is you?"

"It's not me. Trust me."

"What makes you sure?"

David chuckled. "Did you not see what happened today? While you and Agimesh and Taccar were defending us, I stood there like a moron, my feet planted in the ground like a tree. I couldn't do anything to protect her. What kind of guy am I if I can't defend the girl I love? What if we find ourselves in that position again, and no one else is around to fight off the bad guys? What then?" He paused for a moment, calmed his breathing. "Slavandria told me I may have to kill people. That test came today, and I did nothing. Nothing!" He turned away, his gaze on the town. "No. She deserves better than me. Than this. She needs to go home to her family, where she'll be safe, where she'll have all the comforts she's used to. Somewhere she can find someone who isn't afraid to care for and shelter her."

"Don't you think you're being rather harsh on yourself?"

David glowered at the knight. "Don't you think you've asked enough questions? I've made up my mind, and I'd appreciate it if you would respect that." He turned to go inside.

"Gallantry does not include choosing another's destiny," Trog said.

"Stop it!" David spun around, his jaw hardened, his stomach clenched along with his fists. "You don't know anything about her or me!"

Trog folded his arms across his chest, his eyes sharp and focused. "I know she's a free spirit, and you're a configuration of worry and self-doubt." His voice softened, but his tone still held an edge. "You let pride and fear guide you. You let them make your decisions. If you don't learn to conquer both, they will cost you not only the girl you love but your life." Trog walked toward him and laid a firm hand on David's shoulder. "Stop feeling so hell-bent on protecting her and let her make up her mind. She is much stronger than you think, as are you." He removed his hand. "I'm turning in. I suggest you do the same. We have a long trek ahead of us in the morning."

Trog opened the doors. Thunder rumbled in the distance, but it didn't come from the sky. His face tightened, turning all warrior-like. He pointed to the balcony floor. "Get down!"

"Why? What is it?" David squatted, his heart thumping madly.

"Trouble would be my first guess." Trog knelt behind the railing.

The sound of hooves beating the ground and men shouting, drew closer. Lanterns across the square flared to life. Downstairs, the door of the inn opened. The innkeeper, dressed in a sleeping gown, stepped into view, his lantern flickering warm and golden in the dark. Moments later, the horde arrived, thirty or more horses, black as crows, draped in purple fabric, their riders angular and broad. They dismounted and tethered their horses. Purple-gold bandannas hid their hair. Tattoos stained their faces. Hooped earrings glistened in the moonlight while swords and daggers hung from hip and horse.

David gulped, his limbs an earthquake of shattered nerves. "They look the same as the guys on the road today. Who are they?"

Proprietors from several inns made their way into the street and addressed the men.

"Dalvarian rebels," Trog said, "and the men we came upon today on the road were part of that group, soldiers who no longer hold allegiance to the kingdom of Dalvar or its king. They are dangerous."

"What do you think they want?"

"Blood. War. Revenge. I know their type. There is only one side they would ally with in a skirmish, and it won't be Hirth."

A wave of intensity caught in David's chest. His heart fluttered like a hummingbird in flight. "You don't mean Einar, do you?"

Trog nodded. "Aye, I do. I've seen this before. It is not the first time the Dragon King has gathered an army." Trog bopped David on the arm. "Let's try to get some sleep. We need to leave before daybreak if we'll have any chance of avoiding them."

David nodded, but he could tell by the tone of Trog's voice, and the knight's deadly stance, that at least one of them would be getting little sleep tonight.

***

David tossed and turned. Slavandria appeared in the dark corners of his mind, her voice soothing. Tempting.

Come, David. I need you to wake and come to me. I must speak to you right away. It's a matter of great importance to you.

What? What is it?

I need you to wake. I need you to come to the Elthorian manor, now. Her voice called to him like a fresh baked cinnamon bun, warm, enticing. Irresistible. *Hurry.*

David opened his eyes and sat up. Charlotte and Trog were crashed out in their beds. Moonlight streamed through the louvered door. The room was quiet, too quiet. Sleep tugged at his mind, and he lay back down, eyes closed.

David, wake up! Come to me, now!

David rubbed his eyes. "What the hell," he muttered as he stumbled into his clothes and boots. Still groggy, he stood, took one look at his roommates and with an image of the Elthorian terrace pictured in his mind, he whispered, *"Accelero Silentium."*

He shot across space and time at a thousand miles an hour. The terrace came into view, then—

Snatch!

A pale hand dragged him into a caliginous void.

Swirling.

Diving.

Slavandria screeched his name, her voice gripped in tortured pain.

Crazy laughter echoed in the dark. A woman cackled.

Downward.

Spiraling.

Dizziness.

Stomach turning sick.

Oof!

Air pushed from his lungs as leaves, twigs, and moist earth plowed into him. Gasping, he rolled on his back and pounded his chest until he steadied his breathing.

He swallowed and forced himself to remain still. *I'm alive. I'm breathing. I'm okay.*

He lolled his head to one side and scanned the forest glade. Long, thin threads of silver light slithered along the ground toward him. Were the vines moving?

David swallowed, his eyes splayed wide open.

The strands slunk around him, pulling, tugging.

"No! Get off!" He smacked and kicked.

Through his legs and around his arms they wove, binding, constricting. His breath hitched as they lifted him from the ground and slammed him against a tree.

David struggled against his bonds, anger slowly taking over his panic. "What are you doing, Slavandria? This isn't funny."

"Oh, that depends on who's watching."

David jerked his head toward the male voice, his heart skipping all over the place. There was no doubt who it belonged to.

The shadow man from his dreams.

He was a slender man with golden skin, white hair, and piercing turquoise eyes that glistened far too bright for the darkness. He sat cross-legged on a tree stump, curtailing threads that dangled from the hem of his black cloak. Every finger possessed a silver ring. A round, black stone dangled from a leather cord around his neck. Behind him, a tall, willowy woman stood, dressed in a gown of spruce-green velvet. Long, shimmering, black hair tipped in white draped over her waxen shoulders to her waist, a look of satisfaction upon her face.

"My love, may I please have a few minutes alone with him?" she begged. "It would bring me great pleasure to torment him."

The man chuckled. "It sounds devilishly tempting, Avida, but tonight this morsel belongs to me. Is that not right, Your Grace?"

David's heart sank to his stomach as he followed the man's gaze. Two trees to his right, Slavandria struggled against magical constraints.

"Release me, Seyekrad," she said. "You gave me your word this would be a meeting of peace—a meeting to discuss the safety of the realm. Just what do you think you will gain by this outward display of malcontent?"

With a damnable chuckle, Seyekrad unfurled his long legs and eased from the elm perch. He passed by David before moving beside her. She cringed as his long fingers wove through her hair.

"Why, Slavandria," he drawled, "I thought it would be rather evident. You had something I wanted." His fingers brushed her bare shoulder. He stroked her cheek and leaned in, his lips close to her ear. "And now I have him."

David closed his eyes, his heart thump, thump, thumping in his chest. *This is a dream. Wake up. Wake up.*

The man laughed loud and hearty. "Oh, no, dear boy. This is no dream." He snapped his fingers. "Open your eyes and look at me!"

David's lids sprang apart against his will, his gaze riveted to the sorcerer. He swallowed, his throat as dry as chalk. "Who are you? What do you want?"

Seyekrad approached, his contempt as cold as steel. A nauseating, sweet stench of black licorice clung to his every pore. He drew a fingernail across David's cheek. "I am your nemesis, and I want your life."

"Why?" David rasped. "What did I ever do to you?"

The man smiled. "It's not what you've done, boy, but what you're capable of doing. You see, you're like an infinitesimal germ festering in my craw, and like a debilitating disease, you must be eliminated before you can do more harm."

"That still doesn't tell me who you are." His throat hurt as if rubbed raw by sandpaper.

"He's a coward, David," Slavandria said. "A traitor. That's what he is."

Silver threads of fire flew from the man's fingertips, engulfing Slavandria in flames. Her high-pitched scream rose above Avida's cackling. It pierced the air, hanging like a single, endless, tortured note, ramming like a spike through David's soul.

David yelled, his eyes blurred, burning. "Stop it! Leave her alone!" He fought and tugged against his bonds, but they constricted even more.

The flames evaporated. Slavandria hung her head and coughed.

Seyekrad turned to David; a wide, devilish grin stretched across his face. "My, my, you have more fire than I remember." He leaned in, his medicinal breath billowing like a toxic cloud across David's face. "You want to know who I am? Come on. I'm sure you can figure it out. Humor me. Take a guess."

David focused on a path leading into the dark woods. "I don't know. A sucky version of Zorro or Batman?" The words, *Accelero Silentium* echoed in his head.

Nothing.

Nothing except Seyekrad's crazed laughter. "Oh, my. Did you think your juvenile attempts at whatever magic this hellcat gave you would work?"

David thought harder. *Ibidem Evanescere.*

Seyekrad's hand clamped down on David's throat, his spindly fingers curled around David's neck. "Why, you're just a mess of defiance, aren't you?"

A gurgle ushered out of David's mouth.

"Leave him alone," Slavandria said.

"Keep quiet, witch!" Avida stormed across the clearing and slapped Slavandria across the face. "You will keep your mouth shut unless spoken to or I'll kill you myself."

"Go ahead, kill me," Slavandria shouted. "I'm sure my father would love to hunt you down and take your wretched life."

Seyekrad sneered. "Oh yes, good old daddy always to the rescue. Well, not this time, my dear, because for once, it's not you I want. It's this delectable morsel."

"Why? He's just a boy," Slavandria said.

Seyekrad released his hold on David's throat and laughed. "Do you take me for a fool?" He strolled toward her, his hands clasped together as if in prayer. "Did you believe that after all these years, Slavandria, after everything we've been through together, I wouldn't figure it out?" He stroked his forefinger across her brow. "Ah, but you must have because you went to great lengths to hide him. But I found him despite your efforts to keep him secret. Do you want to know how?" A fearful look of curiosity flashed in her eyes. He tilted his head and leaned close to her ear. "I followed you."

The sorceress' skin paled, but she remained silent.

"Oh yes. I know all about Havendale, sweet love of mine. I know about the attempts to hide him from my eyes. Not only did

I find him, but I have also been watching him for quite some time. In fact, we have spent quite a bit of time together, David and I."

Avida cackled from behind a tree. "Yes, we have all become *very good friends.*"

Seyekrad twisted around. "Shut up, Avida, or I shall displace your tongue from your foul mouth!" She sulked into the dark misty shadows of the forest, hissing, and scowling.

"What does she mean, we've become good friends?" David asked, wrestling against his constraints. "I've never seen you before in my life!"

Seyekrad thrust out his right arm; his hand gnarled into a claw. The blue of his eyes faded and turned a fiery milky white.

A fistful of magic punched through to David's brain. A string of images, memories, played in his head like a movie. Mr. Loudermilk's history class. Chess games on the man's front porch. Mowing Mrs. Fenton's yard. Listening to her play the piano.

David squeezed his eyes shut, a desperate attempt to cast the visions aside. "What are you doing?" he cried out. His brain hurt as if pressed in a vise. More movies skipped across his mind like a worn rock over a still lake. Realization began to set in.

No. No. It couldn't be.

David writhed in torturous agony, his head on fire as the image of Seyekrad's face merged with Mr. Loudermilk's.

"No! Get out!" he screamed. Tears flooded down his cheeks. "How could you? You were my teacher, my friend! Why?"

"Because he shifted his allegiance, didn't you?" Slavandria said. "You turned against the realm. How could you, Seyekrad? How could you betray me, my father, and your oath? What did the Dragon King promise you?"

Seyekrad's lip turned up in a wolfish scowl. "You broke me, Slavandria. You ripped my heart out when you cast my love aside …

for Mangus Grythorn! I begged. I groveled for a place at your side, and you denied me. Now I have a place at the Dragon King's side, and I want you to suffer for what you did. I want your spirit to break. You will live long enough to see the light leave the eyes of this insolent pup, this human paladin. Then I will give you to the Dragon King to make of your soul what he wishes. You would make a beautiful shadowmorth."

"Seyekrad, I beg you," Slavandria said with a rattle in her voice. "You don't have to do this. I don't care what you do to me, but let him go."

Seyekrad laughed and laughed. "You still take me for a fool, don't you? Why would I do something so stupid? I know who he is. So does the Dragon King. Letting him go is not an option." The sorcerer turned to David. "Say your farewell, pup. The end doesn't hurt much." He thrust out his arm. "*Torncadum!*"

A ball of black fire swirled in Seyekrad's hand, then shot from his palm and hurled across the open space.

David closed his eyes. His breathing stopped. His fingers flinched, waiting for the impact. He thought of his last words to Lily, his first archery set. Charlotte at Halloween dressed up as a bookmark.

"*Impellaferno!*" Slavandria shouted.

David's eyes flew open.

The spell knocked Seyekrad from his feet and cast him across the clearing; his face engulfed in fire.

"*Aaaargggh!*" he wailed, rolling on the ground. "My eyes!"

Avida jumped from the safety of the darkness, her body surrounded by pale, green light. She turned on Slavandria. "What did you do to him? Undo what you have done or I will kill you!"

"No," Seyekrad said as he struggled to stand. "This loathsome creature is mine."

He staggered toward Slavandria. Waxen layers of skin dangled in strips from the corners of his eyes. "So, this is how you wish to play, is it?" He flicked his fingers. Sizzling strings of magic slithered from his fingertips, writhing like tentacles. "Word of warning. Darkness always devours light."

A blue streak of light shot forth from the depths of the forest. It hit the ground just shy of Seyekrad's feet. A rock shattered. Seyekrad jerked around.

A tall, dark figure passed in the shadows.

Avida screeched, "Who's there? Show yourself."

Seyekrad turned in circles, his eyes searching.

A rustle of leaves drew his attention to the left.

David gasped as another blue streak arced from behind a giant elm and caught Seyekrad on the elbow. Another blue stream of electricity caught Avida in the chest. She collapsed, her body still.

The sorcerer spun around, his aim high and blind. Branches exploded and fell with a splintering crash to the forest floor. Bats high in the canopy of the trees took to flight; two hungry owls followed them.

Another icy blue streak erupted from the dark. Seyekrad spun around and deflected it back toward the source. A momentary cry of pain sounded from the forest depths. Had he hit David's mystery savior? Seyekrad moved toward his assailant.

A shadow moved first to his left then back again to his right. Seyekrad froze in his steps. Sweat poured over the dangling flesh into his eyes. He staggered. "Come out and fight me!"

From the shadows, the figure emerged draped in a cape as black as the night. A single gloved finger pointed at Seyekrad. The shimmering spell hit the sorcerer in the chest before he could block it. He howled in pain and recoiled. Another blue arc hit him, followed by another, and another. Snap, Crackle. Pop. It was like Seyekrad was a fly in a bug zapper. His face turned white. Foam oozed from the corners of his mouth. A final arc and his knees collapsed. He keeled over, face first.

The cloaked figure hurried to Slavandria's side. A little zap and the restraints fell away. Slavandria collapsed in the stranger's arms. Her eyes rolled to the back of her head. "I didn't think you would ever come."

"Shh. Don't speak. I'll be right back."

David's heart thumped, thumped. The familiar voice, soft and feminine, washed over him like a smooth peppermint wave.

The stranger approached. With a quick flick of her finger, the magic ropes disappeared.

His arms ached, his legs trembled. The stranger enfolded him in her arms and eased him to the ground.

"There," she soothed. "It's all right now. You're safe."

His body quaked. Tears fell down his cheeks. He knew that voice as well as he knew his own.

"Lily?"

The hood of her cloak fell away revealing all too familiar turquoise eyes framed in a sea of auburn hair. A gentle smile lit her face. "Hey, you," she whispered, brushing away his tears.

Relief flew out of him like an exorcised demon. He crumpled in her arms and sobbed. "I'm sorry. I'm so sorry."

Lily cradled him in her arms and kissed his forehead. "That makes two of us. What do you say we get out of here, huh?"

"My thoughts exactly," Slavandria said, her shoulders drooping with exhaustion. She knelt beside David and combed her fingers through his hair. "It's time to go back where we belong."

Chapter 21

On the east side of the Domengart Mountains, the first light of day crested over the town of Hammershire. Eric sat with his father in the small hut's kitchen, his mind torn in a million pieces.

"What is tearin' at your brain, son?"

Eric ran his palms over his face then folded his arms on the table. "Father, I need to ask your advice."

"I'm listenin'." The old man scraped at the skin of a potato.

"Suppose you stumbled upon an item of great importance. Returning it to its rightful owner would be a sign of cooperation, of loyalty. You would be praised for doing the right thing, but other than that, your life goes on as normal. Within days, maybe even hours, you're disregarded, forgotten for your deed." Eric leaned over the table, resting on his elbows.

"But let's say you don't return it because you know someone else is seeking it, someone with the power to change the world.

You know if you give the item to this person, you would gain notoriety, respect. Tales would be written of your bravery and courage. Which would you choose?"

"Well, I suppose that depends on the person with the item. Me, I don't care nothin' for the praise and glamor. The way I see it, the best deeds are done when nothin' is expected in return. If ya need all the praise, then you ain't doin' the deed for the right reason."

"But what if you're tired of being passed over, of being ignored and accepted as a fool?"

"Better a fool with integrity, than a braggart with a title."

Eric's father stood and shooed a chicken from the home. "Ya goin' ta help me milk the goats?"

Eric followed his father to the pen outside and grabbed a pail. Deep down, he knew his father was right. Getting honor by giving it directly to the paladin was a selfish reason not to return the necklace to Slavandria, but what of his promise to Sestian? What of his promise to himself? If he didn't seek the paladin, Trog would always treat him like a child. Trog would never entrust him with a chore more dangerous than brushing his teeth in a rainstorm. No. He had to do this. He had to find the paladin. He had to be the one to give him the Eye of Kedge.

The goat bleated and kicked. The pail with its contents smacked against the fence railing.

"Dragon's breath!" Eric ran his fingers through his hair. "I'm sorry, Father."

The man squeezed Eric's shoulder as he passed behind him. "Don't ya worry about it, son. It's just a little spilt milk. It's not like ya killed the goat." He picked up the pail and walked across the yard. "Do what ya need to do, son. Just make sure you don't lose respect for yourself in the process, 'cause in the end, it's you that's goin' to have to live with your choices. No one else. Make sure when you lay your head on your pillow every night, you know you've done nothin' to compromise your principles. Ain't nothin' worth that."

Eric spent the remainder of the day with his father. By the time he tucked into bed, his body ached but his soul had never felt more content. He would find a way to leave Gyllen in the morning.

He would find the paladin, and gain the respect he deserved.

Chapter 22

David's legs felt heavy, like tree roots planted on the wrong side of a one-way nightmare. Lily and Slavandria slipped away, swallowed by a vat of inky nothingness.

No! Lily, wait! Come back! Don't leave me here!

Her voice mingled with the wind as it played with the leaves, whispering as twigs, tap, tap, tapped on his shoulder.

It's time to go.

Your time is nigh.

Be brave.

Wake up.

Wake up.

"David, wake up."

A sharp intake of air and his eyes pinged open. Walls, not trees, surrounded him. Charlotte, not Lily, hovered over him. He pushed her away and scrambled upright, his brain twisted in his skull. His gaze darted from the bed to Charlotte, to Trog. "How?

What?" He gasped for air, the breaths painfully short.

Trog grasped David's shoulders and pressed him against the wall. "Look at me. Breathe!"

David shook his head and sucked in deep, harsh, gasping breaths. "This is — all wrong!" He swallowed hard. "I'm not supposed—Slavandria. Lily." The room spun around him. His whole body shook. "How? I was there. Now—now I'm here."

He couldn't stop gasping for air.

"It was a dream," Trog said. "You're all right now."

"No. Not a dream." He grasped Trog's shirtsleeves. "H-he tried to kill me. Kill Slavandria. Lily saved us." He released his grip. Stared at the ground.

"Who tried to kill you?" Charlotte pressed a wet cloth to his head.

He closed his eyes and counted.

Breathe.

One.

Breathe.

Two.

Breathe.

Three.

The room steadied. His heartbeat slowed to a normal rate. He smacked his dry lips. "Sey—Seyekrad." He leaned forward and found Charlotte's hands. "He's Mr. Loudermilk."

"What are you talking about?" Charlotte dabbed his head again. Worry lines broke out across her brow.

David tilted back his head and closed his eyes. "This crazy evil wizard dude. Said his name was Seyekrad." The word floated from his lips in a whisper. "He pretended to be Mr. Loudermilk so he could watch me." He squeezed her hand. "Mrs. Fenton was there, too, except he called her Avada."

"Avida," Trog snapped, his voice unexpectedly sharp.

David nodded. "Yeah, that." He met Trog's angry, flashing eyes. "Do you know them?"

Trog hauled himself up, his body rigid. "I've had a few run-ins with them. Seyekrad is a defender of the realm, or at least he was." His jaw twitched. Rage settled in his eyes. "I take it by the bruises on your face and neck his allegiance has changed."

David nodded. "He's pissed at Slavandria because she dumped him, and he wants me dead because he thinks I have the power to destroy the Dragon King, but I don't. Right? Isn't that what Slavandria said? I'm here to find a stone, right?" He coughed, his throat as dry and scratchy as a sandbox.

Someone knocked on the door.

David's heart jumped. Charlotte froze.

"Who is it?" Trog said.

"Garret and Gertie, sir. We need to speak with you. It's urgent."

Trog crossed the room and opened the door.

The two G's rushed inside followed by the ever-silent Agimesh and Taccar. The two warriors shut and blocked the door, their faces stoic. Charlotte clasped David's hand tighter.

Trog eyed Garret and Gertie, his arms crossed over his chest, his hands stuck in his pits. "Go on. I'm listening."

"You need to leave Gable right away," Garret said, his eyes dark, serious.

Trog's brow creased in a frown. "Why is that?"

"We know who you are—Sir Trogsdill. Every moppet our age does. And I'd wager every Dalvarian out there knows who you are, too."

"So?"

"They're looking for the person who murdered two of their men yesterday and dumped them in the river," Gertie said. Her hair hung around her straight and narrow shoulders. "If they find you, you and your friends will die."

Anxiety curled its way into David's chest. Charlotte bit her bottom lip. A faint wind blew in through the balcony doors, blanketing the room in a chill.

Their words rendered Trog momentarily speechless.

Heated shouts from the tavern filtered up through the balcony doors. Booted footsteps stomped up the stairs.

Panic soared through Eric.

Garret stepped closer to Trog. "Sir, if you want our help, we need to leave now."

David took a deep breath, and another, his pulse thudding a thousand miles a second. He spun his ring over and over again. Heavy footsteps pounded the floor below.

Trog pointed at Charlotte and David, his eyes too wide, making him look crazy. "Get your things."

They jammed their belongings into their bags and hurried into the hall.

"Agimesh," Trog said, "a little shime magic would be appreciated."

An ethereal mist floated from the ceiling and swaddled them. Beneath them, a swirling vapor cloud rose from the floor, lifting them a few inches and moving them down the hall as if on a conveyor belt. David's stomach tickled. He suppressed the urge to laugh at the absurdity of it all.

Ahead, two Dalvarians topped the stairs, their swords drawn. Charlotte slapped her hand to her mouth. David's limbs went stiff. One by one the goons broke down doors and yanked guests from their rooms. David held his breath. The soldiers stormed past, paying no attention. It was if they were—

Invisible! We're invisible!

David sighed.

Then laughed.

It came out of nowhere, without warning. A release of jitters. He covered his mouth in horror. How could he jeopardize them like that? *You imbecile!*

The Dalvarians turned, their mouths set in straight lines. They moved toward the sound, their weapons poised.

The swirling, floating floor moved faster, carrying David and the others down the stairwell to the first floor. Bearing right, they moved down a slender hall, past the kitchen, and into the washroom. Inside the room, the magic faded. Their sudden appearance startled a young girl with long blond hair and brown eyes. Upon seeing Garret and Gertie, she wiped her hands on her smock, scurried across the room and shoved a chest across the wood floor. Garret opened a hatch. David descended the steps last, entering an earthen room lined with wooden shelves and crates. Overhead, the hatch closed and the chest moved into place. Dust floated from the ceiling.

Charlotte smacked him on the arm. "What was that up there? Were you trying to get us killed?"

"I'm sorry. I didn't mean to. It just came out."

Trog thumped David on the head. "Next time put a plug in it!"

"I'm sorry, okay! I don't know what else you want me to say!"

"Your *sorry* is going to get us killed!" Trog said.

"Oh, and I suppose you've never made a mistake." David's words flew out before he could stop them. He didn't care. Let Trog thump him again. It was impossible to feel any more guilt and anger than he already did.

Trog turned around, his teeth gritted. Charlotte stepped between them, both arms stretched out.

"Stop. We're safe, and that's all that matters."

Trog growled before he plodded through a wooden door behind Gertie and Garret.

David and Charlotte followed and stepped into a tunnel so wide and tall a fighter jet could fit inside with room to spare.

"Whoa!" David traced his fingers over the blue streaks buried within the polished white walls glistening in a fiery pastel color. "This is sick." With every step, the walls illuminated from within, setting the passageway aglow in brilliant white light. "This is crazy. What is this place?"

"The Opal Caverns," Garret said. "Mage tunnels. I'd heard rumors of them as a boy, but never thought I'd ever see them."

"Nor, I," Trog said, his eyes wide and curious. "How did you find them?"

"Foraging for truffles near Brindle Greens. We stepped on a soft patch of earth. It gave way. We fell. We've been mapping them ever since, but I have a feeling it would take a lifetime to discover them all."

"A giant ant hill," Charlotte said, gaping.

David frowned. "Why would mages need tunnels if they can ferry?"

"To hide their traces and shave time when they travel," Trog said.

"Shave time?" Charlotte's eyes narrowed.

Trog nodded. "It's said there is great magic within the Opal Caverns which allows the mages to travel within seconds to anywhere within Fallhollow. But they need key-activated crystals to energize them." Trog's eyes remained steady.

Gertie snorted. "Too bad the mages lost the crystals and the key after the Great War. Some powerful gurus they are."

David stared at a crack in the floor. Realization donkey kicked him in the brain.

Of course. The Eye of Kedge. It's the key.

His pulse raced.

The crystals are at Hirth. Slavandria said so. If he found the stone, then Slavandria could gather the crystals, activate the tunnels and her father would never know a thing. She could form alliances and travel anywhere within Fallhollow. She could work her magic anywhere she wanted, even where forbidden. David grinned, excitement rippling through his veins like mild electrical currents. His eyes met with Trog's. "We have to get to the Doomideen Pass."

Trog nodded, his eyes twinkling. "Yes, we do."

"Why?" Charlotte asked, looking between the two of them. "What's going on?"

"Later," David said.

"Do you have payment for the creature that guards the Pass?" Garret asked. His shoulders seemed stiffer, his jaw tighter.

"Creature?" David asked, flashing a sideways glance at Trog. "What creature? What's he talking about?"

Trog raised an eyebrow at David and then refocused on Garret. "Yes, I have payment. Now, if we could get going, please?"

Garret nodded. "Sure. Let's go."

From a juncture up ahead came laughter and footsteps.

David swallowed.

Moments later, six boys emerged, and from the looks of it, they were primed for a fight.

David guessed them to be around his age, give or take a year or two, all dressed in leather trousers and earth-toned tunics with knives, rapiers, or swords as their accessories of choice.

A lanky, red-headed boy with sharp features and nervous eyes stepped forward.

"What's the news, Rusty?" Garret asked.

"A-all c-clear from here t-to Windybrooke."

Trog stepped forward, his profile strong and steady. "Did you notice if there were scouts from Hirth in the area?"

Rusty's eyes widened to twice their size. His mouth fell open. "S-Sir T-Trogsdill!" He dropped to one knee, his head bowed. The other five boys gaped as well, awe and disbelief written in their expressions. They, too, dropped to their knees and pledged everything from swords to lives.

David snorted and whispered to Charlotte, "What's up with that? Does he poop golden eggs or something?"

Charlotte shrugged, the cutest look of bafflement on her face.

Trog gestured to the boys to stand. "Good heavens, get up. I am not your king or your God."

Rusty stood and shifted his weight from one foot to the other. "S-sorry, s-sir. W-we m-meant nothing by it."

"I don't care for your apology, boy. I want to know if you've seen scouts."

The boy opened his mouth to speak.

A warning caw of a raven echoed in the hollowness of the passage. David and Charlotte covered their ears against the shrill sound. From another passageway flew a blackbird, its body the size of a hawk, its wings as dark and shiny as oil on a sunny day. It hovered for a moment before morphing into a tall, dark-skinned boy with shaggy, black hair, loose-fitting black clothes, and a scar connecting his lip to his ear.

"Whoa!" David said, his knees almost buckling beneath him. His heart thudded like a scared rabbit. "He just—how did he—"

Garret laughed. "Don't tell me you've never seen a shapeshifter before?" He turned to the newcomer and embraced him. "This is Ravenhawk. He watches the Northern Forest for us and keeps us posted on what's happening out there."

"Us?" David's mind spun. "You mean you're all shapeshifters?"

Garret laughed. "No. Ravenhawk and Rusty are the only two shifters in our group. We're simply a group of orphans, made that way by the Dragon King or his minions, and we're looking for payback. Upstairs, we're gutless and weak. We have to be to survive. Down here, we're warriors waiting for the chance to burn the beast in his fire."

Charlotte chuckled and shook her head. "Wow, did I have you pegged all wrong."

"I guess you have to be careful who you reveal yourselves to, huh?" David asked.

Garret scratched the back of his head. "Let me put it this way. If it wasn't for him," he looked up at Trog, "you wouldn't be here right now."

Trog turned to Ravenhawk, his eyes narrowed. "We haven't heard much news of the realm. Do you know anything of importance?"

"My fellow shifters tell me there are armies en route from the north and east by way of the Brindle Sea and the Antylles River. They think it might be a fortnight before they arrive. As for Hirth, almost everything north of Avaleen is burnt, thanks to the Dragon King. Gyllen still stands, but the king and queen are missing. We've got posts set up all near Berg Castle, but the place is swarming with shadowmorths."

Trog rubbed his chin. "That's a bit problematic. We have to make our way north to Gyllen. What are our best routes?"

"Why the dense paths just east of the Domengarts, west of the Elastine Forest. Not much happening there. Not yet anyway. I'm sure that will change once the giant lizard knows you're there."

"And if we need your help?"

Ravenhawk flashed a huge smile. "To fight alongside you and

262

the knights of Hirth? Are you kidding? That would be the most impressive thing ever."

"Do we have your promise on that?" David asked. The realization that he may not have to fight this battle on his own spurred his confidence. A feeling of power rushed through him, and it felt warm, intense. Good.

"Right, you do," Ravenhawk said.

"Then I'm sure we'll make your acquaintance again in the near future," Trog said.

Ravenhawk folded into a deep bow. "I look forward to it."

"Where are you off to, now?" Garret asked the shifter.

"Off to find a roost and a bit of food suitable for this hungry belly. I'm a bit tired of rats and berries."

David's stomach turned.

"You won't find much better upstairs," Gertie said.

Ravenhawk picked her up and spun her around. "Thank you for the warning, lass." He set her down and waved to everyone. "Parting is always inevitable. Until we meet again."

David snorted as the shifter ran toward the secret entrance to the Inn of the Nesting Owls, leaving them to forage on. "Is he always that screwy?"

"You have no idea," Gertie said with a smile.

***

The tunnels grew steeper, colder, as the hours sloughed away.

Charlotte slipped on some gloves she found in her rucksack and huddled under her cloak. "Brrr, who turned off the heat?" Her teeth chattered.

David pulled his cloak tighter around his body. "I know, right? I wish I had some decent socks and my sneakers. My feet are freezing."

A gust of freezing wind dotted with snow whipped and whistled through the tunnel.

"Stay close," Trog said, flakes of the white stuff clinging to his eyebrows and beard. "It won't be long before we're out of the cold."

More than a day passed when they emerged from a hole in the ground, beneath dead brush, leaves, and fallen trees, and onto a rocky ledge. The land dropped away to their right and formed a deep gully. To the north, small towns nestled into the terraced landscape before being overcome by thick, green forest. To the south, the forest opened to rolling hills, meadows, and lakes. Tulipakar and the Southern Forest.

To the left, an icy path rose to a cliff where few scraggly trees grew from crevices.

"Where are we?" David asked. He sat on a rock, shivering, doing his best to ignore the hunger growling in his gut.

"We are at the top of the Domengart Mountains," Trog said. He reached into his bag and tossed David and Charlotte a couple of bruised apples.

David bit into his right away. Charlotte, however, sat on a log huddled beneath her cloak and tore off the skin with her teeth before spitting it to the ground.

"The entrance to the Doomideen Pass is up ahead beyond the tree line," Trog said.

David followed Trog's gaze through a clump of trees that grew skyward. A gust of wind blew thickening snow into his face. David shivered and stood. He stamped the numbness from his feet and coaxed Charlotte to stand.

"I'm so cold," she said, shivering in his arms.

"I know. We'll get out of the wind and cold soon enough, right, Trog?" David shouted the last two words at the knight standing a few feet away.

Trog's cloak flapped in the wind. Snow swirled at his feet. "Stay close to me. Step where I step."

David clutched Charlotte to him.

A sharp, stabbing pain plunged into his brain like a hot poker. He crumpled to the ground.

"Trog! Help!" Charlotte screamed.

Images of Lily and him as a child flashed with uncanny speed in David's mind, like a slide carousel set to hyper-speed. He pressed his palms to his head. "Oh, God! Make it stop!"

"David!" Trog's voice sounded far away, muffled.

The pain pushed deeper, burning.

Four palms pressed to his head. Images of Agimesh and Taccar appeared in his mind. Soothing, mint-cool winds rushed past the pain, breaking it apart, dissolving the ache into smaller pieces. David counted, sucking deep breaths into his nose and out through his mouth.

But the reprieve was short-lived.

It was back, worse than before, burning, searing, plunging deeper and deeper. A high-pitched whine like a jet engine shrieked through his brain. Threads of black and silver light unraveled like threads of lightning. A man's face appeared. Seyekrad.

No. Go away! David thought. There was no controlling his thrashing body.

Green threads spiraled in his brain like fast-growing ivy, thickening, weaving, and wrapping his mind in cool ribbons of wet moss.

Seyekrad yelled. His face disappeared in a sea of green.

The images faded. The pain dissipated. Hands lifted from his head.

David curled into a fetal position and sobbed.

Charlotte cradled him in her arms, her tears mixing with his. "Shh, it'll be okay. You're all right." Her fingers combed his hair as she rocked him back and forth. "Shh."

"David," Trog said. "Open your eyes and look at me."

"No." He cupped his arms over his head, burying his face in their warmth.

"Agimesh!" Trog shouted. "What happened to him?"

"It was Lord Seyekrad, sir. I sensed he desires something of great importance. Taccar and I placed protective weaves in the boy's mind. You have our word we will shield him the best we can for as long as we are able."

"Understood," Trog said. "Agimesh, carry David. Taccar, carry Lady Charlotte. We need to get out of this blasted cold before we freeze to death."

David took in the surroundings as they trudged upward through the trees and scrub, their heads bent to the snow and wind.

In a slight clearing, the path split—the left trail forked upward through a steep, narrow, rocky passage to the treacherous upper slopes—the other veered to the right, snaking along a snow-covered bluff nestled between two black crags. The path ran the length of the mountain range, sloping downward on the other side, the snow replaced by ever increasing greenery.

Trog pointed to a cave half-hidden by a cluster of giant spruce trees, their boughs blanketed in snow. Offset, exposed roots formed the steps to the entrance. Ravens circled and cawed overhead. A faint yet comforting smell of wood smoke drifted from somewhere deep within the darkness. They stepped inside.

Under Trog's instruction, the two shime set David and Charlotte on their feet.

Dark and damp, David found just enough room to move.

"Keep close to me," Trog said.

Taccar picked up a stick and blew a cool but bright flame into the end, and led them down a narrow passageway.

Charlotte's fingers brushed David's. "Are you okay?"

The worry in her voice tugged at his heart. He squeezed her fingertips, thankful for her touch. "Yeah. I'm good." He wasn't really, but what would be the point of telling her his head now had a forest of vines growing inside of it to block a madman trying to kill him? This connection with Seyekrad was his to bear. The further he could keep Charlotte away from it, the better for her.

They made their way through the spiral vein of the mountain and soon came to an intersection. Trog looked both ways and motioned to their right. The tunnel twisted and wound its way downward, then flat-lined before making a steep ascent. Ahead, golden firelight danced on the wall. The smell of cooked meat woke his hungry gut. Trog drew a finger to his lips, stopping at the passage's opening. A gruff voice sounded from around the corner.

"You can step out of the shadows. I have an excellent sense of smell, and the five of you are about as quiet as a rockslide. Come into the light and tell me why you dare to enter the Den of Amaranthine."

The five companions stepped into the spacious cavern. Charlotte clutched David's arm and pointed to the monstrous shadow on the wall.

Bones crunched beneath their feet. David grimaced. Revulsion bubbled up and unsettled his insides. He forced himself to look at the source of the shadow, a hunched-over beast covered in chestnut fur, stirring the contents of a black kettle.

Trog approached the brute, his stride wide and confident. "We're here to request your assistance."

The beast growled. "You want nothing less than any others who have stepped before me. Why should I grant you audience and not make a meal of you instead?"

"Would you make a meal of an old friend?"

David blinked. His head spun. *Trog is friends with this, this thing?*

There was a flurry of movement. The beast stood upright and whirled around.

Charlotte gasped, and her hand covered her mouth.

David blinked, his body frozen in place.

The animal towered at least a foot above Trog. Bright blue eyes set high and narrow just above a long snout peered out from behind strands of copper brown fur. At the ends of his arms and legs were human hands and feet, not paws. Leather arm braces covered both forearms. Strapped to his chest was a leather bandolier replete with a sling, blowgun, darts, and dagger.

The wereman peered over Trog's shoulder at Charlotte and David. Trog shifted to block his gaze. The animal laughed. "I see you haven't changed a bit, Sir Trogsdill Domnall. Still protecting the weak-spirited."

"Someone has to protect them from the likes of you," Trog said. The two embraced.

David shared a confused look with Charlotte, his heart in his throat.

"It's good to see you, old friend," Trog said. "How have you been?"

"Blasted cold and hungry, that's how I am! There's hardly

anything to eat up here now that the snows have come, but let's not talk about me. It's been months. What brings you this way?"

Trog motioned for David and Charlotte to step forward. "Slavandria sent us to you. She said you could help us across the Doomideen Pass as well as tell us where we can find a mage stone, The Eye of Kedge. Have you heard of it?"

"I never discuss business until I meet my guests. Who are the two tasty morsels with the terrified expressions? Have you bought me a meal for old time's sake?"

Shock coursed through David. Charlotte trembled, her grip tightening on his arm.

Trog laughed. "No, they are not food." He turned around. "David, Charlotte, this is Sir Stephen Kavenaugh, a knight of Fauscher."

"I prefer Groote if you don't mind," the wereman said, "as I'm no longer a knight."

David swallowed. Words formed in his head, but his mouth failed to move.

Groote laughed. Firelight bounced off his yellow fangs. "Look at you two, scared as little field mice. Why?"

"Y-you're very scary," Charlotte said, her voice breaking.

"I'm scary? Have you not looked at your companion lately?" He bobbed his head in Trog's direction and chuckled as he strode across the room and pulled down a handful of wood bowls from a corner shelf. "This man is the most lethal knight ever to live." He returned to the center of the room and started filling bowls. "I may look fierce, but he's the one you have to worry about. Me, I'm straightforward. I'll kill you and eat you. Sir Trogsdill Domnall, on the other hand, likes to play with his food before he devours it."

Trog smiled a real smile. A small laugh escaped his lips.

"Don't scare them any more than they already are, Groote." He took two bowls and handed one each to Charlotte and David. "We still have a long way to travel, and they need to feel safe, not wonder if I'm going to slash them in their sleep."

Alarm flitted in and out of Charlotte's face. She stared at her food.

David guided her to a short and wide stalagmite and helped her to sit. "They're just joking," he said under his breath. "Trog's not going to kill us, and he's not going to let Groote kill us either, okay?"

Charlotte nodded. "I know. It still makes me nervous." She sniffed the food in the bowl and wrinkled her nose. "What is this stuff?"

"Rabbit stew," Groote said, shoveling a handful into his mouth. Liquid dribbled down his chin onto his fur. "It's all I've got. Eat or don't eat it. I don't care."

"D-do you have any utensils?" Charlotte asked.

Groote threw back his head and laughed, the sound rich and boisterous. "Does this look like fine dining at Gyllen Castle, lass? Use your fingers, girl. Get a little dirty. Live on the wild side."

David smiled. He couldn't help it. He glanced down at his bowl, his hungry belly shouting *Do it! Do it!* He brought the bowl to his lips, tipped his head back, and let the warm stew slide into his mouth.

Sweet, tender meat all but melted between his tongue and the roof of his mouth. Potatoes. Carrots. He drank in more, chewing and slurping, slurping and chewing. When done, he wiped his mouth on the sleeve of his shirt and belched, loud and long.

Trog and Groote laughed.

"At least someone likes your food," Trog said.

Charlotte stared at David as if he'd eaten a live cockroach.

"Seriously? Can you get any more disgusting?"

"Can you eat already? We've gotta go."

"Why? What's the hurry?" Charlotte brought her bowl to her lips and sipped the broth. Her head tilted back a bit more.

"I know why Slavandria made us come this way," David explained about the crystals and the key, the Eye of Kedge. "Now, all I need to do is convince Groote to give it to me and then we can be on our way to Hirth."

"I don't have it, boy." Groote rummaged through a cloth bag and tossed a leather flask to Trog. "Here, drink up."

The words strangled all hope out of David's body. "What do you mean you don't have it?"

"Just what I said. I lost it in a battle of wits with a scruffy-haired boy with a sharp-witted tongue," Groote said. "It was a delightful challenge.

The wind expelled out of David's lungs. "No." He shook his head. "There has to be a mistake."

"No mistake, boy. It's gone."

David teetered where he sat. He had to remind himself to breathe. What was he to do now?

Trog uncorked the bottle and sniffed. "Bragsworth whiskey. Where did you get it?" He tipped back the flask.

"Off a stupid fool who thought he didn't have to pay the toll. I assume you brought a toll worthy of the five of you passing?"

Trog snapped his fingers. Agimesh and Taccar stepped forward. "They're yours."

Groote laughed. "Well, I'll be a bug-eyed toad. Where did you get this pair?"

"Slavandria," said Trog, corking the bottle.

"Wait," Charlotte said, setting down her bowl. "You can't give them away. They're not your property to give."

"Settle down, Charlotte." Trog stood, his face drawn. "Slavandria arranged this. She knows what she's doing."

Charlotte crossed her arms and turned her angry eyes on Trog. "You can't trade them. I won't let you."

"You have no say in the matter," Trog said.

"But you know it's wrong! No life is worth the life of another!"

"Charlotte," Trog said through gritted teeth. "Sit down and shut your mouth." His tone carried an edge as sharp as the sword on his hip.

David tugged at her arm. She glared down at him, plopped down and scowled.

Groote's ears twitched. He leaned forward. "If Slavandria is worried enough to send shime, then I smell a battle brewing and a nasty one. Tell me."

Trog launched into a retelling of the last five days. Groote sat and listened.

"It's imperative we make it to Gyllen as soon as possible. I'm sure the toll is sufficient for passing, and if you have some food to spare, we'd appreciate a bit to take with us."

"The toll is more than sufficient," Groote said. He stomped across the room, picked up one of many small leather bags and tossed it to Trog. "There are water flasks, bread, berries, and nuts in there, enough to keep your bellies full. The shapeshifters keep me supplied. My only regret is that I wish I could join you in this fight."

"Why can't you?" David asked.

"Because I will die if I leave the Pass. Avida made sure of that when she hexed me."

"Avida?" The name sent chills through David. "W-why did she hex you?"

"She was bored," Trog said, grinning.

Groote chuckled. "It could have been worse, I suppose."

David's muscles tightened. "Why did she hex you? How powerful is she?"

Groote's nostrils flared. "She's an enchantress. She ensnared me when I discovered what she really was. We were a couple. I tried to end things. She punished me. As you can see, she didn't take kindly to rejection."

"Is there a way to break the spell?" asked David. His arms trembled. His thoughts knocked into one another.

"Only if you kill her, boy. Now, go. All of you." He turned to Trog. "You should reach Palindar by mid-night. There is a small cabin there. Take rest inside for the remainder of the night. I will send someone to you in the morning that can help you get through Einar's territory. Do not be afraid of him. He won't harm you."

Trog pulled a lit torch from the wall. "Thank you, old friend. When this is all over and done, I'll send you some Dalvarians to digest."

Groote licked his chops. "I look forward to it."

Trog adjusted the bag on his back. "Charlotte, David. Let's go."

"Wait," Charlotte walked over to Taccar and Agimesh and wrapped her arms around them. "Thank you for watching over us and protecting us. I think you both are very brave for staying behind."

Agimesh lowered his chin. "No, my lady. It is the three of you who are brave. We shall see you soon. I give you my word."

Groote grunted and kicked a bone. "Enough sentimentality. Get on with it before I throw all of you in my stew."

David adjusted the bow on his back and the sash around his waist and edged Charlotte into the dimly lit tunnel of the Doomideen Pass.

"Now what am I going to do?" he asked. "How am I supposed to find the Eye of Kedge?" *How will I ever get Charlotte home?*

"Find the scruffy-haired boy with the sharp-witted tongue," Charlotte said.

David hitched his bag up higher on his back and pushed himself forward. "How am I supposed to do that?"

Trog snorted. "You're the paladin. Figure it out."

Chapter 23

Rains came to Gyllen strong and hard. Farnsworth roused Eric from bed early and made him join a dozen squires in the tournament hall. Along the walls stood at least two dozen pages, their young faces pale in fear. All of them shifted their weight from side to side, their mouths open like hungry little codfish.

Eric rolled his eyes. He hated runt training. He remembered all too well the abuse he took, not only from the knights but also from the older squires. Now he was in the reverse role, and he longed to be anywhere else than battering puny tadpoles half his age.

The training lasted for hours. Two sprouts were taken to the infirmary with mild cuts to their arms. The others walked away moaning, except for one.

He was a young boy with straggly, honey-colored hair and trousers two sizes too big for him, a rope cinched at his waist to hold them up. He followed Eric into the weapons room like a puppy lost from its mother.

Eric sat on the bench and eyed the stripling out of the corner of his eye.

"What do you want?" he said, removing his sparring armor.

"Nothing."

"Why are you standing there then? Run along."

"I can get you out of here."

A tingle rippled through Eric's veins. "Yeah?" he said, removing his greaves. "What makes you think I want to go somewhere?"

The boy shrugged, his eyes following Eric's every move. "I dunno. I hear stuff."

"What kind of stuff?" Eric set the armor on the shelves.

The boy tilted his chin upward, his eyes as big as a deer's and about as innocent. "Sir Farnsworth and Sir Gowran don't let me do things, either. They say I'm too young to be out there."

Eric smiled. "Let me guess. You don't agree?"

The boy shook his head. "Nope. Sestian taught me how to fight."

Eric froze for a second. He knelt down, his face at eye level with the page. "You knew Sestian?"

The boy nodded. "He was my friend. He said the two of you were going far away on a giant quest. He said you were going to go to make the knights proud of you." He lowered his chin and kicked his foot across the ground. "I want the knights to be proud of you, too." He looked back into Eric's eyes. "Can I help make the knights proud of you?"

"Why would you do such a thing? You would get in so much trouble."

"Sestian said you were going. He's not here anymore, so you have to go without him."

Eric swallowed. He glanced down and away, his hand caught

276

in his hair. "Look. I appreciate what you're doing, but I won't get you in trouble, okay?"

"Then I'll scream."

Eric chuckled. "What?"

The boy closed his eyes, tilted back his head and screamed, the sound wailing through the room.

Eric slapped his hand over the boy's mouth. "What are you doing? Hush!"

The boy shook his head and licked Eric's palm.

"Eww!" Eric yanked back his hand and wiped it on his pants. "What are you doing?"

"Let me help you go, and I won't scream anymore."

"No!" Eric swore under his breath.

Another scream filled the room.

"Okay, okay, stop! I'll go! Are you always this annoying?"

"Farnsworth says I'm the most obnoxious prat he's ever met."

Eric stood and rolled his eyes. "Yes, well, I'm going to have to agree with him on that."

***

Eric followed his new screaming companion across the lower courtyard to the buttery. Inside, they moved to the connecting storage room where Eric stood with his hands on his hips, watching the little imp move boxes out of the way of a wooden door.

Eric stared, his mouth open. He closed it. Pried it open again. How many times had he been in this room and never noticed a secret door?

"W-where does this go?" He couldn't believe he was

considering walking through.

Thunder tumbled. The ground shook.

"Sestian said it was the path to freedom, whatever that means."

"I know what he meant."

Eric pressed his ear to the door and turned the knob.

With his heart pounding like a mouse in the coils of a snake, he stepped inside. The space was narrow. Dark. He waited a moment for his eyes to adjust before continuing. "I can't see anything. Hand me a torch."

The Golden light flickered behind him.

"Wow, that was quick." He turned around.

Farnsworth and Gowran stood against the two walls, their arms crossed over their chests.

"Where are you going, Eric?" Farnsworth said.

Eric blinked and flicked his gaze from the knights to the boy cramped behind Gowran. He flinched. Anger clutched his throat. He set his eyes on the snitch, hoping his gaze would burn a hole in his forehead right between the eyes.

He glanced between the knights. Heat, like hot oil, swashed across his face. "You set me up. You told him to do this."

Farnsworth glared at him. "Where were you going once you got out there?"

Eric spat. "Why don't you tell me? I'm sure your little spy has told you everything."

"What did you and Sestian have planned?"

"Nothing!"

Farnsworth shook his head. "Fine. It's your game. We'll play it your way."

He and Gowran reached for Eric.

Eric dodged their grip, turned and fled into the dark passage. Running.

Running.

Such betrayal. How could he have been so naïve?

He ran a shaky hand across his face, his breathing heavy and uneven.

Must get away. Prove my worth.

Wham!

Eric bounced back and hit the floor with a thud. A match struck the wall.

A torch jumped to life. Crohn's face glowed demon-like before him.

Footsteps approached from behind.

"Come on, Eric," Farnsworth said. "Let's go."

Eric pumped a fist against his forehead. His spirit was squashed.

Farnsworth and Gowran lifted him from the ground and led him back the way they'd come. They didn't release him until they arrived at his suite of rooms.

Eric jerked out of their grasp and watched as Gowran locked the door to Trog's room.

"Why are you doing this?" he asked. "Why are you treating me like a child?"

Gowran paused for a moment and stared at him as if the words he wanted to say would spew out at any moment. Instead, all he said was, "I'm sorry," and left the room.

The door locked.

Eric beat his fist on the door and yelled, "You'll be sorry. All of you will be sorry." He turned and paced, his breaths fast and short. "How dare they treat me this way? I'll show them. I will get out of here and do things they only imagined." He fiddled with the pendant around his neck. "Yes, Sestian, they've pushed me too far. You always said rules were for breaking. I'm going to break every one they put on me, and there's nothing they can do to stop me."

Chapter 24

David and Charlotte straggled behind Trog, their feet so tired they could barely place one before the other. After what seemed to be a gazillion hours, they reached Palindar, a small hamlet nestled deep within a forest glen in the Sankara Mountains. Cold and exhausted, they leaned on one another as Trog roused the proprietor, a spindly old man with bony knees poking out from a dingy nightshirt. With oil lamp in hand, he led them down a narrow dirt path and let them into a small cottage with a thatched roof.

"T'aint much," the old man said. "Kitchen, stove, three beds, but it's comfortable enough."

David made his way to the first bed to his right, dropped his belongings, and collapsed. He never heard the proprietor leave.

***

David woke on the floor, his mattress over his head. He tossed it aside and sat up.

"Good morning, Firefox," Charlotte said, staring down at him from a wooden chair.

David yawned and scratched his head. "Morning." He looked around. "How did I get on the floor?"

Charlotte handed him a bowl of oatmeal and a wooden spoon. "Trog put you there. He's been trying to rouse you for the last twenty minutes. When you didn't respond to his last bellowing, he picked up the mattress and tossed you out."

"Where is he now?" David asked, shoveling the food in his mouth.

Charlotte shrugged. "I don't know. Said he'd be back in a few."

Her eyes scanned him, and she smiled that smile that made him forget everything else in the world. He looked away, his body swimming with feelings so intense they were almost obscene.

"You okay?" she asked.

"Yeah." He stood and walked to the window. Pressing his nose against the cool glass, he closed his eyes, wishing the soft pitter-patter of the raindrops would wash away his need for her.

She touched his shoulder and his body electrified. He needed to turn her power off, but how could he when all he wanted was to take her in his arms and never let her go?

"You sure? Because you're acting like you're sick, and I'm the disease."

He had to look at her. He had to convince her she was not the problem. "I'm sorry, Char. I don't mean to be a jerk; you know that. It's just, I can feel the shime's protections in my head fading. If Seyekrad, Mr. Loudermilk, whatever his name is finds me, he'll kill me. The spells Slavandria gave me are pointless against him.

I'm scared. I don't know what to do."

Charlotte wrapped her arms around his neck. "It's going to be okay, David. He won't find you, but if he does, we'll figure something out. We always do, you and me. Right?"

He held her to him and succumbed to the earthquake she caused which was now rattling his bones. After all, if he was going to die, there was no other place he'd rather be.

The door of the cabin flew open, and Trog stomped inside, rainwater dripping from his cloak. He paused for a moment, staring at David, then he flipped back the hood from his face and winked.

"Good. You're finally awake." He strode to his bed. "Both of you. Get your things." He collected his rucksack. "It's time to go."

***

David pulled his cloak around his shoulders to ward off the chill snapping at his bones. The nightmares still plagued him—Seyekrad and Avida chasing him through the woods, taunting and threatening. Beside him, Trog pressed a hand to his side, wincing as his gaze traversed the path before him. The shadowmorth wound continued to bother him, refusing to heal, and despite Charlotte's care, he walked with a severe limp, the hole in his leg from the bolt now three days old. When it came down to it, it would be interesting to see if this great, powerful knight would still be able to protect him—protect Charlotte, when the time came.

They continued for hours without a break. David shook the ache from his legs. Never in his life had he pushed his muscles the way he had the last several days. What he would give to remove them for just an hour so he didn't have to feel the agony.

Charlotte didn't look much better. She'd cut strips from a bedsheet and layered them in her shoes for padding, but she still limped. Still, she rarely complained. Her focus remained more on Trog and the massive wound in his side that refused to heal.

The wide forest road grew narrower until it turned into nothing more than a grassy path shielded by towering trees. Eventually, the path opened up into a sunny glade, a perfect resting spot.

Trog rationed out some of the bread and berries Groote had given them, and they ate in silence. David's tattoo thrummed, the first time he remembered it doing so in more than a day. He spun the ring on his finger and glanced around, his senses heightened, as if thousands of eyes were watching them. Far off in the distance, a gray object loomed within the tree line. David shielded his eyes with his hand and peered into the forest.

"What is that?" he asked.

Trog walked over to him and followed David's gaze. He spat on the ground. "That's Berg Castle."

Crows cawed and rose into the air. David shivered. Einar's lair. Everything in his body told him to run. He was a sixteen-year-old rich kid from the middle of nowhere. What in the hell did he know about saving kingdoms and protecting heirs and finding magic stones?

"D-do you think he can see us?" David asked.

"Maybe, but let's hope not." He walked away. "You two stay here. I need to," he glanced at Charlotte, "you know … "

He walked into the woods.

Charlotte shared a smile with David. "I suppose I should do the same. Will you be okay for a few minutes?"

Alarms went off. The idea of Charlotte alone in the woods with a dragon not far away squeezed the air from his lungs. Still, he couldn't be with her while she peed. That would be too weird. He bobbed his head. "Sure. Go on. I'll keep an eye out."

Charlotte took off in a different direction from Trog and disappeared into the brush.

David picked up a stick and sliced at a small tender tree. He jabbed, danced, poked, and smacked the sapling over and over again as if it would suddenly rise from the ground and wallop him. Intent in his battering, he didn't hear Trog approach.

"So, tell me, Sir David," Trog said with a chuckle, "what has that young sapling done to deserve such a sound lashing from a well-rounded knight such as yourself?"

David spun around and tossed the stick to the ground. "Nothing." Heat rose to his cheeks.

"Ah, do not say it was nothing, Sir David. From what I saw, it was definitely something. Did you fear the little tree would smite you? Take off your head? Perhaps it stood in the ground in an inappropriate manner?"

"No. I was—" He flushed as Trog lifted an eyebrow. "I-I was—practicing."

Trog folded his arms across his chest and scratched his nose. "Why do I feel as I if I am going to regret this? For what, pray tell, were you practicing?"

"T-to fight—like you." It sounded plausible, at least to him.

"Why would you want to do that?"

David shrugged. "Because."

"Inadequate answer."

David bit his bottom lip and stared at the ground. "I saw the way you fought that guy by the river. You're quick. Light on your feet, like a ninja. That guy didn't stand a chance against you. I

284

want to learn how to do that if I'm going to, you know, protect Charlotte." He lifted his chin until his eyes met Trog's. "I froze, Trog. I stood there like an ass. If I can't protect the person I care most about in the entire universe, how am I going to do what I have to do to make sure I get her home? If I can learn to fight and combine that with my spells, I could kick some serious butt."

Trog frowned. "So *kicking butt* is a top priority for you? Are you exalted, placed in a higher station if you battle well? Is knighthood bestowed upon the one who can best pummel his opponent?"

"Yeah, sort of. In a way. Where we come from, if you're a nobody, and you put a bully on his butt, well, you're not a nobody anymore. You're a hero. You're the kid who fought back and won. People look at you differently. They treat you differently. They treat you with respect."

Trog shook his head. "There is much you need to learn, David. Being knightly is not about fighting. It's more about how not to fight. It is a quest for perfection, a search for a higher and more profound order of life. It is godly and goodly, its very fabric intricately woven by threads of compassion and justice. It is also an ugly business and one that should not be entered into lightly nor glorified."

David nodded and stared at his feet, giving his brain time to process the words.

"With that said," Trog continued, "it's time you learned to use a sword. I should have done this sooner, but time didn't permit it. The time, however, has presented itself."

"But I don't have a weapon."

Trog pulled the sword from his sheath and tossed it to David. "You do now."

The weapon fell to the ground. David struggled to lift it with two hands. His arms trembled beneath its weight. He swung it to the right and the left. "This is insanely wicked."

"And deadly."

David stumbled as he brought the sword to rest at his side, his heart in his throat. "I don't want to kill anyone."

"No one of moral character wants to kill, David. Sometimes, it is inevitable, and we have to deal with our conscience later."

"Wow," Charlotte said, walking into the glade, a smirk on her face. "You'd think one of moral character would find other ways to settle a problem without killing. That way they wouldn't have to deal with their conscience at all."

"Everyone at some point in time must come to terms with their morality, my lady. Even you." He folded his arms across his chest and raised an eyebrow as if challenging her.

She met his look with an equally defiant one. "I would never kill someone." Her tone carried an edge of anger, and it hung sharp in the air. "Do you know how many arguments and wars could be avoided if people just listened and talked things out? But, no." Charlotte drew out the last word in one long syllable. "They have to be big bullies and act like they're all that, and start wars over nothing. It's dumb."

Trog dipped his brow. "So am I to understand if an assassin drew forth from the tree line—attacked David at this very moment—you would negotiate?"

"No. I'd try to stop him, but that is diff—"

"How is it different? How would you try to stop him? By throwing verbal threats? Put forth a plea for his life? You would be dead within seconds, and David would not be far behind. Sometimes, my lady, there is no alternative to a fight nor time to pursue a more docile course."

Charlotte crossed her arms over her chest. "Tell that to my brother. He died fighting a war that wasn't his to fight."

"He died to free people from oppression," David said. It was the first time he'd spoken his mind about the matter. His gaze met hers. He hoped she could see his sincerity, hear the sorrow for her loss in his voice.

Charlotte's fists clenched. Her bottom lip quivered.

Trog nodded. "If what David says is true, your brother died for a very noble cause. Outside of those who part this life by accident or natural cause, the rest of us will either perish in battle because we try to take what does not belong to us, or because we defend or take back what does. It is the way it has been since the beginning of time, and it is the way it shall be until the end of it."

Charlotte looked down and kicked at the ground. "It sounds like you like to fight. That you'll make any excuse to do so."

Trog pressed his hand to David's back and guided him to the center of the glade. "Fighting, for me, is not about whether I like or dislike it. It is about necessity. More times than not, negotiations are futile."

Trog pressed his hands to David's shoulders. "Hold your shoulders back. Stand tall."

David's belly tingled as he followed the knight's orders.

"Grasp the sword with both hands, and hold it in front of you."

David did as instructed, his arm muscles burning under the strain.

"Ready?" Trog asked, walking around him, his hands clasped behind his lower back.

"Yeah, I guess."

"Are you sure?"

Alarms went off in David's head. Something was coming, but what? His arms went rigid. His hands tightened on the hilt. He nodded.

Trog spun to his right and kicked.

"Ouch!" David dropped the sword and grabbed his throbbing wrists. "Shit!"

"Pay attention. Watch me, not the ground or some speck in space." Trog picked up the sword and tossed it to David.

He almost missed the catch.

"Again," Trog said, his brow furrowed, his eyes focused. Steady.

David followed Trog's movements.

Trog smacked him on the back of the head. "Move, David. Circle me. Forget about my kicking you. It's the least of your worries at the moment."

David tightened his grip on the hilt and held the sword in front of him, doing his best to ignore the jolt of pain shooting up his arm. What had he gotten himself into? He wanted to learn to fight, not how to be beaten to death by a guy ten times his size.

"Keep your eyes on mine at all times," Trog said. "Never lose connection with your opponent."

Trog lunged forward. David jumped back. Trog smiled. "Why did you retreat? I'm unarmed. You have the weapon."

"Cause you're going to hit me again."

Trog stood still and rested his hands on his hips. "No, I'm not. Lower your weapon and come here. Let me show you something."

David lowered the weapon and walked up to Trog. The knight pushed David on the shoulders, knocking him to the ground. Behind him, Charlotte laughed.

He got to his feet and shot her a look that could light a wick without a match. She covered her mouth, but the smile lingered in her eyes. No sooner had he risen than an explosion of pain shot through his foot. Trog whacked him in the chest.

David hit the ground again, the sword thunking beside him. He hobbled to his feet. "That wasn't fair, Trog. I wasn't ready!"

Trog smiled. "I wasn't aware as your opponent that I was supposed to announce my attack on you." His smiled changed into a serious expression. "Do you know why I knocked you on the ground?"

David rubbed his hip. "Not really."

"Because you did exactly what I told you not to do. You took your eyes off mine. You can't do that." Trog picked up his sword like it was a stick of cotton candy and returned it to the scabbard. "We'll have to come back to sword training later. Let's see what you can do with your fists."

"What?" David froze in place. "You want me to fight you? You're joking, right?"

"I promise to be gentle." There was mischief in the man's eyes.

David didn't believe him for a second. "Gentle? Like you were with my foot?"

"Precisely." Trog grinned.

"Great." David drew in a deep breath and pulled his left fist up beside his head. He pictured the great boxers he'd watched on television and tried to mimic their steps.

The knight stood still, watching David dance around him. "Lift your left hand. It is what protects your face and head."

David raised his fist.

Trog kicked him in the ribs.

David crumpled to the ground, gasping, and sputtering.

Trog bent over him. "Sorry. Did I forget to tell you to keep your elbows tucked?"

The knight was enjoying this lesson way too much.

David got on all fours and stood. "Yeah," he groaned. "You failed to mention that."

"Well, now you know, so stop wallowing and stand up straight. Look at me."

David winced, his hand pressed to his side. "Wallowing? You just nailed me. That hurt!"

"Were you expecting otherwise? That was barely a tap, nothing compared to what a true opponent would unleash upon you. Let's go again. This time, lift your hands, tuck your elbows."

"I can't," David said. "I think you may have fractured something."

Trog's eyes narrowed. "Your opponent will not care if you are in agony. In fact, it is his desire to inflict as much pain upon you as he can. You must not let him, and if he has, you must not let on he has done so."

"But you're not my opponent."

"I am at this moment, and you'd better listen, for you will never find another who will teach you how to retaliate so well. Lift your fists and fight the pain."

"Come on, David. You can do it," Charlotte said.

David raised his fists to his face.

"That's better," Trog said. "Remember, when an attacker comes for you, your first action is to guard your face, the next, guard your ribs. Draw your elbows into your side, like this."

David copied Trog's stance.

"Good. You want to keep your body low and in line. Move around him, but whatever you do, don't bounce around like a convulsive jackrabbit. That was an embarrassment. The whole idea is to let your opponent wear himself out, not vice versa. Pick your line of sight, never take your eyes off your opponent's, focus on his movements, and stay tight to your form."

"I don't see why it matters, Trog. Odds are, I'm still going to get hit."

Trog shrugged and lowered his arms. "Perhaps, but if you're lucky, your opponent will only strike your shoulders, arms, or hips. Your job is to avoid blows to your face and gut." He put a hand on David's shoulder. "Remember, you are not trying to impress your enemy, but disable him. Your goal is not to kill, unless dire circumstances require it, but to inflict as much pain as possible, so he feels far worse than you do when the bout is over. You want to leave a sore reminder he doesn't want to tangle with you again. Understand?"

David nodded.

"Good. We're done. It's time to get moving."

David inhaled a deep breath and returned to his things. Trog may have thought his hits were taps, but the pain in David's ribs disagreed. Still, he'd learned valuable lessons, and for that he was grateful. He flung his bag and bow on his back. As much as he wanted to learn, he cringed at the idea of another training session.

Charlotte stood in the center of the glade, her face drained of all color, her eyes wide. Her lips trembled as she pointed to something across the glade. "W-what is that?" The terror in her voice was palpable.

David and Trog followed her gaze.

Standing in the sunlight at the edge of the forest was a small, wingless creature with piercing ruby eyes. It stood slightly taller than David; its body compact and muscular. Sunlight glistened off its autumn-iridescent scales. Strange gold and red feathers pressed softly against its neck. Two small, goat-like horns jutted from its square forehead; its sinuous, armored pointed tail swished over the cool grass. It looked like something out of one of David's fantasy role-playing games. The dragon scraped at the ground with its sharp claws and snorted like a bull about to engage in battle. It lowered its head.

David froze.

Trog drew his sword.

Charlotte gasped.

The animal's cold stare fixed on David as the creature broke into a gallop.

Charlotte bolted toward David, who stood planted firmly to the ground, too stunned to move. The creature slid to a stop within feet of him, popping up a trail of divots behind him. The beast cocked its head from side to side, assessing the strangers.

David's heart pounded, his chest rising and falling.

Charlotte shoved him back. "Trog, what is that thing?"

"A dragon," Trog said.

The animal and Trog regarded one another.

David gulped. "W-where did he come from? What does he want?"

"I don't know," Trog said.

"You think he's here to help us?" David reached his hand out toward the dragon.

It rumbled.

Trog yanked back David's arm. "Don't. Let him come to you, if that is his choice."

The dragon eyed Trog and moved closer. It exuded a deep, rhythmic purr then snapped open its feathers and scales in a brilliant display.

"Whoa!" David stumbled backward, catching Charlotte before she tripped and fell.

Trog brought his sword to the front.

The dragon arched his tail over his back.

David's eyes widened as the tip of its tail sparked with electricity. "No!"

ZAP!

A small bolt of lightning shot from the tip of the dragon's tail, hitting Trog square in the chest. The knight collapsed to the ground, his body still as dirt. Charlotte and David dove to his side.

"Trog!" Charlotte touched her fingers to the hole in the shirt, the wound still smoking from the blast. She put her head to his chest. "Oh no. No. No! David, he's not breathing!"

The dragon roared and stomped forward. David and Charlotte scurried away.

It nudged Trog with its snout. Several times, the dragon pushed and prodded the knight before. After several times, Trog groaned, his face twisted with all kinds of hurt.

The dragon pawed at the ground and stepped back.

David and Charlotte crawled to Trog's side.

"Oh my gosh, are you all right?" Charlotte uncorked a flask from her bag and offered it to him.

Trog coughed and hacked and pushed himself up to a hunched over sitting position, his knees drawn to his chest, his head tucked between them. "No, girl, I am not all right! My brain is on fire, and my head is pounding!"

"I'm sorry. I don't know how to help you with that. How to treat a dragon attack doesn't seem to be in my mental list of remedies." Charlotte said.

David clambered to his feet and stomped toward the beast that sat on his haunches like a dog, its head tilted to one side.

"Look what you did! You could have killed him! How dare you! Who do you think you are?"

"David, get back!" Trog said, his demand muffled by his knees.

David pointed a finger at the stout animal. "Don't you ever do that again or I will have to—"

293

Oh, be quiet, will you? There is no need to shout. If he had not drawn his sword, I would not have attacked. Besides, I did him no harm.

"Did him no harm? Look at him! You barreled toward him like you were going to —" David froze for a moment. "Wait. Did you just talk to me?"

The dragon tilted his head straight and said, *Yes,* except David didn't hear the low, modulating voice with his ears. He heard it in his mind.

He pressed his hand to his chest hoping his racing heart wouldn't gallop away. "Whoa! I can hear you in my head." He glanced at Charlotte, a finger pointed at the beast. "I can hear him!"

The dragon snorted. *Goodness, settle down. You're hurting my ears with your caterwauling. There is no need to be so loud. I can hear your thoughts as well as you can hear mine. Makes for much better communications, don't you think? It keeps others from hearing.* His red eyes flitted to the north, toward the castle. A vision of a huge, flying dragon appeared.

David gulped. "Oh, yeah. Right. Him." David formed the words in his mind. *What is your name? Why are you here?*

First things first. Help your friend rise and offer him my apology. Then, bring him and the female to me. There is much to tell you in a short amount of time. Shadows move within the Sankara Mountains and the Northern Forest. Berg no longer sleeps.

David turned to Trog and delivered the message. After a few moments, Trog rose, swayed for a bit, and then approached the dragon. "You tried to kill me. Now you wish for me to accept your apology?"

The animal bowed.

The dragon lifted his head, his eyes on David, and mind-spoke once more.

Please tell Sir Trogsdill I meant him no harm. My name is Mirith, son of Sabara and Maldorth. Slavandria told me of your coming, Paladin of Fallhollow. Groote sent for me, but you left Palindar before I arrived. I've been searching for you since this morning. Please tell Sir Trogsdill who I am. I think he will find it of great interest.

David relayed the information.

Trog's eyes narrowed. "That's the son of Maldorth?" He walked around the creature, his gaze never leaving it. "That's not possible. He looks nothing like his father. He has no wings, and he's too small. He has feathers. No resemblance whatsoever."

"Who's Maldorth?" Charlotte asked.

I take after my mother, a Fendox from Braemar, the dragon continued. *Maldorth murdered her because she failed to produce a proper heir. He'd hoped for a nestling of his stature, one who possessed both his elemental power of fire and my mother's elemental power of ice. But my appearance angered him. He saw me as an abomination and tried to kill me. That's when fate intervened and sent this knight to my rescue. Sir Trogsdill Domnall killed my father and spared my life, for which I am forever grateful.*

"Whoa! What?" David said, facing Trog. His skin prickled with excitement. He wasn't sure what tickled him more—the fact he could talk to a dragon, or that the knight standing before him had slain one. "You killed a dragon?"

"One." Trog's eyes narrowed and he stared at the dragon as if trying to make sense of a long forgotten memory. "You?" he said, approaching the beast. "You were the one hiding in the brush. You were the one who healed me when I thought Maldorth had succeeded in killing me?"

Mirith swished his tail. A purr escaped his body.

David nodded. "He said yes."

The dragon turned and displayed an empty patch on his left

flank where a scale had once been.

"He said his scales hold medicinal properties strong enough to counter the most toxic dragon bane."

Trog knelt and touched his fingers to the scar. "I can only imagine the pain you suffered to save my life. Thank you."

Mirith bowed his head.

"I am confused about something, though." Trog stood and scratched his throat. "If you knew who I am, why did you attack me?"

"He said you were going to attack him," David said. "He couldn't allow it since he had to speak to me."

The dragon nudged the knight's hand with his snout.

"He said he's sorry."

"Sorry, smorry," Charlotte said, her gaze ping-ponging between David, Trog and the dragon. "Will someone please tell me who the heck is Maldorth?"

"Einar's son, for the lack of a better word." Trog's gaze skimmed hers and he walked past.

"Wait," David said. "You killed Einar's son?"

"Oh dear God," Charlotte said. "When were you going to tell us this? Did you not think this was important?" She paced, her hands in her hair. And then she laughed, but the sound didn't reach her eyes. "Oh, man, he must be so pissed at you."

"I'm sure that is an understatement," Trog said. He picked up his things from the ground.

"Still," Charlotte continued, "that doesn't explain why Mirith doesn't talk to you instead of David."

David stared at the ground, Mirith's words loud and clear in his mind. The world pressed in all around him, squeezing him, suffocating him as if he were trapped in an hourglass turned upside down and time was running out. "I know why." He lifted his head and stared into her desperate blue eyes. "Slavandria sent him to me through Groote because I'm the paladin and I need Mirith because he possesses the power to do what only one other living soul can do."

"And what's that?" Charlotte asked.

He hesitated for a second, and then said ...

"He can kill Einar."

Chapter 25

The door to Eric's room opened. A young man entered carrying a tray of breakfast. Farnsworth strolled in behind him and waited for the manservant to leave before closing the door. He lifted the silver dome lid of the tray, nodded as if he approved of the contents, and set the lid aside.

"Come. You need to eat."

"I'm not hungry." Eric turned on his left side, his back to the unwanted visitor.

There was a long, perceptible silence in the room before Farnsworth said, "Suit yourself." He crossed the room and opened the door. "Soldiers from Trent and Doursmouth are arriving," he said, "along with others from Banning and Fauscher. A briefing will take place this evening. You are expected to be in attendance. Make sure you are dressed appropriately."

The door latched behind him. The lock tumbled.

He snorted. *They only want me there to keep an eye on me, not because they recognize my worth.*

Eric stood and walked over to the table, his gut gnawing at the intoxicating smell of cured pork and eggs. Outside, sunshine poured over the courtyards. Horses clomped over the battered cobblestones.

Men spoke.

Children laughed.

Dogs barked.

His heart crumbled a bit more. He was a prisoner, forced into servitude. No one considered his feelings. No one acknowledged his ideas. He was nothing to the knights, especially Farnsworth. Just a rabid dog that needed to be controlled.

He picked up the tray of food, walked to the balcony, and dumped it over the rail.

There. Let the dogs scrounge.

At least they were free to make their own choices.

As it was, he was just a pawn, a piece for those with power to move about at will to suit their needs.

Not anymore.

Time was ticking until Eric broke the chains.

And he couldn't wait to see their faces when he did.

Chapter 26

David mind-spoke with Mirith as they trudged to a secluded path northward toward Hirth. He learned of different kinds of dragons, where they lived, and how many there were all over the world of Estaria, not just the realm of Fallhollow. He learned of all the kingdoms of Fallhollow, starting with Braemar, the land to the west that Einar had burned to the ground. A kingdom once thriving with agriculture, gone, destroyed, doomed to a fiery grave from which it never recovered.

The kingdom of Berg had been ruled by a very brave and compassionate king. Its wealth of rivers and access to the Brindle Sea ensured trade to all kingdoms of Fallhollow. What the king collected in taxes he returned to the farms and river towns, providing equipment and vessels to spur commerce and trade. But Einar took the land and murdered all who opposed him, turning their souls into shadowmorths. Trade ceased except for that which he permitted, and farms fell into weed-encrusted memories. The dragon assumed the throne, taking up residence in Berg Castle as if it were built for him.

In the middle of Braemar and Berg was Hirth, a grand kingdom formed from Braemar and Berg at the end of the last Dragon War. It was the seat of power of all Fallhollow and was ruled by a kind and fair king and queen, beloved by all. People came and went as they pleased. Hirthinians were free to set goals and make their own decisions, to live a life of excellence and prosperity. No other land existed anywhere in the world that came even remotely close to its Utopian existence. It was the envy of all the five realms of Estaria, and the focus of Einar's attention, for of all the lands he set out to conquer, Hirth was the only one that denied him his glory. Coupled with the fact the guy who had killed his son lived there, Einar was apparently in a perpetually bad mood over this.

David considered what all this meant, and his stomach churned. Not only was he responsible for finding a magical stone that had just happened to vanish around the neck of some goon, he needed to keep a sorcerer and an enchantress out of his head while avoiding a dragon the size of Texas.

Yeah. This was going to work out just fine.

A soft, almost silent melodic tune floated into David's ears. He stopped walking, his face lifted to the clouds.

"What's that sound?" Charlotte whispered, linking her fingers in his. He gave them a reassuring squeeze.

"The Elastine Forest," Trog said. "One of Einar's prisons. The bells lure you in. Once inside, there is no escape. You're stuck there until the monster decides what he wants to do with you."

"You're joking, right?" Charlotte's words came out rough. She cleared her throat, uncorked a canteen, and tipped it back.

Trog grunted. "Do I have a smile on my face?" He kept walking.

Charlotte wiped her mouth and looked at David. "He's not joking."

David snorted. "Surprise, surprise."

The path grew narrower and the forest thicker and darker, forcing them into a single file with Trog in the lead and Mirith taking up the rear. By late afternoon the path opened into a round glade covered in green grass and bathed in bright sunlight. Pungent cedar lingered in the air. A waterfall roared in the distance. A stream gurgled off to their left. Across the clearing, the path picked up again amidst fallen trees and underbrush.

Trog unhinged his bags. "We'll rest here for a few minutes. I suggest you take care of your personal business while I get more water. We don't have much farther to go before we reach Hirth.

"That's not much of a path," David said, handing Trog his empty canteen.

"Any path farther east will take us too close to Berg and the shadowmorths. We're safer here." Trog wandered off into the tree line.

Charlotte set her bags down beside a boulder and combed her fingers through her hair. "God, I wish that waterfall was closer. I'd jump into the pool beneath it and never get out until this stench washed off me. I've never felt so gross in my entire life."

David paced back and forth, fists clenched, agitated by the increasing pulses and electrical currents zinging between his ring and tattoo. He bit back the icy-hot sensation of blood speeding through his veins.

Beside him, Mirth roared. He lowered his head and popped open his scales and feathers while growling and pawing at the ground.

"Whoa!" Charlotte said, her eyes wide. "What's wrong with him? Why is he doing that?"

"I don't know! Mirith, what's wrong?"

The dragon's voice yelled in his head. *Seek cover. Now! Hide!*

"Why? What's happening?"

Mirith whipped around, his eyes glowing like hot coals, and lunged at him.

Charlotte yelled for Trog as she ran toward David.

"Get away from him!" she shouted at Mirith.

Trog ran from the trees. "What?"

A massive shadow passed overhead. A brisk wind swept the glade, bending the blades of grass.

Charlotte's face turned to the sky. "Oh … my … God."

Trog ran across the glade, the canteens flying into a thicket. He yanked David and Charlotte by their shirts and shoved. "Go! Both of you!"

David found his feet, his nerve. He grabbed Charlotte's hand, scooped up her bag, and ran. He all but threw her over a fallen tree and ducked down, his heart thud, thud, thudding.

Mirith stood in the middle of the glade, his tail swishing, his neck flared out like that lizard that walks on water.

The hiss of Trog's sword leaving his scabbard rippled through David like fingernails across a chalkboard.

Giant black wings twice as wide as a jumbo jet sliced through the air.

David grabbed his bow and nocked an arrow.

The shadow flew over again.

Whoosh. Whoosh.

"Good, God, did you see the scales on that thing? There's no way your arrow will pierce that armor," Charlotte said, "not unless you strap a bomb on the other end."

She was right. What was he thinking? His little arrow would just piss it off. David lowered his weapon, the scene before him playing out like a dream.

Mirith crouched close to the ground. Trog stood nearby, his sword at his side. Two warriors. Bulging muscles. Both ready to fight, defend, and maybe die.

Charlotte peered up at the sky, her hand shielding her eyes. "Where did he go?

As if in answer, the beast circled again, his massive body blocking out the sun. With wings spread and talons open, he dove downward, grabbing the ground as he landed. Trees cracked from the weight of his wings. Chunks of earth plowed up beneath him.

David sat still, paralyzed. Charlotte said something, but he didn't hear. Nothing existed except for the creature before him.

Was he black? Was he purple? The sheen on his scales hinted at both. He was at least ten stories high, the top of his head looming over the treetops. There was a sawtooth on the tip of his nose, horns on its head, and a mace at the tip of its long tail. Armored ridges framed his amber, snake-like eyes and he smelled of rotten eggs and sewer water. He lowered his neck and opened his mouth, exposing sharp, yellow teeth bigger than Trog.

David tried to take a deep breath, but his lungs failed to expand. His chest grew tight, his throat closed up. He tried to look away, tried to blink, but he couldn't. Charlotte grasped his hand. He could sense her touch, but he couldn't feel it. He focused on the tiny dragon and the knight he'd once thought was bigger than life. Against Einar, they were nothing more than miniscule ants.

You have such little faith, Mirith said. *I may be small, but I have something he doesn't have!*

What is that? David asked, his mind barely able to form the words.

Heart! Mirith said, and with that he turned to his right,

charged toward Trog with his head down, and knocked Trog across the glade into the brush a few feet from David.

Charlotte yelled and scrambled over David. "Trog!"

David broke from his trance and grabbed at Charlotte's leg. "Stay down!"

She kicked at him. "I have to see if he's alright!"

A blast of air, followed by a wall of heat slammed into David. Fire.

The glade was on fire.

David peeked over the log as Mirith expelled a long breathy roar. A ring of ice spread across the ground, covering the field.

Einar screeched and hopped as if the cold burned his talons. He swished his tail and hammered the ice, exploding chunks into the air. His body rumbled, and the vibration traveled over the ground. He careened his long neck in David's direction and opened his mouth. Flames billowed inside his throat.

David scrambled toward Charlotte and muttered the only words that came to mind. *"Ibidem Evanescere."*

A crack of lightning filled the air.

Einar elicited a plaintive cry. He whipped around, rage in his eyes, smoke billowing from his right haunch. Mirith smacked his tail against the ground then arched it over his back like a scorpion ready to strike.

Einar's slit-pupil eyes widened. He opened his mouth. Fire flicked between his teeth.

Another electrifying bolt launched from Mirith's tail across the glade, colliding with Einar's jaw.

The black dragon threw his head back and bellowed, fire blasting into the sky.

Mirith flattened his feathers and quills and spun in circles, spinning so fast his body blurred. All at once, he stopped, opened his mouth, and shot copious amounts of water into the air, dousing the flames. Twice he did this until the flames were gone. Einar danced around the puddles, shrieking, electrical fingers zapping his feet. Mirith poised his tail and shot another bolt into the water at Einar's feet.

The black dragon wailed as the blast lifted him from the ground and blew him backwards.

The ground shook.

David thrust his fist in the air. "Yes!"

Einar flicked his tongue and rolled to his feet. He snapped open his wings and took flight. He hung in the air like a kite, a graceful lump of pure destruction.

David broke the invisibility spell and stood. "Mirith? Are you okay?"

Stay back!

David looked skyward. "What's he doing?"

The black dragon spiraled downward, his wings tucked.

David's breath came in short gasps.

At the tree line, Einar spread his wings and swooped over the glade.

David froze, unable to scream. Unable to do anything.

The beast plucked Mirith from the ground and retreated to the sky.

Anguish seized David, his mind filled with Mirith's fear and pain.

"No." David shook his head, anger filling his core. "No! I won't let you kill him!" He scurried to his bow, nocked an arrow and let it fly.

It bounced off Einar's snout like a feather off a ball.

Einar flung Mirith's limp body to the ground, and turned his gaze on David. Smoke drifted from his nostrils.

Mirith's agony. The fear of life slipping away. David felt it all. He clutched his stomach. Dropped to his knees.

Einar screeched, ascended into the sky and disappeared.

"No." David cried. He got to his feet. Mirith was in pain. So much pain He rolled over the log. "Mirith. Talk to me."

Trog grabbed David around the chest and tossed him into the underbrush. "Wait, you fool."

"He's not moving, Trog! I can't hear him."

"Blast you, boy. Shut up and wait!"

"No. He needs me." *Accelero Silentium!*

David dropped beside Mirith and stroked his neck. "Come on. Talk to me. Please."

Trog ran to him and yanked David up by the collar. "Get out of here!"

"He's not breathing. He's—"

Trog picked David up and threw him into the thicket. "The two of you, get your tails out of here. Go!"

David looked at Mirith, his heart torn. Stay or go. There wasn't time.

Choose.

Einar rose above the trees, the downdraft of his wings stirring up dried leaves and dirt.

David grabbed Charlotte's hand and bolted up the steep forest path. Talons scraped the thick canopy above, raining down branches and leaves.

To the left. To the right. Trog guided them through the falling debris.

Einar soared ahead, circled back around and dove straight for them. Trog grappled David and Charlotte to the ground and rolled out of the way as Einar unfurled his talons and grasped nothing but air.

Trog stood, his right hand pressed to his left side, blood trickling over his fingers. "Go!" Trog yelled. A tree lay across their path. "Jump it! Don't stop!"

Charlotte's eyes opened wide. "Trog! You're bleeding!" She headed toward him.

"No, Charlotte!" Trog stumbled toward her. "He's coming back. You have to go. David! Take her. Get to the Field of Valnor, just over this ridge. He can't hurt you there. Take the Haldorian bridge to Hirth. You'll see Gyllen once you leave the forest. Ask for Farnsworth."

"But you're hurt," Charlotte said. "We can't leave you here. He'll get you!"

"Better me than you, now go!"

"But—"

"Damn it, girl, stop your infernal arguing, and do as I tell you!"

David grabbed her hand, his stare pinned on Trog. "We'll come back for you, I promise."

They ran.

Einar followed, bathing them in shadow.

Charlotte resisted David's pull. She slapped at his wrist and pushed at his arm. "Let go of me! Trog needs me!"

She yanked her arm free and ran back toward Trog.

"Charlotte!"

"Go, David! I have to stay. I'm a healer. I can't leave him to die."

She ran back toward the glen.

Einar roared, switched back and sailed after her.

"No. No, no, no, no!" David yelled. His gaze flicked between the dragon and Charlotte.

One arrow after another whizzed from his bow, He waved his

arms. "Hey! You! Over here! I'm who you want. I'm the paladin. Come get me if you can."

"David, what are you doing?" Trog shouted. "Get the hell out of here!" He pushed Charlotte in David's direction.

David shot an arrow, then another at the massive beast, but they might as well have been foam darts for all the damage they did.

Einar whipped and turned. He soared toward David.

"Yes. Come on! Come get me!"

He ran up the path toward the field of Valnor, then veered to his right into the thick of the forest. He had to get the beast away from Charlotte. He had to give Trog time to get her to safety. Which meant going as far from Hirth as possible.

He ran hard and fast, leaving his chances for freedom far behind, and, as he hoped, Einar followed. David raced through the woods, his legs hurdling him over one obstacle after another. Branches whipped across his arms and face, leaving behind ugly red welts. The forest writhed and twisted around him, confusing his path and sense of direction. His sides hurt, his throat was parched and his lungs emptied of breath. Overhead, Einar kept pace, the rush of his massive wings cutting the stillness of the air; his talons scraping leaves from the trees.

David splashed across a wide stream, stumbled, then pulled himself to his feet; his weak legs somehow propelling him forward. Overhead, a legion of smoke-like creatures streamed from Einar's wings and entered the forest. David looked up. "What in the hell are those?" His pulse raced.

He ran. He could hear them closing in behind them, hissing and hacking their way through the trees. Einar's talons brushed the canopy, snapping the trees. The sound of splintering wood ricocheted throughout the forest. David looked up at the broken branches plummeting toward him.

"Oh, sh—" He took two running steps then slammed to the forest floor, his ankle ensnared by a contorted root. He watched in horror as the huge chunks of trees careened toward him. With a painful cry, he yanked his foot free of his boot and rolled away just as the timbers crashed where he had just been.

David army-crawled into a patch of dense underbrush and curled into a ball on his side, and forced himself to become silent to the forest and everything within it. His ankle throbbed, his head buzzed. Flies landed on his face and arms and feasted on the crusts of blood. Every muscle felt torn and wrenched, and every exposed area of skin began to itch.

David expelled a woeful sigh. *What else could go wrong?* Through the leafy green veil, he could see the moon rising in a purple sky. He heard the screech of an owl and saw the small bird wing its way from the forest just as Einar glided downward and dropped catlike onto his feet in the nearby clearing. Innumerable shadows emerged from the depths of the forest and converged on their master.

David cast himself into invisibility and lay perfectly still as Einar fanned his giant wings then folded them across his spine. Through the thicket, he saw the twin horns jutting goat-like from the dragon's forehead. Silver saliva dripped from the corners of the beast's mouth. Each drop smoked and burned through the layers of ground cover. Einar lowered his head and stretched his neck into the forest's edge, the hot breath from his nostrils snorting and turning the leaves on the forest floor. A deep hum like the purr of a cat rumbled from his belly. He swung his head in David's direction until it hung only inches above David's den, and sniffed.

David held his breath. *Go away, go away.*

Huge talons scratched away at the ground covering and threw it aside.

David closed his eyes, his body trembling so fierce he was sure the ground shook with him.

The last of the ground cover blanketing him, flicked out of the way. Large amber eyes stared down at him, but David's reflection wasn't there.

Invisibility was a wonderful thing.

Well, it would be if not for smell.

Einar sniffed and snorted. His nostrils flared. His mouth opened.

Teeth. So many big, sharp teeth.

David closed his eyes, the words *Accelero Silentium* shouting in his head.

Fanged jaws clamped down on a mouthful of brush where David lay a second before.

Einar snarled and snapped. Stomped and growled. Shadowmorths swarmed everywhere, their clicking and hacking eating away at David's sanity. David pressed his hands to his ears, praying the noise would end soon.

Einar tossed his head back and released a long, single foghorn note. The shadowmorths flocked beneath his wings, and with two flaps, the giant beast took to the night sky.

David tilted his head back.

Relax.

Breathe.

In.

Out.

His body itched. Every square inch of it. A red, itchy rash covered his hands and his bare, swollen, bruised foot. With a few grunts and groans he stood and staggered toward the clearing.

Tired and weak, he fell into the thick, cool grass and stared at the stars.

Off in the distance, a girl screamed.

David jolted straight up.

Overhead, Einar passed before the moon, his talons curled tight. Long, flowing brown hair flipped in the wind. The color of chestnuts on a winter's night.

Charlotte.

David stood and threw rocks at the beast. "No!! Let her go. It's me you want. It's me."

He dropped to his knees as the dragon flew away. His sobs gnarled his gut, turned it inside out.

His name carried across the night sky in a single, long, excruciating note. He crumpled, his hands to his ears, and rocked back and forth. Tears fell. His heart ripped. *Charlotte! No! No!*

Einar disappeared.

David continued to rock.

"Why? Why is she gone? Why didn't Trog protect her? He was supposed to protect her. I was supposed to protect her." He pounded the ground with his fist. "This is all my fault. Why did I hide like a coward?" His sobs choked his words. "I should have let him take me. I should have done what I said I would always do. I should have died for her."

Footsteps approached from behind, but he didn't care. Let whomever it was take him. Punish him. Devour him. Charlotte—his first and only love, his best friend—was gone. Nothing else mattered.

Hands, thin as leaves, pressed his back and forehead. Warmth, peace, gentleness flowed like soothing liquid through his veins. He rolled onto his back and stared into the huge round eyes of a tall being as willowy as a spring sapling and as thin as a playing card. Literally. David blinked, his head pounding as hard as his heart. It had to be a dream.

"Who—what—" David said.

A soothing blackness enveloped him. He never finished his sentence.

***

He woke upon a bed in a moonlit room cluttered with strange items. Braided vines hung from the rafters. Piles of river rocks and unusual stones, talons, and teeth, sat in bowls on weather-beaten shelves. Curious, he reached up and fingered the sloughed reptilian skins that hung like party streamers from the ceiling. A high-backed rocking chair stood in the corner, its seat badly in need of repair. David chuckled at the red-and-black inkblot paintings on the wall, and straightened their tilt. High on the windowsills were jars filled with animal bones and teeth, opal spires and amulets, sat upon the windowsill and stone table.

Who the heck lives here?

David startled upright at the knock on the door. He flung his legs over the edge and sat up as the paper-thin stranger entered carrying a wooden bowl and a mug resembling a short, hollowed out tree branch, complete with knots and leaves. He set them on a nearby round table, along with a lit candle, its yellow wax dripping like tears down its tapered form.

"I have brought you nourishment. I figured you could do with some stickies on your insides. I have drawn you a warm bath. It awaits you at the end of the hall. Fresh clothes are on the chest at the foot of the bed. Take your time. When you are done, come downstairs. We have much to discuss." The stranger turned to leave.

"Wait." David said. "Who are you? What are you?"

The stranger flashed a mouth of paper-flat teeth. "My name is Finnegan Aginagin and I am a sestra, an emissary of the mages. You may call me Finn."

"You're a what?"

"Shh," Finn said. "Eat, bathe, dress, and we'll talk when you come downstairs."

Left alone, David devoured his food and hurried down the hall with undergarments, and shirt and trousers in hand. He slipped into the warmth of the tub, and closed his eyes for a moment as the warmth soaked away the ache of his muscles and the itch of his skin. His mind began to drift away, but a vision of Charlotte clutched in Einar's talons had him launching out of the tub and scrambling into his drawers and pants. Why did he leave her? Why? He pounded his fist against the doorframe, and scurried down the stairs, his arms fighting with the sleeves of his tunic.

He followed the clanging of pots and pans into the kitchen. He stood in the doorway, his mouth open as Finn struggled to remove an enormous gargoyle-looking creature that had managed to wedge itself between the ceiling and the top ledge of the cabinets. At the sight of David, the creature dropped its ears, tucked its tail, and leaped out the open window.

"That's right. Be gone with you, you lazy beast," Finn said, snapping the window closed. "Go catch a snoggot."

David cleared his throat. Finn looked up.

"Ah, there you are. Come, come. Sit for a spell." He pulled a chair from the small table and handed David a cup. "I made some juice. Come. Drink up."

David sat down and stared at the bubbling blue-green liquid.

"Go on, go on. It's not going to kill you. That's the last thing I need is another mess around here to clean up. Just watch for the salamander legs. They tend to stick between the teeth."

David gagged on the bile rising into his throat.

Finn smacked him on the back and laughed. "You're too gullible, boy! Why, there's nothing more in that cup than crushed up mintberries and a spoonful of effervescence to settle that stomach of yours. Now wipe off that sour look and drink up."

David held the cup to his lips, hesitated, and took a sip. It was warm, smooth and sweet. He gulped the rest.

Finn smiled.

"Thank you for saving my life." David pressed his back to the wall. "The way I felt last night, I think I would have let Einar eat me if he'd come back."

"Yes, you were in quite a bad fix, I must say. Got yourself all tangled up with the wrong sort, you did. Trying to be brave by provoking the giant reptilian bat, then blaming yourself for something that weren't your fault. Guilt is a strange bedfellow, and one that needs to be shirked, especially since he'll be back for you. Get you, too, if you aren't careful. Them spells you got, they'll wear you down if you don't know how to use them. They aren't meant for human folk, they're not."

"They're not making me weak. I hesitate. I forget to use them and everything falls apart. My best friend might still be okay if I'd just used my head and my spells instead of trying to be some sort of hero."

"Ah, you're one of those who likes to feel sorry for themselves." Finn smacked the table hard enough to make it teeter. "Well, none of that drollness in my home!" He rummaged through a drawer, creating an awful clatter as knives, forks and other utensils crashed to the floor.

David grimaced at all the noise. "What are you looking for?"

"I'll let you know when I find it." Finn tapped his finger to his lips. "Hmm, where did I put it? Ah, yes. Come, come."

David followed Finn down a skinny hallway to a dark, musty room cluttered with misshapen tables and slanted bookcases. A miniature animal with the body of a giraffe, the stripes of a zebra, and the tail and coloring of an antelope, emerged from behind a stack of papers and walked across a ruler bridging two desks together.

David blinked and rubbed his eyes. *What the hell?*

Finn poked through the scattered papers and books, and then said, "Ah, here." He summoned David to his side. "Do you know what this is?"

David looked at what appeared to be a glorified Etch-A-Sketch without the knobs. He shook his head and said, "No."

Finn cleared a space on the table and laid the object on it. "Look into it. If you concentrate, pictures will form in the medium. That is how I found you."

David glanced at Finn, confused. "You were looking for me?"

Finn nodded.

"Why?"

"Why not?" Finn jabbed his finger on the desk. "Look. Go on."

David stared down at the tool. The ink moved fluidly until he could just make out a girl lying on the ground, tree limbs broken all around her. "Charlotte!" He looked at Finn, wide-eyed. "Where is she? Can you take me there?"

"I could, but it would do you no good. Once in the Elastine Forest, one can never leave."

David's throat dried up. His thoughts twisted in his head. "I don't believe that. There's always a way. I have to try."

"Oh, but you cannot. You have a quest to complete."

David tried to hide his shock. "How do you know about the quest?"

"I'm a sestra, an emissary of the mages."

David shrugged. "And?"

Finn rolled his big eyes. "Think, boy."

"Slavandria?"

Finn clasped his hands as if in prayer. "Ah, his brain functions."

"She sent you to me?"

"In a way, she asked me to watch over you. I saw you in the contraption. What I want to know is why you came to Berg Castle instead of going to Gyllen?"

David narrowed his eyes. "What do you mean? I didn't go to Berg. That would be suicide."

Finn's left eyebrow arched. "Really? Then what do you call that?" He pointed outside the window.

David pressed his nose to the glass and looked up at the soaring dark gray walls of a castle. His heart flipped and flopped. Then flipped and flopped again. *No. It couldn't be.* He turned to Finn, his mouth open. "I don't understand. We're right under his nose. How is that possible?"

"Anything is possible with a bit of magic and a little strategic planning. Now that you are in the shadow of the Dragon King, you need to understand that creature never acts on impulse. Every move is thought out with careful precision. Knowing that, you must study his moves, his strategies, before attacking. Today you stay here. You train with me. Tomorrow, you go into the belly of Berg."

Chapter 27

Eric sat alongside Farnsworth, Crohn, and Gowran upon the dais in the Hall of War. The dozens of knights and officers from the kingdoms of Trent, Doursmouth, and Fauscher sat at three low tables arranged around the perimeter of the room, giving the guest an unobstructed view of their hosts.

Farnsworth stood. "Thank you all for coming in our time of need. I will not waste your time by insulting you with mundane talk. It is evident why you have been summoned. As you saw, much of Gyllen is in ruins, our resources and men are few after Einar's attack five days ago. We need your help if we are to defeat him. Never in the past—"

"Excuse me, Sir Farnsworth," said a fair-haired man, "but I thought this was a closed meeting meant only for those with military authority, not mere squires training to shine boots and fetch his master's piss pot."

Laughter erupted.

Eric's skin burned hot.

Farnsworth leaned forward, his fingertips pressed to the table. "Sir Bainesworth, this is our meeting, not yours. If we wanted to invite the scullery maid, it is our prerogative to do so. If you have an issue with this, you are free to leave. Do you have an issue?"

Bainesworth raised his chalice, his stare locked on Eric. "No," he said with a malicious smirk. "No issue. Please. Forgive my interruption."

Eric's blood bubbled like a hot spring beneath his skin. Such arrogance! If he thought he could get away with it, he'd rip the man's eyes out.

Farnsworth continued. "Never in the past has Gyllen sustained such an attack. Einar planned this well and knew when we would be most vulnerable. Many of our people died that night. Many more will, because of him. And the damage does not stop here at Gyllen or in Hammershire. All villages north of Avaleen are little more than graveyards. Our defenses are weak, vulnerable to another attack, and there *will be* another attack. Once Einar destroys us, there will be no stopping him from coming after you."

A loud murmur ran among the men. Gowran barked for silence. Farnsworth continued. "In the past, we fought side by side, defending prosperity and freedom. I ask you now to stand with Hirth and unite in a common cause. If we do not, all we know will cease to exist and fall to this tyrant. Our women and children will become slaves, and we all know what fate awaits us. Join us, not for the freedom of one kingdom, but for the freedom of Fallhollow!"

A thunderous rumble of voices filled the Hall.

"Sir Farnsworth?" a man shouted from the rear table. "Why is King Gildore not at this council meeting?"

Farnsworth shifted his stance. "Our king and queen are missing. Our intelligence suggests Einar may be holding them prisoner, but this has not been confirmed."

"Indeed. And what of Sir Trogsdill? Where is he?"

"What is your point, Sir—"

"Geoff," the knight replied, standing. "News is that Sir Trogsdill has disappeared and is believed to be involved in a conspiracy against your monarchy, working with Einar to dethrone Gildore."

"That is a lie!" Gowran scrambled to his feet, his chair toppling over behind him. "You dare to grace the halls of this castle as an ally but then spout your poisonous diatribe! It will not be tolerated!"

Geoff took a step forward, his fingers toying with the hilt of his own sword. "Then tell us where Sir Trogsdill is."

Farnsworth stretched his arm across Gowran's chest. "Sir Geoff, while it is common knowledge that many within your own kingdom of Fauscher would use whatever is at their disposal to advance themselves toward the throne, it is not the case in Hirth. It is likely Sir Trogsdill was taken while protecting his king. If you believe the wild rumors, you are no ally of Hirth."

The horn atop the watchtower suspended Sir Geoff's words. Three deep blows announced a visitor. The Hall doors opened, and a young page skidded to a halt beside Farnsworth.

"A traveler, sir," he said. "He arrives on foot and appears to be wounded. I was told to tell you that all of you would want to come to the lower courtyard right away."

"Thank you." Farnsworth gestured for Captain Morant to approach the dais and he issued instructions. He then turned to his audience and said, "Please excuse us for a moment, and kindly remain in this room until our return."

Eric departed with the three knights amidst speculative murmuring. They reached the upper courtyard when a man yelled from below. "It is Sir Trogsdill, my lords! He has returned! He's going to need a surgeon right away!"

Eric bounded down the steps, his heart racing. "What are you waiting for? Get the surgeon!" he shouted at the man who'd announced Trog's arrival. "Hurry!" He rushed to Trog's side, the three knights not far behind.

Fresh blood stained his mentor's shirt.

"You look beaten, my friend," Crohn said, helping Trog to sit on the fountain's edge.

Farnsworth knelt. "It is good to see you. We had begun to fear the worst."

Trog winced.

"Lay him down," Crohn said.

Trog moaned at being moved.

"Hold on, my friend. Help is coming," Farnsworth said.

Trog moved his head from side to side. "David—gone— Einar—took—"

"What's he talking about?" Gowran asked. "Can you hear what he's saying?"

The surgeon arrived in his sleeping gown and set his bag of instruments and medicines on the ledge. "Move out of the way. All of ya!" He cut away Trog's shirt.

"Dragon's breath," Farnsworth gasped. "That's a wound from a shadowmorth's blade."

"Yes, and if I don't stitch it now, he might bleed to death. Eric, find a container and get me some water."

Eric ran to the kitchens and returned a few minutes later, water sloshing over the edge of a copper stew pot.

"For the life of me I don't know how you aren't dead," the

surgeon said, cleaning the site. "You must have friends in the heavens."

The healer pulled implements from his bag and laid them along the fountain's edge. From another bag came crystal vials full of tinctures and strange-colored liquids. He lifted Trog's head. "Drink this. It tastes like piss, but it'll cut the pain."

Trog grimaced as he swallowed the yellow-green liquid.

"Eric, keep his head still, insert this strap into his mouth. I would rather him bite this in half than take off his tongue. Gowran, Farnsworth, hold his arms, Crohn, his feet. Keep him as still as possible." He leaned over Trog. "Are you ready, my friend?"

Trog nodded. "Do it."

The scalpel penetrated Trog's skin. His eyes flew wide. His body tensed. A moan escaped.

The doctor hummed. The knife flashed in his agile hands.

Eric swallowed his dinner for the second time as the doctor sliced down one side of the wound and up the other. Trog's flesh hissed as the contents of the vials met with his skin and cauterized the deepest parts of the lesion. He bit down on the strap, his eyes riddled with pain.

Eighty stitches later, the surgeon applied a poultice and dressed the site. He handed additional tinctures to Eric along with instructions.

"He needs bed rest. If he keeps moving around, he's going to continue opening the wound." The doctor laid a hand on Trog's arm. "How do you feel?"

"Like I've been attacked by a dragon." Trog looked up at the surgeon. "How long do I have to stay in bed?"

The surgeon packed up his things and washed his hands in the copper pot. "Anyone else, I'd say at least a week. You, get at least one night's sleep before you're allowed to save the universe, insomuch as it can be saved." He patted Trog's arm. "Good night, sirs. Eric, you know where to find me if you need me."

The three knights helped Trog sit up.

"You heard the man," Gowran said. "Let's get you in bed."

"Pardon me, sirs." A young officer approached. "I apologize for the interruption, but Sir Bainesworth reminds you he and the others await your presence in the Hall."

"Bainesworth!" Trog shouted. "What is that miserable excuse for a knight doing in Hirth?"

Farnsworth turned to Trog. "We called a meeting to ask for assistance. Bainesworth is Fauscher's grand knight. He is here, along with General Vallen, as our allies."

Trog's eyes widened. "You allowed those two on Gyllen's soil?"

"Our defenses are weak. We need assistance."

"So you invited Bainesworth? He has no allegiance to anyone but himself! Tell me, who else have you called?"

Crohn answered. "The best from Doursmouth, Trent, and Fauscher sit in the Hall."

"Trog, it is imperative you keep your animosity between you and Bainesworth separate," Gowran said. "Fauscher is one of Hirth's staunchest allies. They want nothing more than to see Einar defeated as well."

"Fauscher is ruled by a man absent of senses," Trog stated. "He is almost as crazy as the Dalvarian king."

"Regardless, the prospective combined forces of the four kingdoms amounts to ten thousand, more than enough to engage battle with one dragon."

"Ten thousand is nowhere near enough," Trog growled.

"Then perhaps we should do what Slavandria suggests and bring forth the heir to the throne," Gowran said.

Trog glowered at Gowran. "Eric, get me a shirt. Now! I have a council meeting to attend."

Eric met with Trog and the others on the first floor outside the Hall of War. Trog tore the shirt from Eric's hand, slipped it over his head and stormed through the doors. The room fell silent except for the click of boots across the tiles.

"Well, well, well. Sir Trogsdill." Bainesworth's voice echoed in the hall. "How nice of you to join us. Are you well? You seem ill."

Trog snarled. "You have no idea."

Eric suppressed a grin. *Get him, Trog. Gut him and feed him to the dogs.*

"I must say, in spite of your grand entrance, I'm short of feeling honored by your disheveled presence," Bainesworth quipped. "You know how I hate to wait—especially on the likes of you."

"As if I give a damn about what you hate," Trog said, his expression contemptuous.

"You should. You top my list."

"I'm honored, considering I don't give you a second thought."

Bainesworth's lip twitched at the corner. "Watch your arrogance, Sir Trogsdill. You never know where I'll be lurking."

"Go ahead. Lurk. Your fate waits for you on the tip of my sword. Of this I swear."

Bainesworth chuckled. "I look forward to it."

Eric sneered at the evil dripping from the man's tongue. If only he could somehow find a way to shove it back down his throat.

Farnsworth placed a reassuring hand on Trog's shoulder. "Enough of this bantering. We have enough fighting going on outside these walls. We do not need any within."

Bainesworth and Trog settled back into their chairs.

"I offer my apologies to the rest of you," Farnsworth said. "As I said before, Hirth needs your help. I now open the floor for discussion as it pertains to our common goal and nothing else."

A knight from Doursmouth spoke. "Sir Farnsworth, I am concerned about two things. First, while King Gildore is respected to all corners of Fallhollow, he is not our king. Should we ride with you, what does Hirth offer us for our servitude? Second, my understanding, though only by rumor, is that Hirth wishes for us to enter Berg and attack Einar on his own ground. Einar is not your typical enemy, if there is such a thing. There are dark creatures in Berg that we are ill equipped to fight."

"You have raised valid questions," Farnsworth said. "If it is money you are concerned with, let the concern wane. A handsome sum waits for all who ride with us. As to your second item, yes, we have discussed crossing into Berg and fighting Einar there. Our scouts tell us he has already dispatched much of his army all over Fallhollow, making Berg castle and the surrounding lands more vulnerable to our attack. By the time he realizes our presence, it will take him days to reroute his army."

Bainesworth stood. "I must protest. While I am up for a good battle like the rest of us, I can assure you that a blatant show of force will not have any effect on the beast. He will laugh at your childish ways before he slaughters you."

"What do you suggest, then?" Farnsworth asked, clasping his hands on the table.

"Negotiate, of course. I am sure we can reach some sort of agreement that will satisfy both Einar and our kingdoms."

"So you are saying we should not fight?" Crohn asked.

"I am saying we should play out all of our options first. Look around you. This castle is the ultimate lair for Einar. Offer him some treasures. I'm sure he will listen."

"There is only one treasure Einar wants from Hirth and it is not up for negotiation!" Trog said. "Besides, since when does our enemy ever negotiate anything? Need I remind you that Einar has never negotiated. He never will."

"Perhaps you have not offered the correct item," Bainesworth said with venom dripping from his tongue. "After all, what is the honor of a king's life if not to be given for the kingdom?"

Shouts erupted around the room. Trog banged his fist on the table. "Blast you, Bainesworth! You would sell your soul to the devil if you felt you could live an extra day to torture others! What do you know of honor, of protecting one's homeland, one's family? Einar brought war to our land! With malice he has taken our king and queen. Innocents have died horrible deaths, and you have the audacity to sit here among these hallowed walls and tell us we should negotiate? Einar laughs at us and you want us to talk? How dare you take an honored seat at a table of Hirth and cry out for such seditious acts! We will not negotiate with evil. Never!"

"Then you shall die, Sir Trogsdill, for there will be no victory for Hirth should you invade Berg. If you care about anything, your families, friends, then I would reconsider negotiation."

"Bainesworth," Trog replied coolly, "our castle and our lands lie in ruins awaiting an uncertain future. Our people are dying every day. You do what you wish, but my choice is clear. Talk to me again in the afterlife, for in this life, by my honor, I choose to fight!"

"Then you are a fool."

"So be it. At least I will not be remembered as a coward!" The two glowered at each other. It was Trog who ended any further conversation. He gestured to the soldiers standing by the door. "Bainesworth, remove yourself from this room, from this castle, and from this kingdom, and take your knights and General Vallen with you." More shouts filled the room. "Silence," he yelled, turning his gaze back to Bainesworth. "You and your ilk are not welcome here. Eric, escort this piece of filth from my sight, and ensure that he and his men leave. Have twenty of our army ride with them to border of Trent. Bainesworth, if you return, I will kill you."

"I fail to need your chaperones or threats, Trogsdill," Bainesworth gloated. "We will gladly leave you to your demise."

Eric escorted the twelve Fausherians from the hall. Behind him, a chorus of "ayes" erupted from the Hall.

"Fools," muttered Bainesworth.

Eric bit his tongue, the incident in the cloisters repeating in his head. He would have to tell Trog everything: Bainesworth, the High Council, Seyekrad's threat. But all that could wait until morning. Right now, all that mattered was that Hirth was at war.

Sestian would have been thrilled.

***

Eric woke on the floor of the cathedral's chancel. It wasn't the first time he'd awakened there, but it was the first time without Sestian sprawled out on a pew, snoring. It was one of Ses' favorite places to come when he couldn't sleep, his brain on fire with questions no one could answer, like: Where did the universe come from? What happens after we die? Last night, Eric had questions of his own, questions of war, mortality, why he'd lived and why Sestian died. He woke up with stiff bones, a tingling,

327

an arm that was asleep, and no more answers than he'd had when he arrived.

To his right, a side door opened. A sliver of daylight cut across the ceiling and vanished as the door closed. Eric startled. Panic clouded his consciousness. He counted on his fingers. Dragon's breath! Worship day. The priest, altar boys, and members of the choir would soon arrive. He had to leave. Get dressed. He slithered along on his belly, careful not to make a sound. He froze as Farnsworth's voice reverberated throughout the sanctuary.

"I'm sorry to pull you out of bed so early in the morning, Trog, but I needed to speak with you in private."

Eric crawled beneath a table draped in blue velvet and topped with candleholders, gold bowls, and platters.

"Sounds serious," Trog said, his voice heavy with fatigue.

"It is."

Eric lifted the hem of the fabric. Trog sat on a front pew, his elbows on his knees, his hands clasped together. Farnsworth paced in front of him, his arms folded across his chest. His eyes were worried, his face drawn.

Farnsworth ran his hands over his face and covered his eyes before taking a seat beside Trog. His hands clasped between his knees. "We need to discuss Eric, Trog."

Trog glanced sideways at his friend, his eyes narrowed. "What exactly do we need to discuss?"

Farnsworth closed his eyes. "Sestian. Seyekrad. Secrets."

Secrets? Eric stared at Farnsworth's strong, steady face that suddenly looked ragged. Shaken.

"What's wrong with Sestian?" The concern in Trog's voice matched the emotion in his eyes.

Farnsworth sat forward, his shoulders hunched. "He's dead, Trog." His words quivered. "Another casualty of Einar's senseless attack. Eric was with him when he died." His voice righted itself. "Needless to say, Eric is devastated. Angry. It's a lot to process. Of course, he sees me as a cold bastard with no feelings."

"He's young. This is the first time he's experienced death. We've learned to hide our emotions, and grieve when we're alone. His grief is open. Exposed. His feelings are bruised."

"Yes, well, I fear if he doesn't learn to control them, he will set himself on fire with all the friction he creates."

"You've had altercations?"

"It's almost as if he's putting himself in danger to prove a point, Trog. He even ventured to Avaleen on his own to find this paladin Slavandria summoned. Nearly got himself killed in the process."

Trog lifted his head. His eyes looked worried. "How does he know about the paladin?"

Farnsworth frowned. "I don't know. I never got it out of him, but somehow he and Sestian found out."

Eric tried to read Trog's face, but as always he kept his expression completely neutral. Trog leaned back and crossed one leg over the other. "He probably did it to show us he's worthy, Farnsworth. We have kept him rather sheltered."

Eric nodded. *Yes, you certainly have.*

"Are you defending him?"

Trog shook his head. "No, merely trying to explain his *friction* as you put it. He's seventeen. He wants to feel important, like he's done something to contribute, though I think he'd be highly disappointed if he found the paladin."

"Why do you say that?"

"Because I've been with him the past few days."

Eric's heart almost jumped out of his chest.

"What do you mean you've been with him?" Farnsworth said. "Where is he?"

"I don't know." Trog stood and walked around. "We were separated. I was supposed to bring him here, but you can see how well that worked out."

Farnsworth rubbed his brow. "Wait. I'm confused. How did you and the paladin meet?"

"The morning Einar attacked, Eric and I led Gildore and Mysterie to the passageway to Hammershire, but right as I opened the door, Einar unleashed his shadowmorths. Three attacked us. Eric ran across the courtyard. One shadowmorth followed him." Trog dropped his gaze. Stared at the floor. "I had no choice. I had to protect him, so I did, but when I turned around, the two other shadowmorths had captured Gildore and Mysterie. I grabbed Gildore's leg as the shadowmorth lifted him into the dragon's wings. I was certain Einar would keep me hostage, too, but when a shadowmorth's blade sliced my gut, I fell. The next thing I remember was waking up in Chalisdawn." Trog took a few steps and took several long, deep breaths. "The following morn, Slavandria escorted me to the Elthorian Manor in Tulipakar. She said she had a job for me to do. That's when I met our young paladin, a sixteen year-old scrawny thing named David, and his feisty companion, Charlotte."

Eric swallowed. *The paladin is traveling with a girl? Why?*

"Slavandria put them in my charge and left me with the simple task of bringing them here. But I was injured fighting off Einar, David took off into the woods, and the beast took the girl" He faced Farnsworth and stood perfectly still, like a statue. "I failed them as I failed Gildore and Mysterie. The way I failed Gwyndolyn."

Eric's nerves skittered. Gwyndolyn. The author of the mystery letter in Trog's little box of secrets.

Trog's voice trailed off. He rubbed the back of his neck.

Farnsworth placed a hand on Trog's shoulder. "You can't

blame yourself for what happened. Not then. Not now."

Trog spun around. "I swore to protect them, Farnsworth. I let them down. It seems to be a pattern of late."

"No. The only person you continue to let down is yourself, and I refuse to be a part of the pity brigade. You did your best. That is all anyone can ask of any man."

"My best is not good enough!"

Farnsworth's lips pursed together in a fine line. "I refuse to talk in circles with you. There are bigger issues here. Issues you can no longer ignore."

"What issues?"

Farnsworth placed one hand on his hip, the other he used to cup his chin as if in deep thought.

"Trog, the Council is conducting an inquiry into your involvement with Their Majesties' disappearance. Seyekrad delivered the message himself, stating that the Council has reliable sources that confirm your allegiance with Einar. We know this is a conspiracy, and we know it runs deep. Master Camden, Seyekrad, even Bainesworth are involved."

"What?" Trog's spine tensed, his expression contemptuous.

"It is clear they want to discredit you. Find you guilty of sedition. Get you out of the way so their conclave can claim Hirth. Trust me, I've had plenty of time to think about this and it makes sense. Why else would Seyekrad have made the accord with Gildore all those years ago?"

Eric's mouth dropped open. His mind raced. His heart pounded. *Accord? Gildore conspired with Seyekrad?* The thought was mind-boggling. Inconceivable.

Trog stood there, biting his lip, his eyes dark and angry. His chest heaved in and out.

Farnsworth faced Trog, his back to Eric. "I've gone over it in my head a thousand times. Seyekrad promised to protect Hirth from Einar so long as Gildore promised to keep all heirs and the paladin apart."

"Don't go where I think you're going," Trog warned.

"Trog, you and I both know Gildore didn't break the pact. He would never do that, but Seyekrad would. He wants power. He wants the throne. He always has. If my suspicions are correct, he is the one behind the attacks on Fallhollow. He's the one who forced Jared into summoning the paladin. Think about it."

"I don't want to."

Eric shuddered at the hatred in Trog's voice. Last night's tirade with Bainesworth was nothing compared to the monster lurking behind those green eyes at that moment. He'd never seen Trog in such a state. His insides shook as fear crawled inside of him and made itself at home.

"You have to think about it, Trog. Don't you see? It was a test. If Slavandria summoned the paladin and Einar remained trapped, then his plan would fail. No paladin. No heir. But it didn't fail, Trog. Einar did escape. The spell broke. Seyekrad knows the paladin and the heir exist in Fallhollow, and he will stop at nothing until he discovers who they are." He paused for a moment, and then said, "It's only a matter of time."

Trog shook his head. "No. I won't do it."

"Trog, you must. The secret is killing you, and it certainly isn't biding well with Crohn, Gowran, or me. You have to tell Eric the truth."

Eric's heart thumped so loud he thought it leapt out of his chest and drummed on the floor. He placed a hand on his chest.

Trog spun around. "No! I would rather die than divulge the truth!"

"He has to know, especially now. You can't protect him forever."

Trog pushed away. "No!" he yelled. "I vowed to protect him, Farnsworth! I will not throw him in the pit to be devoured by the wolves!"

"For God's sake, Trog! Think about what I am saying. Your blasted pride will put him in more danger than arming him with the truth. You must tell Eric! You must tell him you are Gildore's brother, that he is the only spoken heir to the throne, and more importantly, you must tell him that he is your son!"

Eric's hiding place flipped over as he stood. The toppings clattered to the floor. He stared at Farnsworth and Trog, his mouth open, his heart racing faster than a rabbit running from a fox.

Everyone in the room froze. Even the air stopped moving. The universe had opened a big, black hole, and it was swallowing Eric.

Trog stared, his mouth open, his face drained of all color. "Eric."

"You're—my—father?" Eric jumped from the platform to the floor.

"Eric, please—" Trog held out his arms.

"You lied to me?" He couldn't reel in the anger, not that he wanted to. "After all the lectures you've given me on honesty, integrity, truthfulness; you lied to me?"

"Eric, please. Let's go somewhere so we can talk about this in private."

"What?" Eric clenched his fists at his sides, trying to stop his entire body from trembling. "We're in a church! Confessing your sins before God isn't private enough?" He pushed past Trog and stormed down the aisle.

Trog grasped his arm. "Eric, listen to me. I am a knight, a father, and the king's brother. I will no longer deny it. I cannot even begin to tell you how impossible it seems at times to harmoniously mingle them together. The choices I made were not easy. It was my duty to protect the kingdom, my brother, and you. I was forced to make a decision I never would have chosen otherwise. Someday, you shall have to do the same."

Eric yanked his arm away. "If deceiving the ones you love is required for the positions of knight, king, or father, then I want nothing to do with any of them!"

"Eric—"

"Leave me alone, you hypocritical liar!"

"Eric, I demand you listen to me!"

"Go to hell!"

Eric barged from the cathedral and ran to the stables, tears streaming down his face. *How could he lie to me! How? After all these years! And what about my father, the man who raised me? What happens now? Is he still my father?* His brain hurt. He needed to leave. Go away.

He flung himself on the bare back of a horse and fled from the castle grounds, over the Haldorian Bridge, toward the Field of Valnor and the Northern Forest, anger and hurt festering more by the minute. He tried to wrap his mind around everything he'd heard, but the deception was so deep. They'd all known— Gildore, Farnsworth, Gowran, and Crohn. They were all in on it.

He listened to the sound of his own pulse beating like a drum in his brain. Trog was his father and Gildore's brother, which made both of them royalty. Princes. Future kings. No matter how many times he repeated the information, his brain kept spitting it out. It didn't register. It was illogical, like telling someone everything you say is a lie. The argument goes round and round with no solution, for if everything you say is a lie then you're really telling the truth, but you can't be telling the truth because everything you say is a lie.

His head hurt. His heart was shattered.

In the distance, a whooshing, hissing sound sped through the forest. Panic seized Eric's body. He knew that sound.

Shadowmorths.

The horse whinnied and reared.

Eric tumbled backward. His body hit the ground, his head slammed into a rock.

Hiss. Hiss.

The sound swarmed around him like an army of flying snakes.

Eric tried to focus on the shapes, but bright, white dots clouded his vision. He gasped for air, but his lungs had closed up shop and run away. The hissing grew louder, rushing around his head.

He scurried back, sucking in short, frantic gasps, praying for air to push the thickening mind fog away.

Appendages, light as air, strong as tempered steel, grabbed for him, their jagged tips grazing his ribs.

Pain, unlike anything he'd ever experienced, ripped through him. A hot knife cutting from the inside out.

Tears drained.

Death knocked.

Too tired to fight, he opened the door.

And let it in.

***

Eric remained still, bare chest hot and wet with perspiration despite the chill in the air.

He forced his eyes open and found himself in a small but comfortable bed tucked in the corner of a one-room cottage.

Dappled sunlight trickled through two windows. Copper pots hung above a hearth where food simmered in an iron kettle over a fire. Across the room stood a rectangular table and two chairs, a silver scabbard occupied by its deadly companion, lay on the tabletop. Beside his bed was a high-backed cane chair. An open book lay upside down beside an oil lamp on the table next to him. A few feet away, the door stood wide open.

Eric struggled to sit up. His ribs protested.

He hit the floor, his arms doing little to break his fall. Footsteps stomped toward him. Large, calloused hands lifted and eased him into soft linens. Eric took a deep breath, and then stared into worried green eyes that seemed to hold the heartache of the universe.

"Y-you?" Eric's bottom lip quivered. "Where am I?" He pawed at his chest, his heart in his throat. "Oh, no! It's gone!"

"Calm down, son." Trog sat down in the chair. He wrung out a wet rag and placed it on Eric's forehead.

"No, you don't understand! I lost Sestian's necklace! I have to find it!"

"Are you talking about this?" Trog pulled the filigreed necklace with the dragon eye center from the nightstand drawer and held it up, the pendant dripping from his fingers.

"Yes!" Eric snatched at it.

Trog reeled it back. "Uh-uh. Not until you tell me where you got it." He crossed his arms over his chest.

"It was in a box of Sestian's things, and I want it back."

Trog shook his head. "I'm afraid I can't do that, Eric. Slavandria needs this. It's—"

"I know. It's a mage stone. The Eye of Kedge. She told us about it when we last saw her."

"Why didn't you give it to her if you knew she was looking for it?"

"Because she didn't ask for it."

Trog stared at him, his green orbs locked on Eric's face. "That is very selfish, Eric, especially when you know how it can alter the course of this war."

Eric stared back. He was done being intimidated, especially by someone who had lied to him his entire life. "Don't lecture me on selfishness, *Father*." The word clung like poison on his tongue. "Sestian left it to me. Therefore it is mine to do with as I wish, so if you don't mind, give it back and do something you never do. Trust me."

Trog considered him for the longest time, all the while brushing his thumb over the smooth eye. After several minutes, he tossed the necklace to Eric. "Give it to Farnsworth when we return to Gyllen, understood?"

Eric caught it and draped the chain around his neck. "Yeah. Sure."

Trog stood and walked to the hearth. "How are you feeling?" He ladled some food into two bowls.

"Fine, except for this ridiculous burning in my ribs."

"You were scratched by a shadowmorth's blade. Not enough to bring blood, but sufficient to cause some discomfort." Trog returned to his chair and sat down, handing Eric one of the bowls. "I used some of the same ointments Charlotte used on my wound. Let me know if they help."

Eric's insides fluttered. There was that name again. Charlotte. So unusual. So beguiling. He shifted in the bed.

"Who is Charlotte?" he asked, trying to sound nonchalant. "Is she a healer of some sort?"

Trog nodded. "Yes, she is. Appointed by Slavandria herself. Why?"

Eric shrugged. "I was curious why a paladin would bring

a girl into battle with him, but if she's a healer, then it makes perfect sense."

"There's more to it," Trog said, taking a bite of food. He motioned to Eric with his fork. "Eat. You need your strength."

Eric tried but there were too many questions, anger, happiness, and confusion, floating around inside of him to even think about food. He set his bowl on the bedside table with only a few bites gone.

"I'm sorry for lashing out at you," he said. "I was—am—so angry you'd lied to me. Why? Why didn't you tell me?"

"There were many times I wanted to, son, but I couldn't. The risk was far too dangerous. If anyone else knew the truth, your life would have been in danger."

"You mean, because of whatever deal King Gildore made with Seyekrad?"

Trog nodded. "Yes."

"But why would the king do such a thing? He's never trusted Seyekrad."

"It's a long story." Trog leaned back and ran his hands through his hair.

"So. Have you got some place you need to be?"

"Don't take that tone with me, Eric."

"Then don't call me son if you have no intentions of treating me like one." Eric crossed his arms and stared at his father.

"Fine," Trog said with a deep, heavy sigh. "It was seventeen years ago. You were a baby, no more than six months old, when we heard rumors of Einar amassing an army so he could attack Hirth. Gildore dispatched several legions to seek proof of such an army. I took five men with me and headed east. Several weeks into the journey, we encountered a dragon in the Northern Forest—a vile creature who resembled Einar right down to his sinewy tail. In a very short time, the black beast managed to slay all five of my men. In the end, the dragon lay dead on the forest floor. By some miracle, I survived, though not without suffering my own wounds."

"The one on your neck and your back," Eric said.

Trog nodded. "Once I regained my strength, I continued my search, eventually meeting up with a small regiment from Doursmouth and Trent. About three months later we discovered the location of two outposts filled with Dalvarian rebels. I returned home to report what I'd discovered. That is when I found out your mother had been murdered."

"Murdered?" The word stuck in his throat like an ice pick. "By who?"

"No one knows, but we suspect Einar sent someone to do what he couldn't. Queen Mysterie found her floating in the fountain. She'd been stabbed through the heart."

Eric swallowed hard, pretending not to feel the anguish caught in his chest for a woman he never knew, a woman he should have known. He stared at his lap and fiddled with the sheet. Poor Trog. His nightly visits to the fountain weren't just sentimental journeys. He was there to pay homage to his wife and the mother of his child. Eric's heart fell into his gut, Trog's drawn face almost unbearable. He knew Trog. He knew him well enough to know he blamed himself for her death. All these years he carried around his own guilt. Guilt for not being there to protect the woman he loved. Guilt for angering a dragon to the point he would seek revenge over the death of his own son.

Blinking back tears that burned to escape, Eric asked, "What was she like, my mother?"

Trog stared at a spot behind his son. "She was unlike any woman I've ever known—beautiful. Spirited." He glanced at Eric and smiled ever so slightly, as if the memory pleased him. "A mirror image of her sister, Mysterie."

Eric's heart almost jumped from his chest. "What! They were twins?" He pushed himself up a little more so he was straight up and down on the bed.

Trog nodded. "Identical."

"Dragon's breath! No wonder you look at the queen like … " Eric caught his words before they flew out of his mouth.

"It's alright, Eric." Trog stood and looked out the window. "It is difficult sometimes to see her and not see Gwyndolyn. In moments of anger or frustration with Gildore, my tongue has been known to slip and call her by her sister's name. She understands. Both of them do."

Silence filled the room except for the crackle of the fire. Sunlight was fading, and a brisk breeze wafted through the open door, carrying with it a hint of rain. Trog closed it and poured a cup of wine.

"Anyway, before my return to Hirth, Gildore received word that a few hundred of Einar's troops were marching their way across Berg toward Hirth. He sent a messenger to Chalisdawn to ask Slavandria for help, but she was gone. Desperate to save his kingdom, Gildore met with Seyekrad. The sorcerer made him an offer. He would place a spell around Gyllen to protect it from an attack by Einar and his shadowmorths. In exchange, Gildore would ensure no heirs to the throne existed within Fallhollow, and that upon his natural death, the throne would revert to Seyekrad. Should the terms break, so would the protections."

"I don't understand? You're the king's brother. You're an heir. I'm an heir." Saying the words out loud still didn't make them real.

Trog leaned against the kitchen table. "Yes, and no. Gildore

340

was barely two years old when I was born. Our mother died giving birth to me, and our father fell ill from grief, but not before he proclaimed me dead as well, or so the story goes. I was taken to live with Gowran's family. For fifteen years, Father lingered in a comatose state, tucked away from the world, not knowing one person from the next."

"Who took care of King Gildore?"

"Father's best friend was Sir Falwyn, Farnsworth's father. Farnsworth was the same age as Gildore so it only made sense to move Falwyn's family into the castle to care for Gildore. Of course, my brother and I grew up knowing the truth, Sir Falwyn made sure of it, but according to royal papers, I was dead. It wasn't until my adoubement ceremony two years after Gildore became king that we dared tell Gowran and Crohn the truth. What I didn't know until a few years ago was that Slavandria and Jared documented our *holy* births (he rolled his eyes at the words) and our official records are stored in the mage vaults in Avaleen. If need be, I could assume the throne without question."

"Wait. Are you telling me that Seyekrad knows who you are?"

"No." Trog sipped his wine and walked over to the hearth. "The documents are locked up tight in Jared's personal vault, protected in ways I can't even fathom."

"But still, you're the king's brother. How could Gildore make the promise to not have any heirs in Hirth when you're obviously here?"

Trog faced Eric. "When you were born, the king and queen still did not have any children. Convinced they would never have any, Gildore appointed you as the heir apparent upon your birth. The ceremony was private and overseen by Jared and his two daughters."

Eric's mouth hung open in shock. "Wait. Jared ordained my

title? Why would he do such a thing?"

"Their sacred Book of Telling requires Hirth to have an heir to the throne at all times. Since I was the official heir to the throne, but didn't want to be, and you were my son, thus third in line, you were appointed, I was removed, and Jared was happy."

"But there was still an heir in the kingdom," Eric said, his eyes pinched in confusion. "Me."

"Yes, but you're also a mage-appointed heir, meaning your identity is kept secret until such day it needs to be revealed. Your presence, however, can be detected with the right kind of magic. Crooked magic, Slavandria called it."

"Crooked magic?"

"Trickery, Eric. You see, according to Gildore, there was another caveat in place. The mages' sacred book states that Jared has the authority to summon the paladin in a time of war. He would then join forces with the heir of Hirth to return stability to the land. However, he couldn't enter Fallhollow unless the heir was present, so, Seyekrad, in his greediness, made sure that didn't happen. In short, Seyekrad got tired of waiting for Gildore to die. He caused enough chaos to force Slavandria to summon the paladin, and waited to see what would happen."

"Wait." Eric winced as he leaned forward, his mouth open. Understanding clicked in. "So when the paladin arrived, it triggered a trace to show up. Seyekrad saw it but he doesn't have a clue who it belongs to?" He laughed. "What a dolt! He must be going insane!" Eric took a deep breath, giving his brain time to absorb everything. After a few moments he chuckled. "So much for the mages not interfering in the lives of men, eh?"

Trog pulled a sour face. "They interfere far more than they will admit."

Silence fell over the cottage. Eric picked up his bowl and

finished his dinner, the story of his life weaving around in his mind. There was still a piece that didn't make sense.

"Sir." Butterflies scurried in his belly. No matter how he tried, he couldn't call Trog *Father*. "Why didn't you raise me as your own?"

Trog scratched his nose and sat forward, his elbows on his knees, his hands clasped together. "The night before I returned home from my skirmish with Maldorth, someone from Einar's camp killed your mother and left a message carved in her arm." He stared at the floor, his jaw tight, his hands clasped so hard his knuckles were white.

Eric gulped. "W-what did the message say?"

Trog's lip twitched. "You killed my son. Yours will be next." Trog stood, his chair scraping across the floor, and walked away. "Of course, Gildore did the only thing he could to keep you safe. He put you in the care of the blacksmith. When I discovered what had happened, I wanted to scoop you in my arms and whisk you away. But I was a knight. I couldn't run. Even if I had, Einar would have hunted us down and killed you." Trog pulled the rectangular table from the wall, and propped his foot on the rung of a chair. He withdrew his sword from his scabbard and examined it, running his fingertips along the sharp, double-edge. "It was the hardest thing I ever did, letting you go. I used to sit by the fountain and watch you play with the other boys. You know, you knew how to wield a stick better than anyone. When you were five, I took you as my page. The rest of the story you know."

Eric smiled, memories of his childhood streaming in his mind. The years with Trog hadn't been that bad. He'd never been beaten. Trog very seldom yelled at him. Of course being on the receiving end of *the look* was far worse than any lashing he could have received. Knowing what he knew now, it made sense for

Trog to be hard on him. He expected more, wanted more, for his son. If only Eric had known sooner.

Thunder rolled closer. The wind whistled through the trees, neither one loud enough to conceal the sound of booted footsteps approaching the rear of the cabin.

Trog held a finger to his lips and approached the door, firelight glinting off his sword. "Stay put," he said as he slid back the bolt and stepped into the night.

Eric tossed off the covers and flung his legs over the edge of the bed, his ribs on fire. Using the chair to steady himself, he took a deep breath and stood. Glancing around, he found his own sword on the shelf above his bed. He grasped the hilt, stifled the moan clogging his throat, and shuffled to the open door.

There was no movement. No sound. He peeked around the doorframe. No Trog. Looking both ways, he stepped onto the narrow porch, the cool night air sweeping over his goose-bumped skin. A rustle sounded in the brush to his left. His heart raced. A rough hand clamped over his mouth.

"I thought I told you to stay put!" Trog whispered in his ear. "Get inside—now!"

Dark figures moved from the shadows of the trees. Human. Their garments were as black as the masks concealing their faces.

Eric squirmed out of Trog's grasp. His face hot, his hand gripped tight to the hilt of his sword. He sensed a presence behind him. He waited, held his breath, then spun and kicked at the intruder's chest.

The assailant flew backwards and crashed to the ground. Behind Eric, swords clashed. He glanced over his shoulder as Trog brought down his weapon, splitting a man's skull clear to his eyes.

Red droplets sprayed Eric's arms and face. Vomit rose in

his throat. He staggered back, leaned over the rail and hurled his dinner. More footsteps approached from behind. A glint of metal flashed out of the corner of his eye. Panic back-flipped in his stomach. *Who were these people?* He ducked as a sword cut the air above his head. Heart thumping, he whirled to his right, and sliced his assailant's neck. Blood spattered across his face. He gagged, fell to his hands and knees, and retched.

Shadows swarmed. A few steps from the porch he could make out the sounds of a struggle, feet shuffling through dirt and brush. He heard agonizing moans, the clanging of swords. Eric lifted his chin as Trog twisted and elbowed a man in the face. Eric winced at the loud, meaty crack.

A foot connected with Eric's side, and he yelled, clutching his ribs. Another blow bashed his chin, sending him sprawling. He coughed. Blood oozed from his mouth in a string of spit.

"Get him inside," a voice said, "and bring that mongrel of a knight, too."

Eric was hoisted to his feet and shoved inside the cabin. He caught himself on the rear wall, and pressed his head to the cold stone, trying to pretend he couldn't feel the pain screaming in his chest. Trog stormed in the room seconds later, his hair wild, his face smeared with blood from a pulped nose and a gash across his forehead. He barged forward, lashing out at the men in his way, and positioned himself before Eric, his weapon raised.

"Step away from the boy!" ordered one of the men. "Drop your weapon! Now!"

Outside, booted footsteps clomped over the wooden planks of the porch. Eric looked up and gulped as a man with blond hair, dressed in black-and-red leathers, crossed the threshold. The men moved aside to let him pass.

"Bainesworth," Trog growled. "I should have known."

The knight smiled. "I always love seeing that stupefied expression on your face when I get the best of you. Now move aside before I order my men to kill you where you stand."

"What?" Trog said. "Are you not man enough to do it yourself?"

Eric flinched and glanced around the room at the twenty or so warriors armed with swords, daggers, and an array of lethal weapons, that could rip their lives away in an instant. Was Trog crazy? What happened to *Don't taunt your enemy?*

Bainesworth shoved Trog. "Get out of my way."

Trog pinned the tip of his sword on Bainesworth's throat. "What is it you want?"

Eric pushed off the wall, his sword at his side.

Bainesworth's gaze shifted from Trog to Eric. "I want your squire."

"You can't have him."

Bainesworth's eyes locked with Trog's. "It wasn't a request."

"Then you will have to kill me first." Trog lunged. Bainesworth twisted, his torso barely escaping Trog's sword.

"Lower your weapons!" Bainesworth shouted to his men. "This miscreant is mine." He drew his sword and brought it down in a sweeping arc, the blade glistening in the firelight.

Trog spun out of the way and kicked, dislodging the weapon from Bainesworth's hands. He lunged and rammed his fist into the browbeater's gut, his own sword clanging to the ground. The two men grappled on the floor like wildcats, rolling, flipping, grunting and growling.

Bainesworth punched Trog's face. The sound reverberated off the walls. "Grab the boy!" he shouted to his men.

Trog grasped Bainesworth around the neck and flung him on the bed, the man's weight shattering the frame. He plucked his sword from the floor and rushed Eric's assailants, disarming them both. Others advanced. Trog picked up a fallen sword, and with a double-handed swing, robbed two men of their heads.

Eric stared, wide-eyed, as one of the heads rolled past him and stopped, its eyes still open and staring up at him. His stomach churned. The room began to tilt. He stumbled back against the wall, needing something to ground him.

The hiss of an arrow sang through the air and lodged in Trog's shoulder. Two more struck him in the chest, propelling him backward. Blood saturated his clothes.

No! Anger spurred inside Eric, fueling what little strength he had left. He stumbled to his feet, grabbed a sword and charged the archer. But his muscles trembled and gave way as he swung, and he fell. A masked ruffian plucked him from the floor and threw him over his shoulder. Through swollen eyes, he saw Trog—his face beaten, his own wounds open and bleeding profusely—propped like a ragdoll against the wall.

Bainesworth wiped the blood from his mouth, knelt down and grasped Trog by his hair. "You have twenty-four hours to deliver the paladin to Einar. Do so and you can have your squire. If you don't, he'll come back to you in pieces." Bainesworth shoved Trog's head against the wall and motioned to the men behind him.

Outside, the cold rain hammered against Eric's naked skin. "Why are you doing this?" he mumbled. "You know he'll never turn over the paladin. Not to anyone."

Bainesworth laughed. "Of course not. But he will seek him out to warn him. When he does, we'll be in the shadows, waiting."

Eric raised his gaze to meet Bainesworth's. "You think too highly of yourself."

"And you talk too much."

The pommel of Bainesworth's sword connected with his face. Out went the moonlight.

Chapter 28

David crouched, invisible, in the brush, mere feet away from a guarded passageway at the base of Berg castle. He didn't want to go into Berg, but he had no choice. Finn had somehow restricted David's movement and now he had the ability to ferry only within the immediate vicinity, leaving no option other than to enter the dragon's lair. Then again, according to Finn, everything David sought lay within the castle walls. David hoped he was right. Otherwise, he was going to end up as a piece of barbecued meat at a dragon cookout.

Finn tapped him on the shoulder, smiled, and ran at the guard by the doorway, buzzing like a swarm of giant bees. The guy ran down the hillside, hands flailing in the air.

Finn opened the door to the castle. David darted from the tree line and crossed the threshold into darkness, adjusted his quiver and bow, and closed the door behind him.

"*Andor.*"

He squatted on the ground in the dark and pulled the tinderbox from his pocket, removing everything except one wax-and-sulfur-tipped spunk Finn had given him. He struck the flint across the steel and after several frustrating attempts, a fire flared. "Finally," he mumbled. He seized the only torch from an iron sconce on the wall and held it to the small flame; the oiled wax caught right away, and the spunk died. He waited a moment for the metal box to cool before placing the items back in his pocket.

David eased along the corridor, sliding his flattened palm along the damp, chilled stone. His booted footsteps tapped against the slate floor, and with every step he took a sense of dread permeated from the walls. The passage twisted and turned several times before coming to an end. An arched wooden door studded with iron bars stood ajar, beckoning him into the blackness beyond. Goosebumps scattered up his arms. His spine prickled as he wiped the sweat from his hands, pulled his knife, and pushed on the door. It swung open on well-oiled hinges.

Whew! Could he get any luckier?

He found the next room to be a large, circular space, void of windows; the air was cold, damp, and thick with a musty odor. Empty shackles hung from the walls. An unadorned door punctuated the wall opposite him. He took a step forward.

Crunch.

He lowered the torch. Scattered about the floor were what looked to be human teeth and skeletal remains of fingers and toes. In the center of the room, a large rat, the size of his foot, lay twitching on the floor while two others twice its size fed off its warm entrails. David gagged and dropped to his knees before puking. A rat scampered toward him and feasted on his vomit.

"Oh, God, that's disgusting." He stumbled to the wall and wiped his mouth onto his sleeve. His throat burned, his eyes watered. Then his torch gave a brief flare and burned itself out.

"Oh, man! You've got to be kidding me!"

He hugged the wall, thankful for its cool embrace, and inched toward the door. David held his breath and listened. The surroundings took on an eerie silence. He continued along the wall until his fingers met with the doorframe. He hesitated, wiped his sweaty palms on his pants, and pushed open the door. A step later he tumbled down an unseen set of steps.

"Ow! Ouch! Umph!"

He landed on his back, his knife and bow inches from his face.

David lay still, afraid to move. His body felt broken, his muscles wrenched and torn. Somewhere in the distance he heard muffled voices. He got on all fours and collected his weapons. A blind search of the landing revealed a handrail and a second set of steps. A shiver ran through him. He inhaled a deep breath and descended into the unknown, the thought of Charlotte's face, her hair, her laughter, driving him on.

The steps spiraled before emptying onto a lantern-lit corridor flanked on both sides by iron cages. The air held a pungent scent of straw and dirt. Up ahead, two men argued over who was going to kill a prisoner.

Heart racing, David whispered, *Ibidem Evanescere*, and moved down the corridor. He stopped just short of the two disheveled guards and studied the layout.

The corridor, flanked on both sides by more cells, continued some distance ahead, coming to an end at a chained door embedded with a small window. To his left, opposite the guards, a set of wooden steps led straight to a tall door, unadorned except for wide bands of iron. Keys dangled from a column at the base of the stairs. To his right, in a cell behind the guards, stood a man shackled at the wrists to the dungeon wall, his forehead planted against the unforgiving stone. His hair, knotted together with sweat and dirt, hung to the top of his bare, broad shoulders. Shredded trousers hung from his hips. Multiple, scabbed, thrash marks crisscrossed over his back, and from the sound of his erratic breathing, he was in a great amount of pain.

An ear-splitting screech sounded from the top of the stairs as the door creaked open. David ducked into the cell across from the prisoner as if doing so would make him less detectable. Two men conversed on the landing above before one strode off and the other descended the steps.

"Kofghan! Get the prisoner to his feet! You two imbeciles—get out!"

Heavy footsteps pounded the steps as the guards fled upstairs. The door shut behind them. The imposing man—about the same age and size as Trog—stepped off the bottom rung and removed his gloves. David gulped, unsure if the red tinge on the man's black clothing and leather armor was there by design or if it was blood.

A gargantuan specimen of a creature, sickly green with freakishly long, pointed ears and wart-like growths all over its face, appeared from the far-reaching corridor of empty prison cells that streamed beyond David's view. He snorted and grumbled obscenities under his breath as he approached.

"Yes, sire."

"Open the door. I wish to have a conversation with our guest."

Kofghan fumbled with the lock then stepped inside and jerked the prisoner around, leaving his chained arms above to twist like a grapevine. The prisoner gasped, but neither screamed nor struggled.

He was an older man, his lean and angular face covered in bruises. Gashes, crusted in blood, crisscrossed his chest like roads on a map. The pair of deep-set blue eyes, however, spoke of wisdom, intelligence and perseverance. They also apparently recognized with loathing the flaxen-haired man before him.

"Bainesworth," the prisoner said. "I thought I smelled your traitorous stench."

"Gildore." Bainesworth placed his gloves on the bench inside the cell. "What a surprise."

David straightened. *Gildore! The king of Hirth? Seriously?*

"I doubt that," Gildore said, his voice rough and scratchy. "Where is my wife?"

"Where else but the Elastine Forest, but let's not concern ourselves with such trivial matters." Bainesworth turned, his palm wrapped around the pommel of his sword. "Where might I find the heir to the throne of Hirth?"

Gildore said nothing.

Bainesworth backhanded his captive's face.

David strangled the yell in his throat as Gildore crumpled.

Kofghan yanked Gildore's head back by the hair. "Ya will ad'ress y'er audience as 'nstructed!"

Gildore snorted. Blood trickled from his mouth. "When you bring me someone worth addressing, then I shall do so."

Bainesworth pulled his sword from its scabbard and pressed its silver tip against Gildore's throat.

"What? Are you going to kill me with my sword?"

"*Your* sword?" He flicked a glance at Kofghan as if looking for confirmation.

"Aye, 'tis the pris'ner's, sire. He 'ad it on 'im w'en 'e arrived."

"Really," Bainesworth said, taking a step back, admiring the weapon. "Remarkable. A true Hirthinian sword forged specifically for its king. No wonder Einar insisted I use it to interrogate you."

Bainesworth pivoted, cutting the air with the blade with the ease and smoothness of slicing a warm fig. The tip of the blade slit Gildore's cheek.

The king winced but volunteered no other sound.

Bainesworth remained poised, his left hand to his side, the tip of the sword pinned to Gildore's throat. "Where is your heir?"

Gildore closed his eyes.

A matching slice appeared on Gildore's other cheek. David flinched. How the king could remain quiet blew him away.

"Hmm." Bainesworth dropped the sword to his side. "I suspected as much. I told Einar you would resist." He shook his head and motioned to Korghan. "Release him."

The shackles opened. Gildore stumbled a few feet forward and collapsed to the hay-covered earthen floor.

Bainesworth flipped Gildore onto his back, and knelt, the sword resting across one knee. "Let's try a different approach, shall we? It has come to Einar's attention that you have betrayed a certain wizard's trust and as such, opened your kingdom to a long, overdue attack by Einar. You alone are responsible for the deaths of your people. Why would you do such a thing?"

"I don't know what you're talking about." Gildore's dry voice grated like sandpaper over a rock.

Bainesworth stood and paced the cell. "Is it not true you accepted Seyekrad's promise to protect Hirth from an attack by Einar so long as you expelled your heirs to the throne?"

"What?"

"And did Seyekrad not explain the pact would be null and void should Slavandria ever summon the paladin, thus revealing the presence of an heir, your heir, within Fallhollow?"

"You're mad, Bainesworth. I have no children."

"Liar!" Bainesworth kicked Gildore in the ribs. "If you know what is best for you, you will cease with this charade and tell me where I can find the heir to Hirth. Where is your son?"

"I—have—no—child."

Bainesworth shoved Gildore's face to the floor. "You obstinate fool! Perhaps you need a bit more persuasion. Kofghan! Fetch the boy!"

The creature lumbered off and returned moments later with a battered boy about David's age and height.

Bainesworth grasped the new prisoner by the back of the neck and shoved his face hard against the bars of Gildore's cell.

Gildore's swollen eyes widened. "Eric!"

"Sire!" Eric's raw, flesh-torn fingers tightened around the bars.

Bainesworth flung him across the corridor into David's cell and locked the door.

Gildore rolled to his knees and stood. "So help me, Bainesworth, if you hurt him in any way—"

Bainesworth pinned Gildore to the wall. "You'll do what? Kill me? Try." With a swift elbow blow to the head, Gildore fell with dead weight to the ground. He didn't move.

Bainesworth sheathed his weapon and collected his gloves. "Kofghan, lock this door. For the next twenty-four hours, you are to guard the dungeon entrance. Do not return until I send for you. Go!"

The creature cursed as he lumbered away and climbed the same steps David had descended earlier. Bainesworth glanced over his shoulder at Gildore, spit, and said, "Fool," before climbing the towering steps. The door above closed and the bolt slid into place.

Downstairs, David said the word, *Andor* in his head, and

materialized inches from his cellmate.

Eric startled and scuttled back. Dark hair hung in strands around his swollen face.

Bruises covered his face, his arms, his torso, and his left shoulder looked funky like it wasn't set in the socket right.

"Shh," David said. "Keep it down before that ape and his pet troll hear you."

Eric used the bars as leverage and struggled to his feet. "Goblin," he said. "His pet goblin." He studied David the way a fox would view a cornered rabbit. "Who are you? How did you get in here?"

"You wouldn't believe me if I told you. Let's just say I'm a friend."

"Really? Who sent you?"

"Slavandria, sort of." David stepped closer, his gaze on the Eric's arm dangling like a limp vine from its socket. "What happened to your arm?"

Eric winced. "Dislocated."

"Ouch. It looks painful."

Eric groaned. "Well, it's certainly not pleasant." He cast David a sideways glance. "What do you want, anyway? Why are you here?"

"I'm searching for something, a necklace, about the size of my fist."

Eric's eyes widened. A tired smile twitched at his bruised lips. A weary laugh trickled out of him. "I don't believe it. You're him. The paladin. You're who I risked my life for." He turned his head to the wall and sighed. "Someone shoot me now."

David stiffened. "How do you know who I am? Who are you?"

Eric pressed his back to the bars. "Eric, squire extraordinaire, or so I'd like to think. Slavandria and Trog told me about you."

David's breathing did a hop and a skip. "Trog? You've seen Trog? Is he okay?"

Eric nodded once. "He's been better. He's angry about what happened to you and your friend. He blames himself, of course."

David hung his head. "He shouldn't. It was my fault what happened." He looked at Eric. "I can fix it, though, but I need to find the necklace and give it to someone named Farnsworth. Then I can search for my friend."

Eric clung to the bars of his cage. "What if I told you I can help you find the necklace? Can you get me out of here?"

David's breath hitched. "Do you know where it is?"

Eric closed his eyes; his face contorted in pain. "Bainesworth took it, and since it wasn't around his traitorous neck, I would assume it's upstairs somewhere."

"Can you get upstairs?"

"What's in it for me?"

David shrugged. "I don't know. Fame. Glory. Knowing you did something to save mankind?"

Eric winced as he adjusted his position. Here it was, the chance to prove himself to Trog. Somehow it didn't seem to be such a top priority anymore. Still, if the boy could get him out of the castle, he could get help for Trog. Get him back to the castle to have his wounds cared for, that is if he wasn't already dead.

"How good are you with those magic spells?"

David rubbed his nose. "I know them well enough to steal back what I need and to get us out of here."

"Do it, Eric." Gildore's voice cut through the stale air. "But fix that shoulder first." The king groaned as he stood. "Come here, boy. Get me out of this cage."

David incanted himself out of the cell and, using the key

from the wall, opened the cell and released the king of Hirth.

Gildore patted him on the arm. "Thank you, young man. What is your name?"

"David, sir."

"It is a pleasure to make your acquaintance." He stood before Eric's cell. "Open this door, please."

David did as asked. The king approached Eric, and examined his shoulder. "Where did you last see Trog?"

Eric relayed the events at the cottage. When done, Eric looked at the king and said, "He told me about what happened after I was born."

"Everything?" Gildore said.

Eric nodded.

"Good. It's about time. Now let's see what we can do to pop that shoulder back in place." He turned to David. "We'll need your sash."

Alarms ping-ponged all over David. *Do not remove the sash*, Slavandria had said. He shook his head. "Sorry, I can't." He removed his shirt. "You can borrow this if you want."

"That will work."

He handed it to Eric who teetered on his feet for a second before putting a sleeve in his mouth. He studied the solid wall in front of him as if it was a mountain and he was standing on the precipice waiting to jump.

"Steady yourself," Gildore said. "The initial blow will howl through you, but then it will be over." He patted Eric on the back. "You can do this."

David's eyes darted between Eric and Gildore. "W-what's he going to do?"

"I'm going to set my arm." Eric took a deep breath, steeled himself, then ran forward, twisting his body at the last minute.

His shoulder slammed full force into the unforgiving stone.

Crack!

David squinted his eyes shut, the thought of what just happened paining his own shoulder.

An almost inhuman, guttural cry sounded from behind the lump of cloth. Eric dropped to the hay floor, rocking back and forth with tears rolling off his chin. He spit the cloth out of his mouth and cradled his arm while muttering a string of cuss words.

David took his shirt back from Gildore, and pulled the fabric over his head. His nose wrinkled at the wetness in the sleeve. *This is so, so gross.*

"Are you better?" Gildore asked. "Can you help David?"

Eric nodded. "Yes, I think so."

"Good. While you're up there, find my sword and bring it back. I swear it will be the last time anyone uses my own weapon against me."

Eric smirked. "Trust me. I plan to bring back as many weapons as I can carry." He looked at David, a sly grin working its way to his lips. "Are you ready to work some magic?"

A rat squeaked and scurried along the edge of the wall. David sucked in a breath and steeled his nerves. "Ready as I'll ever be."

Chapter 29

Eric studied the steep steps, the wooden door at the top lost in the shadows. He wiped his sweaty palms on his trousers.

"This will be interesting."

"Why?" David asked. The hesitation plucked his nerves. "What are you thinking?"

"That door is sure to be guarded. Even if we do get past the sentries, I fear we won't last long. I'm sure that beast knows every scent, every sound in this castle and in the forest around it. He'll detect us right away, regardless of your skills."

David snorted. "If that were true, I wouldn't still be talking to you, would I?"

Eric stared at David, his mouth empty of a retort.

"Yeah," David grinned. "That's what I thought." David began to climb the steps. He glanced over his shoulder. "Are you coming or are you going to stay behind and let me take all the glory?"

"Don't get cocky," Gildore said. "You may have the power to

pop in and out of rooms, but you're not exactly built for combat."

David rolled his eyes. "Yeah, so everyone keeps telling me."

Eric climbed the stairs, wincing with each step. "You heard the man. Let's go, magic boy."

David scowled. "Don't call me that."

"Why? That is what you are, right? All bang and no pow."

"Screw you." David ascended the stairs. At the top, he pressed his ear to the door and listened.

"Well?" Eric asked. "Are we alone in the universe?"

"Will you shut up!" David whispered. "I can't hear anything with your mouth running."

He continued to listen. Hearing nothing, he lightly tapped on the door.

"Oh, that's good," Eric said. "Alert them to the fact that we're behind the door." He tapped his forefinger to his head. "Smart."

David glowered at Eric, his fingers balled into fists, his lips curled up in a snarl. He wanted nothing more than to knock the smug look from this jerk's face, but that would solve nothing. He wasn't worth it. Bullies never were. He exhaled, drew back his anger, and put his ear back to the door. Convinced there was no one on the other side, he gave the door a push, but it didn't move.

"It's locked, imbecile," Eric said.

"Nah. You think? And do me a favor when you talk. Face the other way. Your breath smells like a rat crawled in it and died."

"And I guess yours smells like jasmine in springtime? Now, are you going to open the door or not?"

"Yeah, I'll open it. I just have to remember how."

"You're a magician. Can't you do a simple trick like open a door?"

"I'm not a magician!"

"Well, it's about time you admitted it."

David groaned. "God, do you ever shut up!" He squeezed his eyes shut trying to remember the words Finn had taught him. After a few minutes he snapped his fingers, placed his hands on the door and said, "*Tradoreo.*"

He passed through the door like a ghost and shivered. "Whoa, that was freaky."

"Hey, Mister I'm-not-a-magician," Eric said. "You want to open the door?"

Not really. David shook his arms and legs, ridding them of the remnants of the incantation, then slid back the bolt and released the hound.

Eric's gazed traveled up and down David's body as he crossed the threshold. "I'm not even going to ask how you did that." He glanced around, bolting the door behind him. "Well, this is interesting. A tower."

Holding onto the rail, Eric climbed the winding stone stairs. Sunlight filtered through dusty windows. Somewhere high above, a door screeched open.

"Crap!" David whispered to Eric. "We're going invisible. Don't talk." He grabbed Eric's arm and muttered, *Ibidem Evanescere!*

Footsteps pounded the stairs. A looming shadow appeared on the wall. They pressed their backs to the wall as a guard passed by. He tested the door, gave a final look around and went back the way he came. The door closed and the stairwell returned to blissful silence.

David sighed and said, "*Andor.*"

Eric doubled over at the waist, gagging like a finger had been shoved down his throat. "Please tell me we won't have to do that again." He staggered up the steps. "I don't think I can take it."

David laughed. "Having trouble with that one, are we? Wait

until I have to transport you."

At the top of the stairs, David pressed his ear to the door. "There's something out there," he whispered, his heart racing, "but I can't make out what it is."

"Move. Let me listen." Eric pressed the side of his face to the door and covered his other ear. "Sounds like the kennels at dinner time."

"What do you think it is?"

"I don't know, a dragon maybe?"

A fist tightened around David's lungs.

Eric continued. "The only way you're going to find out is to do that walking through door thing."

The knot in David's stomach tugged tighter. "Easy for you to say. You haven't come face-to-face with that thing."

"No?" Eric said, his brows drawn together. "See this gash on my back?" He twisted so David could see "That's where Einar tried to pluck me from my horse. See this scrape on my ribs? That's where a shadowmorth's blade grazed me. Trust me. I know what that beast is capable of."

David swallowed, and looked away from Eric's torso covered in shades of purple and blue. How the kid managed to walk around baffled his brain. He ran a shaky hand across his face.

"Okay. I'll pop over to the other side, see what's there, then I'll come back to get you." David sucked in a deep breath, made himself invisible, and walked through the door.

David wasn't quite sure what happened next, whether it was the burning of his ring, the intense thrumming of his tattoo, or the cinching of the sash around his waist, almost to the point of pain. One thing was certain—they were all warning him of the big, black dragon sprawled on a stash of jewels no more than fifty feet away from him, chowing down on a pile of dead animals.

David stifled his urgency to run, to escape the horror nipping at his limbs. The beast was freaking huge, like *oh my God, holy shit* big. If he sat straight up, his head would burst through the frescoed ceiling, which rose so high up, it probably touched the sky. The dragon's body took up a colossal portion of the room, as well as two others, the walls once dividing them reduced to rubble.

Einar scooped up a mouthful of food and tossed back his head and swallowed. A shiver rippled through David. *That'll be me if I'm not careful.*

He stepped to his left, toward the long, wide hallway that led into infinity. *How freaking big is this place?*

Einar shifted and whipped his head around. David froze. The monstrosity's nostrils flared. His amber eyes sharpened. His jawline tightened. A rumble from somewhere deep within his belly vibrated the floor. The dangerous, terrifying animal craned its neck, and keeping it low to the ground, sniffed like a dog for a treat.

David stood petrified as the dragon's head came closer and closer. Puffs of smoke drifted from Einar's snoot. David threw a hand over his mouth and nose. The toxic smell of rotten eggs gagged his stomach, burned his eyes. He wanted to cry, run, dart to the dungeons for fresh air, until he saw it, the Eye of Kedge, dangling from the hilt of a sword sticking out of a floor vase. But how was he to get it? The vase sat between two jeweled thrones that rested on a dais behind a pile of jewels.

Behind Einar.

David's heart pounded, the enormous dragon eye blinking not more than two arm's lengths away. He pressed every inch of himself to the wall, too paralyzed to move. He held his breath. *Go away. Please go away.*

The dragon snorted and shot out a baby flame big enough to

set a small house on fire. Sweat exploded all over David's body. His throat closed. His lungs screamed for air. He bit his lip and shut his eyes. If he was going to die, he didn't want to see it happen.

A rustle from the mound and David's eyes sprang open. Einar scooped up another heaping mound of food and swallowed.

David ordered his body to move, to flee back into the tower.

He spoke the spell in his head, coughed with his mouth closed, the sound muffled by his sleeve, tears streaming down. He reappeared in the tower and held up his hand to Eric. "Don't talk." His voice came out as a raspy whisper. "Einar. In there." He pointed to the door.

"What?" Eric stared, unblinking, his chest rising and falling.

Taking a steadying breath, David whispered the layout of the room as well as certain items of interest. "I can't get them on my own. We need a distraction, which means you and I will have to go invisible again, and I'll have to drag you through a solid wood door. Thing is, you can't get sick. You can't make a sound no matter how much you want to puke." David removed his boots.

"You don't worry about that," Eric said. "All you need to do is get me in there. I'll take care of the rest."

David wiped the sweat from his brow and shook the nervousness from his hands.

Breathe in. Out. In. Calm. Exhale. Peace, except for the glob of nerves that refused to move no matter how many times he swallowed.

"Okay, wingman," David said. "Let's fly."

***

David and Eric materialized behind the velvet drapes framing the thrones. David clamped his hand over Eric's mouth.

Eric clawed at David's arm. *Get off of me!* he mouthed. He dismissed David with a swish of his hand. "Go. What are you waiting for?" he whispered.

David gritted his teeth and stepped out from behind the drapes, still shrouded in invisibility. Eric, however, was as visible as a deer in headlights. David gulped and crept forward.

Einar lifted his head from beneath his wing and sniffed the air.

David froze. Did he put off some sort of odor that Einar sensed?

Einar raked his tail across wood and jewels. He rose to all fours, his nostrils flaring. The floor vibrated. The walls shook. The dragon brought his long neck around, his enormous head within feet of David. His amber cat-like eyes blinked. His mouth opened.

Crap! Fireball!

David spotted an alcove a football field away.

Accelero Sil—

"A-choo!"

No! David's heart thumped against his chest. *Please tell me Eric did not just sneeze!*

Einar pivoted all the way around and roared, the sound so high and sharp it could cut glass. The dragon ripped the drapes from the wall, the fabric stuck to his talons.

Shit. This was so not in the plan.

David shed his invisibility, picked up a nearby vase and threw it at the beast. The dragon whipped around.

David ran. "Come on, you overgrown lizard. Come get me!"

Einar bounded from his bed, and then looked behind him at

the sword. He belly-flopped and curled his tail around the vase.

"Oh, no, you don't!" David yelled, nocking an arrow. "Get off your lazy ass! Don't you know who I am? I'm the paladin, you foul-smelling winged bat."

The arrow sailed into Einar's thigh.

The beast bellowed and thundered toward David.

David ran. "It's all yours, Eric!"

Boom! Boom! Boom!

Earthquake.

David zigzagged past broken columns and shards of marble no longer fixed to the walls. Einar followed, the ceiling raining plaster dust. And there was fire. Lots of fire.

David rolled into a massive two-story room stuffed with carved furniture and thousands of books, and snuffed the flames on his trousers. Huge doors punctuated the walls to the right and left.

Which way do I go?

The doorway exploded, along with the entire wall, as Einar burst through.

David plowed through the door to his right, heading back toward Eric.

Einar screeched. Heavy stones shattered and crashed in the hallway. Walls behind him fell. David flicked a hurried glance over his shoulder. Einar was right behind, and a huge fireball hung in his throat, ready for launch.

Accelero Silentium! He crammed into Eric.

The Eye of Kedge hung from Eric's neck. Gildore's sword in his hand.

"Hold on!" David grabbed Eric's sleeve. *Accelero Silentium!*

They tumbled into the cell with Gildore, weapons clanging around them. Upstairs, Einar wailed and stomped. Dust fell from the ceiling in the dungeon.

Andor!

David staggered to his feet. Sweat poured from his brow. "We have to go. Now!"

Eric tossed Gildore his sword.

High-pitched screams filled the tower.

"Shadowmorths!" Eric said. "Get us out of here!"

David grabbed Eric and Gildore's arms.

Wisps of smoke appeared at the top of the stairs.

Ibidem Evanescere! Accelero Silentium!

They jerked forward like fish caught in the gut by an invisible hook and slammed into the moist forest ground where David last saw Charlotte and Trog.

Gildore puked.

Eric grasped David's shoulders. "Don't ever do that again!"

"They're coming!" David said. "Where do we go?"

Eric wiped the sweat from his brow. "There!" He pointed to an open field at the end of the path. "The Field of Valnor. Einar can't touch us there!"

David grasped Eric and the king. "Hold on! *Accelero Silentium!*"

Air whipped by in a roar. They slammed into the ground, rolling and tumbling over rocks hidden in the green grass.

A swarm of shadowmorths massed around them, thick like bees swirling and hissing and hacking.

Icy hot electrical bursts surged from David's ring through his veins to his tattoo. The sash tightened. A dome of pulsing energy formed around the field, a membrane of air and electrical currents.

Zap!

Zap!

The shadowmorths popped like mosquitoes on a bug zapper. Their bodies disintegrated into vapor and disappeared.

Einar screamed in tortured agony, the guttural sound thrummed the trees, like plucked strings on tree trunks. More shadowmorths hissed and snarled through the forest, rapidly approaching from the south and east.

Soldiers, clad in black leather armor from head to foot, emerged from the trees. Horses pounded the ground. Trolls lumbered along the outer flanks, backhanding trees, flinging them in the air like toothpicks.

Gildore stood. His scabbed lashings oozed droplets of blood over a skin covered with bruises. He limped forward, his jaw tight, his eyes unsettled. "There must be a hundred of them. David, take us to Gyllen."

David stared at the encroaching forces, panic doing backflips in his belly. "I-I can't. I can only transport us to places I can see or where I've been."

Shadowmorths swarmed overhead, their forms darkening the sky. The cacophony of their hissing and screeching grew louder, penetrating.

"We'll be safe here, sir," Eric said. "We're in mage territory."

"We're only safe from the dragon and his minions, not from them." Gildore nodded toward the soldiers marching toward them. "David, get us to that bridge!"

He pointed to a stone crossing near a huge waterfall.

"Yes, sir!" He grabbed the king and Eric. "*Accelero Silentium!*"

Nothing.

He spoke the incantation again.

Still nothing.

Panic infiltrated every pore. *No. This can't be happening! Not now!*

He ran through the gamut of spells he knew to see if any of them worked.

Nothing.

He gulped, his breathing coming in short bursts. "I can't get any spells to work. I don't understand."

"Of course," Eric said, his teeth gritted. "It's mage territory. You can't use magic here. It's protected! We'll have to run for it!"

A line of soldiers on foot broke into a run toward them.

Gildore yelled in agony.

The painful cry ripped through David. He turned, his gaze pinned by the dagger stuck in the king's thigh.

Gildore stumbled forward, dragging his leg behind him.

"No!" Eric cried.

David's heart raced. Panic set in. Soldiers rushed forward. Getting nearer.

Gildore grasped the hilt of the dagger with both hands and pulled.

Eric yelled, "David! Give me your sash! Hurry!"

Blades flashed in the sunlight. A solid line of black death raced toward them.

David flicked his gaze from the encroaching enemy to the king, and his lungs collapsed.

Eric hurled a string of obscenities at David, picked up Gildore's sword and spun around, slicing two men across their stomachs in one swipe. Sweat flew from his brow as he whirled and danced around his opponents, droplets of blood raining down around him.

"Damn it, David! Move your ass! Do something!"

David's feet unhinged from the ground. He sprinted to the king's side, and ripped off the sash. It was the least he could do to bind the wound. Pain, unlike anything he'd ever felt before, shot through his brain. Sharp. Stabbing. Burning. He collapsed, his body no stronger than a spaghetti noodle.

The ring and tattoo fell silent. The remnants of the shime's woven jungle snapped and unfurled. A voice hurled in. A voice he didn't want to hear ever again. Seyekrad. The mage had found David, and he was coming for him.

Eric tugged at him and shouted, "David, get up!"

Yes, David. Get up, Seyekrad mumbled in David's mind. *I see you. I'm coming for you.*

"No!" David cried, his palms pressed to the sides of his head. "Leave me alone!"

"David!" Eric grabbed him by the shirt and sat him up. "Pull it together. We have to go!"

David draped his arm around Eric's shoulder and stood. If only he could focus. If only the magic man inside his head would quit slicing up his brain.

A new group of men on horseback charged across the stone bridge. An army of at least two hundred stormed the field and clashed with the soldiers from Berg.

Swords hissed. Metal clanged.

David's body shook as a horse raced toward them and circled round them twice before the rider dismounted. He was dressed in blue leather armor, a shield emblazoned with an eagle perched above a raised bull tacked to his horse. Stringy red hair hung over his eyes. A maelstrom of emotion flooded through David. A good guy, come to save them.

"Your Majesty!" the man shouted.

"Gowran! You've got to get him out of here!" Eric helped the king onto the horse. "He needs a surgeon."

Eric stepped aside as the knight mounted the steed. "I'll come back for you!" Gowran pulled a dagger from his calf. He hurled it through the air, catching a would-be assailant in the neck. The fighter dropped at David's feet.

David stared at the blood pooling where he stood, blood that once sustained a life. The man's eyes lay open, vacant. He swallowed the bile in his throat.

The king and his rescuer retreated at breakneck speed. Eric picked up a sword from the ground and ran it through a raging militant. He whipped around, his eyes dark and dangerous. "What are you waiting for? Put that bow to some use, will you?"

David willed his arms to move, but they couldn't. Wouldn't. There was so much blood. Death. War. More bodies fell around him.

Somewhere behind him a sword hissed from its scabbard. David looked over his shoulder into the eyes of the man who had tortured the king in the dungeons of Berg. David's mind raced. What had Gildore called him?

Bainesworth.

"Well, well, look at you," the man said. "So you're what all the fuss is about. What a scrawny bag of bones."

What? How did he know—

Bainesworth threw a punch, the fist hard against David's left cheek.

Lights flashed before David's eyes. His brain exploded. A kick to his back and he met the ground, face-first.

"It's time for you to die, paladin."

An invisible forced tugged David's gut. He rolled out of the way, the sword plunging into the ground where he had just been. He heaved himself up to his knees, tightened his fingers around the shaft of an arrow, and stabbed it into Bainesworth's calf.

The man growled in pain.

David scrambled to his feet and picked up his bow lying a few feet away.

All around him men fought with fists. Swords clanged.

Arrows flew from above. A raven circled overhead, cawing, then landed among the chaos and morphed. Five more winged shifters followed.

Ravenhawk!

Overhead, Einar circled, his shadow turning the field into night. Fire scorched the forest. but failed to penetrate the membrane of magic protecting the field. The dragon whipped and roared and snatched at the protective shield with his talons. Electrical currents zigzagged through the air and sparked up his legs.

The beast arched his back and wailed. Everywhere around David soldiers shouted and screamed. Sweat, drenched in blood, dirt, and grime, clung to indistinguishable faces.

Eric's voice rang out through the chaos. "Behind you! Look out!"

David spun as the blond gladiator swung his sword in a downward arc. A bull of a man rammed into the warmonger, knocking him to the ground. David's breath hitched. Could it be?

The man whipped his head around, his piercing green eyes glaring from beneath a curtain of dark-brown hair.

Trog!

"David! Eric! Get out of here! Go!". The injured knight lumbered to his feet, his face battered. Bruised. One eye was almost swollen shut. His nose smashed. He staggered as he walked. His right arm dangled at his side, the weight of his sword pulling his shoulder down.

And the shadowmorth wound was open. Again. David stared, his feet incapable of movement. "What happened to you?"

"I happened," muttered the blond cretin.

Trog shoved David aside and brought his weapon up to meet Bainesworth's.

The two blades glinted and clanged. Seyekrad's voice edged into the recesses of David's mind. *Ahh, there you are.*

Pain, followed by bright lights, exploded like fireworks within him. David gasped for air but his lungs failed to fill.

Rasp.

Slurp.

Dizzy.

The sorcerer moved across the battlefield like a force of nature, wind swirling around him, the violence of it thrusting men aside like rag dolls. He drew back his hands, balling them into fists before thrusting blinding balls of silver flames into the membrane protecting the field.

Sparks flew across the magic skin exposing veins of electrical currents. A sizzling discharge collapsed the shield, leaving the air thick with an acrid odor of burning flesh

Einar circled, roared and breathed fire onto the field.

The world erupted into chaos.

Eric spun and dodged an onslaught, his moves choreographed with precision. Up. Down. Around. Thrust. His jaw was firm and tight, his eyes, steely. Sweat drowned his hair as well as his bruised and bleeding torso.

Trog plowed forward, slashing and hitting anything in his way. How he remained on his feet was a mystery.

David stumbled, Seyekrad's voice far too loud in his head.

A wall of energy— silver black and pulsing—formed around David in a sweeping arc. Seyekrad appeared before him, his lips curled in a sneer. His eyes were creased with laughter. "You stupid boy. You thought you could outsmart me. You thought your friends could save you?"

David was suspended in the moment. His nerves shattered into a thousand pieces.

Seyekrad stepped closer.

David glanced at the bridge. *Accelero Silentium! Ibidem Evanescere!*

Seyekrad laughed. "It didn't work then, it won't work now. Prepare to die."

Tentacles of black magic streamed from Seyekrad's open palms and lifted David high into the air. He dangled face-down like bait on a hook.

David's stomach left his body. His heart stopped.

Einar screeched and dive-bombed him, his mouth open.

David twisted his head and stared wide-eyed at the raging inferno coming at him. Millions of images flickered and faded, a hurricane of memories swirled through his soul. He braced for the attack.

Spears of ice shot through the sky.

The beast bellowed and tumbled away; his body lit up like a firework on the Fourth of July.

David scanned the pandemonium for the source of the attack. It came from a little stout dragon with autumn-colored feathers for a mane.

"Mirith!"

From the thick of the battle emerged two women.

Tears swelled in David's eyes. Emotion exploded from every pore.

"Charlotte," he whispered. "You're alive."

Einar screeched, and came around again, his wings outstretched, his mouth wide open.

A courage David had never felt before surged in his chest. His best friend, the love of his life, was okay.

More ice bolts sailed past his head and pierced Einar's left haunch. The dragon somersaulted backward, his protest like thunder reverberating in a tin can.

David struggled against the magical weave holding him in the air. He had to get down. He had to somehow put an end to the madness. Green mist appeared out of nowhere on the ground. Avida emerged from within the brume and cackled as she swung Charlotte by the hair, pitching her across the battlefield and raking her over dead bodies. Slathering her in blood and death.

Rage ignited like a furnace within David. He reached for his bow, but it was gone. He spotted it on the ground, not far from where the shifters were battling. Frantic, he shouted to Ravenhawk who was having too much fun ambushing the bad guys, and then pecking their eyes out. With a nod, Ravenhawk clasped the weapon in his talons, flew it to David and held it steady while he nocked an arrow. David shifted as much on his side as he could, and took aim at Avida.

His tethers swayed him from side to side, a willow in a hurricane.

"Come get him, Einar!" the sorcerer shouted. "Feast."

Shadowmorths swarmed from the trees. From the flames of the forest, Einar emerged.

Blood rushed to David's head. The world throbbed. His pulse tripped.

Three ravens landed in nearby trees and shape-shifted. Ravenhawk grinned. He held up a batch of darts and shouted at David, "We'll stave off the minions. Kill the witch!"

The shifters loaded their dart guns and fired at the wispy creatures.

The sound of a thousand fingernails dragged across an invisible blackboard. Time slowed.

David re-nocked his arrow.

Aimed.

Released.

The shaft lodged in Avida's back. The witch screamed and flailed, but held tight to Charlotte's hair.

Seyekrad paused in his tormenting, his eyes on his precious pet.

In the lull, David took another shot. The shaft passed through the back of Avida's neck and out the front. She hit the ground, still as a rock.

To Charlotte's right, Bainesworth held a sword over Trog's chest.

David let another arrow fly.

Bainesworth lurched back as the projectile found its mark. The goliath of a man fell to the ground.

The magic strands corded tight around David and whipped and battered him into the canopy with the force of a speeding train.

Loud cracks sounded around him. Pain singed up his legs, his arms, his back. Bone after bone snapped like bubble wrap in his fingers. A scream expelled from his lungs and into the air, the sound curdling the nerves in his own ears.

Einar swooped in, his mouth wide open. David stared into the inferno.

He tried to move his legs, his arms, but he might as well have attempted to move a mountain. He lay on his back, straddled over two limbs, as hot tears streamed down his cheeks.

I love you, Charlotte.

Lightning bolts lit up the sky. Crackling blue threads helixed around Einar. More electrifying projectiles bombarded his body from nose to tail.

Seyekrad's connection broke. A horn blew.

"Retreat!" bellowed a voice.

White, pulsating threads swirled around David, enveloping him in a comforting cloud of pale resplendence. He floated downward, as if one with the air, serenity taking root within him.

But black cords invaded, harnessing all the light. It battled for his soul, raising him upward in a cold, suffocating, ebony vapor.

"Let him go, Seyekrad!"

Slavandria's voice drifted over him like a warm breeze. White energy pulsed downward, rolling and curling like clouds cascading over mountaintops. It wrapped David in a cocoon, binding him as he floated toward the Haldorian Bridge, over the Édes Falls.

Flashes of white, black, and blue light sparked everywhere.

Einar screeched like a freight train skidding off its tracks. He banked and flew back toward Berg, the shadowmorths in pursuit.

Seyekrad bellowed, "I will kill you for this, Slavandria!" He vanished in a glistening black fog.

David touched down on lush, green soil, his emotions as paralyzed as his body.

Horse-drawn wagons clattered across the bridge, making their way to the battlefield.

Slavandria knelt at David's side and finger-combed his hair. "I'm sorry I took so long to get here."

"It's okay," David said. Tears slipped from the corners of his eyes, exhaustion settling in. "Where's Charlotte?"

"She's coming." Slavandria stood as a wagon pulled up beside her. She raised her arms to the sky. Pale light shimmered from her palms and spread out in all directions, forming a shimmering dome. "I'll be right back," she said, looking down at him with a tender smile.

A group of wounded men limped toward the lorry. Eric

shambled along the outer rim, his shoulder dislocated again. Blood and dirt covered his body. He wiped his arm across his face and collapsed on his back next to David.

"Hey," he said.

David blinked. "Hey." The inability to move forced another tear down his cheek.

An awkward silence passed between them.

"Thank you for what you did out there." Sincerity choked Eric's tone, turning his voice into something unrecognizable.

Confusion swarmed David's battered mind. "What did I do?"

"You put an arrow into Bainesworth. You saved Trog's life."

David swallowed, his throat dry as cotton. Somehow being thanked for stealing another's life did little to fill the growing emptiness in his soul. He was a murderer. No matter how he spun it, the truth remained. He was changed forever. The demons of war had seen to it.

Eric winced as he rolled onto his side and pushed himself up on one elbow. He fished the Eye of Kedge from around his neck, and placed it around David's. "You saved us back there. In Einar's castle. On the battlefield. None of us would be alive right now if it wasn't for you. You deserve the glory, not me. You deserve to give this to Slavandria."

Eric stood with the help of an attendant and made his way to the back of the cart.

David stared into the sky, watching the wispy clouds float along oblivious to the horrors on the ground beneath them. He'd come so close to dying, to being devoured by a raging inferno. To getting Charlotte killed.

As if hearing her name on his mind, his best friend, the love of his life, collapsed beside him, and sobbed. He wanted to hold her, comfort her. If only he could move his arms. If only

378

he could say the words hovering on his lips. But there were four men swarming around him, getting instructions from Slavandria where to take him once inside the castle. And then Eric was back, speaking soothing words to Charlotte, and helping her to her feet.

David's heart tightened and squeezed at the way Eric's eyes scanned her face, the gash on her forehead. The way he swept her messy, tangled hair caked with filth and blood from her temples. Who did he think he was, this Abercrombie and Fitch wannabe?

The men lifted David into the wagon. His heart relaxed as Charlotte scuttled from Eric's arms and lay beside him, her hand on his chest. A strange calm settled over him.

And then he was asleep.

Chapter 30

David woke in a canopied bed in an enormous room, twice the size of his, back home.

Moonlight slipped through the open balcony doors. A fire burned in the hearth, while lanterns flickered upon the end tables.

Slavandria sat beside him, watching.

He yawned and ran his palms over his face, then stared at his limbs as if they belonged to someone else.

"You fixed me. Thank you."

Slavandria smiled and nodded. David returned the smile.

"How do you feel?"

"Like I've been beaten with a two-by-four." He swept his palms over his face and stared at the ceiling. "Where's Charlotte? Is she okay?"

"I'm right here," Charlotte said, stepping into the room from the balcony, the moonlight silhouetting her body clad in a pale blue sleeping gown. She fell into David's bed and curled up next to him.

He wrapped his arms around her and kissed her forehead. "Hey, you," he whispered as he inhaled the scent of her. "Are you alright? I'm so sorry I left you. I thought if I led Einar away from you and Trog, he'd leave you alone."

Charlotte put a finger to his lips. "I'm fine, and I know why you did it. It was a good try."

He combed his fingers through her hair. "How did you escape?"

Charlotte circled a finger on his chest and nestled her face in the crook of his shoulder. "Mirith, mainly, but I don't want to talk about that now. In fact I don't want to talk at all. Is that okay?"

David stroked her hair. "Yeah, that's fine."

They slipped into a comfortable quiet, David finding comfort in the need to say nothing. He let out a heavy sigh, releasing the tension that had held his body hostage for over a week. It was a relief to breathe. To feel safe. To know they were going home.

A knock at the door and Lily peeked inside. "Do you mind if I come in?"

Her voice hugged his entire being. Her eyes held a tear or two as she bent over and kissed his forehead. It hit him suddenly that he didn't blame her anymore for not telling him sooner who she was. He would never have believed her anyway, if she had told him of a real world complete with faeries, shapeshifters, and dragons. Some things a guy just had to experience for himself.

Lily sat beside him her long fingers curled around his hand. "Honey, I'm so sorry."

David shook his head. "No. I'm the one who should apologize." He closed his eyes for a half second. "I should never have doubted you. It's just everything happened so fast, and I felt so helpless, and I knew you had answers, but you weren't telling me."

"I know. You have every right to be angry with me. I hope you can forgive me."

David sat up and wrapped his arms around her. "There's nothing to forgive, I get it now, but there is one thing I need to know. How was Seyekrad able to take over Mr. Loudermilk's body without you knowing?"

Lily stood. "He and Avida used very dark and undetectable magic, something called naching. Long ago, wizards used it to kill their victims and then take over their bodies in order to infiltrate enemy lines. Our father banned the practice after the Great Dragon War as part of the peace plan. I never suspected Seyekrad would do such a thing. He was a protector of the realm. Father used him for reconnaissance. He trusted him."

"We all trusted him," Slavandria said. "I'm sure Father will be quite livid when he discovers the truth."

"He's going to still try and kill me, isn't he?" David asked. "Seyekrad, that is, not your father."

Slavandria nodded. "I'm afraid so, but the next time, we'll be ready for him."

David considered her words. Something inside his soul ripped apart. Fear and desperation clung to his nerves, and he swallowed. "What about my parents?" he asked. "Have you heard any news?"

Lily smiled. "Yes. They have been found, and are resting comfortably."

David's skin tingled. Emotion bubbled up from his toes. "W-when can I see them?" He sucked in a deep breath, determined to ward off the raw emotion coming to life within him.

Lily swept his hair out of his eyes. "Tomorrow, David. They've been through a horrible ordeal, as have you. Is that okay with you?"

A tear fell, followed by another. He swept them away.

He nodded and took a ragged breath. As much as he wanted to see them, he understood pain and tiredness. Besides, he'd waited almost seventeen years. What were a few more hours? "Yeah. That's okay." The thread of worrying about Seyekrad finding him slipped away.

Lily kissed him on the top of the head. "Good. Why don't you get some sleep? It's been a long day. Charlotte, come with me, honey. You need to rest as well."

Charlotte kissed David on the cheek and stood. "Thank you for today," she said, squeezing David's hand. "I would have died if you hadn't killed that witch. It didn't sink in until now."

David stood and engulfed her in his arms. Holding her felt like a breeze funneling through his lungs. His right hand threaded in her hair, his lips pressed to the softness of her neck. "I'd die for you, Char. Always."

Charlotte looked up at him, her eyes glistening. "Me, too." She rose on her tiptoes and kissed him softly on the lips. "I'll see you tomorrow."

David let her go, his entire being frozen in the moment. The moment when everything was right in the world. The moment when love did indeed, conquer all.

Lily and Charlotte filed from the room. Slavandria approached him and gently clasped his shoulders.

"I'm very proud of you, David. Eric told me what you did to rescue the Eye of Kedge from Einar. I cannot even begin to explain to you the value of what you have done, and there are no words that can tell you how much I appreciate what you have accomplished."

"I take it the pendant is safe, then?"

Slavandria nodded. "Yes."

"And Trog and Eric? Are they okay?"

"Yes, they are fine. So is Mirith, but it will take some time for them to heal. Trog's wounds, especially, are critical." She paused, and then said, "You saved Trog's life, you know."

David nodded. "Yeah. I just wish I'd had another choice."

"Sometimes we are left with no other choice. It is sad, but true, but you have plenty of time to come to terms with it. Right now, you need to sleep and dream of a happy reunion with your family. Good night, David."

Slavandria slipped from the room and closed the door behind her.

David curled up on his bed and stared at the patterned fabric above him. His life and everything in it had changed. There was no doubt it would continue to change, but this time, he was ready.

He closed his eyes, snuggled into his pillow and succumbed to the feeling of peace spreading through him. He'd done it. It was over.

Tomorrow, he and Charlotte were going home.

Life didn't get much better than that.

ACKNOWLEDGMENTS

Next to writing a query letter, I think the Acknowledgement section is the hardest part for me to write. I don't want to leave anyone out, yet to thank everyone who has influenced me throughout my life could turn into a mini novella. With that said, I will try to be concise, and hope that everyone will understand.

To my Lord and Savior, Jesus Christ, and His heavenly father, thank you for providing me with a stellar imagination and an extraordinary gift to weave words into vivid pictures and timeless tales. I should have listened to 'the calling' ages ago, but as you know, I'm a classic pantser and you're an awesome plotter. Thank you for being patient while I traveled around the sun to get to the moon. The trip would have been much shorter if I'd listened in the first place. All I ask is you cut me some slack. I was a teenager. Forgive me.

To The Sisterhood of the Traveling Pens. Ladies, I don't know what I would have done without all of you. For the past few years you have seen me through some rough spots, and you've been my friends and encouragers when I didn't think I could go on. Each of you holds a very special place in my heart. I'd like to give a special shout out to Julie Reece and Sheryl Winters for putting your eyes on Dragon King for more times than you probably wanted. Your suggestions were spot on, and I can't thank you enough for being such awesome betas.

To The Sixteen to Read group. Thank you for the beta reads, the incredible inspiration, laughter, friendship, and wealth of information and wisdom you provide on a daily basis. Each of you are the cream and sugar in my coffee.

To Aimee at J. Taylor Publishing - thank you for the first professional read through of my story, and pointing out all its horrendous flaws. Because of you, the novel went into a massive re-write and emerged as a piece of work I'm proud of. I owe you so much more than a few words in the back of a book. Thank you for everything.

To my very, very special beta reader and friend, Jennifer M. Eaton. Who knew when we met on Nathan Bradford's site all those years ago as beta readers that we would both be published authors now, and true-life good friends? You have read this story so many times and banged it up and knocked it around until it became what it is today. You were never afraid to shake me and ask, "What were you thinking when you wrote this rubbish! You can do better than this!" Thank you for putting up with the tearful phone calls, the exasperating emails, all of my drama, and for holding my hand and believing in this story from the very beginning. I couldn't ask for a better beta reader or friend.

To my publisher, Georgia McBride and Month9Books - I can't thank you enough for taking a chance on me and this story. Your support has been more than anything I could have asked for. Georgia, you are super woman, and your enthusiasm is catching. If only you could bottle up some of that energy and give it to me.

I also want to give a special thank you to my editor, Sarita Amorim. You are an editing queen. Thank you for taking my story and making it tighter and richer while staying true to the voice of my story and characters. You rock my world.

To the design team who put together my kick-butt cover – wow!! I am still blown away every time I look at it. You completely exceeded my expectations. I bow to your greatness.

Thank you to everyone who ever read or suffered through a

reading of the first (horrendous) draft of this story, and didn't roll on the floor laughing when I said, "Someday, I'm going to get this published."

To Dunkin' Donuts, Martini and Rossi and the makers of Lindor Truffles – I couldn't have written one word without you.

To my dearest friend, Diane Englund – you were and still are my angel. You left this earth way too soon, but your spirit will remain between the pages of this book and all those to come.

To all my teachers who told me I should become a writer. Thank you for believing in me.

To my son, Kevin – you always gave me your unbiased, unapologetic, sometimes sarcastic and always candid opinions of this story ever since this adventure started. You were my first fan, even when the story was worse than awful. Thank you for being my sounding board, my midnight reading partner, and my co-plotter. Because of you, shadowmorths exist. Fist bump.

To my son, Bryan – thank you for the countless laughs at my expense due to horrid character development and/or plot mistakes. You always made me laugh until my sides hurt and tears poured down my cheeks. More importantly, you taught me not take me too seriously. Thanks for all the stress relief. Trog smash, baby.

To my daughters, Clarissa and Heather, thank you for believing in me and my dream, and always being there to encourage me when I wanted to give up. Heather, I'm still waiting to see what hair color you come up with. After all, a deal is a deal.

To Mama, thank you for instilling in me a love for the written word. You always pushed when I needed it, and never let me give up. I wish you were here to share this moment with me, to see my dream come to fruition. Instead, I'll imagine you flitting around heaven telling everyone how proud you are of me because that's the kind of mom you were. Thank you for everything. I love you and miss you so much.

To Daddy, you were a man of few words, but the ones you did speak stayed with me all my life. It is my memory of you that breathed life into Trog, and you shall forever remain my real-life knight, hero and inspiration. I love you, Pops.

Last but not least, to my husband, Tom, who spent far too many days and nights alone while I ventured off with my imaginary friends. You are my rock, my foundation, and while we may not always see eye to eye, there is no place else I'd rather be. It seems you're stuck with me and all the voices in my head. Just remember. I'm not crazy. My mother had me tested.

To everyone else, including present and future readers and fans – you are awesome! Thank you for being a part of my crazy life, and for reading my story. I hope you enjoy it and come back for books 2 and 3 in the Chronicles of Fallhollow trilogy. Big squeezy hugs. Until the next time.

A Note from the Author

Wow! I don't know about you, but I'm out of breath! Can you believe David, Eric and Charlotte escaped Einar and lived to tell the tale? Are you anxious to find out what happens next?

If so, please sign up for my newsletter where you'll get all the latest info about The Chronicles of Fallhollow trilogy, including cover reveals, bonus content, and maybe even a few giveaways. All you have to do is click the link. http://bit.ly/1K7K5EU.

And if you want to chat, you can find me all over social media. Head over to my website to find my links. http://www.j-keller-ford.com.

Thank you so much for reading IN THE SHADOW OF THE DRAGON KING. I hope you enjoyed the story.

Word of advice: stay safe and be on the lookout for dragons. There's no telling when a magic portal might open near you, which makes me wonder … if one did, would you be prepared?

J. KELLER FORD

J. Keller Ford (known to all as Jenny) is a scribbler of Young Adult and New Adult speculative fiction. As a young Army brat, she traveled the world and wandered the halls of some of Germany's most extraordinary castles in hopes of finding snarky dragons, chivalrous knights and wondrous magic that permeated her imagination. What she found remains etched in her topsy-turvy mind and oozes out in sweeping tales of courage, sacrifice, honor and everlasting love.

When not torturing her keyboard or trying to silence the voices in her head, Jenny spends time collecting seashells, bowling, swimming, screaming on roller coasters and traveling. Jenny is a mom to four magnificent and noble offspring, and currently lives in paradise on the west coast of Florida with a quirky knight who was silly enough to marry her, and a menagerie of royal pets. Published works include short stories, The Amulet of Ormisez, Dragon Flight, and The Passing of Millie Hudson. IN THE SHADOW OF THE DRAGON KING is her debut novel and the first installment in the Chronicles of Fallhollow Trilogy.

OTHER MONTH9BOOKS TITLES YOU MIGHT LIKE

SUMMONER RISING
WITCHING HOUR
TRAITOR
SERPENTINE

Find more awesome Teen books at http://www.Month9Books.com

Connect with Month9Books online:
Facebook: www.Facebook.com/Month9Books
Twitter: https://twitter.com/Month9Books
You Tube: www.youtube.com/user/Month9Books
Blog: www.month9booksblog.com
Instagram: https://instagram.com/month9books
Request review copies via publicity@month9books.com

Someone should have told her.
You can't control the creatures
you let into this world.
SUMMONER
RISING
LAWS OF SUMMONING 1
MELANIE MCFARLANE

SARAH HOGLE

WITCHING
HOUR

DRAGONRIDER CHRONICLES 3

Traitor

NICOLE CONWAY

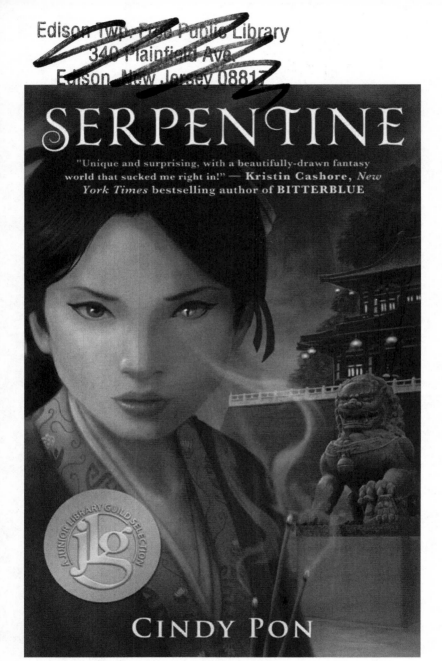

SERPENTINE

"Unique and surprising, with a beautifully-drawn fantasy
world that sucked me right in!" — **Kristin Cashore**, *New
York Times* bestselling author of **BITTERBLUE**

A JUNIOR LIBRARY GUILD SELECTION
jlg

CINDY PON